SHADOW OPS: BREACH ZONE

"Cole's managed to cover a hero's journey story, a quest story, and now a running battle interspersed with a romance. It works spectacularly . . . *Breach Zone* is Cole's best novel yet, and it's the perfect end to the trilogy."
—*io9*

"[The Shadow Ops series is] a set of three excellent, action-packed novels that combine elements of contemporary magic and superhero fiction with the type of atmosphere genre readers usually only get in military SF . . . *Breach Zone* is such a tense and action-packed ride . . . Full of desperate, back-against-the-wall combat scenes. Right from the start, it feels like a 'last stand' type of story."
—*Tor.com*

"*Breach Zone* is filled to the flanks with action, intrigue, and simply all-out mayhem . . . A book that you simply shouldn't miss."
—*Fantasy Book Critic*

"Cole wraps up the Shadow Ops trilogy with a magical battle royal . . . Action-filled, adrenaline-powered adventure." —*Publishers Weekly*

"Shadow Ops is a scary good series. I'm not sure 'military fantasy' existed as a genre before Myke Cole, but I know now that I want more."
—*King of the Nerds*

"A stunning novel . . . Well written, emotional, exciting, and a superb end to the Shadow Ops trilogy." —*The Qwillery*

"Cole has really impressed with a stunning all-out war novel that never disappoints. This series is arguably one of the definitive military fantasy novels and delivers an excellent payoff that's well worth your time. Highly recommended." —*The Founding Fields*

"Executed brilliantly . . . [Cole] seamlessly blends the realities of the modern military with the imagination of D&D to mind-blowing result." —*Staffer's Book Review*

"Pulse-hammering action . . . Myke Cole has outdone himself."
—*52 Book Reviews*

continued . . .

PRAISE FOR

SHADOW OPS: FORTRESS FRONTIER

"For fans of military fiction and fantasy, the Shadow Ops series is the best thing going. Not reading it would be a crime against good fiction."
—*Staffer's Book Review*

"[Cole] proves that an action blockbuster can have heart and emotional depth, while never skimping on the fireworks and explosions."
—*Fantasy Faction*

"Propulsive . . . Highly entertaining . . . Reads like an intense game of Dungeons & Dragons."
—*Kirkus Reviews*

"This action-filled adventure holds the reader's attention with occasional glimmers of hope that someday the oppressed magic-users might finally force those in power to respect them."
—*Publishers Weekly*

"It is a book that will have something for fantasy readers of every kind and pays homage brilliantly to Tolkien's legacy . . . Myke Cole is an absolute gift to urban fantasy and military fantasy subgenres."
—*Fantasy Book Critic*

"This book is awesome . . . This is one heck of a whirlwind ride, and right now, Myke Cole's Shadow Ops series is quickly becoming the best that military fantasy has to offer. Top-notch stuff."
—*The Founding Fields*

"There are some truly surprising twists and turns . . . If you enjoyed Myke Cole's debut, you should love this sequel." —*Tor.com*

"This generation's *The Forever War* . . . Myke Cole is the most exciting SFF author to come along since Joe Abercrombie."
—*Neth Space*

"The action is again pretty much nonstop, the narrative is tense, energetic, and above all *convincing*." —*SFBook Reviews*

GEMINI CELL

MYKE COLE

ACE BOOKS, NEW YORK

THE BERKLEY PUBLISHING GROUP
Published by the Penguin Group
Penguin Group (USA) LLC
375 Hudson Street, New York, New York 10014

USA • Canada • UK • Ireland • Australia • New Zealand • India • South Africa • China

penguin.com

A Penguin Random House Company

GEMINI CELL

An Ace Book / published by arrangement with the author

Ace Books are published by The Berkley Publishing Group.
ACE and the "A" design are trademarks of Penguin Group (USA) LLC.

For information, address: The Berkley Publishing Group,
a division of Penguin Group (USA) LLC,
375 Hudson Street, New York, New York 10014.

ISBN: 978-0-425-26964-0

PUBLISHING HISTORY
Ace mass-market edition / February 2015

PRINTED IN THE UNITED STATES OF AMERICA

10 9 8 7 6 5 4 3 2

Cover illustration by Larry Rostant.
Cover design by Diana Kolsky.
Interior text design by Laura K. Corless.

necessaries: shower and a fresh uniform, the clunky, slow-as-molasses computer system used to file his report, the last-minute tasks and questions, the traffic on the drive home, inexplicable given the odd hour.

It was three hours before he was finally on his way up the stairs to home. He turned the key roughly in the lock in his excitement, making the old door creak as he opened it before he remembered the late hour. Sarah and Patrick would be asleep. He slowed down, but too late, he could hear Sarah stirring from the bed in their loft above the living room, surrounded by her paintings. Moonlight would be filtering in through the huge bay window overlooking the Chickahominy River.

Patrick's room was off to the side on this floor, but the boy could sleep through anything, and Schweitzer let his seabag thump to the floor without bothering to slow his roll.

Sarah appeared at the top of the stairs, cuffing sleep from her eyes. Her pink hair was tousled, and she wore only her panties and a T-shirt featuring one of the Japanese comic-book characters she was so crazy about. Sleeve tattoos covered slender, muscular arms.

The open door drew the air from inside the apartment toward him, and the rosewater smell came with it, filling him with love and lust simultaneously. Sarah was his wife and mother of his child. Her strength had pushed him through training and the many ops that followed. She was a hundred times smarter than him and good at everything she touched, from word games to musical instruments. It had taken him a long time to accept that someone he admired so much could love him, but he managed it. But everything else aside, she was in her underwear, her tight hips and long thighs exposed. Her small breasts strained against the tight T-shirt.

He went to her.

"You're home." Her voice was sleepy as he folded her into his arms, one hand cupping her ass, the other in the small of her back. He held her close, inhaling her scent, steeling himself for the confrontation, trying to just love her for a while. He stiffened in his trousers and tried not to grind it into her. Now wasn't the time. They had talking to do.

"I'm home," he said, "and for a while. We're stood down. Maybe two weeks."

She relaxed a bit as he buried his face in her neck, kissed his way up to her earlobes, moved to her mouth.

She responded coolly, pushed away. "You're okay?"

He gestured down at himself. "I'm fine, baby. How's the P-Train?"

"Sleeping. He made a painting for you."

"Like his mommy."

"Is it really two weeks this time?" she asked. She reached down, and his lust surged as he imagined she was reaching for his crotch, but her hand moved past to the cargo pocket on his thigh, where she tapped his ruggedized smartphone through the fabric. He'd been on leave before. They rarely let him go the full length of it without calling him back to action.

He nodded. "Chief's covering for me. She promised."

Sarah stepped away from him. "Bullshit."

"Baby."

"No, Jim. Give me one good reason why it'll be different this time."

He opened his mouth, closed it. He didn't have a good reason. This op had felt different. It wasn't the biggest firefight of his career, but it was close. Was it the corpses? The secrecy? Something made him believe that *this* time, he would get the R&R he deserved.

"I don't know if I can keep doing this." The words struck Schweitzer like a blow. He'd known they were coming. He just hadn't expected them so soon.

"Baby, come on." He reached for her.

She stepped away. "Jim, you are never, *ever* here. I get that what you do is special. I get that it's important. I get that it makes you happy, but I have to be happy, too. Patrick has to be happy."

"I can make you happy, baby," Schweitzer said.

"I don't need you to *make* me happy. I'm not one of that brood of hens out there." She gestured out to the rest of the apartment complex, at the invisible host of navy wives, asleep in their beds, a few beside their husbands, most not.

"The show turned into a major commission," she said. "Bethany wants me to continue exhibiting there. She sold my two biggest pieces, and she's willing to front me money to keep things running."

"That's fantastic!" He tried to keep his voice upbeat. "How much?"

"Depends on sales, but she's putting up forty large for an advance."

"Holy shit, baby! That's amazing! I knew this would happen!" He moved toward her again out of instinct, then checked himself as she tensed.

"Yeah." She ignored the compliment. "This is my point, though. I can make myself happy. I can take care of myself."

"I know it, ba . . ." He stopped himself from using the diminutive. *You know it, but you've got a funny way of showing it. Stop calling her that.*

"This is the thing you don't get, Jim. I don't *need* to be with you. I *want* to be with you. That was always the way, right? That was why it worked."

Schweitzer's stomach fell at her use of the past tense. She had the right of it. There were so many shrinking violets in Virginia. Weak women who wanted nothing more than a fighting man to take them away from their lives and give them a role in a household. Church on Sunday, Memorial Day barbecues with the other navy families, bitch-and-stitch sessions while the husbands were away. Schweitzer hated those women. They would go silent on movie dates when he tried to deconstruct the plots with them. Stare blankly when he handed them a book he wanted to read and discuss.

Not Sarah. She was his equal. Everywhere, from the bedroom to the Scrabble board, she kept pace, challenged him. She didn't need him. She didn't need anyone.

But she *wanted* him, and that had always made him feel

more special than anything else. More than his special-warfare pin. More than his Bronze Star. More than the knowledge that not twelve hours ago, he had taken on an army of powerful mercenaries, kicked them in the teeth, and survived.

"You have to want to be with me, too," Sarah said. "I don't want you to have to choose between the job and me, but . . . that's what it's coming to."

"Sarah." *No more calling her "baby," you idiot.* "I . . ."

"Why do you do it, Jim? What do you get out of it? I mean, apart from the adrenaline rush."

He thought for a moment and decided to answer honestly. "I'm good at it. Really, really good at it. It's like you with the painting. You touch it, it's amazing. You don't even have to try. I know you do, and damn hard, but that just makes a good thing better."

She nodded. She did know. She was the only person who did. "I know you don't want to work a desk job. I know you want to do something exciting that makes a difference. I can even handle the danger, Jim. Even with Patrick, I can handle that. I know you're not made to sit in an office. Hell, that'd drive me crazy. I get it.

"It's the being gone that's killing us. It's the never being able to tell me where you're going, or when you'll be back. It's me having to second-guess every person with a foreign accent who says hi to me in the grocery store. It's this . . . scrutiny."

The art world had made Sarah many foreign contacts: Russian dealers, Chinese collectors, Middle-Eastern high-rolling buyers. The government didn't take kindly to SEALs interacting with foreign nationals off the job. Every time Schweitzer joined his wife for a dinner with them, he spent the next day filling out forms for his security officer.

"That's the life, Sarah," was all he could say. "That's what you have to put up with to get to do this."

"No, Jim. That's what *you* have to put up with. I don't have to put up with anything. I am choosing to put up with it, which is the part I think you're not getting."

Frustration boiled over. He glanced at the door to Patrick's room and kept his voice low with a will. "Sarah, damn it. I love you. I can't be without you. What do you want me to do?"

Her expression softened, she took a step toward him, her dark eyes reflecting his own, the love there plain to see. "I love you, too. I love you too much to change you, honey. You want to save the world? You want to drive fast cars and sling a gun? Do it. Become an EMT. Join a police force. Hell, join a SWAT team. Open up a firing range or a gun shop. Become a fireman. Anything. Find the most dangerous thing you can possibly do that keeps. You. Home."

"There's also . . . Pete," Schweitzer added, unable to meet her eyes. His brother, at rest in Arlington Cemetery, the naval special-warfare pin and the Congressional Medal of Honor engraved on his headstone. A hero the likes of which Schweitzer could only hope to match. Pete had been so proud that little Jimmy Schweitzer had joined up, had made it through training, had pinned on as a SEAL.

How could he turn his back on that memory?

"Pete's dead," Sarah said. "We're alive. Patrick and I are alive."

He knew that. He knew it keenly. But it didn't banish his brother's memory, the expectation that had hung in the air since Pete's final op had gone sour.

She looked down at the hardwood floor. Dirty by Schweitzer's standards, but Sarah wasn't the clean freak in the relationship, and he was never home to tidy up. A maid was beyond their modest means, though maybe, with Sarah's new commission, that would change.

If he could keep her.

Schweitzer's heart surged with love for her, terror at the thought of losing her and Patrick. But above it all hovered fear over leaving the navy. If Schweitzer wasn't a SEAL, then what made him matter in the world? Pete's ghost hovered in his mind's eye.

Sarah looked up at him from under the neon pink of her dyed bangs.

He went to her, and she didn't resist him this time, folded into his arms, moaning softly as he crushed her to him, running kisses along her neck, the line of her jaw. "I'm sorry, baby," he said, not caring if the term slighted her. "I'll fix it, I'll fix it. Contract is up in a year. I won't reenlist." Even as the words came out in a rush, he knew they were wrong.

But he still heard himself saying, "A year's not so long." Yet he knew that it was long, and was glad of it, because it would give him time to think. He couldn't lose Sarah. He'd scoffed at the idea of "the one" until he'd found her, and now he couldn't let her go.

But his job wasn't a small thing either.

She met his kisses now, sucking hungrily on his lips. Aggressive where other women were timid, knowing where other women let him take the lead. She thrust one hand down the front of his trousers, squeezing the base of his cock, pulsing her hand low enough down to be tantalizing, high enough up not to hurt him, touching him with a familiarity that spoke of the years they'd spent together, learning one another's bodies.

"I love you," she husked, as he slid one hand over her ass, sliding his fingers behind her underwear, pushing it down her thigh, finding the edge of her sex and running his fingers over it. She moaned again, crushing into him. Schweitzer nearly wept with relief. For now at least, she was here. For now, she had forgiven him.

Patrick would sleep through a rocket attack, but it felt wrong to do this so close to him. "Come on," Schweitzer whispered in her ear, taking her by the wrist to haul her up the stairs. Sarah stood rooted to the spot, one hand still pumping him, the other sliding up under his shirt, over the ridges of his stomach and over his chest. "Uh-uh." She bit her lip, shook her head.

Schweitzer smiled, reached down around her waist and scooped her up over his shoulder. She squirmed, kissing his neck as Schweitzer crested the landing and tossed her onto the bed.

He climbed on top of her, surrounded by her paintings;

haunting watercolor marshscapes of the land rolling around their home, populated with sunbursts and puffs of flame that hinted at serene intelligence. The big bay windows let in the moonlight, limning her body in silver, making her nipples into stars, her eyes into wave tops.

He paused, holding still as she pawed at him. At long last she stopped and they stared at one another. Schweitzer willed his emotions through his face, hoping she could feel them, see them written on him.

"I love you," he said again, just in case the look wasn't enough.

She smiled, her brows drawing together, her eyes sad but reconciled. She nodded, and he knew it had been enough after all.

So he fell on her, making her wet, making her cry out, making her understand how much she meant to him.

The line between the two of them blurred, until Schweitzer forgot where he left off, and she began, and they were one thing, sweating and moving and drowning in love.

He woke in the darkness, suddenly alert, rising through all the layers of drowsiness to heightened vigilance, as if he hadn't been asleep just moments before. The moonlight still filtered through the bay window, turning the dust motes in the air to dancing silver, making Sarah's skin an alabaster wonderland. She slept, her head propped on her arm, snoring lightly.

The digital clock on the nightstand told Schweitzer he'd only slept for two hours. He flopped back onto his pillow, the scent of Sarah's hair wafting up from the bedcovers, calming him.

Calming him, but not nearly enough. Schweitzer had dealt with this since he'd first joined the teams. The sudden bursts of hypervigilance, the screaming certitude that he was *not safe.* When it overtook him in public, he'd find a corner to put his back in and wait it out, taking deep breaths, hoping against hope that no one would try to talk to him.

When it happened at home, especially at night, there was no hope of sleep. The wizard had prescribed him pills for that (and confided that most of the guys took them), but they were in the bathroom, and he didn't feel like getting out of bed right now.

Schweitzer had rolled on scores of targets since he'd earned his pin. When they'd integrated with the Coast Guard to run ops against domestic targets with a nexus to terrorism, he'd seen some bizarre and disturbing things. A tipoff on a shipping container supposedly harboring an antiaircraft missile system and its crew turned out to be packed with Korean sex slaves. The women had been at sea for weeks without food, drinking rainwater from their bundled clothes, soaking the stuff up where it leaked in through the container's cracks. When that ran out, they started drinking their own urine. By the time Schweitzer got to them, they'd begun eating one another.

The sight haunted him, but less than the images flashing through his head of the refrigerated corpses, lying in silent rows on those stainless-steel racks, as if they were patiently awaiting something. As if a shouted command or the touch of a button could make them spring into action. That weird moment, when the darkness had come alive . . . that was just a flash of nerves.

But it had felt so *real*.

Schweitzer shrugged the thought off. If they weren't supposed to talk about it, then thinking about it wasn't going to help any. He turned back to Sarah, reached out, and touched her hair. He'd told himself he'd fix this, but all he'd done was bought himself time. Sarah wasn't the type to make idle threats. When she said, "I don't know if I can keep doing this," she meant that she couldn't keep doing this.

Her or the navy. Exactly the choice he'd dreaded as the realities of the life he'd chosen had crystallized.

It would have to be her. Schweitzer knew that in his bones. The thought filled him with a fear so powerful that he shook. He wracked his brain, going over the career choices she'd laid out for him, adding a few of his own. What could he do? Who could he be?

In training, he'd learned that to look too far into the distance was to lose focus on what lay right before you. On an op, that was as good as suicide.

Cops were a dime a dozen. Even the best blended into the background of workaday slogging. Schweitzer had found a way to be special. How could Sarah love him without that? How could Patrick admire him?

And Pete. Always Pete, pinning on his crows when he'd graduated. *Proud of you, bro.*

Stop it! Schweitzer told himself. *You're going to put work over your own family. What the hell is wrong with you? Fuck the navy.*

But the questions wouldn't quit.

He stared at the ceiling and fought the question, trying to calm his spiking pulse, to push back the rising knot in his stomach. This was a thing he couldn't shoot, couldn't kill. There was only the hard call, consequences any way he turned. You ran ops by the numbers. There was a right way and a wrong way. Here? Nothing but choices.

A shadow danced past the window, blotting out a section of the starlight, leaving Sarah shrouded in shadow. He heard a faint patter, as of raindrops, but more regular. He brushed Sarah's hair from her face again, waiting for the cloud to pass.

It didn't. The shadow hung, motionless. The patter was steady, distant. He sat up, his anxiety banished by the sudden calm that came over him when a firefight was imminent. His heart slowed, steadied. He froze, listening carefully.

The patter. Rotors.

It was four in the morning. His apartment wasn't on any aviation route he knew. In all his years of living here, he'd never seen or heard a helicopter go by, especially so late. He supposed a military helicopter could be doing a training run, but they always ran in pairs. This was a single bird.

And something more. Something odd about the sound.

Not just rotors. Muffled rotors. He was sure of it. He threw back the covers and raced to the window, trying to track the object's position, following the path of the moonbeams before the side of the building intercepted them. If it was a helo, it was very high up, probably over the roof.

He ran to the gun safe under the bed, keying in the digital code. The beeping of the keys woke Sarah, and she propped herself up on an elbow, sleep fleeing from her eyes as she took in Schweitzer's posture, the gun in his hand. The magazine was already inserted, and he chambered a round before grabbing his pants from the floor and leaping into them.

"What's going on?" Sarah asked.

"I'm not sure," he answered. He felt suddenly silly. Loading his pistol because a helicopter happened to be flying over his house? Maybe it was overkill, but his senses were screaming at him, and he'd survived in his job all these years because he always trusted them. He looked down at the pistol and remembered the axiom he'd learned in training. *If you need it and don't have it, you'll never need it again.*

Sarah's eyes narrowed, and she swung into a sitting position, nearly as alert as he was. Schweitzer didn't scare easily, so when he showed concern, she took it seriously. "Patrick," she began.

"I'm going to check on him," he said.

She nodded, and he moved to the top of the stairs just as light thumps sounded on the roof. More shadows streaked past the bay window, too fast for him to see what they were.

Patrick.

Schweitzer's son's room was just below them, the window facing the same side as theirs.

The need to check on his son nearly blotted out his senses, and he raced down the stairs, taking them two at a time, the traction of his bare feet the only thing keeping him from falling over.

His feet slapped down on the hardwood floor just as he

saw shadows moving across the gap between the floor and front door, backlit by the sconce lighting in the hallway outside. He cast a quick glance at Patrick's door, shut tight, and took a shooter's stance, stepping behind the stairwell for cover. The thin wood wouldn't stop even a nine-millimeter round, but it would obscure the line of fire. Cover was cover. He thought briefly of calling to Sarah and dismissed it. Whoever was on the other side of that door would hear him.

Sarah thought differently. "Honey?" Her voice was edged with panic.

"Stay there, sweetheart!" he shouted back. *The hell she will.* That was Sarah Schweitzer up there.

The door exploded.

A breaching charge was overkill for a flimsy, residential door, but they'd used one anyway, shivering the wood and fiberglass into fragments, sending the brass mail slot spinning over Schweitzer's shoulder to career off the wall, ringing like a bell.

Schweitzer ducked behind the staircase long enough to prevent the flash from blinding him, but the boom was loud enough to leave his ears ringing, the sound of the door fragments settling and Sarah's screaming all coming to him as if from a long way off.

The temptation to empty his magazine into the doorway was strong, but he resisted it. He'd breached many a door in his day, rolling behind the wall and allowing the enemy to expend precious ammunition into an empty doorway. Schweitzer squinted into the entryway, waiting for targets to present themselves. His mind screamed at him to rush to protect his wife and son, but the calm center, the part that had been honed by years of training and experience, knew that the best way to protect them was by dealing with whatever came through that door.

Who the hell was attacking him and his family? Why? Those questions would have to keep. Right now, all he knew was that they were dead men walking. He sighted in his pistol, covering the doorway.

A brief pause, as the assaulters waited for him to shoot,

then an arm appeared around the doorjamb, clutching a metal cylinder in a black-gloved hand.

Schweitzer fired. The round tore through the wrist, the arm jerking, the cylinder fumbling and falling to the floor just outside the door, hissing out a plume of gray-green-tinted gas into the hallway.

Another impossible shot. Another perfect hit.

Artistry.

Shouts in the hallway, and four men stumbled into the room, fumbling respirators up and snapping them into place onto their black helmets. They wore state-of-the-art body armor, submachine guns swinging off tactical slings. Black body suits beneath.

The same outfits worn by the men outside the shipping container.

Security was a constant theme in the life of every operator who worked domestic operations. Their identities were carefully hidden, the fact that they were military members the only thing known about them. Personally Identifying Information like phone numbers, addresses, and family data was guarded as if it were classified.

But somehow, the Body Farm had found him.

Later. For now, work.

He fired again, putting a round through the bridge of one enemy's nose as he did his respirator up, spinning him in a tight circle that sent him spilling into his buddy, throwing them both to the floor. The enemy beside the fallen men looked up, eyes widening as he spotted Schweitzer, jerking up his weapon and firing.

Schweitzer didn't bother dodging. The shooter hadn't even bothered to get on the sights, and the rounds flew harmlessly wide, thudding into the wall beside Patrick's door.

Schweitzer fired again, punching through the shooter's balaclava and throat, sending him to his knees, hissing through the hole in his neck.

The last man standing wisely didn't bother with his gun, and instead closed the distance, pulling a knife from his chest sheath. He'd thrown out his left hand as a sacrifice, showing good technique, but Schweitzer was in his domain now. He knew the ground, he had the drop on them. He was doing what he'd been born to do.

Schweitzer ignored the distracting hand, letting it slide over his shoulder and allowing the knife to fill his vision. As it came down, he caught the man's wrist, turning the bones to rub painfully against the glove's Kevlar protective plating. The man cried out, and the knife fell to the floor, burying the tip in the hardwood and quivering there as Schweitzer closed the remaining distance, close as a lover, jamming the pistol barrel up under the man's chin.

He fired, sending the helmet spinning off the man's head and spraying the last remaining enemy with his brains, just as he shrugged out from under the corpse of the first man Schweitzer had shot, and got to his feet.

Schweitzer grinned at his stunned expression, the slow terror dawning across his face. "You knocked on the wrong door," he drawled, pushing the corpse into him.

Six more men rushed into the room and Schweitzer's grin died.

Schweitzer had just enough time to roll behind the stairwell before a shower of rounds tore into the wall. They were well equipped, and good shots by transnational standards, but they would have to do better than that.

A moment later, they did. Bullets whistled through the staircase, one catching Schweitzer's thigh, a burning hammerblow that dropped him to one knee. He didn't have time to see how bad it was, to worry whether or not he'd bleed out. He fell onto his side, the thigh wound screaming as it impacted the floor, and leaned around the staircase bottom, firing.

He caught one enemy in the ankle, the man crying out and falling. Another salvo of bullets shredded the staircase. Something heavy and hot fell on Schweitzer, cracking a rib. He grunted and fired again, catching a man in the abdomen, hopefully below his body armor. The smoke filling the room made it impossible to tell where his rounds were impacting.

A high shriek came to him from a few feet away. "Daddy!"

Schweitzer allowed his focus to crack, his eyes to come off the gun sights and toward the sound.

Patrick stood awake in the doorway to his room, his footed pajamas showered with dust, his blond hair a tousled mess, his face pink and eyes shining with tears. "Daddy!" he shrieked again.

As one man, the enemy turned toward him.

Schweitzer's heart leapt into his throat. "Patrick! No! Get back in . . ."

The stuttering salvo resumed. The muzzles of the enemy guns flashing. Patrick flew back from the doorway, snatched by an invisible hand. A streak of blood traced the floor, an arrow pointing the way he had gone. The door to his room danced, ripped off its hinges and spinning in the air, blotting out Schweitzer's view of his son.

And then the door covered Patrick, burning, rocking on its edges. His son screamed no more.

Schweitzer screamed for him. His vision swam. The pain of his wounds vanished. He leapt to his feet, shrugging off the wreckage of the stairway, sliding on the floor slick with his own blood. *He's okay,* his mind told him. *If you can get to him fast enough, you can save him.*

A part of him knew it couldn't be true, that no four-year-old could survive that many rounds. He silenced that part. Another part came alive.

That other part propelled him to the burning door over his son, firing madly, all attempt at accuracy forgotten. He snarled, the world disappearing. The room, the smoke, the enemy, all gone. Nothing existed other than the red tunnel that encompassed the ground Schweitzer had to cover to reach Patrick's side.

He ran as if through molasses, Patrick's door growing no closer. Something struck him in his side, his shoulder. He stumbled, sank, kept going. *He'll be okay. You've still got time for CPR.*

He heard a shriek and allowed himself a look over his shoulder.

The balcony to their loft bedroom sat above the staircase, offering Sarah a clear view of Patrick's doorway. She called her son's name, leaping out over the ragged hole left by the now-burning ruin of the staircase. The guns moved toward the ceiling, spitting rounds into the recessed-can lights, showering all with plaster dust, sparks, and shattered glass. Sarah plummeted, slamming into one of the enemy. Something bright and metal flashed in her hand. Schweitzer blinked and realized it was the tiny, hook-bladed knife she used to cut canvas. The lacquered wooden handle was probably two inches long, the blade scarcely longer.

A mother wolf, she bore the man to the floor, plunging the flimsy blade into his neck above the collar of his body armor, covering herself with a bright spray of arterial blood. *Oh, baby. I knew you wouldn't stay still.*

The man writhed away from her, his finger clamped on the trigger, the gun uselessly spitting rounds into the ceiling. Sarah screamed and stabbed him again and again. He shuddered beneath her.

Her target dispatched, she looked up, eyes lighting on Patrick's door, not seeing Schweitzer before it. She got to her feet, began to run for her son.

A bullet slammed into her, lifting her into the air, throwing her back into the ruins of the staircase. She spun in the air, twitching, eyes narrowing in shock and agony. Blood misted the air as Sarah disappeared, vanishing into the burning splinters, her body limp.

For the first time in his life, Schweitzer was frozen in the midst of battle. The corpse of his wife before him. The corpse of his child behind him. Which way to turn. No way. There was no way. *They're not okay. They're not okay. They're not okay.*

The image of the refrigerated container of corpses flashed in his mind, but this time Patrick and Sarah's still, blue-lipped bodies lay on the steel racks. *A lot of corpses in one day, huh?*

More hammerblows, this time in his gut. Schweitzer took a few steps backward, tried to hitch a breath, couldn't.

The red tunnel turned gray, narrowed. He couldn't see Sarah. He tried to turn to Patrick's door. Couldn't move.

He looked down.

His chest was smeared with blood, the skin blistered, dotted with splinters.

Below it, he could make out the jagged yellow-white protrusion of his sternum, hovering over the gap that had once been his abdomen.

The curve of his rib cage held the ribbons of his abdominal muscles, hanging in flaps over the dark recesses of his gut, laid open by what must have been a considerable volume of fire. Long gray-blue ropes had uncoiled from inside, draping down to his knees. He watched, numb, as they slid farther. *Sarah? Sarah? I'm hurt.* His mouth worked. He felt something warm and sticky sliding down the corner.

The tunnel narrowed farther, his vision blurring, the edges of what little he could see going indistinct. He didn't have time for this, he had to get to Patrick, but he couldn't move.

One of the enemy stepped into his field of vision. He was still spattered with his comrade's brains, the last of the original four who'd come in. He stepped close to Schweitzer, intimately close, eyes slits of rage. Schweitzer could smell the sour stink of his breath through his balaclava. He was a coffee drinker. Smoker, too.

"We knocked on the right door, asshole," the man said.

Schweitzer could feel the cold firmness of a gun barrel shoved underneath his chin. He tried to punch the man, smack the gun down. Fight. Anything. He couldn't move.

Sarah.

Bang.

CHAPTER III
AWAKE

There was no pain.

That was the first thing Schweitzer was conscious of. Nothing hurt. He was neither cold nor hot. Neither closed in, nor spread out. No smells. No sounds. No sensations. There was simply nothing. Nothing but this certainty; he could think. He was himself.

He was alive.

Sarah. He felt for her, strained to hear a snatch of Patrick's cries. Where were they? Where was he? He still couldn't move, but now it wasn't because his body wouldn't obey him. He couldn't feel a body at all. There were no muscles to strain, no mouth to grimace with.

Am I dead? Is this what death is?

The thought filled him with panic. He'd learned long ago not to dwell too much on death or what it would be like. That was a short road to madness in his line of work. But in his weak moments, he'd imagined the things he'd learned in church or debated on the middle-school playground. Death would be a lake of fire, or a cloud covered with angelic harpists, or a simple end to everything.

But never this. Never consciousness without action. Never life without life.

An eternity of this would drive him mad.

He struggled to calm himself. If he was thinking, he was alive. Maybe he was in a coma. Maybe they would find a way to revive him. And if they could revive him, maybe they could do the same for Sarah.

Oh God, Sarah. Patrick. Oh God.

He fought against the thought, the panic it inspired. It seemed he was a disembodied mind. His stomach couldn't turn over. His balls couldn't hike into his abdomen. But panic he could feel.

Rosewater. He smelled rosewater. He tried to flare nostrils he couldn't feel, to sniff air into nasal passages he no longer possessed. Nothing.

He struggled to track the scent, to follow it. There was only darkness.

And then it was gone.

In its place, a presence. It enveloped him. It gripped him, draping him like a lover in the afterglow, tendrils dug into every cranny of his floating consciousness. Stifling.

He struggled, whirled, tried to throw it off, but how could he, with no body to move?

The thing probed, licked at him, pushed in. It drank his thoughts, digging into his secrets, his memories. The violation was total, he was laid bare before this thing, could feel it exulting in its knowledge of him, its raping of the long years of his history. It sifted his past and pressed closer, hungry.

Years in the SEALs had taught him to adapt. *When you're under fire, you don't just sit there. You get off the X. Moving the wrong way is still moving.* His physical senses were gone, the rosewater scent a teasing ghost that tricked him, a phantom limb of a smell. He had no body to use, or if he did, it was full of traitor nerves that would not report or obey. He relaxed, stopped trying to reach out to his dead physical self. He drove his consciousness in reverse, seeking the presence. He pushed back into it, and recoiled.

It was cold, ancient. Though his physical senses were gone, his consciousness still clung to them as parameters to define his experience. The presence felt like dry parchment, gray ice, jagged bone.

Its malevolence was plain. It bore no goodwill. It held him like some giant tick, a cuttlefish latching onto its prey.

He felt its surprise that he reached back for it, felt it take his measure.

And then it spoke.

No words. There was simply a vibration in his mind, the tremors of communication that his consciousness registered as speech. It was as if an army of discordant voices spoke at once, from a field of distances—some shouting in his nonexistent ears, some calling softly from the bottom of a well. It spoke in a hundred languages. Some he understood, some were hauntingly familiar, some impossibly alien. It was sensual, mocking, harsh.

It was legion.

You are with me now, and we will make a mighty work together.

Schweitzer tried to follow the voice, perceive the speaker, had to forcibly fight his instinct to try to see it physically. He tried to answer, had no mouth to speak with. He roiled first with frustration and finally fear, until at last he forced the panic away, focused back on his floating consciousness, and reached out to the thing again.

How . . . ? he managed. His mind fell back on instinct again and tried to talk through an absent mouth.

Good, the thing answered. *You are a quick study.*

How are you . . . ? Where am I?

There is no "where." We are together. We are one. You were once called James Schweitzer. That name is lost to you now.

The thought made the panic spike. He tried to calm himself, think the way he had once spoken when backed into a corner, conjure some of that swagger. *Then what are we calling me these days?*

The voice laughed, or thought a laugh. It resounded in his

mind like the cracking of dried twigs. *You are called nothing. When you are called at all, you are called through me.*

And who are you?

I am Ninip, the thing said, intoning its name like a priest with a blood offering, *and I am war.*

There, again, the barest hint of fragrance. Sarah's homemade perfume, maddeningly close, the origin masked by the confused darkness.

Sarah! he cried out. *Patrick!* He strained his mind, the same poor facsimile of hearing through which the presence spoke to him. If he was dead, maybe they were here with him. Maybe they could answer.

But it was Ninip's voice he heard, the grating rasp of chains dragged over stone.

They are lost to you, the presence said, the tone suddenly crooning, sympathetic. He felt its touch again, warming now, a reassuring arm across his nonexistent shoulders. *I am your family now.*

Schweitzer shrugged the arm away. *Bullshit. How the fuck do you know?*

I know death, Ninip said. *Soon, you will, too. For now, you must trust me.*

The scumbags Schweitzer routinely operated against enjoyed kidnapping for ransom nearly as much as they did arms sales and blowing stuff up. The first rule of negotiation was always proof of life.

Bullshit, he said. *Show me bodies.*

He blinked into the darkness, or tried to. If he could smell Sarah's perfume without a nose, then maybe he could see her without eyes.

You doubt the darkness. Ninip sounded tired. *The new ones always do. You still cling to the tinctures of life. Very well. Look upon the world again, for all the joy it may bring you.*

Schweitzer's vision went from black to white. Sensation followed. His muscles locked, tensed over sturdy bones. His eyes blinked, and his nostrils flared. He lolled a dry tongue, thick in a parched mouth. He flexed fingers.

He could feel his body responding to the commands he sent it, but there was something wrong. All his senses came to him at a remove, as if he were hearing about the world thirdhand, a tale told by an expert narrator who, for all his skill, couldn't capture the spirit of the thing.

Look, Ninip commanded.

Schweitzer blinked again. The whiteness flickered into static, then slowly began to resolve into color and depth.

He was lying on a metal table, surrounded by men with guns leveled at him.

He sat up, his torso rising effortlessly, no sensation of his abdominals engaging or his thighs flexing to compensate.

The presence stayed with him. The feeling of envelopment, of intrusion, didn't fade in the least. Ninip's being was so close to him that he imagined he could hear the thing breathing.

Inside him. Ninip was inside him, in his heart, in his head, in the atoms of his flesh.

They shared his body. Two souls in a single shape.

Am I possessed? His thoughts now gave voice inside his own mind, and Ninip heard and answered.

Some call it so, but they are fools. You are bonded. You are wed. You are better.

Schweitzer looked around the room.

It was a hospital, but secured like no hospital he'd ever seen. The room was windowless, about twenty feet across and bare save for a wheeled standing desk covered with computer equipment. The door looked to be made of solid steel, with locking bars that would make a bank vault look weak. To either side, tall red tanks stood, lines running to nozzles placed around the room, tiny blue pilot lights burning below them. A broad red button stood beneath a plastic flip-up shield beside the door.

Whoever built this place wanted to be able to burn whatever was inside at the touch of a button.

Soldiers surrounded the table, carbines leveled at Schweitzer's head. They were kitted out for war, helmets, heavy body armor, grenades. One of them held a flame-thrower, blue pilot flame flickering from the tip.

At their head stood an older man, wild white hair and whiskers giving him a reasonable likeness to Mark Twain. He wore an immaculate lab coat with a plastic badge clipped to the breast pocket. It showed only his face, the Department of Defense seal, and a single name: ELDREDGE.

The man scowled, frown deepening until his eyes positively blazed hatred. He hunched, fingers hooked into claws. Shadows danced between his legs and beneath his armpits, haloing him in curling black mist. The shadows cavorted around the soldiers' boots, writhed about their weapon muzzles, dripping red at the edges, tinting all in blood.

The man said something, a barking sound, the coughing of an angry monkey, his teeth glinting wetly as his lips parted. The recesses of the room bent and wavered, fading in and out of focus, making Schweitzer doubt their stability. The table was a shelf beneath his buttocks and thighs, his feet dangling out over an abyss.

He looked down. A threadbare hospital gown flapped off him, tattered and filthy. The air vents hissed, rasping filthy gas into the room. Maybe poison.

This is the seen world, the felt world, Ninip said. *It is not so pretty as you left it.*

This isn't the world, Schweitzer said. *You're a fucking liar.*

And as he said it, so it was.

He felt his vision peel at the edges, the veneer lifting ever so slightly, until he could discern the filter, thinner than onionskin, draped over his senses.

There were two souls sharing his body, two sets of senses perceiving the world. This horrid landscape of foul smells and threatening visages was Ninip's view. Schweitzer shuddered to think of a life lived on this brutal plain: every movement a threat, every sound a warning, every touch a blow.

He rebelled against the perception, reaching out with

his spirit to peel away the layer that filtered his sense of the world.

He felt the presence dig in, tendrils chafing against his soul, clutching and pulling, struggling to hold on to its control over their shared perception. It battered his consciousness, closing their shared eyes, clenching their shared hands.

Stop, Ninip said. *A comfortable lie is still a lie. I am showing you the truth. Do not exchange it for the duped sleep of the contented.*

Schweitzer ignored it, chipped away, pushing back. At long last, he gave an inward shout, and the veneer fell away, the world coming into normal focus again.

The man in the white lab coat frowned down at him, but he did not scowl. The soldiers around him came into stark relief, the shadows gone, their uniforms familiar. The hospital gown was clean and blue. The air vents ran smooth and silent in the background, blowing sweet, clean air.

You are a fool, hissed Ninip, *and you will reap a fool's reward.*

The man in the white coat leaned in close. "Can you hear me?" His voice was gentle.

Yes, Schweitzer responded, realized he was speaking internally to Ninip, that his lips hadn't moved. Schweitzer struggled, sucking in air, forcing it down his windpipe, feeling his lungs inflate, puffing out inside his chest cavity, then forcing them to squeeze the air up and out again, choking the muscles of his throat down around the air as it pushed out of his mouth.

"Yes," he said, recoiled at the thick croaking that came out, not even close to a human word.

The man's eyebrows arched. "Very impressive. It takes most of our . . . new arrivals much longer to master even the rudiments of speech."

Schweitzer felt sick panic, looked down, yanked up the hospital gown.

His stomach was whole, a long trail of sutures running

a railroad-track pattern from just above his crotch to the base of his sternum.

His skin was hairless, the white-gray of a fish's underbelly.

He flared his nostrils, smelled the stale, antiseptic odor of the room.

But the scents weren't guided to him by his breath. He stilled himself, watched his torso.

He wasn't breathing.

You have not been listening, Ninip said. *You are with me now. We are a fortress. We are mighty, and together we shall have the gate of our enemies.*

That's nice, Schweitzer said. *We're also dead, aren't we?*

The memories flooded him. Patrick crumpling beneath a burning door. Sarah falling backward through the air, a bullet chewing through her tender flesh, blood misting the room.

A pistol barrel jammed beneath his chin. *We knocked on the right door, asshole.*

An explosion. Darkness.

Schweitzer lowered his head.

He felt Ninip curl around him, could imagine the presence as a serpent coiling about his shoulders, forked tongue flicking in his ear. Grief subsided, anger heightened, rising until his muscles bunched.

We will avenge you, Ninip said. *We will avenge your family. Our vengeance will be legend. Our enemies will sing of it for generations.*

Schweitzer found himself leaning into the voice. The thought of vengeance sang in his soul. The fuckers who'd killed him, killed his family would pay. Somehow he'd cheated death. Maybe it was only to give him a second chance to make things right.

We have a new life together, Ninip whispered, *and we will see the butcher's bill paid in full.*

Schweitzer raised his head, blinked again, met Eldredge's eyes.

"You must have a lot of questions," the man said as the

soldiers around him slowly lowered their weapons. "Let me start with the first one. Moving isn't living. Thinking isn't living. You are dead, James Schweitzer."

"How?" He exhaled.

Eldredge patted his shoulder. "It will take time to master speaking, and you'll likely never be fully capable," he said. "Pushing air over your vocal cords came naturally before. Now you have to force it."

It wasn't an answer. Frustration spiked, and Schweitzer clenched a hand on the stainless steel of the table's edge.

And felt it crunch in his grip. He looked down to find the metal crumpled in his fist, balled like tissue paper below his dead, gray knuckles.

A mountain, Ninip crooned, *a river in flood. We are mighty.*

Schweitzer felt the power surging through him. The strength bunched in his muscles, coursed through his tendons. He looked back up at Eldredge, the man suddenly looking old, tiny, and frail. Schweitzer could break him in half with no effort, all he had to do was reach and . . .

He battered the lens aside. Ninip again. His seeing, his thoughts, his hungers.

Not so fast, Schweitzer said.

They are toys, Ninip said. *They cannot harm us. They are made to be our slaves.*

They are people, Schweitzer said, *and we're not enslaving anyone. That went out of style a long time ago.*

He felt Ninip's sigh. *My grandfather told me that repetition can teach even the donkey. I will repeat the lessons until you learn.*

Good luck with that, Schweitzer said, straining against Ninip's influence. The eagerness to test his newfound strength on Eldredge didn't abate, but he managed to hold it in check, surging just below his skin, making his fingers twitch.

"How?" he managed again.

"Well," Eldredge said, shrugging. "Honestly? Magic."

The older man stepped aside. Behind him stood another

man, thick beard neatly trimmed, dark eyes regarding Schweitzer with open curiosity. He wore the long shirt-robe and baggy trousers common to the hill tribesmen in the lawless steppe around Afghanistan and Iran. He was thin, his head looking too big for his shoulders. A small kufi capped his wild shock of black, tightly curling hair.

The air around him shimmered, swirled, as if some barely visible river coursed about him. Schweitzer shook his head, but it was not Ninip's influence this time. Whatever he was seeing was true to the man before him. Eldredge paid it no notice; nor did any of the soldiers.

"This," Eldredge said, "is Jawid Rahimi. He is . . . well . . . he is a Sorcerer, and he has raised you from the dead."

Hello. Jawid's voice echoed in Schweitzer's mind, penetrating into the space that he shared with Ninip. *Hello to both of you.*

It was the language of Jawid's thoughts. Schweitzer could hear the Pashto beneath, the slow and painstaking translation into the halting English that reached him. It was like listening to two men, one talking slowly after the other.

Jawid did not share the space with Ninip and Schweitzer, merely spoke into it, but Schweitzer could sense the channel that connected them, could see the swirling current about the Sorcerer focusing forward toward him.

This one is strong, Ninip said to Jawid. *You have done well.*

Jawid said nothing, but Schweitzer could feel the Sorcerer's fear at Ninip's words, felt him withdraw slightly, drawing back up the channel he had created.

Sarah and Patrick, Schweitzer said hurriedly. *Where are my wife and son?*

They are meat, Ninip snarled, *and we are steel.*

Fuck off. Where the fuck are they?

You mewl and whine like a kitten, Ninip answered. *You cry for milk and your mother. You are with me now. We are a storm.*

Jesus, give it a rest. Jawid, what happened to my family?

He knew the answer before Jawid gave it, could feel it in the Sorcerer's link to he and Ninip. *They . . . they did not survive. I am sorry.*

Though Schweitzer had known this, had seen it, the grief still came anew. He lowered their shared head, cradling their head in their hands, the emotion setting their shoulders shaking, physical motions performed out of habit. They had no tears, their shared cheeks would not redden.

Disgusting, Ninip said. *They are better off, beyond the bags of flesh that held them prisoner.*

Where? Schweitzer asked. *Where are they now? Are they in heaven?*

I don't know, Jawid answered. *I only found Ninip.*

Where did you find him? Schweitzer shouted. *Maybe they're in the same place! Send me back there?*

I cannot. I . . .

Jawid is a fool, Ninip said. *An ignorant goatherd who cannot spell his own name.*

Shut the hell up, you don't . . .

No . . . Jawid cut in, *he is right. I cannot read and write, and I am not good at stories. I will show you.*

Schweitzer's vision blotted out, his mind swept along the current of Jawid's magic, drowning even Ninip's curses. His vision returned to the grainy static, flickering and wavering, the colors finally running together into unbroken white.

Slowly, the field dissolved, a scene resolving beneath it.

A little boy, shivering beside a goat path, scrawny, filthy, arms wrapped around his knees. Behind him, a hut of scavenged wood, plastic sheeting, and corrugated metal has been ransacked, set alight. There are corpses among the wreckage, the boy's family.

It's you, Schweitzer said.

Yes, Jawid answered. *My father was proud. He would not pay the warlord for the privilege of herding in our own ancestral range. They left me to starve. How could a little boy survive in the hills that ground the Russians and the Americans both to powder?*

The little boy standing, tears streaking clean trails through the dirt covering his face. The air beginning to eddy around him, shimmering, visible only to him. The little boy crying out to the world beyond, reaching for his family.

And finding something else.

A hand stretched out from the afterlife, grasping his own, hungry for life, following the sound of his voice back into the land of the living.

My grandmother told me of the jinn, Jawid said. *I put the first one in a stone and carried it with me. It made me run faster than the wind. Fast enough to hunt hares on my own.*

The boy, face red with blood, sheltering under an overhanging rock, chewing hungrily on the body of a rabbit.

That was how they found me. Hard men with eyes like flint, dirty white turbans trailing over Russian military fatigues. They carry guns, grenade launchers. They kneel before the boy, offer him food, their eyes crawl over him with a hunger that made Schweitzer recoil.

What could I do? I was a child. I wanted nothing more than a family again.

The boy, eyes kohled and lips rouged, dressed in a woman's gown, sitting in the lap of one of the hard men, a finger idly stroking his hair.

Abdul-Razaq told me he loved me, and I told him of my jinn-in-a-stone. Some of the Talebs wanted to kill me, but others saw the power in what I could do, they made me reach out again and again. I made amulets, talismans. The jinn made the Talebs strong, or swift, or able to see in darkness. It made our little band mighty. Until . . .

A gun battle. The boy shivering again, from fear this time, hiding behind a boulder as explosions sound around him.

One of the Talebs leaping over him, the amulet about his neck sending him fifty feet in the air. The sniper takes him anyway, the huge round nearly severing his head.

American soldiers. Special Forces by their gear, surrounding the boy. One of them kneels, takes the boy's shoulders, speaks gently. He knows what the boy can do. They have gotten it from a captive Taleb.

The rear hatch of a C-130 slowly closing. A female medic smiles at the boy, checking him for lice, giving him shots, antibiotics. The shudder as the huge plane takes off, the bumpy ride through the long hours before the hatch lowers again, the light of the American sky flooding in.

They have given me a home, here. I still bring the jinn, but now . . .

. . . I am the amulet, Schweitzer finished for him. *My body.*

Schweitzer's vision went white again as Jawid's magic withdrew, then resolved back to the room, Eldredge looking at Jawid, his brow furrowed with worry.

"No problem," Jawid said to Eldredge in heavily accented English. "I am telling him how he came to be."

"Ah." Eldredge turned back to Schweitzer. "So, there it is."

That's what you are, Schweitzer said to Ninip. *One of these jinn.*

A goatherd's name for a thing he cannot understand. I was a god and king both, in my time. It pleases me to live again.

Sarah, Patrick. The images flashed through his mind, a bullet knocking his wife back into the wreckage, the burning door covering his son. The thought of this unlife without her . . . He didn't think she'd like this existence, but he was powerless before the impulse, so strong it blotted out even Ninip's presence for a moment. If there was even a chance that he could see her, could talk to her . . .

Schweitzer sucked in air again, working the bellows of their lungs, tensing the muscles around their larynx. "Make . . . Sarah . . . live."

Eldredge and Jawid exchanged a worried glance.

"I cannot do it for everyone . . ." Jawid said. "They were not . . . strong enough."

Lies, Ninip said. *They were not useful enough.*

"Why?" Schweitzer asked.

Eldredge nodded to Jawid, who stepped back. "You served your country in life, Jim. We were hoping you'd continue to do so now."

"What?"

"The Gemini Cell has been engaging in some experimental operations based on Mr. Rahimi's rather . . . unique capabilities. You will find you now have some capabilities of your own. Your memories, your skills, didn't pass with your life, Jim. You are still a SEAL. This is why the Cell doesn't work with taxi drivers or chefs. We make warriors, Jim. Warriors the likes of which this world has never seen."

He has the right of it, Ninip said. *The world has never seen the likes of us.*

"Let me show you." Eldredge waved to two of the soldiers, who slung their carbines and stepped aside to reveal a dressing mirror set into the wall. "Look at what you are now."

Schweitzer stood, felt the energy course through their legs, the muscles tensing, ready to respond to his commands. He wanted to run, to leap. He knew they would run faster than he'd ever gone in life, jump higher than any living man could.

Through me you have these gifts, Ninip said. *Together, we are a mighty work. Alone, you rot.*

Schweitzer forced them to walk, slowly, deliberately, the soldiers parting around them, until they stood before the mirror. He stripped away the hospital gown and surveyed himself.

He recognized his body, still lean and hard from grueling training, the buoy swims, the beach runs, op after op in sixty pounds of gear.

They'd done the best they could with his stomach. The sutures were a Frankenstein mess, but they were solid and holding.

They'd had less success with his face.

The bullet had entered through his chin and sheared off the back of his head. It had tumbled en route, shattering the bone behind his eyes, nose, and mouth. He raised a hand to feel the surgical steel they'd used to provide the armature that had once occurred naturally, his skin stretched taut over it, stitched with the same wide white sutures along his false mandible. What remained of his face stretched out, flattened across the metal surface beneath, looking as if his old self had been painted across a slightly curving canvas.

His eyes were gone. In their place, soft silver light played in the sockets, glowing gently, eddying like the air around Jawid's shoulders.

He gestured to the twin flames. "Eyes."

"Magic." Eldredge shrugged. "We don't understand why it happens when a soul is paired with one of Jawid's jinn, but it always does. We tried leaving the old eyes in at first, but they always burned away. Now we just cut to the chase and take them out."

Schweitzer gazed back into the mirror.

"Monster," Schweitzer said.

"Only to your enemies," Eldredge said. "To the rest of us, you're a hero."

CHAPTER IV
OUT WITH THE BAD AIR

Steven Chang looked down at the tiny tube emerging from his chest. A three-sided bandage hid it from view, letting air escape from his reinflated lung, preventing it from drawing any back in with each breath.

In his years with the teams, Chang had seen far worse but never on himself. The sight reminded him that he was dizzy, nauseous. He swallowed, felt faintness swamp him, put out an arm to steady himself against the hospital wall.

You're not a SEAL, Master Chief Green had said to him in Coronado. *Fucking slant-eyed piece of shit. You can wear that pin, but you didn't fucking earn it. Don't you ever forget that.* In addition to being a racist, Green was a mean drunk and he'd been drummed out of the navy shortly after, but his words stuck with Chang, and down the years he'd never been able to shake them.

The doc told him that the bullet had broken his ribs, driving them into his lungs, a hidden wound that could have easily killed him had it not been for Schweitzer's quick thinking.

Jim Schweitzer, the first smiling face since graduating

the SEAL basic course known as BUD/S, the first friend
he'd had in the teams. The man who never doubted him,
even when he doubted himself. The same friend who'd had
his head sheered off by a bullet while Chang slept soundly
in an air-conditioned hospital room. SEALs were closer
than brothers. His had saved his life, then died hours later.

*You couldn't have done anything. Don't do that to your-
self.* But saying it over and over in his head didn't make
him feel it. If he hadn't gotten himself shot, if he had
trained harder, fought harder.

You're not a SEAL. Green hated him for his race, but
that didn't make him wrong. Chang tried to take a breath
to steady himself and winced at the fiery agony in his
chest. He doubled over, panic racing up his spine to burn at
the base of his skull. He was no stranger to fear, he knew
how to put it aside, but that didn't address the root cause.

Weakness. He could see Green's disgusted face in his
mind's eye.

Chang looked up, nodding at one of the nurses, who
frowned in concern. "I'm fine," he whispered. *You're not
fine. You're weak and Jim's dead and it's your fault.*

He straightened, composing his features before moving
the rest of the way down the hallway to the outpatient
room. The sign outside the room read SENTARA PRINCESS
ANNE, MED SURG—3.

I can't let you go, the doc had said. *I need to keep an
eye on you.* But one look at Chang's face had convinced
him. Chang might be a lousy SEAL, but he was a good
friend. He owed Jim this much.

He turned the handle and eased the door open, stepping
into the immaculate hospital room. It looked more like a
hotel, complete with banal art and a fake potted plant in
the corner. Four beds lined the walls, all empty save one.

Sarah Schweitzer was awake.

She lay on her side, a huge swatch of white gauze taped
over her abdomen. The round had struck her hip and rico-
cheted off the bone, tumbling upward to take a sizeable
bite out of the meat below her ribs. What it hadn't done

was pierce any vital organs. Chang didn't doubt she was in pain, be he also didn't doubt that she'd live.

And the pain she felt was nothing compared to what she was about to feel. He braced himself against the wall, watching his T-shirt bunch and rise around the tiny tube, fighting against dizziness again.

Lock it up. She's not going to hear it from some jerkoff chaplain. She never believed in God. It needs to come from you.

She looked up as he shut the door, struggled to rise, winced at the pain in her side, and lay back down.

"Steve!" Her voice trembled, her pink hair a slash across her eyes. God, she was beautiful. Jim had always talked about what a firecracker she was. A true SEAL's wife. He'd deserved her.

It should be him here, not me. The thought flooded him, dampening his smile. She frowned as she saw it. *Damn it, you will be strong for her.* He grinned until he felt like a store mannequin, and made it the rest of the way to the bed, pulling up the metal-framed chair beside it.

"Hey, Sarah. How're you holding up?"

"I've been kidnapped," she said. "This isn't a hospital. This is a fucking jail. Nobody will tell me anything. I have to see Patrick . . ."

"The P-Train is fine," Chang said. "He just needs to rest is all. So do you." A lie. Patrick was badly burned, with one arm broken in three places where a round had passed clean through. That didn't even count the damage the experience had done to his still-forming mind, but it wouldn't help her to hear that. "He's in pediatrics. Doc says you can see him tomorrow."

He silently prayed she would stay focused on the good news, be too distracted to ask him about Jim, give him time to get his nerve up to . . .

"Where's Jim?"

Focused as a laser. She could have been a SEAL herself. His heart sank. *Try not to fuck it up too badly.*

He opened his mouth to answer, closed it. He paused,

tried to form words again, but it was no use. Jim was dead and he was alive and the world would never be right again. The silence at last dragged on long enough for her to have her answer.

"Oh, Steve," she said. He felt her fingertips brush his knee. Her voice broke. "Oh, Steve. You poor kid. I'm so sorry."

He heard her sobs, felt her hand shaking. In the midst of all this, she was sorry for him, only worried about how keenly he felt the loss. It was too much.

He pitched off the chair, wracked with sobs so hard they doubled him over. His knees hit the reflective tiles of the floor, and he fumbled for her hand, grasped it tight, heedless of his fingernails digging into the backs of her knuckles, his wounded lung singing in agony as the hitching sobs shook his ribs. She reached across, a move that he knew must hurt her equally, wrapped her arm around his head, drew him close.

They lay like that, her on the bed and he slumped on the floor, the room filled with their hitching breaths and exhalations, the pouring out of sorrow, the whispered "I'm sorry," and "I'm so sorry," and "I won't leave you alone."

It was Chang who said the last, and when he looked up at her again, he realized how deeply he felt it. This woman and her son were the last he had of Jim, and he couldn't bear the thought of them struggling, with grief or anything else. He knew Sarah was tough as nails. Hell, Chief told him she'd stabbed one of the assailants through the neck with her canvas knife. She didn't need his help, but that didn't lessen the urge to give it. He'd loved Jim, and that meant he loved her, too.

They cried and cried, and Chang couldn't remember when they finally stopped, exhausted and dried out, no tears left in them.

"What happened?" she asked at last.

"I don't know," he answered lamely. "They're still trying to piece everything together. I just got discharged from medical an hour ago."

"And you came straight here." Her eyes went wet again.

"I wanted you to hear it from me." *Bullshit. You needed someone to lean on. You don't want to be alone either.*

"Terrorists? Criminals? Who were they?" Sarah was a SEAL's wife. She knew the list of bad guys lined up to take their vengeance on her husband was a mile long. "How the fuck did they find us?"

"I have no idea. We'll find out, Sarah. We'll find out, and we'll make sure it never happens again."

She tried to sit up again, slumped down grimacing in pain. "You do that, Steve. You make sure those fuckers pay. They hurt my boy."

"I swear to God, Sarah. We'll take care of them." *Others will do that. I will sit on my ass and "convalesce."*

"You got any other family in the area?" he asked. "Anyone close? I doubt you have to worry about it, but it stands to reason we should warn them."

"Just my sister, out in the Shenandoah Valley. Hours away. Middle of nowhere."

"Okay. I hate to put this on your plate, Sarah, but we need to start thinking about relocating you as soon as you're discharged. Whoever these guys were, they were able to pin down a team member. That means they've got some intel. I'm not trying to scare you, but . . ."

"No." She shuddered with grief, spasms crossing her face until she bit down, swallowing them. "No, I appreciate it. You're right. I just can't . . . I just can't deal with all this right now."

They were quiet for a moment.

"Oh God." She sighed. "I've got so many phone calls to make. I've got so many people to tell."

Chang patted the air with his palms. "Please don't do that. Not for a while."

She stared at him. Her expression said she understood the why of it, but that didn't make her like it.

"This is life with the teams," he said. "Schweitzer wasn't just gunned down in a barroom brawl gone bad. This was a hit by an organization. They're asking you to hold off on talking about it until they can get on top of this, figure out how Jim's identity got leaked."

She stared at him, tears forming in the corners of her eyes, spilling down her cheeks.

"You want to get these guys, don't you?"

She nodded silently.

"You're not alone." He reached out and grabbed her hand again. "I'll be with you every step of the way through this. Promise."

She looked up at him, gratitude and determination mixing in her beautiful, dark eyes. "I appreciate it, Steve. I do." He believed her, but that didn't mean she needed him.

She swallowed, steeled herself. "I need to see his body."

Chang started, stomach doing flips. He'd been hoping she wouldn't ask that, had known she would. He stalled for time. "What? I mean, do you think it's rea . . ."

"I need to see him," Sarah said again. "I need to . . . I need to close this. I can't leave until I do."

Chang had been grateful when they refused to show him his teammate's body. He had asked because he knew what was expected of a brother SEAL. But the thought of Jim's body, cold, gray, and dead, the gaping wounds covered up by gauze or sewn shut, turned his stomach. He loved Jim, he couldn't bear to see him dead.

Sarah was braver. "I need to see him," she repeated. "I don't care what he looks like."

Chang bit down on the tears again, swallowed hard. He struggled to draw breath, to find the words to tell her.

"Sarah, he got chewed up pretty bad. They . . . they shot him in the head." *Shut up, you idiot! She doesn't need to hear that.*

Sarah didn't bat an eyelash. "I said I don't care what he looks like. I need to see him."

Chang swallowed again, winced at the pain in his chest—and said it. "You can't."

She managed to sit up this time, wound or no wound. Her eyes were hard. "What the fuck do you mean 'I can't'? Why can't I?"

"There's nothing to see. He got . . . he was . . ."

"What the fuck do you mean there's nothing to see? How the fuck can there be nothing to see!?" She was yelling now, and Chang felt himself shrinking into his chair. He couldn't bear to see her in pain, but this anger, this was a hundred times worse.

He realized his posture and sat up straight, cheeks burning with shame. She wanted it unvarnished, then that's what she would get. "They mangled him, Sarah. They cut him to ribbons. There was nothing to preserve. As soon as they got what was left back to base, they cremated him."

CHAPTER V
LOADOUT

Physically, Schweitzer stood before a stainless-steel work-bench heaped with instruments of war. Eldredge stood with his arms folded as an armorer arranged the gear, added more. Internally, Schweitzer huddled inside his own mind, spiritual arms wrapped around intangible knees, head down and weeping. Sarah and Patrick gone. This . . . thing sharing his body. His own life snuffed out and replaced with . . . what?

Confusion and grief blotted out his senses. *Oh, Mom. First Pete and now me. I'm so so sorry.* Was his mother looking down on him now? Did she feel grief? He gritted his spiritual teeth as he shut out the legion of questions his new existence raised. But he couldn't shut out the faces whirling through his mind. Sarah, Patrick, Steve Chang. Pete. Always Pete. *Proud of you, bro. Always knew you'd make it.*

Schweitzer had always ignored the tiny sliver of his heart that secretly hoped that, when he finally gave up his last breath, he'd see Pete again. He'd known the priests were wrong but could never kill the hope they were right.

Were they? What was . . . this? Where was he now?
Who was he now?

Lock it up. Dead or alive, you're still a SEAL.

Sniveling like an infant. Ninip shuddered around him,
oozing contempt. *Death is the gateway to strength.*

He felt his spirit buffeted by the jinn, knocking him
against the inner walls of his own body. Images began to
replay in his head, blotting out the faces of his friends and
family. A hostage-rescue op in the Colombian jungle, Schweitzer springing from a tree branch like a jaguar, bearing
his target to the damp earth, gloved hand clamped over his
mouth, knife plunging into the enemy's throat again and
again, hot blood washing over him. Turning a corner in an
abandoned warehouse in Greece, coming face-to-face
with three armed thugs, as surprised as he was. Pistol flying out of its holster almost of his own accord. Three head-
shots in as many seconds, three bodies crumbling lifeless
to the concrete floor.

Artistry.

Schweitzer had always allowed himself a nod of cold,
professional satisfaction at a difficult job well-done, sustained himself with the knowledge that his family and the
families of his brothers-in-arms slept safe in their beds
because of what he did.

But this time, the images were accompanied by an exultant thrill, a naked and simple joy, the chest-thumping
predator lust of bloody victory. SEAL training had worked
overtime to kill that kind of thinking. Quiet professionalism trumped heroic pride in his line of work.

It felt wrong. It felt fantastic.

What the fuck are you doing?

Showing you the truth, Ninip answered. *The truth of
what you have done, of who we are together.*

Schweitzer pushed back against Ninip, felt the jinn give
ground, swarm back in. He could swat the reaching tendrils of the presence from his mind, but he was a man with
only two spiritual hands, where Ninip was an octopus.

He shook his head, blinked, clung to the conscious world before him.

Eldredge stood beside the armorer, looking over the panoply laid out on the workbench. The SEAL teams had always gotten their pick of the latest and greatest war gear the navy could buy, but this was special.

Pretty. Schweitzer could feel Ninip's excitement, the presence reaching out to their hands, tensing the trigger finger.

Ninip's tendrils dug deeper in his memories, matching the image of the weapons before them to Schweitzer's knowledge of guns, from shooting skeet with his father as a little boy, all the way to his first qualification with the M16 in boot camp, to the slow building of his deadly skill in the CQB shoothouse. The presence shuddered in excitement. Schweitzer observed Ninip, soaking up every detail, reaching out to touch the jinn even as it touched him.

Schweitzer thought of the bloodlust sensation the jinn had sent coursing through him, choreographed to scenes from his past. Whatever this demon wanted, he wanted the opposite. All good ops started with intel. Knowing your enemy was the first step.

New to you, eh? Schweitzer asked. *Who the hell are you, anyway?*

Who I am is as useless as who you are, Ninip answered. *There is we, and that is all that matters.*

He felt Ninip pressing to stretch his filter across their joint senses again, shadows gathering in the corners of the room. Schweitzer fought back against it, boosting his own energy into their shared body, struggling to keep his view of the world.

I'm thinking things would go a lot easier if we made an effort to get along.

Schweitzer could feel Ninip's anger and frustration. It was not used to being defied. *Let's try this again,* Schweitzer said. *Who are you?*

I am a god, Ninip answered. Schweitzer's vision went

white, then to static again, as it had when Jawid had shown him his story.

It resolved into an image of a muscular man, back to him, standing atop a stone pyramid. His dark skin was festooned with jewels, dangling from his crown, from the collar that stretched to the tips of his shoulders, from the trimming of his leather boots and broad belt. Tight black ringlets of hair hung to his waist, shining with oil.

Guards stood to either side of him, nude except for bronze helmets and hide shields. Their bronze-tipped spears pumped into the air, matching the rhythm of the throng of people at the pyramid's base. The crowd was sallow-skinned, with hooked noses, black hair and eyes, matching the guards' and the jeweled man standing before them, arms outstretched, soaking up their adulation.

I ruled them. The greatest warrior of my age. And now I am joined with the greatest warrior of yours. And we will rule again.

Schweitzer's vision returned, crystallizing into Eldredge, arms folded across his chest, regarding him frankly. "Jim? Are you with me?"

The speaking was coming more easily now, but it was still difficult to consciously do what had always been unconscious. "Talk . . . jinn."

Eldredge's eyebrows drew together. "Ninip? What does he say?"

"Eh . . . gypt . . . Sumer? Old."

Eldredge shook his head. "You are the first Operator we've had who could communicate with us. I'd love to get some interview time. Do you think . . . Ninip would be willing to talk to us?"

Old fool. We will drink his blood, Ninip said. *You bray like a donkey with this animal. Take the weapons! Let us go!*

Schweitzer felt their shared hands twitch toward the war gear, threw his will against Ninip's, struggling to pull their limbs back into place. *Calm the fuck down! We can't just shoot our way out of here. Everyone has guns like these.*

We are greater than the best of them, Ninip said. The bloodlust surged again. Schweitzer felt a phantom pulse, as if his dead heart raced with excitement. It was heady, addictive. He pushed against it.

There are hundreds of them, and they're the good guys. Calm down and let's get our bearings first.

Schweitzer felt Ninip pause, relax the fight for their shared hands and arms. *We shall see what the cattle offer.*

"No talk," Schweitzer managed.

Eldredge shook his head. "See what inroads you can make. This is the first . . . communications we've ever had with a jinn since the program began. I'd love to see what we can do with that. The jinn do not speak with Jawid willingly."

"Other . . . Op . . . rators?"

"Were not strong enough to grapple with . . . with what Jawid calls jinn. They became . . . uncommunicative."

Schweitzer didn't like the sound of that.

"The world is changing, Jim. It has been for some time. Jawid isn't the only person with his . . . abilities. What Jawid does . . . this summoning, is particularly rare, nearly singular. But there are most certainly others. Those who can call fire. Those who can fly. Those who can heal flesh or tear it. The Gemini Cell is looking into what these phenomena are. Sometimes, they manifest in decent people, folks who are cooperative, who want to work with us. Sometimes, these powers manifest in . . . bad people, criminals, terrorists. When that happens, we need to take action. Fight magic with magic, if that makes sense."

"Me," Schweitzer said.

"Yes." Eldredge nodded. "The souls of the dead linger about the body for a time. Paired with a jinn, they remain. The union creates a magical being powerful enough to go toe to toe with the magical beings that threaten us. You are the heart of a new and growing Supernatural Operations Corps."

Idiot prattling, Ninip said.

Shut the fuck up and listen. Even now, dead and reanimated, sharing his own corpse with a malevolent spirit, he could barely believe Eldredge's words.

"Maj . . . ick," Schweitzer managed.

Eldredge nodded. "We call it the 'Great Reawakening.' We don't know what it is yet, but we know this: Magic is coming back into the world."

"Back?" Schweitzer asked.

"Yes," Eldredge answered. "We now believe that there was a time like this before, roughly a millennium ago. We're not sure why or how, but it raises the troubling possibility that this . . . thing . . . is orbital, or ebbing and flowing like a tide. And that means things are going to get a lot worse before they get better."

Schweitzer felt the force of the statement swamp him. His training answered. Failure to accept reality ran ops off the rails, got good men killed. The untrained, the average, froze when disaster unfolded around them; SEALs responded to events, not their perception of them. Life wasn't fair. Sometimes it didn't make sense. You didn't worry about that. You determined where the fire was coming from, and you got off the X.

He could feel Ninip's appreciation. It weighed his thoughts, replaying them, considering them. *Your way of war is . . . different. We have much to learn from one another.*

It flashed him an image of a man, naked save for a bronze helmet, shield, and spear. He strode out from his place in the front line of an army, beating his chest and shouting at the enemy, brandishing his spear. He shouldered the weapon, grabbed his testicles and penis, thrusting his pelvis forward, shaking his manhood at the enemy.

Schweitzer imagined the response such antics would get in his day. He pictured an infantryman sighting down on the posturing warrior from behind a rock, taking his time to line up his sights, easing back the trigger.

And as he thought it, the image materialized, blotting out his vision and Ninip's at once. The American soldier braced his shoulder as his rifle bucked, the posturing warrior's bronze helmet flying, a tiny red hole appearing in his forehead, the back of his head exploding, spraying his comrades with fragments of his skull.

He felt Ninip's amazement. *That kind of shit doesn't fly nowadays.*

The jinn didn't answer, only replayed the image again and again. Schweitzer clawed through it, struggling to reengage with Eldredge.

"There'll be some training," the old man was saying, regarding him from beneath frosted caterpillar eyebrows. "It never takes long. The soul remembers most of what it knew in life. We want to get you in the field as quickly as possible."

"No," Schweitzer said.

Eldredge looked up at that. "No?"

He could feel Ninip's surprise. *You said we would hear his offer.*

Shut up. I've got this.

"Why?" In life, he'd fought for his country, for the mass of citizens he would never meet and see. But while that moved him, they were always an undercurrent, a theme that never truly touched his heart. There was pay, there was advancement. There was the house he wanted to buy, the records he wanted to break. There was the immense pride in knowing he did things no one else could do. There was his mother, alone on the West Coast.

But most of all there was his family. A son he wanted to make proud. A woman for whom he still felt the little-boy impulse to impress and protect.

And now they were gone.

"Why?" Schweitzer repeated.

"For your country," Eldredge said. "To do good."

Schweitzer felt Ninip's contempt. The jinn understood the words, but not the concepts behind them. He dug in Schweitzer's memories, replaying old civics classes, the pledge of allegiance, the Constitution, the abstract notion of pledging one's allegiance to an idea instead of a leader.

Madness, the jinn said.

Schweitzer felt only nostalgia and sadness. "I . . . dead."

"You're still an American," Eldredge said. "You pledged yourself to the navy. That oath still holds."

Today, Master Chief Green had said, *you erase your old life. You put away everything you knew or sought. From this day forward, you belong to your country. You belong to one another.*

Chang, Biggs, Ahmad, Perreto, even Martin. What would they see if they saw him now? How would they react to his ash-colored skin, the pools of shimmering silver where his eyes had once been?

"No."

Eldredge scratched his head. "Jim, I don't think you fully appreciate your position. We'd prefer your cooperation, but if you force our hand, we can simply have Jawid compel you."

That goatherd cannot compel us to do anything, Ninip said.

No, he can't, Schweitzer agreed. *If he could, we wouldn't be having this conversation. He wouldn't be trying to motivate me. Us. Whatever.*

Schweitzer shrugged their dead shoulders.

"The Gemini Cell does deadly work, Jim. Our Operators tread paths that even the teams you used to run with shy away from. You know better than anyone that these paths *must* be gone down, Jim. If you won't walk them, then we'll have to send others. Living men. Men with families, wives, and sons. Men like who you once were."

The words sent a spasm of grief through him, but Schweitzer was careful to bite down on it, send it funneling inward to boil beneath the jinn's contempt.

Eldredge was right. He was dead. His family was gone. Nothing in the world would change that. The most he could hope to do was what he had always done. He remembered the motto of the Air Force pararescuemen who had medevac'd Chang off the deck of the freighter: *So others might live.*

Schweitzer had taken a similar oath when he'd pinned

on his trident. It was who he was in life. It was who he was in death as well.

He said nothing, but he knew that Eldredge had already won.

Eldredge mistook his silence for defiance and smiled, folding his arms across his chest. "All right. What do you want?"

"Sarah. Patrick . . ."

"They're gone, Jim. Jawid's abilities don't allow him to . . ."

Schweitzer was already shaking their shared head. "Who kill?"

Eldredge froze. "We don't know. We're still trying to find out. I can promise you that when we . . ."

"I find," Schweitzer said, batting aside Ninip's scorn. "Me."

"Jim, you're an Operator, not an analyst. You don't know how to find them."

"You find. Send me."

Eldredge nodded thoughtfully, stroking his moustache. "I'll take it up with the director."

He lies, Ninip said.

I know, but it's a start.

Schweitzer made them nod, allowed Ninip's eagerness to move their shared body forward to the workbench. The armorer stepped back, stopping only when Eldredge put a hand on his shoulder. "Show our newest Operator what we have for him."

The armorer forced himself to take a step forward. Schweitzer could feel the fear in him, taste it in his breath, smell it emanating from his pores. He felt himself instinctively leaning toward it, muscles responding to the scent, coiling to spring.

The armorer was a big man, wearing the navy uniform that Schweitzer had known and loved all his career. But Ninip's senses addled his own, and he saw only a weaker being, ripe for the kill. Ninip exulted, taking control of their shared limbs, balling the hands into fists, raising them.

Eldredge's own fear began to mist the air, his eyes widening. Schweitzer followed his gaze to their hands.

Their gray fingers had lengthened, the bone sliding out, piercing the fingertip, tapering into four-inch claws, the ends jagged and yellow, sharp enough to pierce flesh, tear it.

Ninip threw his presence forward, pulsing the image of the claws rising, falling, rising again, trailing gore. Before Schweitzer could stop it, the jinn had taken control of their arm, raising it over the armorer's head. The man leapt backward, Eldredge with him, shouting.

Schweitzer struggled to pull the arm down. *Stop! What the hell are you doing?*

But he already knew. The predator joy was coursing through him, shouting in his dead nerves, trilling in bones. It felt right. It felt . . . alive. All he had to do was close his eyes and let it take control.

The arm froze, trembled. He battered himself against Ninip, felt the jinn fighting to strike the men.

Idiot! Coward! Let me . . .

His vision went white again, overlayed with images of throats laid open, hearts plucked still beating from human breasts. Schweitzer pulled with all he had. Their body shook with the effort. He was barely conscious of a low groaning escaping their shared mouth, could just make out Eldredge's widening eyes, his fear stink abating.

Slowly, the arm began to lower.

Ninip raged. No words now, just an incoherent animal scream.

Schweitzer's vision cleared. He saw guards flooding the room, spreading out along the walls, sighting their weapons at him. Flamethrowers, large-bore shotguns. Two carried axes.

Eldredge jerked his chin at the guards. "We can't kill you, Jim, but we can render your body . . . inoperable. The dead don't die, but they also don't heal."

Ninip's madness sobered somewhat at the words. His fight for control over their body eased.

"Okay," Schweitzer said, pinning his arms to his side. "I okay."

He met Eldredge's eyes. Whatever he was now, he wasn't an animal. He wasn't a murderer. "I okay," he repeated.

Eldredge waved the guards back, awe etched on his face. "I believe you, Jim."

Eldredge put his hand on the armorer's back, tried to move him forward again. The man wouldn't budge. Eldredge finally gave up and stepped up to the workbench himself, extending a hand. "I believe you."

Ninip flashed an image of Eldredge's wrist, grasped, pulling the old man over the workbench, the claws coming down into the back of his neck. It thrilled him, made him shiver with anticipation, but Schweitzer fought it down. He reached out, took Eldredge's hand. He clasped it quickly, released it, not trusting his ability to hold Ninip at bay.

And in a tiny square not covered by armament, caught his reflection in the stainless-steel surface of the workbench.

The claws were retracting, as were horns and spines, protrusions of yellowed bone sprouted across his body. Their jaw had lengthened, the dead tongue lolling from it, the muzzle of a corpse wolf bent on the hunt. Their teeth were daggers, razor stalactites overhanging their shrinking jaw.

Within moments, he was himself again, as much as a dead man could be. But in that moment, there had been nothing about him remotely human.

He pulled back the shared hand, staring.

"That is the jinn," Eldredge said. "It is a form . . . useful in the field, in tactical contingencies. At other times, we find it counterproductive. I have never seen an Operator rein it in before. Once loosed . . ."

Once loosed, we rule, Ninip said, *as we were meant to.*

Schweitzer continued to stare at his hand, the slit tips of his fingers where the claws had been. "Why?"

"We don't know," Eldredge said. "All jinn were once

human, that much Jawid is sure of. But the time they spend in the beyond changes them."

Humanity is weak, Ninip said. *Tearable meat and breakable bone. What we are after is greater, purer. And the longer we tarry in the void, the stronger we become. It purges us, distills us. Our form becomes perfect. Better suited for the fight, the hunt. Stop thinking of yourself as a man. Start thinking of yourself as half of a god of war.*

The jinn surged, and Schweitzer felt as if he were being pushed from his own skin. He gritted his spiritual teeth, struggling anew to keep the demon in check.

Eldredge frowned, reached into his pocket, and lifted out a small length of chain, raised it in front of Schweitzer's face.

Sarah and Patrick smiled at him, the beginnings of brown rust forming in the depths of the etched lines that made up their faces.

"I was told you carried this with you everywhere you went. I see no reason that should change."

Ninip raged anew, shrieking. *Baubles from a life beyond us. It will hurt us. It will make us weak!*

The jinn still fought for control of their body, but now it struggled to pull away, to move as far from the etched talisman of Schweitzer's past life as it possibly could.

He was not letting the demon take him now. It would not rob him of this.

He shouted silently, pushing back with all he had, shooting the arm forward to snatch the dog tag from Eldredge's hand, lift it over their head, settle it around their neck.

As soon as the metal touched skin, the demon quieted, the voice receding to a low muttering.

Schweitzer swore he smelled the faintest whiff of rosewater.

The guards along the walls lowered their weapons for a second time, visibly relaxing as Eldredge waved a placating hand. "We thought that . . . a focus from an Operator's life would help them maintain control. It never worked."

"It works," Schweitzer said, grappling with grief, feeling the phantom touch of Sarah's hair. Ninip went silent under the onslaught of memory: cool sheets against his skin. Patrick laughing as Schweitzer tossed him in the air, a tattooed arm hooked through his. Paintings. Haunting watercolor marshscapes of the land rolling around their home, populated with sunbursts and puffs of flame that hinted at serene intelligence, knowing faces hiding in the flickering luminescence if you just looked hard enough.

"It works."

CHAPTER VI
ROSE TRAIL

Sarah Schweitzer floated above a field of rose petals. Her body was folded, a budding flower yet to bloom, legs intertwined, heels nestled against her crotch. Her hands were loosely curled, thumb and forefingers touching, resting on her knees.

It was quiet here, the gentle dark shutting out grief and loss. Somewhere in the distance, water trickled. She relaxed into the cotton comfort of half sleep. A vague sense of urgency tickled her, a feeling of loss, the knowledge that something terrible had happened to her. But that was outside this sphere of calm, this blanketing dark, broken only by flickering starlight and the low moan of the wind.

She pushed away from the horror, burrowed deeper into the peace she had found. But the wind would not let her be. It swept across the plain, sweeping the loose petals into the air, spinning them into a broad path, arcing out from where she floated, moving off into darkness.

The wind carried the petals' scent to her, faint and sweet. It reminded her of something. Something wonderful she had known, a piece of who she was. But it brought the horror with it, carried her a step closer to the knowledge of what lay beyond the protective walls of the dark.

She shook her head, her center lost. She tried to push the petals away. She shut her eyes tight. She pinched her nostrils shut against the smell.

The wind picked up, behind her now, drilling between her shoulder blades, pushing her a step forward.

When she opened her eyes, the path of rose petals was still there. She stood on it, her nose filled with the rose scent, the horror of what had happened drawing nearer. She pulled away, trying to retreat back into the dark, but the wind would not be denied. It howled across the field, pushing her forward again, knocking her a couple of steps farther down the path.

"Fine," she said. "Give it a rest."

She walked, the path rising higher and higher, the petals giving slightly, a tight weave that kept her steady, springing gently with each step. The darkness, the stars, the wind, the water, the field all vanished, and she walked through a nothing filled only with the path and her body, the only sound the steady pulse of her beating heart.

There was no light at the end of the path. The void merely stopped, the nothing becoming a tiny patch of something, a dot in the distance, growing larger.

The horror swirled around it, convalesced into a knot of pain and memory. She tried to pull away, but the wind was there, waiting to drive her on. It howled urgently, icy against her neck.

She stepped forward, the something growing larger still. A child was crying in the distance, calling for his mommy. She knew that child, loved him. The horror coiled around his cries, the memory she struggled not to face.

And then she was close, and the something resolved into a man. A lean line of jaw. Soft gray eyes. A dimpled chin. Strong shoulders.

The man grew, blotted out her vision, the child's cries becoming screams.

The petal path connected them, a wavering umbilicus, the steep scent of the roses nearly overwhelming her.

She knew the smell. She'd daubed it behind her ears, on her wrists. A daily ritual to welcome the sun.

She knew the man. His name was Jim.

She loved him.

Sarah woke crying, the dream reverberating in her mind, making her bones ache.

Jim. She lay back on the pillow, shut her eyes, willed herself back into the dream. To see his face. She hadn't had a chance to say anything to him.

Patrick's screaming. She bolted upright. Leapt out of bed. She couldn't go back there. Couldn't hear that sound again.

Patrick.

She raced down the hallway of their Navy Lodge suite, threw open the door to his room.

Patrick lay on the little bed Steve had bought for him, a tiny thing in the likeness of a dark blue car, headlight eyes shining, grill of a mouth grinning welcome.

His body was covered in gauze bandages, the burn gel beneath staining them yellow. He'd managed not to upset them in his sleep, and that was good. His arm was lashed along his side, looking tiny despite the huge cast enclosing it, cartoon animals cavorting across its pink-and-orange surface.

Sarah restrained the urge to kneel beside him, to hear his breathing, to smell his hair. She couldn't risk disturbing his sleep. Not when it was so rare these days. She stared at him a moment longer, her little boy who must now grow up without a father, who must learn too soon what horrors the world had in store for him. She bit back tears at the thought, sadness over Patrick's losses, the scars he would bear into adulthood, rage against the nameless, faceless enemy that had done this to them, against the government for asking her to be silent, for denying her the voice she needed to grieve.

A gentle knock on the door, almost a brushing of fingers, scarcely heard. Sarah went rigid, adrenaline dumping into her system. She winced as her tightening abdominals aggravated the gunshot wound, healing cleanly but slowly.

Don't be an idiot, she said to herself. *Do you think that if someone were coming to hurt you, they'd bother to knock?*

She shook her head, biting back tears again, absorbing the realization that she would always be like this, jumping at shadows, looking for the enemy hidden behind every corner. Like Jim. *Oh God. Sweetheart, how did you do it?*

She shook herself, took a deep breath and went to the door, looking through the peephole, fighting back the premonition that she would see men on the other side, prepping assault weapons while they tightened the straps on their body armor.

Instead, it was Steve Chang, looking winded and sad, a brown paper shopping bag dangling from one hand. She tried to square the image of this man, lost and bewildered, with the grinning warrior who'd spent half his weekends drinking beer with Jim on the apartment stoop or walking alongside the Chickahominy, Patrick squealing from his shoulders. Seeing his strength fade in the wake of this tragedy terrified her, galvanized her to be strong. He wasn't an enemy, and it was good to not be alone. That was something.

She opened the door, relief flooding her, swept him into a hug. "You idiot, you scared the shit out of me. Why didn't you ring the bell?"

"Little guy's sleeping, right? Didn't want to wake him." Of course he didn't. Steve might have been hurt badly by Jim's death, but it didn't change who he was at his core, summed up by the tattoo along his rib cage, alongside his blood type and serial numbers, block letters reading SO OTHERS MIGHT LIVE.

"How's he doing?" Steve asked, setting the bag on the counter, the contents making a clinking sound.

Sarah shrugged. "I don't know, Steve. How can I know? He's breathing. He eats. He poops. He knows who I am. I'm grateful for that much."

Steve frowned. "He screaming? Crying? Nightmares?"

She shook her head. "That's what scares me. He's . . . not catatonic. He talks, he asks for things . . . food, the potty, but he doesn't ask questions. He doesn't ask what happened. He doesn't ask about his bandages. He hasn't . . . he hasn't asked where his father is." She swallowed hard, bit back tears. She was so damned sick of crying.

Steve pulled her into him, stroked her hair as she cried against his chest, feeling the valve of his air tube tickle her nose. Being so close to the wound should have put her off, but it only made her feel closer to him, a reminder of their shared experience.

"Shh," he said. "It's okay. It's normal. You can't expect him to be . . . like he was after this. It's going to take time."

She leaned into him, so grateful for the warmth, the solidity of his body. Weak and broken-looking as he was, it still held the fear at bay. Steve knew her grief, truly shared it, the only man who was remotely as close to Jim as she had been. "I'm going to take him to see a child psychologist, but the doctor said he needed to heal more first."

Steve nodded. "That sounds about right."

She cuffed at her tears with the back of her hand. "What's in the bag?"

"Mixed greens in a bag, couple of chicken breasts. Bottle of cheap wine. I figured you wouldn't be up to cooking."

"Oh, Steve. Jesus. You didn't have to do that. I'm not an invalid."

Now it was his turn to bite back tears. "I didn't do it for you. I just . . . I don't want to be alone."

"Of course," she said. "Let me just grab a recipe off the Internet. You know what a lousy cook I am."

"Yeah." He smiled. "Enough not to trust you with the recipe selection. Get your laptop and leave the rest to me."

He watched her while she went to the couch to retrieve her computer. "You been sleeping?"

"Too much," she said. "All I want to do is sleep. I know that's the first sign of depression, so I'm fighting it. Only allowing myself eight hours a night, no matter how I feel."

"Not sure that's the best plan. What do you do when you're up?"

"Stare at blank canvas. Stare at Patrick. A lot of staring. Besides, it's the dreams." She shuddered. "They're awful."

"Nightmares? That's normal."

"Not really nightmares. Just . . . vivid dreams. They're more sad than scary."

"About Jim."

"Of course. I never talk to him, I never even really see him . . . I just . . . I keep feeling . . ."

"What?" Steve asked, folding his arms across his chest, taking care to keep them clear of his wound.

"I dream of roads, Steve. I dream of paths that always lead to him. I know it's crazy, but I can't shake the feeling that he's alive."

CHAPTER VII
OP TEMPO

The armor was almost as light as clothing. Schweitzer could feel the thin layer of liquid beneath the fabric, weight shifting gently to redistribute itself with his movements.

"Shear-thickening fluid," Eldredge said, "stronger than any Kevlar or ceramic you've ever worn. Light and completely maneuverable when you're not under fire, but the moment it gets hit, it goes solid. The harder you hit it, the harder it gets."

This is not armor, Ninip said.

Yes, it is, Schweitzer replied. *They were experimenting with this stuff before . . . before all this went down. It's the best stuff there is.*

He could feel Ninip's contempt. The jinn flashed him a mental image of a man, soaking wet, pierced by arrows. Schweitzer flashed back an image of a raging torrent, sweeping those arrows aside. Ninip dismissed the image. *We do not need it. We cannot be killed.*

Eldredge went on. "We hope that, without trauma, you can last forever. We've never had an Operator with us long enough to . . ."

"Rot?" Schweitzer asked.

Eldredge looked embarrassed. "We're reasonably certain that the magic prevents it, but we're equally sure that your body no longer heals. It can be damaged beyond repair. It can be shredded or burned. You can be destroyed."

Schweitzer felt Ninip's disdain. *Never.*

"Then?" Schweitzer asked.

"We don't know. Jawid has never recalled the same jinn twice, so it stands to reason that you go on . . . somewhere else."

Was he talking about heaven? Religion had always come to Schweitzer through preaching and reading, rendering God into some textual abstract. He knew what God was supposed to look like, what heaven was supposed to be like, if his Sunday-school readings were to be believed, but the resonance was never there. Sarah's open contempt for religion was the final nail in the coffin.

Ninip crept forward as Schweitzer thought about it, leaning in to probe at the memories of the pictures in the young Schweitzer's Vacation Bible School Primer. Schweitzer didn't bother to fight as the jinn followed the thread, starting with John 3:16, then down the rabbit hole through sermon after confession after Bible study. He drew back, aghast. *This is the faith of your people?*

One of them, but the biggest.

You worship a wounded weakling nailed to a piece of wood and bleeding out his life. He is no warrior.

That's kind of the point.

How can you be so mighty, have such incredible weapons, then sway in a cult that reveres peace above all things, ruled by a broken dead man?

Schweitzer shrugged internally. *We've never gotten a whole lot of points for consistency.*

You worship a jinn. Like me.

It's not the same thing.

Is it not? He was slain. On the third day, he rose again. How is that different?

Schweitzer paused. The truth was that he didn't know

anymore. He'd always taken all these things for granted: Magic wasn't real. Dead was dead. There was no heaven.

He was wrong about the first two. Maybe he was wrong about the third.

He was about to ask Ninip where Jawid summoned him from when Eldredge spoke.

"Now, your targets are on the other side of that wall." Eldredge gestured to a seamless barrier of cinder block, some twenty feet high, extending the full width of the room. Cameras were set into the corners of the ceiling, tiny black insects hiding in pockets of gloom. "Get over there, assess, and discriminate. Only take down the red targets. Beat thirty seconds."

An LED readout on a display at the far end of the room was just visible over the top of the wall. The face lit up with huge red block numbers indicating the countdown.

Schweitzer hefted the carbine slung across his chest, nestling the stock into the sweet spot of his shoulder, finger indexed along the upper receiver. The carbine had been modified to accept .50 caliber rounds. The huge bullets required an extended magazine, not just long, but wide, a plastic drum extending from the weapon. Schweitzer hefted it. He knew that it would be impossibly heavy for any normal man to fire accurately, but those days were behind him now.

Schweitzer looked up at the wall before them, eyes roving across the seamless surface. *They clearly expect us to get up that.*

Leave it to me, Ninip answered.

It'd help if you . . .

A buzzer sounded and the LED numbers began to tick down. Ninip engaged the shared muscles of their legs and set their body leaping forward, barreling toward the wall, head down. Schweitzer lifted their head, tried to slow them, turn them aside before their skull shattered against the hard surface. Ninip growled and pushed back.

Schweitzer pictured their lowered head smashing into the wall, coming apart like an eggshell. Ninip swatted the image aside, showing Schweitzer only blackness.

He said we can't heal, this is a really bad . . .

Ninip's presence contracted, pulsed, channeled into the muscles of their legs. They took a galloping leap, squatted deep, and sprang.

Schweitzer felt the ground vibrate as they left it, saw the walls of the room rush by. The length of the wall shot past them, five feet, then ten, then fifteen. Schweitzer marveled as he planted their hand on the top, felt the gritty, uneven surface of the cinder block take their weight, and vaulted over to the other side. Then the world rushing past them again as they fell, landing in a crouch on the dirt floor just as the first targets popped up.

No, not targets. Black shapes, low and surging like waves, deep rumbling rising from sable throats.

Eldredge had set them down in a pack of dogs.

They were the same animals Schweitzer had run a dozen ops with, sniffing out explosive materials, turning corners for the team, risking their lives to distract dug-in enemies, drawing fire so their human masters could bring their guns to bear in safety.

Their names had been deliberately meek: Tripoli and Jennifer and Strawberry. They'd been a mix of breeds, mostly Belgian Malinois, happy and playful off the job, steel-eyed killers on it.

Schweitzer knew how his new form must smell to them, the thick reek of chemical preservative riding over the more familiar smell of dead flesh. Alien, threatening.

They lunged.

Ninip seized control of their arm, thrusting it forward and up, claw extending from a rigid finger, angling for the animal's belly. Schweitzer pulled the claw in, curling the hand into a fist that slammed into the dog's chest, cracking a rib and sending it rolling and yelping across the floor.

He could feel Ninip's attention turn to him, coiling with contempt. *It is a dog,* the jinn said.

They were full members of our unit, Schweitzer replied, conjured images of the SEALs jumping with the animals strapped into their harness, playing with them at unit barbecues, pinning medals on their collars after successful ops. *They were family.*

You were fools, the jinn spit.

Another dog lunged for their ankle, fastening his teeth around the armor, biting down hard.

Schweitzer kicked the leg back and forward before the dog could put pressure behind the bite, moving even as the jinn began to drive their hand down.

The dog whipped through the air, jaws ripping free with an audible click, teeth flying out of its mouth, trailing threads of blood. The rest of the pack hung back, snarling threats that masked fear.

Kill them, Jawid's voice rang in his mind.

No thanks, Schweitzer replied. Even contorted into snarls, their black muzzles were a whisper of the life he had known. They had been weapons, yes, but also comrades.

Ninip said something, but it was lost in the buzz of the barking and the hissing of the air vents, drowned by Schweitzer's focus as the first real target finally did pop with a loud thunk, wood reverberating against its metal housing.

The superhuman run and jump had taken Schweitzer by surprise, but as soon as the man-shaped piece of wood slid into view, he was back in his element. The carbine popped into its familiar spot on his shoulder, finger brushing the trigger, easing out the slack even as the weapon came up, eye dropping onto the sights. *I've got this.*

Red target. Engage.

Ninip slid aside, releasing their shared limbs to Schweitzer's control. The first target was only twenty feet away. At that range, the high-caliber round obliterated it, leaving a smoking shower of splinters. Schweitzer fell into the old groove instinctively, grateful for the familiar space, a shred of the known in the strangeness that had become his world. Ninip shared that space, marveling at the precision of his movements, the firm ease with which he let the trigger slide forward until he felt the slight click of the reset, keeping just the right amount of tension to hold it there. His eyes narrowed, his shooter's vision alert for threats, moving, moving, never settling. Contact right. Red. Turn, sight, fire. The target exploded, and Schweitzer moved through the wreckage, the front sight post the only point of clarity in a blurred world. Bang. Bang. Single shots. Each impacting in the tiny triangle where he'd put them all his professional life.

Impressive, Ninip said. Schweitzer ignored him. This killing space had always been his refuge, the immediacy of combat shutting out all distractions, giving Schweitzer the only true peace he'd ever known, his mind surrendering to the reptilian repetition of move, sight, shoot. The irony was one only other SEALs ever understood, that there in the midst of the maelstrom of battle was the only real rest they ever truly got.

He felt Ninip ingesting his experience, absorbing his skill. He shuddered internally, tried to shrug the presence away. Ninip laughed. *We are one. Will your hand deny your arm?*

Both are dead, Schweitzer said.

One of the dogs found its courage and leapt for them. Schweitzer was too absorbed in his shooting dance to react. Ninip seized the moment to lunge, moving them with lightning speed, throwing the carbine down to hang by its sling, reaching out to snatch the leaping animal out of the air.

Schweitzer strained against the jinn, but Ninip already had the momentum, bringing the dog down across their knee so quickly and with such force that the animal nearly broke in half.

The rest of the pack scattered at the sound of the dog's final yelp, and Schweitzer shouted inwardly. *You fucking bastard!*

The outpouring was unforgivable in his line of work. SEALs succeeded precisely because of their ability to maintain professionalism no matter what horrors unfolded around them. Schweitzer's concentration broke just as his wide shooter's vision caught a target springing up, so close he could feel the air stirring over his elbow. Too close to take a shot. His mind switched the action, immediately moving to drive the carbine butt into the head-shaped top of the board.

But Ninip blotted out his senses, the jinn's filter sliding across his eyes. The hangar-sized room suddenly slid close, the cameras gleaming targeting lasers, painting Schweitzer's forehead. Even the wooden target had changed, painted now with a mad grin, a malevolent clown smile showing razor teeth. Schweitzer's nose filled with the copper smell of blood, making his mouth water. Anger swamped him, an animal need to escape the suddenly tiny room, slaughter anything that stood between him and the exit. His training receded to a splinter in his mind, dominated by the jinn's feral presence.

It was the antithesis of how he'd always fought. No professionalism. No cold precision. Only red, raw rage. Was the target red? He couldn't concentrate enough to tell.

He felt their shared throat flex, jaw unhinging, dropping until it touched the bottom of their sternum. Their tongue whipped out, lashed around the target's neck, yanking the wood toward them. He gave in to the passion of the fight, and their head whipped forward, snake's jaw snapping closed. He felt their teeth, dagger huge now, punch through the rough wooden outline simulating a man's shoulders, upper chest. Ninip thrilled within him, drowning in animal joy, jerked their neck, tearing the top of the target off, ragged shreds of wood following like entrails. The terrified yipping of the dogs sounded all around them.

Schweitzer felt himself slipping away, a grain of sand drowning in a sea of the jinn, howling in predatory exultation. The room was close as a womb, the chewed wood in their mouth gobbets of flesh, the splinters blood spray. Ninip spit out the mouthful and howled just as two more targets sprang up, almost slapping them in the face, painted grins alive now, mocking him. Schweitzer felt the scythe claws extend, arms sweeping up to form a brief X before their face, then the muscles in their arms engaged, sweeping them down again, shearing the targets in half along the waistline.

Ninip was all. The jinn turned, eyes sweeping the dogs, cowering now against the edges of the room, as if by pressing themselves hard enough against the walls, they could pass through them. Their beating hearts and flowing blood were not human but were still far more interesting than the wooden targets.

Ninip stalked toward them, taking his time, savoring their animal terror.

Schweitzer was horrified. His entire life he'd thrown himself at challenge after challenge. Some had gone down easy, some he'd had to wear away. But they always fell. Ninip swept him away like a tsunami.

Schweitzer dug deep and pushed back against the jinn. Ninip pushed back briefly against him, then sullenly gave way. *Now you have seen what it is to fight.*

Schweitzer's vision slowly returning to normal, the room resuming its normal size, the targets shredded wood once again. Schweitzer could feel Ninip's coiled strength. He knew that the jinn hadn't really fought him, didn't doubt that it would have beaten him if it had.

Schweitzer looked up, noted the countdown on the LED clock: five seconds remaining.

A buzz and click indicated a steel door swinging open at the far side of the room, four soldiers entering through it. Two held carbines at the ready, the other two carried what Schweitzer was beginning to see as the ubiquitous flamethrower and fireman's axe.

"Let's go," one of them said, jerking his head toward the door. The man's eyes swept the wreckage of the targets, the broken remains of the dog in the center of the room. He looked up at Schweitzer, shook his head in disgust, motioned to the door again. "Move."

Schweitzer recognized the curt bravado for the fear it sought to mask. A moment later, he realized this was more than just experience. He could smell the man's fear, a thick, ammonia odor like stale piss. Ninip smelled it, too, and Schweitzer tensed himself to push back against the jinn, but the presence made no move.

"Where?" Schweitzer asked.

"Cold storage," the man with the axe said. "Cool your heels for a bit while we decide what to do with you."

Cold storage turned out to be a stainless-steel refrigerated unit that looked like a restaurant meat locker. It was completely featureless save the omnipresent red nozzles that told Schweitzer the room's contents could be incinerated with the touch of a button. These were interspersed with other, smaller protrusions, brushed-chrome knobs with tiny holes in their tips. Schweitzer began to examine one, then realized that his heightened senses could pick up the cold emanating from them, along with the slightest whiff of oil. Liquid nitrogen likely, or Freon. If they weren't in the mood for burning, they could freeze him solid.

Chill air fogged the room, emanating from louvered vents ringing the walls. Schweitzer knew he was cold, could sense the temperature, but there was no discomfort. His senses still functioned but reported at a remove, a secondhand story.

Why are they trying to freeze us? Ninip asked.

A dead body rots, Schweitzer said. *They're trying to preserve us.*

We do not rot, Ninip said. *I see to that.*

Guess you can't be too careful.

You are too careful. It is cowardly.

Yeah, wish we were brave like you. You sure showed that dog who was boss.

It was an animal. You mourn it as if it were your betrothed. Do you fuck dogs in your armies?

Schweitzer didn't bother responding. Ninip was silent for a moment before trying again, his tone conciliatory. *You fight well. Your rifle is impressive.*

It's a carbine. You need to pay closer attention.

Still, you kill at a remove. I will teach you valor.

No thanks. All valor does is get folks killed.

Don't be a fool, valo—

Dude. Shut up. Your way of fighting is millennia in its grave. There's a reason it didn't survive. War isn't chest pounding and reciting lineage. War is teamwork and professionalism. War is workmanship.

When Ninip finally replied, his tone was thoughtful. *I am a lord, a god.*

Yeah, I've run with guys like that. They make lousy warfighters. A Saudi prince once tried to get me to carry his rucksack. I laughed at him. Rank and privilege might fly at the Marine Corps ball, but on an op, how good you are is all there is.

Ninip considered that. *You are a footman.*

Schweitzer laughed. *We're all footmen. Even our officers had to suck sand in BUD/S. Nowadays, footmen are all there is. You're a lord? Good for you. I'm an American. We don't kneel to lords.*

Ninip was quiet for a good while after that. Schweitzer liked that even less than his predator binges. Evil, insensate rage was simple, loud. A quiet, thinking enemy crouched in the dark came at you when your guard was down. *Your woman, your child. They keep you weak. Even in battle they are with you. Even though they are gone.*

Schweitzer instinctively moved their shared hand to their chest, held up the engraved dog tags. Sarah and Patrick stared back at him. Was the rust deepening already? For now it made the lines of their faces stand out in starker relief, but it wouldn't be long before it crossed the line from help to hindrance.

They keep me going. He could still smell the rosewater, so faint it was barely a whisper of a scent. He closed his eyes, tried to visualize it, a path leading back to her, but the smell seemed to come from everywhere at once.

How long have you been dead? Schweitzer asked.

I cannot mark the sun. A very long time.

What's it like outside a body? It's different, right?

It is . . . chaos. There are many of us there, but the

strong know their own. Only the greatest of us can find our way back to the few like that goatherd who can speak to us. It took me a long time to learn how, but I did.

This is what you came back for? To kill people?

There is nothing there. Here, there is light, and speech, and the rush of the wind. There is . . . life. Killing is still life.

Schweitzer pictured Ninip, stranded in darkness, the millennia ticking by. A chord of sympathy sounded in him, and he felt the presence shudder in anger at the touch of it.

Is that where Sarah and Patrick are?

Ninip shrugged. *I suppose. I know of no other place. I was like you, believing in priests' bleating promises. There is only the storm, and it is nothing like the stories.*

We call that purgato—

I know what you call it, Ninip said, conjuring up the image of Schweitzer's first Bible, dog-eared, child's scrawl in the margins. Schweitzer tensed in revulsion at the stolen memory. *It is the prattling of shavepate divines seeking to wring gold from their betters. Only merchants lie more than priests.*

And only jinn lied more than merchants, Schweitzer thought. Ninip's entire perception of the world was a membrane of falsehood pulled over their collective eyes. *If you can reach out, you can reach back, right? You can help me find Sarah and Patrick.*

Impossible, Ninip said. *The dead are legion. All but the strongest are whirling in panic, they know nothing but the storm, hear nothing but their own shrieking.*

Goddamn it, you can try!

No, I cannot. Were this body to be destroyed, we would go back to the maelstrom together. You would be lost and no closer to being reunited with your wife and child. Your heaven is a lie. You do not reunite with your beloved dead.

Bullshit. Show me.

Show yourself, the jinn said. He felt Ninip's presence

slide aside, a void stretching out within him. Schweitzer turned into it, fumbling blind through the blackness. He recognized the void from his first moments of death, before Ninip had spoken to him. It was the deepest dark he'd ever known, not the painted black of the inside of his living eyelids, but the true night of a space devoid of even the concept of light.

The void stretched out for what seemed an eternity, then Schweitzer caught a sudden glimmer, a hint of palest light, the tiniest whisper of sound. And the smell of Sarah's perfume. Schweitzer reached out toward it, moving through the black toward the source, Ninip laughing outright at his excitement. At last the sound crystallized, became something with a name.

Screaming.

Ninip was right to call it a storm. A tangle of whirling limbs stretched across Schweitzer's vision. Ethereal, spinning bodies, sliding around and through one another, howling terror as they circled, tossed by some invisible tornado current. All SEALs developed a healthy respect for the sea, came to know it as intimately as a fickle lover, as likely to kill as kiss. This then was a sea, violent and storm tossed, made of people.

The scent of Sarah's perfume led toward it.

The ocean of souls was so vast that Schweitzer couldn't begin to take it all in. *You'll never find them in there. Not if you spent the rest of eternity looking.*

Ninip's voice softened. *You cannot have them back, but we can avenge them. That is something.*

Schweitzer bit down on his despair. *Whatever. What the hell do you know about family?*

I had nine wives, twelve sons.

No daughters?

Ninip snorted. *Some. I did not keep them.*

Schweitzer felt his anger rise, sensed Ninip's satisfaction as the jinn felt it, too. *You go ahead and do your whole animal angry valor dance in here. When we run an op, you let me drive. That hunger does no one any good. It's a waste of fucking time.*

No, Ninip replied. *It is the nectar of what we have become together. You mock it now because you do not feel it. But you will, and soon.*

CHAPTER VIII
TRIAL RUN

Their cell was featureless, no chairs, bed, toilet Schweitzer simply stood, talking internally to Ninip, feeling the jinn continue to dig in his memories. He was aware of his body's functions, the fatigue in the leg muscles, growing stiffness in the joints. He set their shared body pacing, keeping it limber, the glycerol they'd used to replace the blood in his veins flowing.

After a long time, panels slid aside in one wall, revealing a reinforced transparent panel that opened on a featureless gray hallway. Schweitzer could see military personnel pacing there, two guards outside his door. Beyond them, a ready room buzzed with activity, huge screens taking up an entire wall. Eldredge stood there, writing on a clipboard. Jawid was seated in what looked like an aircraft pilot's chair, electrical leads flowing under his robes, plastering his head. His eyes were closed.

Good morning. Jawid's voice echoed in Schweitzer's mind. It was halting, hesitant. Schweitzer could tell he was translating someone else's words.

Is it morning? Schweitzer asked.

It is. The sun has not yet risen.
Is it good?

Jawid went silent at this, and he saw the Sorcerer turn and speak quickly with Eldredge, who glanced toward the cell. At last, the old man shook his head.

Yes. It is good, the Sorcerer finally answered.

Ninip stayed silent, but Schweitzer could feel him circling the edges of the channel opened with Jawid, sniffing at it, reaching tentatively toward the Sorcerer. He felt Jawid's wariness and concentration, ready to push back against the jinn.

To what do we owe the pleasure? Schweitzer asked Jawid. He liked the banter, there was something in it that made him feel tied to who he had once been. If it puzzled his handlers, then so much the better. He was dead. They could put up with a little snark.

We're ready for you to go to work. Your first run, Jawid said.

Schweitzer shrugged off the images of carnage Ninip projected. The jinn shivered with anticipation.

So, you're putting me . . . us . . . on an op?

We are, Jawid answered.

Good, Schweitzer said. *Then you can explain to me how this leads to the people who killed Sarah and Patrick.*

In the room across the hall, Jawid opened his eyes, had a short conversation with Eldredge.

This is your trial run, the Sorcerer said. *We need to know that you are in control, that you can respond to tasking. Do this well, and we'll send you after the people who killed you*—a pause as Jawid listened to Eldredge, then the Sorcerer focused his attention back to Schweitzer—*just as soon as we have good information on where they are.*

Schweitzer gave Ninip just enough rein to fuel him with anger, channeled the rage down his connection to Jawid. *You tell Eldredge I'm not fucking around. This is your free one. The next op better be working a lead to whoever did this to my family. It had to be the Body Farm.*

He could feel Jawid's confusion, Ninip's frustration

with the delay. The jinn knew there was slaughter once the mission was launched and was bristling with impatience to get started. The emotions hit him and scrambled his thinking; he dug deep and found his center. Ninip could wait. *The Body Farm. Tell Eldredge that's who killed me. Ask him to talk to my old lieutenant. Name's Martin Biggs. We ran an op . . .*

Jawid cut in, speaking quickly. Schweitzer could faintly hear Eldredge's voice in the background and realized he was hearing through Jawid's ears. *We know about that. That doesn't mean we know who exactly did the deed or why. We're working on it. You of all people know how networks like this operate. There's no way to do it quickly.*

The words gave Schweitzer pause. He had always been patient as a spider, sizing up dangers, stoically accepting hard realities, taking the time to plan. Pushing like this wasn't him.

He turned his attention back to Ninip, noted the jinn's increasingly frantic scratching at the channel linking them to Jawid, a cat pawing at a sliding glass door. He recalled his reaction to the slaughtering of the dog. He was losing the bubble. When his guard was down, he was making the jinn's ways his own. Not good.

He took a moment to center himself. Okay. An op. By the numbers. That was the best way to slow down and do a thing right.

What's the op? Schweitzer asked.

KC, Jawid answered without any hesitation. He hadn't needed to translate for Eldredge that time, which meant that either he'd been prebriefed or all the ops the Operators were sent on were Kill-Capture missions.

Target? Schweitzer asked.

Schweitzer felt Jawid push deeper in, and his vision dissolved to white, then resolved to a closer view of the wall of screens. Seeing through Jawid's eyes. He still felt himself, could still see his own surroundings in his peripheral vision, as if Jawid had turned his perspective into a set of binoculars Schweitzer could peer into.

The center screen was a pastiche of photographs, all showing a bald man with a wide jaw and deep-set, kind eyes. He had the look of a man who spent a lot of time frowning, but in concern rather than anger. A politician, or an aid worker. The only full-body image showed him to be thick around the middle, and in the corporate uniform of blue button-down shirt and khaki slacks. Painfully nondescript.

This target was nominated by the code name JACK-RABBIT, written across the bottom of the screen.

Your target is a cultist. Jawid was translating again. *He leads a group of people who believe him to be the second coming of Jesus Christ. They walk the border between religious and terror group. They poisoned a meat shipment last year. Seven people died.*

Schweitzer remembered the news story. He flashed the memories toward Ninip, but the jinn batted them away, entirely focused on Jawid.

They are currently planning an attack on a subway system, Jawid added. *Gas.*

How much time do we have? Schweitzer asked.

We don't know. Not much.

Okay. Where are we hitting him?

The pictures of the man vanished and were replaced with an image.

Ninip had at last grown frustrated with his stalking of Jawid. Schweitzer could feel the jinn rifling his memory again, grasping at touchpoints that explained what he was seeing, stumbling down the web of concepts that linked to it: satellites, photography, space travel, computers.

The image was a satellite view of a building on a waterfront. Schweitzer had seen shots like this in briefings for scores of ops. Large structure, corrugated steel roof, piers leading up to the walls. Dockside warehouse or fish-processing plant. Another building stood across a wide avenue, air-conditioning units, water tower, and elevator mechanism on the roof. Probably residential. Industrial and residential this close together meant a major city. The superdense Western architecture gave it even odds for New York or London.

This is the location, Jawid said. *We have eyes on, and will insert you once we know Jackrabbit is inside.*

What else is in there? Schweitzer asked.

It doesn't matter, Jawid replied.

Of course it matters! You don't hit a target blind.

Ninip finally stirred at this. *What does it matter? He is a target.*

Schweitzer felt the seductive thrill of the bloodlust, struggled with it before forcing himself to say, *No way. I've never run an op with this lousy a targeting package. This isn't sufficient detail to go on. I need a lot more. What assets do we have? What's around that building? What's the layout?*

Schweitzer could see Jawid speaking to someone out of view, then arguing with Eldredge. At last he came back. *He is a criminal. He has killed many people. You will have a map. There is no need to worry about your surroundings. Just remain in the building.*

He's alone? Schweitzer asked.

He will have his supporters. Other criminals.

How many? What are they packing? Where are they located? This is bullshit.

Jawid sighed, then spoke slowly and deliberately, careful to deliver the message verbatim from Eldredge. *You do not understand what you are. This is the reason for the Gemini Cell: to hit targets where we don't have the intel to risk a team with homes and families who'll ask questions. We need a ghost to materialize out of the darkness, push this button, and vanish. That's why you're here, Jim. That's who you are.*

The words stopped Schweitzer cold. Ninip shook his head. *You still cling to life. You are more than that now. We do not need to know what faces us because nothing can stop us. We need not fear death, because we are death.*

Schweitzer had been caught up in the old preop battle rhythm. It had been a touch of the familiar, an anchor to the life he'd lost. Jawid's and Ninip's words rekindled grief in him, and he gave himself a moment to acknowledge it before squashing it. *Lock it up. Dead or alive, you're still a SEAL.*

Still, it was stupid to go in unprepared. He couldn't resist another question. *What about squirters?*

If anyone runs, we will see to them. We'll have eyes on from the air, with limited cover.

No team? Schweitzer asked.

You are the team.

Ninip exulted. The primitive love of combat, the glory-seeking, was as infectious as the jinn's bloodlust. Schweitzer fought it down. He might be a possessed corpse, but an op was an op, and cold professionalism was what was needed. *Let me review the map.*

You can review it in the air, Eldredge answered through Jawid. *We've got a short window. We're going now.*

The helo, the weapon, the weight of tactical gear, all were notions of the life he had known, reminders that Schweitzer's new world wasn't total strangeness. He trotted out along the flight line, his first steps in the outside world since his . . . reawakening? Rebirth? Animation?

The moon was bright in the sky, blotting out the spray of stars, shining like crushed glass farther out. A warm breeze rocked thin pines, carrying the scent of box elder. He was definitely still in the Mid-Atlantic, and probably still in Virginia. Another handle on his old life. Another reminder that he was still James Schweitzer.

He could feel Ninip's contempt for the idea. *In the beginning, I was the same. That man is dead. The sooner you accept that, the sooner you can start being what you are.*

No way. They brought me back because I'm supposed to be a god of war, right? Ninip grinned at the expression. *Well, that comes from my memories, my training. Those things are part of me. You want Jim Schweitzer the SEAL? You get Jim Schweitzer the man, the whole package.*

Ninip was silent at that, and Schweitzer turned his attention to the helicopter.

Two men sat in the cabin, feet dangling out over the side. They held the now-ubiquitous flamethrower and fire axe, insurance for his makers should he decide he wanted to stray outside mission parameters. Ninip snarled, the expression reaching their shared face, contorting the stretched surface into a twisted horror. The men slid inside the helo, weapons at the ready. Ninip's killer's litany began to flash through Schweitzer's mind, and he fought it down yet again. *Save it for the op.*

The men scooted out of the way, crowding as far as they could against the far cabin wall as Schweitzer leapt in easily, ignoring the rattail and carabiner one of the men offered him. He slid to the cabin edge, dangled his legs over the side. The rotors spun up, and the helo began to rise. One of the men called out to him. "Sir, I need you to come inside. You're not clipped in and we can't risk you fa . . ."

Schweitzer raised one shared hand, and the man's voice died. Schweitzer turned his attention to the ground, beginning to broaden in his vision as the helo rose. He could feel the shared thighs and abdominals tightening with inhuman strength, keeping them perfectly balanced as the helo banked. They could have stood tiptoe on the edge of the cabin floor and not fallen out. Ninip's power was amazing.

The ground blurred beneath them as the helo leveled off and picked up speed. Death hadn't taken Schweitzer's internal compass, and he judged them heading east before the woods gave way to coastline, and the helo beat out over the ocean before turning north.

New York, then.

Schweitzer could feel Ninip watching through their shared eyes, awestruck. It was one thing to read Schweitzer's memories secondhand. It was another thing to experience it. *We are flying.*

Schweitzer shrugged. *We've been at it for over a century now. Not all it's cracked up to be, honestly. You should see our delivery vehicles.*

He smiled as Ninip retrieved the memory of the submersible, parsing the weight of the water pressing on his wet suit, the dull throb of the motors as the vehicle propelled his team along the ocean floor, fish scattering out at their approach. Ninip's awe was palpable, his presence pulsing with it.

An hour into the flight, Schweitzer realized he could barely hear the rotors. The usual roar was a dull patter, even quieter than the modified helos he'd roped out of his entire career, quieter than the machine that had delivered the Body Farm's hit team to his door. He fought against the surge of anger, but Ninip stoked it, forcing it on until Schweitzer could feel the rage pulsing in his glycerol-filled veins.

Ninip caught the idea. *Let this be our blood. It will serve.*

"On target in five!" the crewman called to him. "We'll set up a pattern and extract you in twenty minutes. If you get slowed down, give us a call."

Ninip grinned. *We will not be slowed.*

Schweitzer watched the ground rise as the helo banked again, slowed, descended, the picture from the satellite image slowly matching up to the reality unfolding beneath him. Schweitzer felt the old familiar thrill, the anticipation before the drop, the sudden calm and focus.

"Throw ropes!" one of the men behind him shouted. Schweitzer could hear him muscling the thick hawser into position. Schweitzer stood their shared body up, toes out over the edge, put out a hand to stop him. He heard the man freeze, the dull thud of rope dropping to the deck.

Ninip didn't bother to speak, his lust a silent rising in all of Schweitzer's senses. The building's roof looked impossibly small, a postage stamp in a field of gray.

"Sir . . ." the man began.

Schweitzer jumped.

Ninip's instincts leapt into control of their shared body, beating down Schweitzer's effort to go belly down, pointing their toes, flexing their hamstrings until their thighs rose above their pelvis. Instead, they folded in their arms and legs, bent their head, and arced through the sky, an arrow racing toward its target. Schweitzer knew he should be frightened, but Ninip's confidence suffused him. He felt alive with the heady power of the creature at the top of the food chain. They would strike that building headfirst, split it in half, and rise laughing from the rubble.

Ninip unfolded them at last, angling their body outward. Schweitzer felt them slow, the roof speeding toward them, the draft against their body moving them in at an angle. He overcame the instinct to shut their eyes. That was for the living.

Their core muscles engaged again, their feet cutting through the racing air, slicing through the pressure as if it were nothing, getting their soles underneath them just as the roof arrived to embrace them.

They hit.

Schweitzer felt the muscles in their legs tense, taking his weight, sending tremors up through their shared skeleton. He felt Ninip's presence focus inward, coiling around the fragile bones, holding them together by sheer force of will.

The corrugated metal surface didn't fare as well. Their boots punched through, the cells of fluid in the armor hardening at the impact, locking around their ankles. The concrete beneath receded, sending a spiderweb of cracks spreading out until they disappeared beneath the whole surface of the steel above.

And then they bounced out, heels ripping the rents wider, tucked their head, and somersaulted until the momentum was spent, coming up into a crouch just before the freight elevator housing. Schweitzer asserted himself, smacking down the jinn's bloodlust. *Let me drive!* Ninip growled, but acceded as Schweitzer popped the carbine up into the sweet spot, getting on the sights as they rose, scanning the roof for threats.

You got infrared on these guys? Schweitzer sent up to Jawid. *We must have made a pretty loud bang when we hit.*

A loud bang on concrete with fire-retardant foam, Jawid sent back. *We're not seeing any indicator they heard it. The building has central HVAC. It's pretty loud.*

Schweitzer turned his attention to the outside world, could hear the loud humming of the climate-control system, the elevator mechanism, the gantry cranes. *I think you're right,* he sent. *Looks clear, we're moving.*

Pent anger flared in him. He knew this target wasn't responsible for his family's death, but it didn't matter. It would feel so good to do *something* with all this . . . *Stop,* he told himself. *That's Ninip talking. You're a professional, and this is a job, nothing more.*

But the jinn's influence could not be denied, and he felt the carnivore lust in the back of their throat as he moved to the elevator-housing doors, swelling their tongue, lengthening it until they were forced to open their mouth, let it slap against the helmet's faceplate.

Report, Jawid said. *Status?*

Ninip sent a feral growl back up the link, and Schweitzer felt the Sorcerer's fear traveling back down.

On deck and in position, Schweitzer managed. *Entering the elevator shaft.*

Jawid tried to link Schweitzer to his vision, give him a look at the map, but Schweitzer was pulled along by Ninip's eagerness and rejected the image. *That shaft leads to the . . .* Jawid began.

Shut up, goatherd, Ninip growled.

Schweitzer reached out, their fingers brushing the seam between the doors, their fingertips responding, claws extending, prying between. Schweitzer couldn't hold back the growl as Ninip engaged the muscles of their shared arm, peeling back the three inches of steel as if it were cardboard. The metal shrieked, opening just enough to admit them, and Schweitzer slid them into the cramped, dark space beyond.

Their vision compensated instantly. In life, his NODs had lit the darkness with a pale green hue, a tunnel that distorted distance and depth. Now he saw in red, the outlines and details of his surroundings as clear as if it were broad daylight.

The giant metal cylinder of the elevator's mechanism

dominated the room, thick steel cables wrapping around it to descend through the floor. Schweitzer brushed past the controls on the wall, and Ninip immediately moved them into a squat, clawed fingers prying at the machinery's base.

Dude, Schweitzer said. *Chill. There's a goddamn hatch.* He forced their head to turn to see it, thin outline barely visible at the machine's edge. Ninip's feral impulse almost turned him back to the machinery anyway, but Schweitzer pushed them back to the panel, allowing the jinn to rip it from its moorings, hurling it over their shoulder.

Whatever floats your boat. We're not going to surprise anyone this way.

Warriors do not skulk like thieves, Ninip answered.

With the prospect of battle so close, Ninip was becoming harder to control, his influence so strong that Schweitzer found himself swept along. All this power, locked into one tiny body, it was only fair to let it out to stretch its legs.

They dropped through the hatch, landing on top of the elevator on the balls of their feet, silent for all Ninip's efforts to throw caution to the wind. The jinn ripped open that hatch as well, dropping them into the elevator below. Their vision compensated again as they fell into the lighted space, a single uncovered fluorescent bulb washing all in harsh white.

We're making a lot of noise, Schweitzer sent to Jawid.

I know, Jawid replied. *So far, so good.*

Before Schweitzer could process their surroundings, Ninip was clawing at the seam in the elevator doors. The metal came apart, scraping loudly against the housing. Their swollen tongue found the seam between faceplate and helmet, forced through. Schweitzer could see it lashing the air before them, gray and impossibly long.

This was not the SEALs' way. The clumsy noise of their entry was an affront. They had paired him with Ninip to bring his years of training to bear, but it was buried in the jinn's raw eagerness for blood.

Status? Jawid asked again. Ninip's eagerness overcame him, and Schweitzer felt himself pushed to the very edge of his own body, his presence shrinking as Ninip's enlarged to fill the darkness they shared. He felt the boundary of his own corpse, felt himself slipping across it. Cold washed over him, biting deeply. He heard distant screaming, the chorus of billions of shrieking voices tangled together. Schweitzer clung to their shared space, forced his way back into it.

Are you on the second deck? Jawid again, urgency in his voice. *We need your position.* Schweitzer could not answer, his energy funneled into the fight to cling to his corner of the ground he still held in his own corpse.

He felt Ninip give grudgingly, a fraction of their shared space opening to him. He slid gratefully into it as the jinn ripped the elevator doors from their moorings and leapt into the hallway beyond.

Schweitzer managed to get the carbine coming up, head down on the sights. They were already moving, the painted cinder-block surface of the walls sweeping by them, spaced by green metal doors at regular intervals.

Status! Jawid said. *Where are you?* The Sorcerer again forced the floor plan of the building down the link between them, but Ninip batted it aside again, picking up speed. *On the second deck, passageway outside the elevator. Moving to junction on north side,* Schweitzer sent to Jawid.

Shouts. Silhouettes at the end of the hallway, moving toward them.

Contact, Schweitzer sent up to Jawid. *Multiple . . .*

Ninip hauled on the trigger and the carbine barked. One of the silhouettes spun, dropped. Schweitzer had no idea where the round had impacted. SEALs took pride in knowing precisely where each round was placed, making them as effective with a .22 as they were with a monster-caliber weapon like the one they were holding now.

But Ninip would not be denied. The jinn drew on the fragments of gun lore he had learned and hauled on the trigger again, sending a large-caliber round digging into the floor a foot before the target. The silhouettes vanished, the shouts louder.

Ninip threw back their head and answered them, their

shared throat constricting to let out a howl that channeled all of the jinn's predator joy. Schweitzer knew that howl didn't sound human, knew it would cause the hairs of whoever heard it to stand on end.

Your boy is out of control, Schweitzer passed up to Jawid, felt Ninip's scorn as the jinn leapt forward. Return fire now, the whining of rounds streaking off the walls. Amateurs, then. One lucky bullet clipped their side, the liquid armor hardening at the blow, sending the round skimming off. Even the glancing hit would have put a normal man on the deck, but their magically augmented core locked up, keeping their body stable, moving them forward as if they'd never been hit.

A door flew open off their elbow. Schweitzer had been so focused on maintaining some purchase on his body that he hadn't noticed his shooter's vision taking over, his eyes beginning to rove instinctively in search of targets. The widened range caught the door, the face of the man beyond, contorted by rage, swinging a long-handled engineer's wrench.

Ninip took the reins, reaching out one clawed hand, raking their enemy's stomach open. The man's face went white as his guts came out, filling Schweitzer with a queer sense of déjà vu. Not long ago, he'd worn the same expression, staring at his own life falling away from him.

Ninip lashed the lengthened tongue out, curling it around the man's neck, yanking him in. Schweitzer felt their jaw unhinge, their neck tensing as their head jerked forward, the jaws clamping on the man's face. It collapsed under the pressure, the screaming cut off, the bones crunching as their jaw muscles engaged, and the jaws snapped shut. Blood filled their mouth, their throat convulsing to gulp it down, spraying over their shoulders, trickling down behind their armor.

Their skin tingled at the touch. The metallic taste was ambrosia. Schweitzer knew he should be horrified, but he could barely feel the edges of himself in the midst of Ninip's exultant storm.

He threw the carbine back into the sweet spot, hoping the familiar battlefield drills would anchor him, but it was useless. Ninip pushed the weapon back down, gnashed their teeth, and flexed their claws. *We do not need it.*

Schweitzer drowned in the bloodlust as they raced the rest of the way down the hall.

The man they'd dropped was kitted out in secondhand gear. An amateur playing at war. The .50 caliber round had punched a dime-sized hole through his sternum. He stared sightlessly at the ceiling, lips still trembling.

Ninip put their boot on his throat and stepped down.

A rusted steel railing stood before them, flaking green paint, metal staircases descending from either side. Before them was a broad gallery that had likely once been a factory floor. It was now somewhere between a camp and a hospital. Foam bedrolls were laid out at regular intervals, some still sporting rumpled sleeping bags. Three steel, wheeled worktables stood in the center of the room. Each one bore a body wrapped in bloody bandages.

Men and women were scrambling from the gallery floor, dressed in the same patchwork military clothing as the corpse under their boot, wielding the same secondhand weaponry. The stink of fear was sharp in the air. The enemy did their best to look determined, but it wasn't working. Schweitzer could see the panic on their faces.

Save one.

A man in a suit stood beside the worktables, bald head reflecting the gleam of the fluorescent lights. His face was warm and open, his forehead creased with concern as he bent over one of the bandaged bodies.

Jackrabbit.

Contact Jackrabbit, Schweitzer sent to Jawid. *Engaging.*

Jackrabbit looked up at Schweitzer and Ninip, his face registering resignation, sadness.

But not fear.

With that gaze, something punched through the cloud of Ninip's hunger. The jinn snarled, and Schweitzer felt the current more closely, as if it were another presence, made of the same stuff as the jinn itself.

Jackrabbit reached a hand toward them, and the current intensified. He frowned. Whatever he'd expected to happen, it hadn't.

Schweitzer felt one of the liquid cells on their shoulder go solid as a bullet impacted. Jackrabbit crouched, gathered his current in, then his thighs bulged impossibly large, splitting his pants along the seams, and he jumped.

He cleared the hundred feet between them easily. Schweitzer had enough time to slash to his left, laying open the throat of one of Jackrabbit's followers, and then Jackrabbit's arc brought him down onto the railing, his muscles returning to their normal size.

Schweitzer got the carbine up, not bothering with the sights at this range. The gun kicked.

Schweitzer felt the current intensify and Jackrabbit's side folded inward, his rib cage suddenly gone to jelly, sucking the shirt with it to create a notch that let the round pass harmlessly through. Then the flesh shot back to its normal position with all the spring of a released rubber band, and he was upon them.

Schweitzer let the carbine drop onto its sling and took Jackrabbit's fists in their balled hands, claws sinking into the backs, screeching against bones gone suddenly dense and hard as steel. Jackrabbit's current rose, and his hands swelled to the size of bowling balls, until even Ninip's magical strength broke and they stumbled backward. Schweitzer could see the crowd gathered behind Jackrabbit, watching, expectant.

Jackrabbit came on, his current a pungent cloak around them. One giant hand receded into a stump, a spike of bone shooting out, flattening into a cleaver edge, so sharp it gleamed like metal. He crouched.

"And now they send the dead after me," Jackrabbit said. "You do realize my answer isn't changing. It won't change no matter how many innocent people you kill."

Schweitzer only had time to capture the image, send it up to Jawid before Ninip growled and launched them forward.

"I'll be sure to send your head back to your bosses," Jackrabbit said, stepping into the attack. Ninip brought their claw down into Jackrabbit's shoulder, but the flesh went tacky, allowing their hand to sink to the palm before holding it fast.

Jackrabbit bladed away from them, raised the cleaver, brought it down on Schweitzer and Ninip's opposite arm. The shear-thickening fluid was designed to harden at the supersonic impact of a bullet. The bone cleaver sliced through it like ripe fruit. Schweitzer could feel it sink deep into muscle, slamming hard into the thick ball at the top of their humerus, splintering halfway through before grinding to a stop.

Ninip howled in rage and snapped at their opponent's face, but Jackrabbit's neck snaked away, suddenly flexible as rubber.

The angry animal act isn't going to cut it, Schweitzer said. *Let me take this.*

Ninip's answer was an incoherent snarl and a projection of solid red across their vision. He felt the cleaver twist, widening the wound until the fibers of the muscle gave way and their shared right arm hung useless at their side. Jackrabbit was smiling at them now from the top of his plastic neck, dancing just out of reach. "Does it hurt?" he asked. "Can you even feel anything?"

He's going to cut us to pieces, Schweitzer shouted. *This body doesn't heal! Are you trying to lose?*

Ninip growled again, but he felt the jinn give way. Schweitzer leapt to control their body, dropping their center of gravity and letting their lower half fall. Their boots shot forward between Jackrabbit's legs, their shoulders and head hitting the floor.

Their claws, still embedded in the Jackrabbit's shoulder, took their weight, yanking down. Jackrabbit was only able to yank his head out of the way before his elongated throat smashed flat into the concrete floor.

Schweitzer wrenched their clawed hand up, slicing through Jackrabbit's flesh and popping free, dragging chunks of something purple and wet. The speed with which Jackrabbit's body shifted and changed made it impossible to be certain, but he guessed it was the top of his target's lung.

Jackrabbit sprawled on the floor behind them, his tide focused inward now, probably repairing the damage Schweitzer and Ninip had just done. Schweitzer leapt them onto his back, thrust with their good arm, the clawed fingertips digging into Jackrabbit's back. He could feel the brief resistance of Jackrabbit's rib cage, then they were punching through, reaching upward, fingers scrabbling, even as Jackrabbit's current changed focus, and his shattered ribs became spikes, punching into Schweitzer and Ninip's wrist and forearm.

At last their hand closed around Schweitzer's target, felt the tough meat pulsing against their hand. He grunted and yanked back with everything they had. Jackrabbit's heart came free in a spray of red so deep, it bordered on purple, and he pitched forward on his face.

Schweitzer stood, feeling the heart beating in their hands. With the threat neutralized, fatigue gripped him, the effort of battling Ninip for control of their shared body hitting home at last. The jinn felt it, and surged forward, battering Schweitzer aside and spinning them to face the men and women clogging the hallway behind them, going slack-jawed at the sight of their fallen leader, lying face-down in a spreading pool of blood.

Ninip grinned, held the beating heart aloft. Schweitzer watched Jackrabbit's followers' wide eyes fix on it. He knew the fight had gone out of them. They were lambs for the slaughter.

Jackpot, Schweitzer managed to send. *Jackrabbit down*.

Then Ninip crouched, snarled, leapt into the midst of them, good arm already going to work.

Schweitzer tried to pull him back, lacked the strength. Ninip knocked him aside and leaned into a shove that sent

Schweitzer scrambling to hold on to his slice of real estate in their shared body.

Schweitzer felt the faint pulse of Jawid's attention. The Sorcerer was saying something, but he didn't care what. He turned inward, curling into the blackness, trying not to sense what the monster wearing his skin was doing.

CHAPTER IX
ASHES TO ASHES

"Come on, little man." Sarah's knees ached from the hours she'd spent on all fours, only the hotel's thin carpet between her and the concrete beneath. Patrick twirled the toy truck idly in one hand, looking at it as if it were some strange living thing that he wasn't sure would hurt him or not. He was silent, as he had been for hours now, had been for over a month since the hospital had seen fit to let him come home.

Panic swamped Sarah for the hundredth time. The therapist said it would take time, but the thought of Patrick never coming out of this semicatatonia was always hovering at the back of her mind. It was enough that Jim was gone, that she hadn't had a chance to say good-bye, that she wasn't sure if the people who'd done this to him wouldn't soon be coming for her. That there was no way to avenge herself on them, no answers, and no resolution. The thought of caring for Patrick alone, while he was like this, filled her with exhaustion so bone deep that she just wanted to curl up in a ball and sleep. She choked back tears, conjured the image of the man beneath her, gurgling out his life as she plunged the canvas knife into his neck again and again. Anger. That was good. Anger she could use.

She clung to the emotion desperately, reeled it in, directed it at herself. *Lock it up. That's what Jim would have said. Crying won't solve anything. Patrick needs you strong. The only way to lose is to quit.*

So she swallowed, ground her knees into the floor. The pain jolted her into action, and she smiled the warmest mommy smile she could muster, making rumbling noises as she pushed Patrick's trucks along the floor. He had loved them all his short life, and he would again.

Her cell phone buzzed a reminder, and she gathered Patrick into her arms. "Uncle Stevie's coming over soon. You want to play with Uncle Stevie?"

Patrick looked up at that, some glimmer of excitement in his tiny face. "Stevie," he said.

Relief flooded her, and she fought back tears again. Thank God for Steve, their rock in all of this. The one connection to the family the navy claimed to be, had instantly ceased to be the moment Schweitzer's corpse had gone cold. She was sure the navy wives would take her in, hold her hand, talk mealy-mouthed bullshit about God and plans, fling a chaplain at her. This was the thing about religious types she hated so much. They never missed a chance to proselytize. No tragedy was sacred, no setback off-limits. They would solemnly enter your private space, regal and pompous as crows, full of righteous self-importance. Then, when she was at her weakest, they would tell her why the unacceptable was acceptable, why it was okay that she'd lost the love of her life because an invisible man in the sky (and it was always a man, wasn't it?) had willed it.

Sarah's fingers itched for the canvas knife. She'd gladly plunge it into the throat of any god who'd done this to her, to her son.

Her cell phone's message indicator had a large red 5 in the upper right corner. They were voice mails from her mother, from Peg, her sister in the Shenandoah Valley. She often went weeks without talking to either of them, but a month was a stretch. She'd put Peg off with a short, "Things are complicated right now. I promise we'll talk about it later." Her mother she hadn't spoken to. She didn't trust herself to hear her mother's voice and keep her composure.

The doorbell rang, and Sarah set Patrick down, went to answer it. The panic rose in her again, the state of hypervigilance Jim had called "living in condition yellow" screaming at her to slow down, that she didn't know what was on the other side of that door, that she had to be ready.

Sarah mourned this most of all. When those men had come into her home, they'd pulled back the curtain on a world she'd always suspected existed but was able to ignore. It was a world where human lives were truly fungible, where death was meaningless and random, where being good and hardworking and loving your family meant absolutely nothing, where you were utterly powerless to keep anyone safe.

Sarah knew this was the space Jim had lived and worked in, that once that curtain was yanked aside, it could never be closed again, not really. *Oh God, Jim. I don't know how you did it*.

She paused at the door, fought against the urge to use the peephole. She knew it was Steve outside, not some armed thugs sent to finish the job they'd started. But the demons whispered to her from behind that open curtain, refused to allow her to let her guard down. Her hand was shaking as she forced herself to throw the latch, turn the doorknob, open the door at a normal pace.

Steve stood in the hallway, a steel can under one arm. She saw a glimmer of her face reflected in his dark eyes, knew that he alone could read her expression, the tremor in her hands, could truly understand the guarded twilight that would be her life from now on.

The tube had been removed from his chest and he looked healthier now, standing up straight, with color in his cheeks. She was embarrassed to admit how relieved she felt to see him, his nightly presence in her home an addiction. Steve brought peace with him, bags of groceries and toys for Patrick. More importantly, he understood the value of being quiet, of simply being in the room and letting Sarah grieve on her own. He respected the space her grief required, had an uncanny sense of when it was okay to move into it, to provide comfort when she was too weak to hold herself up.

Very few people could understand what Jim was to her, to the world. Steve was one of those few. He brought calm, he brought companionship, he brought the last shred of her husband that didn't live in her dreams of rose-petal trails.

"Uncka Stevie." Patrick stood and toddled over to him, holding up his truck.

Steve knelt, setting the can down at his side. "Hey, guy! Is that your truck?"

Patrick nodded shyly, holding it out to him.

"Thank God," Sarah said. "He hasn't said a thing all day."

Steve reached out for the truck only to have Patrick snatch it away, suddenly shy. He picked the boy up instinctively, hoisting him in the air. Patrick nestled against his chest, his expression losing some of the confused distance it normally wore these days.

"You feel like his daddy," Sarah said, the truth of the words making her throat swell.

"Yeah, well," Steve said, embarrassed. "I guess all guys feel sort of the same."

She'd been so happy to see him that the can had gone unremarked. It hit home now, the silver lines of its exterior suddenly coming into sharp relief. It shone from the floor, a cylindrical metal star.

"Is that what I think it is?" she asked.

Steve set Patrick down on the floor and tousled his hair as the boy clung to his leg. "It's his ashes."

She started to pick them up, stopped. Somewhere along the way, she'd brought a hand to her mouth, looking like a stupid girl. She dropped it with an effort. "Oh, my God," she breathed. "How did you? You said that . . ."

"Yeah, they weren't going to turn them over. They gave me every excuse in the book. They didn't have them, they'd gotten mixed up with others. They were still doing testing. The hush-hush bullshit can get pretty damn thick at times."

She finally bent and picked up the can, saw her funhouse reflection in the curving surface. She'd overcompensated for its anticipated weight. She had to clutch it to her chest to stop herself from tossing it in the air. Even with the metal, it was . . . was this all that was left of Jim? A pinch of dust? "It's so light."

It was quiet after that, until Steve's voice finally broke the silence, reminding her that she'd been staring at the can in her hands for . . . she didn't know how long. "Anyway, that's what there is. I'm sorry there isn't more, Sarah. I guess we can . . . well, we can have a funeral now."

"How did you get them to stop stonewalling?"

"Good old-fashioned pain-in-the-assery. I begged, I pleaded, I made accusations. I went to the chief and made an impassioned speech. I played on her sense of obligation to you. I shamelessly portrayed you as a wailing woman on the brink of suicide, which, I should add, is perhaps the biggest lie I've ever told."

"But none of that worked, did it?"

He looked at the floor, rubbed the back of his neck. "No. None of it did."

"So, how?"

"I threatened to go to the press. I said I'd tell any paper that would listen about how the navy treats the families of fallen warriors. It won't do my security clearance any favors but . . . ah, hell. I'm not so sure I want to do this anymore, anyway. Not after . . ." He trailed off.

Jim would never have even considered that, she thought, *not for an instant. No tragedy, no injury could have ever stopped him from being a SEAL.* She looked at the fear in Steve's face, knew it would never leave. He was a fighter, to be sure, but every fighter had their limit. He'd found his, and coming up against it would haunt him the rest of his life. For the first time in their long friendship, she pitied him.

But the pity was overcome by the wave of comfort and

gratitude that followed as he helped her put Patrick to bed, ordered Chinese delivery, sat in the living room, and ate with her in silence, watching images of a world they'd both left behind flash across the flat-screen TV mounted to the wall.

Sarah came to, her head on his shoulder, a tiny strand of drool trailing from the corner of her mouth to anchor on his shirt. She'd dozed off. She snorted, swallowed, swatted groggily at the air. She thought briefly of sitting up, but the solidity of his shoulder felt so good, the warmth radiating through his shirt against her neck lulled her back down, and she found herself nestling against him contentedly.

"You went out there for a little while. You must be exhausted." His voice sent tiny vibrations through his shoulder that buzzed her soothingly along her neck. She sighed.

"I haven't slept more than a couple hours at a stretch for God knows how long. Having you around helps."

"Well"—his voice was thick—"that's good. I'm glad to know I'm helping."

They sat like that in silence, and after a moment, he rested his head against hers. The move shocked her at first, but it was more warmth and more not-aloneness. He smelled faintly of the ready room, of gun oil and ripstop fabric seasoned with sweat. They were familiar smells, and she let herself sink in them.

"So," he said, "I guess we'll have to plan a funeral."

"Not yet, Steve. I'm just . . . I just can't face it right now."

When he answered, his voice was pinched. "I think it would be for the best. You need . . . closure here. You can't just hide out in this apartment forever. You have to get on with things."

The words stung, even as she acknowledged the truth of them. She thought of the boy crying in her dream. This felt like that. The necessary horror she dreaded facing, knew she had to.

"I know," she forced herself to say, "and I will, just . . . not soon."

She felt him tense. "You said you needed to get closure.

I fought like a mad dog to get these ashes for you, so you could have it."

She sat up, hating him for pulling her out of her precious brief moment of warm contentment. Her tiny spot where everything was, just for a short time, okay. "That's why you got them? So *I* could have closure? Jesus, Steve. He was your best friend. He was your . . . 'battle buddy,' or whatever the hell you call it."

His eyes narrowed, some of the warrior coming into his face. He couldn't have been more different-looking from her husband, but that expression nearly choked her with nostalgia. "It's different for us," he said. "You accept it from the time you graduate. You train for it. You know it's coming. You can't do what we do and not lose people."

Anger became hot in her throat. "Oh, really? Was this the same Steve Chang who cried like a baby next to my hospital bed? Maybe you need more training, tough guy."

His expression changed, the anger and determination morphing to something else. *You're hurting him.* But she couldn't stop herself. Because anger wasn't grief. Anger wasn't fear. And anything that wasn't those things was something.

"That's not fair," he said.

"Life isn't fair, or hadn't you noticed? It's not fair that I lost my husband. It's not fair that Patrick lost his father. It's not fair that your fucked-up little excuse for a brotherhood won't or can't figure out who the hell did it or why. The sea doesn't care about you, Steve. Or did you forget your favorite quote?"

"This is the first time I've heard you mention Patrick," he said. "What about him, Sarah? He's young, but that doesn't mean he's stupid. He knows his father is gone. He knows that the people who killed Jim hurt his mommy and hurt him, too. You think you're scared? What about him? Maybe you don't need closure, Sarah, but he does. He needs some kind of thing that will tell him that this makes sense."

"This doesn't make sense!" she almost yelled, and turned it into a snarl that she prayed wouldn't wake her son.

"You're right, it doesn't, but Patrick isn't an adult. He's not ready for that kind of revelation. He needs a world that's safe and ordered. He needs to believe that his father is in heaven surrounded by puppies and baby ducks and that he's watching him always. He needs the bullshit religion you hate so much. He needs to feel safe."

The words fell like hammerblows. Sarah knew he was right. She'd been so caught up in her own grief that she'd forgotten that Patrick was grieving, too. She'd focused on playing with him, trying to restore some sense of normalcy. But Patrick's mind was clear enough to understand that nothing would ever be normal again. It was up to her to define a new normal for him. She'd failed to do that.

The anger leaked out of her, leaving her only the grief and terror. She clung to its departing threads, unwilling to admit she was wrong just yet, to give way to the sobbing she knew bulled up against the dam of this stupid argument.

"Patrick's not your problem. You're not his father. This isn't your job."

"Fuck you," he said, the warrior pushing the hurt aside, taking full possession of his expression. Here was Steve Chang the SEAL, her husband's strong right hand, the fighter who kept the monsters at bay. God, he was beautiful.

"Fuck you if you think this isn't my job. You're not the only one who lost your family, Sarah. Jim was a brother to me, and the teams were brothers to both of us. I lost both when he died. This medical leave is purgatory. I can't go back when it's over. You know that. You're all I have, Sarah. You and Patrick are all that I have."

She stared, saw his expression shift, knew what he was about to do. *Oh God, Steve. Don't. Please don't.*

"I love you," he said. "I've always loved you, Sarah. I promised Jim a hundred times that I'd take care of you and Patrick if anything happened to him, and I mean to keep that promise. You were always the woman I thought I could never have, that I'd have to go on loving you from a distance for the rest of my life. Maybe this is the one good thing that comes out of this whole disaster."

A hundred retorts rose to her mind, that this was grief talking, that he didn't know her well enough to love her, that the fact he thought she needed taking care of was proof that he didn't know her at all. But she stood frozen to the spot, unable to work her mouth, dumbly realizing that this was the first time since Jim had died that someone had told her they loved her.

She felt the first tears fall, cursed herself, unable to stop them.

"Oh, Sarah," he said. "Oh, baby." He went to her, pulled her into his arms.

Don't call me "baby." Only Jim called me that. But she said nothing. Because as her hands came up to push him away, they found the taut solidity of his arms.

The spike of arousal hit her out of nowhere. Whoever Steve was, he was a man, and she had forgotten that she wanted a man, thought that she'd never want one again. She realized now that she had been wrong, that the hunger had crouched hidden, waiting to spring the moment the right touch triggered it. And was it wrong? Jim was dead. There was no manual that spelled out how long a widow had to wait before finding someone else. There was no rule that said it couldn't be his friend. There might be some who'd turn up their nose at the prospect, but fuck them; Sarah Schweitzer had always lived life on her own terms.

She slid her hands across his broad back, the thin fabric of his shirt gliding over sturdy muscles, heat bleeding into her hands. No, it still felt wrong. She wasn't sure she was ready.

She pushed against the lust, fought it down, but it was tangled now, wrapped up in the grief and rage and despair. And love. Yes, love. She loved Steve, she knew that. It was a different love than what she and Jim had shared, and she realized that she'd been trying to figure out what that love was, what it meant. She hadn't had time, she hadn't had energy. This was a different love. It wasn't the kind of love that should make her feel a hot pulse between her legs, that should make her open her mouth, let the tip of her tongue graze his neck, drinking in his smell.

But it was love. And in the hell of the last month, it was what she needed more than anything.

And so she surrendered to it, giving herself over to the simple pulsing word in her mind—*good good good*—grasping at the sensations of pleasure that she'd thought lost to her forever, letting him push her down on the couch, taking his tongue into her mouth. Her body fell into familiar rhythms, stripping off his shirt, running her hands over the hardness of him, softer now with his time convalescing, but still a SEAL's body in its roots.

She let her body work, it knew how to make love. She retreated into the tangled knot of emotion boiling within her, crawled into the heart of the love and lay inside it, luxuriating as the wanting drove her limbs, stripping off her pants, so hurried that it barely could be bothered to pull her panties aside before guiding him into her.

And then her body claimed what was left of her senses and all there was were stars and warmth and someone moaning from a long, long way away.

CHAPTER X
COLD STORAGE

They put him back in cold storage.

Schweitzer didn't remember much about the extraction. Sated, Ninip retreated into the darkness of their shared inner world, resting in his fashion, sluggish from the blood that soaked their armor to the knees, covered the walls like the effort of an art student whose ambition exceeded his abilities.

Death was Schweitzer's job, and he'd seen plenty of it. His second op after joining his team had been taking down a safe house used by narcoterrorists in a godforsaken stretch of South American jungle. It had been hot like a bad dream of hell, and as the fresh meat on the team, Schweitzer had the lucky job of breaching the door. His finger trembled along his carbine's receiver, ready to show his brothers that breaching and tac-pro wasn't the only thing he was good at.

So, of course the place was empty.

Of the living.

The bad guys had been questioning some members of the gang who they suspected of informing on them. Their remains were strung along the ceiling like Christmas lights, razor wire looped around their throats. They'd been splayed open with machetes, slit down the middle and stuffed with what looked like rotting fruit. Insects were nesting inside them, the heat swelling what was left of the gray flesh to balloon-sized, malignant cauliflower.

It was Schweitzer's first test, and he'd passed, but just barely.

"Six-pack of Coronas says the FNG blows chunks." Martin had laughed. He'd bet the Fucking New Guy would lose it, and Schweitzer had been proud when Martin had been forced to pay up later. But the image of those corpses stayed with him, as much a reminder that he was a SEAL as the pin on his uniform. Because if he could look at that and find a way to go on, then he was hard enough for anything.

But Schweitzer had looked at the red slurry Ninip had made of the people in that warehouse and realized he was wrong.

The fear he had always been able to look in the eye was staring him down. It had become huge beyond imagining, a freezing blackness filled with the tangle of endless limbs, a chaos of screaming voices, bullying anything but raw terror into submission. Sarah and Patrick were somewhere in there, condemned to that horror. He never believed he would hesitate to go after them, be cowed by the thought of that spinning endlessness, of not only losing them but the last shreds of himself. But he was frightened, truly and deeply.

He felt Ninip's presence stretching itself luxuriously, and Schweitzer realized the root of his horror. Standing in that corrugated metal shed, watching the heat of the jungle do its work on those bloated flesh-flowers, Schweitzer realized what he was. It was in the killing that the SEAL distinguished himself from the enemy. Schweitzer killed with a professional's precision, a cold calculation made holy by its service to his country's cause. It was what made him an artist instead of a thug.

He'd fought against Ninip's insensate rage, but a part of

him had reveled in it, drunk on the power of an apex predator, a video game played on the easiest setting, his enemies powerless grist for the mill of his might. He hadn't
fought hard enough. He hadn't dug deep enough. He'd
stood knee-deep in the gore the jinn had created and realized that maybe he wasn't so different from the men who'd
strung those people up. Worse than a thug.

A monster.

Ninip's voice was smug, *I told you I would teach you
valor.*

That wasn't valor. That was slaughter.

*You think because you are . . . what do you call it, a
"professional," that you are not a killer? We are no different.*

*We are. I'm interested in justice. You're interested in
your appetite.*

*Justice? Would you have arrested that man, like one of
your police? Do you think justice would have held him?
He would have been free in moments.*

*We'd be stronger if we did it by the numbers. That's
what my training is for. You can only go so far fighting like
a wild animal. True warriors are professionals.*

Footmen, Ninip scoffed.

Schweitzer didn't answer. Eldredge stood outside the
reinforced glass, arms folded, chin in one hand. Jawid was
saying something to him, shaking his head.

Schweitzer thought of Sarah and Patrick again, lost in
that maelstrom. His hand went instinctively to the dog
tags, pulled them out from behind his blood-spattered
armor. Ninip didn't even bother trying to control their
shared arm, only watched smugly as Schweitzer traced the
lines of his family's faces with a gray fingernail. The rust
seemed thicker, their likenesses fading into the pitted
metal. It had only been a day or two, was it possible for
metal to oxidize that fast? Was there something in the
touch of the armor or his dead flesh that destroyed it? He
felt a spike of grief. This was the last he had of them.
Would he forget their faces? He reached out for the smell

of Sarah's perfume, the phantom limb of their connection that he'd sworn he sensed before. Nothing.

Ninip had lived in that maelstrom, had spent countless years in that spinning hell.

What was it like? Schweitzer asked.

Ninip stirred, shrugged. *I told you. It was blind panic. A storm unending.*

No, I meant what'd you do all day? You just . . . floated around?

Ninip sighed contentedly, ignored him. He felt the presence turn a shoulder.

If Ninip could read his memories, then maybe the process worked in reverse. Schweitzer tried to center himself, imagined himself in a lotus position, legs folded, hands on his knees. He visualized sending his mind out to Ninip's. Nothing happened. It was ridiculous to even try. Ninip was a being of magic. What could Schweitzer do?

But he felt Ninip stir. *What are you doing?*

Look, I have no idea how long we're going to be stuck here before they run us again. Talk to me. I'll go crazy just . . . sitting.

That is what it was like. That is what I did.

What?

Went crazy. Schweitzer felt the jinn reach out to him, and his vision went white, a blank canvas that the jinn began to decorate with images from his life. It was the storm of souls as Ninip had seen it when he was imprisoned there, the screaming was louder, the clamor of voices running together into a hum. The crush of bodies closer, an ocean of faces rushing past, all genders, races, and ages, all wearing the same openmouthed expression of horror.

You catch glimpses of their thoughts, Ninip said. *You pass through them, you share them, but only for an instant.*

Schweitzer could see it now, the moment upon moment of recognition, of shared experience, each as quick as a camera's shutter click, before whirling to the next. For years, for millennia.

Ninip. Churning, spinning, snatching at the brief shreds

of contact. On. Off. On. Off, until his own voice joined the chorus, and the screaming was all, seeping into his soul and rooting there. The scream becoming the animal howl that Schweitzer heard him utter in the warehouse corridor.

And then, blue flashes in the mass, lines reaching out, strings of words, voices not screaming. The magic. Sorcerers like Jawid reaching into the storm to draw the jinn out. All of the souls surging toward the shred of humanity, the splinter of the life they'd known. They crawled over one another, clawing aimlessly as the gale churned them over and over and away. Ninip, snarling, pushing with everything he had, reaching out to clasp the hand that was extended along that blue path, to talk back. To let them know he heard them.

That was Jawid, Schweitzer said. *That's what it looked like.*

Not Jawid. There were others. Are others. From time to time, they reached out to us. Less often, one of us would find a way to answer.

One of the spinning souls detaching from the rest, semiopaque, a broad-shouldered woman with a long stretch of dreadlocks reaching down her back. Pulling herself forward, sliding into the line of blue, rocketing down it, vanishing from view.

Into life.

Ninip. Watching. Learning.

And finally, the next flash. Words, Jawid's voice this time. The monster howl, the animal rage, Ninip channeling it, forcing it into motion, falling into that blue highway that led back to Schweitzer's cooling corpse.

And for the first time in an eternity, the kernel of something blossoming deep in the sliver of Ninip that hadn't been lost to those years in the storm. Hope.

As the vision faded, Schweitzer felt the edge of that hope go sour.

What happened?

We happened. Now there is only us.

No, I mean, what did you want to happen? Schweitzer

projected the hope back at him, felt the jinn recoil from it, the gorged lethargy beginning to ebb.

That. That is nothing.

It's not nothing. What did you want? What did you think you'd see?

The presence retreated from him, and Schweitzer followed, the SEAL in him knowing to press the advantage. *What? You're disappointed. You didn't think you'd wind up . . . here, in me. You expected something else.*

Schweitzer reached out again, and this time he felt the edges of Ninip's experience, his memories. He snatched at them, and the jinn pushed him back, angry now. He felt Ninip gathering his strength, remembered the sensation of being pushed out of their shared body, the screaming chaos ready to take him in. The fear came again, but this time he felt some of the old training take hold. He acknowledged the fear, let it pass through him, turned back to Ninip. *SEALs fight as a team. None of us can do the job alone. That's how wars are fought now.* Schweitzer pushed memories back at the jinn now, hours and hours of school circle chats, pages and pages of loose-leaf-binder paper, extolling the virtues of teamwork, of the warrior brotherhood, of leaning on the man next to you. He recalled and showed Ninip planning sheets, fire-team breakdowns, each operator in his or her position, with their specific job: the pigman, the breacher, the intel weenie, the overwatch, the comms geek. Each alone, still SEALs, but together, a symphony capable of accomplishing wonders.

He could feel Ninip absorbing the information, considering.

We have to work together. He projected more images. Barbecues on Chang's deck, Chang giving presents to Patrick on Christmas. Ahmad playing singles volleyball against Sarah on the lawn outside their home. Schweitzer on the phone with Perreto, giving him advice, listening as the Coast Guardsman complained about his girlfriend. More than a team, a family.

We have to be tight. He shuddered at the thought of

being close to the black soul that had been responsible for the massacre back in the warehouse. But even if Ninip was his enemy, ignorance served no one. *If we're going to be the god of war you want us to be, we have to be like that. So, tell me*

He felt the jinn pause, gather itself. He could feel the anger shifting from smolder to burn, readied himself for the assault that would shove him out of their shared body.

But Ninip only sighed, and Schweitzer's vision went white once again.

He saw through Ninip's eyes, the red filter gone. Ninip lies on a bed of dried reeds, a thin white cloth draped over him. The bed is on a raised dais in the center of a cavernous room built from sand-colored blocks of stone. The walls have been painted in garish colors, stylized figures in rows, carrying jugs of water, palm fronds, spears. Crude scribbling is interspersed with the paintings, tiny, blockish pictograms, little shapes marching in orderly rows on their way to meaning.

The room is open at one end, admitting a bright sun through thick columns to pool around him, but Schweitzer can tell that Ninip is cold. A beautiful woman bends over him, a white gown leaving one brown breast exposed, a jeweled black wig hanging down to either side of her heavily kohled eyes. She holds out a dried gourd brimming with water. Ninip reaches out a hand, trembling, withered, ancient.

A younger man, still in the prime of his life, kneels at the bedside, speaking. His face is dark with concern, but the look doesn't reach his eyes, and he strokes his braided beard impatiently. He is covered in jewels, a short sword curving like a whip along his side.

He cradles Ninip's head gently, holds out a small fig, glistening with oil.

He is trying to get Ninip to eat it.

He told me I must eat something.

Your son.

Ninip's silence was answer enough.

Ninip, taking the fig in shaking hands, forcing it into his mouth, knowing the oil didn't smell like olives, eating it anyway. The beautiful woman kisses his forehead. His son sits with him, and Ninip stares at him, taking in the contours of his face, loving him with a fierce heat.

But the younger man's eyes are set on the sun, rising past the columns now, spreading its glory across the kingdom below.

He was impatient. Ninip's voice was flat. *I lingered too long.*

And you wanted revenge?

Ninip shook his head. *I lingered, weak. I would have done the same. I wanted to see him. The* En *told me he'd had a vision, that my boy would be a poor ruler. I had him poisoned as recompense. All priests are liars. But I wanted to be certain. All men have their time to die, and this was mine, but how I wanted to see my boy rule.*

That writing was nothing Schweitzer had ever seen before, certainly not Egyptian hieroglyphics. Probably older. Ninip's civilization was likely lost to history. It was possible there was a way to find the answer, but Schweitzer wouldn't even know where to begin.

The priests lied. They told me that the peasants would eat dust and scraps, but there would be offerings from my family, burned at the altar each day. I would still live as a king, as a god. But there was only . . . you have seen.

I'm sorry.

Ninip stopped at that. Schweitzer felt the presence bunch, retreat. Schweitzer began to ask him what was wrong, stopped himself. Whatever the customs Ninip had known in his past life, Schweitzer doubted sympathy was high on the list.

I had a son, too, Schweitzer offered.

I know. But it is your wife you remember, her perfume you still smell.

Yeah. Sarah and I had years to bond, Patrick was still new. We were still learning one another. He was just becoming a person when . . .

The jinn's voice was softer. *You will have vengeance. It will be glorious.*

Thanks. And when we're done, we'll go check out your home. We'll ask Jawid to look it up. Archaeology's come a long way. Maybe we can find something. As soon as Schweitzer said it, he knew it was a mistake. Ninip reached out, tapped Schweitzer's understanding of archaeology, surveyed the images of digs, sarcophagi behind Plexiglas, old men in pith helmets dusting at lengths of desiccated bone.

Ninip growled. *There is nothing. Ashes. Do you see what comes of clinging to the past? Why moon over old loves? Children? There is only the path ahead, and we gain neither gold nor honor by looking elsewhere.*

The thought made Schweitzer sad in his dead bones. He felt the weight of their shared body suddenly, dead muscles moving, glycerol-inflated veins sliding under gray skin. All of it driven by the magic of the jinn.

We'll find who killed them, who killed me. We'll make them pay. We'll find out what happened to your son, to your kingdom.

And then? Ninip asked.

There'd always been a plan before. Make the next rank, see Patrick into adulthood, grow Sarah's career. Keep the country safe. Do his twenty, then see what retirement held for him.

We see to our pasts, Schweitzer said. *We settle scores and close loops.*

Ninip didn't answer, and in the dark space they shared, Schweitzer could feel the jinn shaking its head.

CHAPTER XI
THE NEW NUKE

After two hours, they came to fix his arm.

Ninip was sullen, annoyed that he'd shared himself with Schweitzer, and the jinn skulked in the darkness, ignoring him. Schweitzer passed the time alternately trying to reach out for the smell of Sarah's perfume, or to touch Jawid. The connection between Ninip and himself was clearly bidirectional, and he knew there was a way to reach out to the Sorcerer, but he couldn't figure out what it was.

Then the door to their cell slid open with a hiss and puff of gas, admitting four men. Two were their old friends, Mr. Flamethrower and Mr. Axe. The other two wore medical scrubs and surgical masks and pushed a wheeled steel table set with shining knives, clamps, probes, needles, and a generous coil of thread.

Ninip briefly contemplated attacking them, but Schweitzer resisted, and the jinn seemed content to let it go. The men in scrubs approached him carefully and began examining the damaged joint where Jackrabbit's bone cleaver had nearly cut the arm away from their body. Schweitzer tried to look over as they worked, but the men were too close. He could feel the bone and muscles being cinched into place, staples being put in, thread sewing shorn fibers back together.

Schweitzer was amazed at how comforting it was just to have people close, to be touched. He waited for Ninip to chastise his weakness, but the jinn only sulked, lost in whatever passed for reflection with his kind.

"How look?" Schweitzer managed to say. He tried to contort the stretched face into a smile and found the structure wouldn't allow it.

One of the medical technicians looked up at him, eyes widening behind the safety glasses, eyebrows disappearing up behind the hairnet. "It's looking good, sir. We can fix it."

"Thut," Schweitzer said, frowned, tried again. Slowly this time, deliberately flexing lungs and larynx. "Thanks."

The man smiled behind his blue face mask. "It's our pleasure, really."

Schweitzer badly wanted to talk with someone who wasn't either Eldredge or Jawid, but the man had already bent back to his work, this time producing a blowtorch and what looked like a caulking gun filled with some kind of sealant. A plastic joint was set into place, and Schweitzer could feel them working away for another two hours, until they finally stepped back and nodded in satisfaction.

The man stepped around him now. Schweitzer felt him make an incision in the back of his neck. "What?"

"Just a little something so we'll know where you are. We had it in your armor before, but Dr. Eldredge decided it would be safer here. Just sit tight, this'll be over in just a sec."

"Take time. No hurt," Schweitzer said.

The man chuckled. "That's right. I'm not used to patients who don't feel pain."

But he still did his work quickly, and a moment later, the back of Schweitzer's neck was stitched shut, and the four men left.

At the door, the med tech turned back to him, shot a thumbs-up. Schweitzer waved.

Ninip tested the arm. It swung stiffly, but it swung. The fingers moved. The hand opened and closed. The wrist and elbow bent and turned.

Shortly after they left, Schweitzer felt something open within him, and Jawid's voice sounded. *What happened?*

We did as you asked, Ninip answered.

Schweitzer felt Jawid stretch down the link between them, reaching for their memories of the op. Ninip pushed against him, but Schweitzer recalled as much as he could, passing it back up the link while Ninip snarled and cursed.

Schweitzer felt Jawid's horror as the Sorcerer reviewed the images, his emotion slowly rising to a crescendo that Schweitzer knew meant he had seen the massacre at the end.

Dr. Eldredge will want a word, Jawid said, and closed the link.

A moment later, Eldredge appeared outside the thick, transparent pane, now fogging slightly from the temperature differential of the warmer hallway outside. He looked at Schweitzer for a long time before a squawk box conveyed his words into the refrigerated cell, giving the gentle voice a tinny, antiseptic quality punctuated by static.

"How are you doing, James?"

That is not our name, Ninip said.

Schweitzer ignored him, doing his air-pushing dance again. "Good."

"I'm looking over the after action, talking with Jawid. I've got some concerns. It's imperative that you work together with your partner, but I've already told you that some of our past subjects have found these unions to be overpowering. It's your work in tandem that makes you powerful. It's critical that you hang on."

Schweitzer thought of the cold abyss, the storm of souls as Ninip pushed him out.

What will you do without me? Schweitzer asked, but the jinn was silent.

"Why?" Schweitzer managed.

Eldredge frowned, then laughed. "I have to admit,

James, you're the first one to ever care. In the history of this program, I never had an Operator ask me a question."

"Not ans . . . er," Schweitzer managed. That was a longer word, harder to form. He was getting better.

"No, it's not an answer," Eldredge said. "I'm sorry."

Schweitzer stepped closer to the window, Eldredge backing away with each step, until the doctor's back was against the corridor wall.

"Ans . . . er," Schweitzer said, "or no work."

Eldredge sighed. "It's control, Jim. The jinn are . . . feral. You're the brains of the operation. The discipline. When Operators go monolithic, they lose their . . ." He paused, frowned again.

"Use," Schweitzer finished for him. He recalled Ninip's rage, his lust. Animal cravings, driving him to kill as animals do.

Eldredge smiled ruefully, spread his hands. "The dog tags, do they help?"

Schweitzer moved their hand to the chain, froze as Ninip struggled to push it down. Eldredge watched with interest as Schweitzer struggled through, raising the hand by inches until it closed around the etched medallions.

"Yes," Schweitzer said. "Help."

Eldredge nodded. "That's good."

"Why, kill." The next word seemed impossible, so Schweitzer broke it into two. "Jack . . . rab?"

Eldredge's forehead creased. "For the same reason we've sent you on every direct-action op when you were alive. He needed to die."

"He . . . magic." Ninip was perking up now, paying attention.

"Yes, James. He was a Sorcerer, not unlike our Jawid. Only, his magic is different."

The warping body, the cleaver hand. "How?"

"We're still figuring that out," Eldredge said. "For now, we call it Physiomancy. Jackrabbit had the ability to manipulate living flesh. So, you can see why you were particularly effective against him." The current, focusing on him. Jack-rabbit frowning as the expected effect didn't materialize.

"Why, kill." Schweitzer recalled Jackrabbit's words. *And now they send the dead after me. You do realize my answer isn't changing. It won't change no matter how many innocent people you kill.* He tried to put steel into his clumsy croaking. "Why?"

"Because we asked him to come in. We offered to help him control it, to help him understand it. He refused."

Schweitzer began to work his throat again, but Eldredge held up a hand. "Before you go indignant on me, let me ask you something. Let's say that a very ethical and intelligent friend, someone you trust implicitly, were to come into possession of a particularly virulent and contagious strain of Ebola, or a small megaton nuclear warhead. Do you think it's okay to just let him keep it? Without supervision? Without the government's getting involved?"

Eldredge paused to let Schweitzer answer, then went on at his silence. "Jackrabbit could enter a room and kill every-one in it in less than thirty seconds. He could tear off your head with a thought, make your heart jump out of your chest by snapping his fingers. He'd drawn a group of followers who thought he was the messiah. Those were the men you killed back there. Religious fanatics who called Jackrabbit Jesus because he had the power to heal. But what he didn't show them is that he also had the power to kill. That's why we had to stop him. Let me show you something."

Eldredge stepped into the command center across the corridor, shooed a soldier away from a computer terminal, and began tapping away at it. A moment later, pictures began to appear on the one big screen Schweitzer could make out through the glass. They were soldiers, direct-action operators like he'd been in life, judging by their gear.

They were mutilated. It was worse than what Ninip had made him do. One of the men had simply been turned inside out, the blue-gray of his organs still in perfect place, his face a bowl of gore. Another had been stabbed to death by his own skeleton, the bones projecting through his ragged skin, making him into a literal pincushion.

"There are more like Jackrabbit," Eldredge said, calling up more images. "More every damn day."

The screens scrolled by: an older woman, head thrown back under a sky crowded with dark clouds, lightning coiling around an outstretched arm. A young man in a smart suit, standing in a parking lot covered with twinkling frost extending from his fingertips. A little girl sitting Indian-style in a cemetery, a hint of mischief in her eye, surrounded by hundreds of the newly risen dead.

Eldredge walked slowly back to the glass, folded his arms again. "That's what you stopped, James. You wouldn't let a private citizen have possession of a nuke. Jackrabbit *was* a nuke. That's what magic is. That's why we have to keep it under control."

Ninip reached for Schweitzer's memories, but Schweitzer beat him to the punch, pushing him away and funneling the images to him. Einstein and Oppenheimer, Fat Man and Little Boy, START and SALT. Mushroom clouds. Radiation sickness. Doomsday.

They have such weapons? Ninip asked. *They must give them to us!*

I told you about teamwork, Schweitzer replied. *These weapons take a pretty big team.*

We made short work of this Jackrabbit. With these, we will make short work of nations.

"You swore to protect the American people," Eldredge went on, "and that's what you're continuing to do. The Gemini Cell is born of magic and dedicated to understanding and curtailing it. Single Operators for now, but once we perfect it, I'm confident we can start running fire teams, just like you used to do. You'd like that?"

Schweitzer realized that he would like that. The thought of snapping back into the puzzle that only his expertise could complete appealed to him. Ninip scoffed. *We need no team. We dispatched this supposed new nuke and thirty more besides.*

Schweitzer ignored him, focused on Eldredge. "Sarah. Patrick."

"I haven't forgotten that part. Look, James, you know that developing intel takes time. You don't just snap your fingers and come up with reliable sources. It takes time to put them in place, to cultivate them, to get them to produce. I promise you that we are making this a top priority."

"Show," Schweitzer said.

Eldredge looked confused. "Show you what?"

"Intel."

"Jim, you're an Operator. You get a targeting package. You don't get the intel behind it."

Schweitzer stepped forward, their forehead touching the glass lightly, the silver fire of their eyes boring into Eldredge's. Slowly, he raised their shared fist, jerked a thumb at their chest.

"Not Operator.

"New nuke."

CHAPTER XII
WALK OF SHAME

Sarah opened her eyes, taking in the bare expanse of the bedroom wall, off-white paint, tiny fingertip smudges where Patrick had touched it. In that brief moment of disorientation that comes on waking, she imagined that it had been an erotic dream, that the feel of Steve's body against hers was a phantom, one she could shrug off, the byproduct of being horny, lonely, desperately needing to feel loved.

But she felt the familiar ache from the tops of her thighs to the bottom of her ribs. The gentle slope of the mattress that indicated a shared bed, the slow rhythm of his breathing, the heat of his body.

It wasn't a dream. She'd betrayed Jim. *Don't be stupid. He's dead. You have a can of his ashes on the kitchen counter. He's dead, and you're alive. He'd want you to move on, to take care of yourself.*

But the feeling sat in the pit of her stomach, rising through her throat until tears pricked at the corners of her eyes. Dead or alive, she'd betrayed him. She'd loved another man while her son slept less than fifty feet away.

Oh God, what if I'm pregnant?

*Stop it. You're so stressed-out, you've missed your period
already. If, by some miracle, that happens, you'll deal with
it then.*

She felt Steve stir and went rigid against the sheets. She
couldn't turn, couldn't bear to see him. *Please, just think
I'm asleep. Just get up and go.*

But Steve didn't get up and go. She felt the mattress
shift as he turned, threw an arm over her, tracing his fingers down her shoulder, gently cupping her breast. She felt
his breath dust her shoulders, his lips brushing the nape of
her neck, placing gentle, fleeting kisses there. Even without seeing him, she knew he was smiling.

She didn't move, hoping against hope that he would
think she slept, lose interest. A moment later she felt him
stiffen, grind himself into her ass, press his body against
the full length of her. This time, her body didn't respond.
She lay frozen, her mind desperately searching for a way
to stop this, to reset the broken boundary. *You'll break his
heart.*

He'd said he loved her. In hindsight, she had been a fool
not to notice it before. But she couldn't let a moment of
weakness and desperation turn into a commitment. She
had to pull the Band-Aid off now.

She was still searching for a strategy when he noticed
her stiffness, her failure to respond. He pushed back from
her, propped himself up on an elbow. "Sweetheart, what's
wrong?"

"Don't call me that," she'd said before she could stop
herself.

Now it was his turn to freeze, but only for a moment. She
heard him throw the sheets back and get out of bed, felt his
heavy tread on the floor as he came around to face her.

He was magnificently naked, the early-dawn light
striped by the blinds across the scar on his chest, running
into dozens more crisscrossing his body, a tale of battles
going back years. He was slowly losing his arousal, his
manhood dangling as he crouched down to eye level. He
looked determined. He looked terrified. "What?"

She sat up, wrapping the sheets around herself, covering her nakedness. He looked grim at that.

"You know what. I won't say you took advantage, Steve. It takes two to tango. But I was lonely and I was hurting and I shouldn't have done that. It wasn't right."

He reached for her, eyes going maudlin. "It was the rightest thing we've ever done. It was a long time coming."

"No, Steve. We're both fucked-up by this. We're leaning on each other, and . . . things get confused when you do that."

Angry now. "You're not pulling that teenager shit with me. 'Oh, I'm so confused!' That went out in high school. We're grown-ups."

"I'm not saying I'm confused. I'm saying you are. You don't love me, Steve."

The anger condensed. "Don't tell me how I feel. I love you and I love Patrick and I always have. I'd die for you."

"Please don't make this any harder than it is. Just go. I'll call you when I've had a chance to sort all this out."

"And what the hell am I supposed to do while you're sorting things out?"

"You just said we were grown-ups, Steve, figure it the fuck out." His face fell, and she instantly regretted the words.

"I'm sorry, Steve," she said. "I know . . . I know you feel differently. But like I said, it takes two to tango, and I don't want to dance just now. Please understand that."

"What about Patrick, huh? What are you going to say to him when I'm not here? When I stop coming around? He needs me, Sarah."

Sudden anger spiked in her belly, rising up her spine until her scalp burned. "Patrick is *four*. We're the adults. It's our job to make responsible decisions. I make the decisions about what to say and what not to say. I decide what he knows and doesn't know. It's my job to take care of him. I'm his mother, his blood. You're not."

Steve stood, his body tensed, a storm cloud gathering behind his eyes. For a fleeting moment, Sarah wondered if he'd strike her. But he only stared, the rage yielding to sadness that showed in the cast of his eyes, the cut of his shoulders. He opened his mouth, said nothing, then stormed out to the living room, where she heard him gathering his clothing, discarded around the couch in their eagerness to get them off. As he did the belt on his jeans, she heard Patrick open the door to his room, heard the patter of his feet on the floor as he ran to embrace Steve's leg.

She rose, sheet still wound around her, went to the doorway in time to see Steve kneeling, hugging Patrick to him, tears running down his face. "Hey, hey little guy. It's fine. It's okay."

Patrick said nothing, face buried in Steve's shirt. *He knows he's leaving. He's already lost one man. Don't do this to him.* But she couldn't let him stay. Someone had to be the grown-up. It's what Jim would have done. He had the strength to make the hard calls, to do what was right even when it hurt.

"Sweetheart," she said, "come to Mama."

Patrick looked up, eyes wide, didn't move.

Steve swallowed hard, disentangled Patrick's arms, stood. "Go on, man. Go to your mother."

Patrick gave him a long look, sniffed.

"It's okay. I'll be back soon." This last he directed to Sarah.

She took a step forward, and Patrick went to her, already crying.

Steve gave her a long last look and left, the door slamming shut with a bang that sounded strangely final.

She held Patrick for a long time, only aware that time had passed by the rhythm of his body changing as crying softened to whimpering and finally to sleep, his head resting against her shoulder, one small fist bunched, knuckle in his mouth.

She came back to herself then, her stomach feeling hollow, an ache of panic and sadness in the small of her back. *Did I do the right thing? Should I have let him stay?* But any way she turned the question over in her head, she came back to the same answer. It was wrong. She didn't love Steve, not the way he needed her to. It wasn't right.

She carried Patrick gently back to his room and laid him in his bed. She knew she should keep him up, try to engage him, the doc had said that constant sleep was a sign of depression, that he had to be made to fight it. But she didn't have the energy. She needed to sit and think now.

A few of her effects had been salvaged from the wreckage of her old apartment, among them an old bottle of her favorite bourbon, in its customary place on top of the refrigerator. She snatched it up, grabbed a dirty glass out of the sink, and poured herself a generous helping. She sat sipping it, warm and caustic and tasting strangely different at this early hour, as if the light of dawn had flavored the liquor somehow.

She looked at her reflection in the brown liquid. Even with the fun-house distortion, she could still see the dark half-moons under her eyes, the hollowness of her cheeks. She looked hard. She looked mean.

She thought of Patrick, nestled against Steve's chest, sobbing.

The anger flared again. *Goddamn you, Jim. Everything was going so well. Why did you have to die?* She knew that wasn't true, remembered the tongue-lashing she'd given him on their last night together. But it didn't matter. Time, distance, and drama had erased the bad memory, leaving only Jim the saint, handsome protector, father, and lover. Oh God, how she missed him.

For a moment, her strength failed, the misery doubling her over until her head rested in her hands, palms pressing into her eyes until her vision became a kaleidoscope of shimmering brown-black arcs, merging and overlapping.

She pressed harder, sinking into the dull pain in the back of her eyes, her head clearing, some of the misery and panic abating. The lines in her vision continued to aggregate until they became a uniform blackness, silent and blessedly devoid of anything. She floated there, as she had in her dream, grateful for the chance to simply exist, to occupy a space where crisis didn't dog her, where no one depended on her.

In her college days, she'd studied abroad in Tokyo, three months sweltering in that beehive of a city during the hottest summer on record. The oppressive heat had stifled all efforts to paint, and her professor had taken pity on her, taken her to a mountain temple, high up where the air was cooler. There, he'd taught her zazen, a seated meditation that he said would help her reach inward, find the art inside. She didn't know if it helped the art, but the cool air was nice, and she did a fair bit of good work up there.

Later, she'd discovered the lotus position, and sat in it daily, thinking of that tall mountain, the pine tops waving in the breeze below. She wasn't sure if it did anything, but it was a pleasant break from sitting at her easel.

In her mind, she assumed the position now, floating in that blackness. *Like in my dream.*

And as in her dream, she felt the wind pick up, only it didn't howl now, it brushed her cheek gently, as it had on that mountaintop all those years ago. She looked down, and the pine tops waved below her, only now instead of needles, they were covered with rose petals, wafting the gentle smell of her perfume upward. The tallest trees snaked a line above the rest, leading inexorably outward and upward.

To Jim. She knew it.

In her dream, the wind had insisted. But now it seemed content to let her contemplate the path, make her own decisions.

She let her eyes wander along it, watching the rose pines wave. She could feel Jim's outline, somewhere at the other end of a walk she didn't have the energy to make, even in her mind. *Oh, Jim, you bastard. I'll get past this. I'll get over you eventually.*

But I don't want to.

And with that, she took her hands away from her eyes, and the blackness began to recede into swirling colors as the world poured back in. And for a moment, as she sat blinking in the light, she heard a faint echo. A tremor. An unshakable certainty that, as she'd reached out along that path, he'd reached back.

Jim was alive. She was absolutely sure of it.

She shook her head, flopped back on the couch. Ridiculous. Worse than ridiculous, desperate. Just because she wanted a thing didn't make it so. She couldn't wish her late husband back to life. Jim was dead, and that was that. She had to accept that, no matter what wishful visions she had.

But you never saw the body.

There is no body. Jim's ashes are in that can on your counter.

She stood, turned. The can sat where Steve had left it, the curved surface reflecting the growing light as dawn came on in earnest. She walked over to it, hesitated, clasped it. *What were you expecting, for it to pop open and Jim to come out?*

She lifted it. It felt so light, almost empty. How could Jim's huge, solid body be reduced to this? She shook it, heard the ash and a few larger fragments rattling around inside. That couldn't be all of him, no way. *Maybe they lost most of him. Maybe they just gave you a ceremonial amount.*

But the certainty stayed with her. This wasn't Jim. This couldn't be Jim.

Jim was alive.

Maybe she was going crazy, but she didn't care. It wouldn't hurt to check. The tragedy couldn't be compounded. She had nothing to lose.

She snatched up a scissor from the kitchen, headed to the hall closet.

The navy had used the mutual assistance fund to rent this extended-stay suite. When they'd first moved her here, she'd been in a daze, unable to do anything for herself. Steve had seen to the salvage of her effects, making sure to retrieve her paintings and art supplies, all of which were bundled into the bedroom closet. After that, he'd rifled through what else he thought she'd need, some cookware, the china they'd gotten for their wedding.

The laundry bag, packed full.

She threw open the closet door, found the thin, black bag and yanked it open, digging frantically. At last she found what she sought, pulling out the bedsheet.

You didn't get to live a SEAL's life without picking up some nervous habits. Jim was a clean freak. He never went anywhere without a small pack of wet wipes. When they'd taken Patrick to DC, he'd used a paper towel to grasp the poles in the metro. He'd have done the same to touch door-knobs if Sarah hadn't challenged him to face his pathos.

But he hated it.

So she indulged him a bit. And every time they made love, when she rose to use the bathroom, he stripped and changed the sheets, damp with their sweat, her juices, his seed.

She stared at the black sheet, the white smudge plain as day. She knelt, cut out a generous perimeter around it, stuffed it in her pocket.

Crazy. Fine. Jim was crazy with his paper towels. It didn't hurt anyone, didn't stop him from being a god of war. She could be crazy, too, could allow herself this one small thing.

She thought of Steve's body pressed against her, his sighs in her ear. *I will make this right, Jim. I will find out what happened to you.*

Patrick was still groggy as she dressed him, fell promptly back asleep on her shoulder as she went to the counter, snatched up the can of ashes, cradling it in her armpit like an expensive porcelain vase, and headed for the door.

CHAPTER XIII
ONE GOOD THING

Whatever powers Ninip granted Schweitzer, keeping track of time wasn't one. They stood naked in the center of the refrigerated cell. The armorer had come and collected his cast-off armor earlier, left shaking his head at the damage to something he apparently prized.

Schweitzer realized with an internal smirk that he should have asked for a watch.

He didn't need to sleep. Didn't need to eat.

There was nothing to do.

So, he asked Ninip, *what'd you like to do on weekends?*

The jinn didn't see the humor, but Schweitzer felt his shifting emotions, sullen anger, sadness, predatory hyper-vigilance.

Asking about Ninip's son had apparently hit the jinn where it hurt. Schweitzer hadn't meant to. He had his own dead to remember. Sarah, Patrick.

Peter.

He realized with a start that he hadn't thought of his brother since he'd died. He'd . . . he'd forgotten him. Schweitzer felt his spiritual stomach clench in amazement. He'd carried Peter's memory with him on every op he'd run since he'd first gotten the word.

He'd pictured Peter alongside him, a ghosted outline of how he'd looked in the last photo the networks had shown of him, tall and broad-shouldered, chin dimpled like a cartoon superhero. Pete had worn his hair long, his beard a bird's nest the military allowed only to special operators. Schweitzer had been afforded the same luxury once he pinned on, but he'd kept to uniform regulations, in part to sketch some boundary between himself and his brother. After Pete died, Schweitzer had stopped shaving.

Images began to flash in his mind. Master Chief Green shouting at him as he low crawled in the Coronado sands, telling him he wasn't as good as his brother, that he shamed that legacy. Peter punching the qualification pin into his chest, the short stab of metal and the feel of hot blood trickling behind his blouse, then sweeping him into his arms. The crush of his strength, beard scratching at his cheek, the smell of sea salt and the Skoal he perennially chewed. Navy smells.

Pete pushing him back to arm's length. *Proud of you, bro.*

The news reeling below Pete's picture while Schweitzer sat horrified beside his mother in their living room. FOUR SEALS CAUGHT IN FIREFIGHT. SURROUNDED BY INSURGENTS.

Some stuttering lieutenant at their door, delivering the news that Pete was out of contact, that they didn't know what happened to him. A clueless chaplain trying to force his atheist mother to pray as she sat down hard, the news already finishing the job the cancer had started.

Biggs repeatedly denying Schweitzer's request to go in. *You're a SEAL, damn it. You don't jump in the shit without a plan. We'd need months to figure out this target, and you're too damn close to this anyway. Let the QRF handle it. That's what they do.*

But the CH-47 carrying the Quick Reaction Force had been hit by high winds rising suddenly out of the steep

Afghani ravines. By the time the mess was sorted out, there were seventeen dead in all.

He'd been worried about that uncle-shaped hole in Patrick's childhood. But that was past now, wasn't it?

He wondered what Pete would say if he could see him now, the gray-skinned Schweitzer. The Schweitzer whose face stretched across a steel plate, eyes burning silver, zippered scars running up him like the stitching on a baseball.

He tried to imagine Pete's ghost as he had a hundred times before, tried to sketch the thatch of his sandy beard, the ridge of his nose, jagging sideways since it had been broken in high school.

Nothing. If Schweitzer was a ghost himself, then he was shunned by his own kind.

Pete was gone now, swirling in the screaming morass of bodies out in the void. Like Patrick, like Sarah.

Ninip stirred, and Schweitzer realized that the jinn had been observing his thoughts, collecting them. The violation made him tremble. *You get a nice look?*

A warrior clan, the jinn said. *I was the same.*

Schweitzer marshaled an angry response, then stopped as he realized the presence wasn't mocking him. He felt none of the contempt that had become a thematic undercurrent since he'd first awoken to the shared confines of his own corpse. It was an odd ripple emanating out from Ninip. It felt strangely like sympathy.

You are new to death, Ninip said, *and so it is understandable that you cling to life. Eons in the void taught me that life is a fleeting thing. There are regrets, yes. Loops to close, as you have said. But in the end, there is only what you are at your roots. That is the only thing that does not change. A man can be anything: a farmer, a potter, a scribe. They are all equal in your American eyes. So, why not a warrior? It is the root of who you are. In this we are the same. Your brother, you and I. This is why we are joined, why you remember him so keenly. It is a piece of yourself. Do not grieve. Let the branches do as the root commands. You are a warrior.*

Fight.

Ninip was silent after that, leaving Schweitzer to think, the low buzz of the refrigeration units droning in his ears. He was so deep in thought over Ninip's words that Jawid had to speak twice before Schweitzer noticed that the Sorcerer had opened a link to them.

Tomorrow we will do some demonstrations on the range.

Nope, Schweitzer said.

He felt Jawid's surprise, hesitation. He latched onto the emotions, tried to reach back up the link that connected him, felt the brush of . . . something before Jawid jerked away.

What do you mean? the Sorcerer asked.

I'm out of my fucking mind here, Schweitzer answered. *I want some books.*

Jawid's shock was palpable, reverberating down to him. Ninip sniffed at it, but it wasn't fear, so the jinn sat back and listened. He knew better than to turn away knowledge now.

Books? Jawid asked. *Why do you want books?*

To read, Schweitzer answered, *or maybe I'll build a fucking fort out of them.* He remembered Jawid's origins, the man wasn't literate.

Schweitzer softened his tone. *There's nothing to do in here.*

None of the others have complained.

Well, I'm not like the others.

I don't know where to get books for you.

Bullshit. This has to be a military facility. There's an MWR. A library. Figure it out.

I don't . . .

Look, there has to be some quid pro quo here. You want me to do a dog and pony show for you. Fine. I want books. I'm not doing jack without 'em.

What sort of books? Shock had melted into confusion.

Anything. Magazines. Comic books. Romance novels. Just something to read.

I have a Qu'ran. It's a King Fahd. Can you read Arabic?

I thought you couldn't either.

I can't, but I know the words by heart.

Even if he could, a goatherd that reads is still a goat-herd, Ninip said.

The truth was, Schweitzer could read a little Arabic, had learned the ligatures' rudimentary meanings in Pashto, Urdu, and Farsi as well. But it was only what he needed to read signs, sift through recovered documents, leaving the detail work to the pointy heads in intel. He'd read the Qu'ran in English a few times, but there was no way he was getting through it in Saudi Arabic.

Well, I can't read it either, Schweitzer said to Jawid.

More confusion, then the connection closed.

I would like to know more of your nuclear weapons, Ninip said. *Ask for a book on that.*

Schweitzer smiled. *Yeah, I bet you would.*

Sometime later, Eldredge appeared again outside the glass with an armload of books. "You really are a special case," he said, his Mark Twain moustache twitching up in a smile. "I never thought I'd see the day."

Schweitzer didn't bother to try to return the gesture. They hadn't rebuilt the ruin of his face for smiling.

"This is all I could come up with on short notice," Eldredge said, "but I'll bring more tomorrow. Any special requests?"

Schweitzer thought about this. What he wanted most was to feel connected to the world. "News-pper," he said.

"Easy day," Eldredge answered. "Anything else?"

Anything would be better than the interminable dark-ness, Ninip pacing like a caged animal beside him. "Bio. His-tree. Com-ik. Bat . . . man."

Eldredge smiled again. "Would . . . Ninip like anything in particular?"

Ninip tried to push Schweitzer aside, take control of their mouth, but Schweitzer pushed him away. The jinn let him. Words weren't his strength. He would have asked for a manual on nuclear technology. Schweitzer thought of the jinn's spouting about valor, his constant exhortation of the warrior ethos, his contempt for his daughters. He smiled, the expression not reaching his physical face as he did the air dance again to form the words, "*Little. Women.*"

In the end, Eldredge didn't bring the Alcott book, but he did manage to scrounge up a biography of Andrew Jackson and a couple volumes of Foote's history of the Civil War. These all rested on top of a large coffee-table volume, the red binding cracking with age. THE ART OF WARFARE IN BIBLICAL LANDS was written across the front in flaking gold. "You said Ninip was old," Eldredge said. "I thought he might be interested in this."

The books were pushed in one by one through a slot that sealed shut almost seamlessly as soon as it was no longer needed. The room was featureless, so Schweitzer sat them cross-legged on the floor and opened the books across their lap while Eldredge watched from the window. Schweitzer felt Ninip crowding forward to examine the books; he showed initial interest in the Foote, until Schweitzer shot him images of the old rifle mechanisms, the lumbering, breach-loading cannons. Ninip compared them to the carbine they used on ops and laughed.

Schweitzer then turned to the coffee-table book, leafing through hand-drawn sketches of wall carvings and statues showing warriors at their trade. He skimmed through the chapters, Hyksos, Sea Peoples, Old Kingdom Egypt, Akkadia, Babylon, Assyria. Men with horned helmets in reed boats, round shields and curving swords. Crude glyphs portraying naked men with braided beards and beaked noses, depicted in profile, spears across their shoulders.

He became lost in the familiar rhythm of reading, the words sliding past his vision, the messages forming in his mind. It made him feel human, alive. He was so engrossed in the act that it was awhile before he noticed the jinn was silent and still, looking out through their shared eyes, feeling their shared finger tracing across the surface of the pages.

That one, the jinn said. Reaching out and taking control

of their hand, thumbing back through the pages to a broad color photograph, age washing it in sepia tones, blotched with rust-colored foxing. It showed an archaeological-dig site stretched out over a broad, sandy plane, wide pits dug to show the broken remnants of walls, so badly weathered that it was hard to distinguish between what was turned earth and what was archaeological find.

But there were some prizes. Another photo showed two men posing beneath a stone relief depicting warriors in file holding body-sized shields and wearing crested helmets. Another showed a statue of a winged lion with the head of a crowned man, his beard braided and set with rings.

Ninip looked out over the ruin of the buildings, long gone to seed, mostly mixed with the earth they were being dug out of.

All gone, the jinn said.

Is that your home? Schweitzer asked.

I cannot tell, Ninip answered, his voice mournful.

I'm sorry, Schweitzer said. *You were . . . in the storm a long time. I thought you understood that.*

It is one thing to know it, Ninip said. *It is another thing to see it.*

Schweitzer pictured looking at their old apartment, torn to pieces by the attack. He imagined having to take in that sight, look out over Sarah's and Patrick's graves . . .

Sarah's and Patrick's graves.

He looked up to find that Eldredge had returned, observing him from behind the glass. The man stared back at him, eyes bright. "What does Ninip think?"

Schweitzer shrugged, tapped the book. "Sad."

Eldredge's expression changed. "Yes. I imagine he would be."

Schweitzer thought briefly of asking Eldredge to show him Sarah's and Patrick's graves, but wondered if he'd pushed it enough for one day. Letting the Gemini Cell's secret weapon out in public would be a stretch, and he didn't even know what had been done with his family's bodies. He made a mental note to ask.

When Schweitzer glanced up, Eldredge had gone, and opaque shutters had louvered down to cover the transparent pane.

Schweitzer sat on the floor and let Ninip read intently through the book, stumbling over the English, accessing Schweitzer's command of the language to forge on. He could feel flashes of recognition from the jinn at random images, a series of glyphs depicting women carrying jugs of water, a reconstruction of an ancient chariot. Ninip was so intent that Schweitzer finally ceased his own contemplation of the text and stepped back, observing as the jinn reconciled himself with this window on his past.

These are . . . stories. We had singers who did the same.

This is history. Some of it's guesswork, but most of it is true. People aren't making up tales here. The goal is to give the truth, based on evidence.

So it is real. That is what . . . archaeology is. It is your evidence.

I'm not an expert, but that's the general idea.

Nothing is left. Everything we built. It is dust.

Everything everyone builds is dust, sooner or later. Don't take it personally.

Who is there now?

Where?

Ninip moved their shared hand, leafing the pages back to the first photograph of the dig site. *Here.*

Schweitzer looked at the caption below the photo. *That's Iran. Enemies. A mad priest rules there.*

Ninip nodded. *Does this mad priest honor us? Are we remembered?*

I don't know. I don't think so.

I would go and see.

We keep running ops for the US, you'll likely get your chance. But this is my body, so I get first crack. We close the loop on whoever did this to my family, then next stop is Tehran.

Ninip was silent then, and Schweitzer, tired of reading, explored his new senses. He marveled at the control he had

over them, able to feel the surface of the floor beneath
them with a clarity he'd never known. He could feel subtle
gradations in temperature through the tile, in the air
around them, colder nearer the vents that pushed the chill
air into the room. He could shift spectrums by squinting
their eyes, see the cold as dark blue cones descending from
the vents, even catch a human-shaped outline of heat
through the thick surface of the door.

You did all this . . . in the storm?

Ninip shrugged. *I did nothing in the storm. All of this
is . . . new. It is what we are together.*

Schweitzer closed their eyes, pushed all his attention out
into their ears, focused on listening. At first, the thrumming
of the chillers drowned out all sound, but after a moment, he
found he could adjust their hearing as he adjusted their
vision, focusing it deeper on other sounds. The chillers
faded into a thematic buzz as Schweitzer dialed in on the
low hum of the electrical wiring in the walls, which eventually receded into the distance, giving way to the gurgling of
liquid moving through pipes.

Then, voices. The guard outside was talking to someone. Schweitzer focused on the speech.

Soft, whispers, but graduating to murmurs a moment
later. He found his ability worked too well, locking in on
the specificity of tone, letting the words hum by. As Schweitzer tried to adjust, the speaking stopped, replaced by
what sounded like slurping. Were they eating?

A sucking, popping sound. Not eating. Kissing.

Schweitzer's amusement roused Ninip to at least pay
attention. Here he was, a living corpse in one of the most
secret programs in the American military, and his guards
were making out on shift. People were people, anywhere
you went. He'd never forget the day Chang got caught fool-
ing around with one of the corpsmen assigned to the sub
they were to deploy on. The skipper knew SEALs played
by different rules, but it was one of his own, and he was
ready to go to general quarters over it.

Chang had sat on the edge of his rack while Ahmad had

grilled him, reminded him of the consequences of that kind of breach of discipline. At the end of the tirade, Chang had shrugged. "What do you want, Chief?" he'd said. "We're about to spend God knows how long dragging ass through the Horn of Africa while a bunch of . . . misguided but well-intentioned religious devotees try to kill us. Might be the last chance to get my dick wet ever. You're just mad because I got the shot and you didn't."

Schweitzer had laughed his ass off. Chang had even managed to crack a smile out of Ahmad's normally iron visage. She'd gone to talk to the skipper, and that was the last they heard of the matter. The corpsman stayed on the pier. As far as Schweitzer knew, Chang never talked to her again.

Put monkeys with needs in charge of a secret and highly dangerous government program, and they still acted like monkeys with needs.

Ninip was paying attention now, his own reaction shifting between amusement and rising arousal. Whatever else might bore him about humanity, base lust was a thing he understood. Schweitzer felt the jinn's filter begin to slide over their vision, pushed it back. He knew how Ninip saw the world when he was hungry for blood. He didn't want to think about how it looked when he was turned on.

But even if he had more control, Schweitzer still had a monkey's soul. He justified the eavesdropping by practicing fine-tuning of their hearing, sliding along the spectrum of high and low sounds, through the popping of lips coming together and parting to the low rustle of hands sliding over clothing, of breathing going ragged, of the sharp clacking as weapons slapped against the wall.

Man, they were really going at it. He'd lost track of time, but this had to mean it was in the wee hours, and there was no one else around. Schweitzer had seen it before, guards turned on by the prospect of making out at work. It would be an intense burst, followed by pushing away, shaking of heads, then walking along like everything was normal. Hell, he'd practically done it with Sarah in a Victoria's Secret dressing room once with the sales attendant just outside the door.

Ninip was pressed into their shared body now, asserting himself in the tension of their limbs. Schweitzer could feel the claws beginning to extend slightly, their tongue swelling again. There was a line between lust for blood and lust for sex, but it was a thin one even for the living, and it seemed to have all but vanished for the jinn.

Before Schweitzer knew it, they were standing, the book sliding off their lap and landing with a muffled thud on the floor. He could feel the jinn's agitated presence all around him, as nasty and inappropriately intimate as when his fellow nonrates watched porn together in their liberty hours at the end of boot camp.

The ragged breathing broke with the smack of wet skin parting, and Schweitzer heard the flat rustling sounds that heralded the pushing away he'd known would come. Now, soft words of devotion, or maybe promises of what would come later, and one of them would walk off. Schweitzer tuned their hearing lower, guessing at the softness with which they would be uttered, tried to poise himself to catch them.

But what came was at a much higher register, a woman's voice raised in anger. Schweitzer ran their hearing up to the higher frequency, then dampened it as the voice grew louder, was answered by a man's. He caught only a single word, "smothering." This tryst wasn't a moment of shared passion, it was a moment of weakness, regretted and now going sour.

He sniffed the air, caught the sick, bitter scent of fear. The voices came more quickly now, the man's low tones. Cursing. A slap ringing out, loud as a gunshot to Schweitzer's augmented hearing.

Before he knew what he was doing, Schweitzer had moved them to the shutters, begun clawing at the seams between them.

Ninip frowned, annoyed at having his voyeuristic thrill interrupted. He pulled their shared hands back. *What are you doing? This is their affair. Let them have at it.*

There's nobody to break it up. Someone is going to get hurt.

Ninip only looked at him, and Schweitzer saw the situation as he knew the jinn saw it, a couple of peasant foot soldiers, squabbling over something beneath his notice. The event was only notable in its capacity to amuse.

But the shouting and scuffling was growing louder. He'd seen lover's tiffs spin out of control, ruin careers, lives. There was a dull thump which he knew was a human head rebounding off the wall. This was going ugly, fast.

Schweitzer tried to wrench their limbs back to their work on the shutters. He wouldn't be able to get there fast enough if he had to fight Ninip the whole way.

Fortunately, the jinn was nothing if not predictable.

Schweitzer dug in his mind for the worst images he could imagine, a male soldier murdering a female, knocking her head into the hard floor until her brains leaked out her ears. Screaming, blood, eyes wide in horror.

Ninip surged. The jinn abruptly reversed course, pouring his energy into their shared body, Schweitzer's purpose suddenly going from half to double.

He drove them at the shutters, getting the bone spikes of their claws into the seams, yanking down with all the big muscles in their arms, feeling the metal joint in their shoulder engaging, the stitches pulling taut. The doctors had done their work well, the limb held as they strained. The metal was strong, stronger than anything Schweitzer had encountered before. They pulled, felt their muscles engage, lock, straining the tendons and bones beneath. At last, he felt something break in the mechanism as their magical strength overcame the strength of the metal, bending it aside with a shriek.

An alarm sounded, a low trumpeting behind a machine-woman's voice, calmly issuing instructions. Through the transparent panel revealed by the parted metal, Schweitzer could see lights flashing from metal cages set into the ceiling, spinning their orange warnings across the white paint of the walls.

Schweitzer stopped to consider the transparent pane, definitely not glass, palladium most likely. He wondered if they could break through the thickness, but Ninip had no time for such cares. The jinn threw their shared body into it, magically enhanced bones reverberating at the impact, sending them shuddering back. The jinn charged forward again, driving with the horns this time, and Schweitzer felt the impact almost snap their neck.

Calm the fuck down! We're not going to . . .

But as the jinn pulled their shared body back for another charge, Schweitzer could see the faintest white spiderweb of cracks in the transparent material. He let Ninip have his head. It would be a fight to control the jinn once they got through, but it was better than letting whatever was going on outside escalate into something worse.

Even as he battered them against the palladium pane, felt it begin to give under the repeated blows, a part of Schweitzer echoed Ninip's doubt. These people were his resurrectors, but also his jailers. Any obligations he'd had were absolved when the bullet had gone up through his chin and sheared off the back of his head.

But that wasn't right. Ninip had talked about roots and branches. He'd said that combat was the root of the warrior. But Schweitzer's instinct reminded him that it was something more. Any thug could be a warrior. Schweitzer's wars were sanctified. His roots ran deep in soil called paladin, guardian. The roots told Schweitzer's branches to preserve, to defend.

So he did.

A final blow and the pane gave, the fragments holding together as they punched through, leaving a shattered cone of an ovipositor that birthed them onto the hard floor of the corridor outside their cell. The chill fog followed them out, dissolving in the warmth of the free air.

Schweitzer had been partially right. His guard had been

a female. Her uniform was rumpled, her carbine sling twisted around her back, hung up in her magazine punches, the weapon wedged uselessly between her legs. Blood trickled from the corner of her mouth, a bruise already forming over one eye. She looked dazed.

The man was a civilian. His khaki pants were unbuttoned, his white shirt rumpled beneath a skewed tie. An ID badge, much like Eldredge's, was clipped over his pocket.

His eyes were already going wide with terror, face drained of color. The guard was fumbling with her weapon, desperately trying to haul it into use, succeeding only in getting the stock stuck under the lip of her body armor. Ninip's filter snapped into place, and Schweitzer saw them as they appeared to the jinn, tiny, weak, ripe for the hunt.

He reversed course, dug in with everything he had, hauled back against the jinn. Ninip howled and fought back, beating Schweitzer senseless against the walls of the darkness they shared. His vision went red, then black, then white, his hearing filled with an inhuman scream that he belatedly realized was issuing from their own mouth.

But Schweitzer hung on. Ninip raged, pushed like a tidal wave, but only succeeded in holding their shared body crouching on all fours, tongue reaching, darting in and out of the distended jaw, gnashing dagger teeth.

And then the jinn turned inward, slamming Schweitzer up against the perimeter of the space they shared, forcing him through it. He felt the void gaping behind once again, heard the boiling chorus of screams. He turned his attention from controlling their shared body and refocused on remaining inside it.

But the jinn was strong enough to multitask. He occupied Schweitzer with half his attention. With the other half, Ninip took control of their limbs, rose, turned toward the guard and her assailant.

Schweitzer managed a brief foray at their shared mouth, uttering a single word. "Run."

But they weren't listening. Their eyes were cast over

Schweitzer and Ninip's shoulder. Ninip followed the direction of their gaze, saw Mr. Axe and Mr. Flamethrower barreling toward them. Axe hung back while Flamethrower took a knee, leveling the nozzle, blue pilot light blazing malevolently below. Schweitzer watched Mr. Flamethrower's finger drop down to the trigger and begin to tense.

Ninip howled again, too lost in the swell of predatory lust to understand what was about to happen. There was no way to reach them in time. Ninip was in the cattle chute of his own senseless rage, but Schweitzer knew the fuel gel moving through that nozzle would heat the air around them to twelve hundred degrees in an instant.

It couldn't kill them. As far as Schweitzer knew, nothing could.

But reducing their shared body to ash would do the trick. He thought of the void, the swirling storm of souls, and shuddered.

Ninip gathered himself to spring, and Schweitzer redoubled his efforts to hold him back. Mr. Flamethrower was just doing his job. If they were to be destroyed, it wouldn't be in the act of hurting innocent men following orders.

Ninip turned to fight him, and Schweitzer turned to the darkness. Maybe, somehow, he could find Sarah and Patrick again in that tangled hell.

A sharp voice. No heat. Tension slowly leaking out of the corridor.

Schweitzer looked up. Eldredge stood beside Mr. Flamethrower, one hand on the weapon's barrel, gently pushing it down. His eyes were fixed on Schweitzer, but he was speaking to the soldier in low, gentle tones.

The jinn battered him again and again, shoving him to the limits of their shared space. Schweitzer dug in his memories, thrusting images at Ninip, napalm reducing jungles to ash, fuel air bombs bursting over Afghan villages, metal turned to dust in seconds. Humans screaming, burning, dying. Over and over again. He sent the images, felt Ninip's attack lessen in response, until the jinn finally took his meaning, dialed back his madness, until the slow ebb of his passion left them on all fours again, shaking in the corridor while Eldredge and his men looked on.

When Schweitzer at last was able to focus on seeing the world outside their body again, he noted the wide peripheral vision he always slipped into when on an op was still in place, giving him a view of the guard and her attacker, gaping in shock, no doubt processing the thought that the flamethrower would have incinerated them just as easily as it would have the monster that crouched before them, that Mr. Flamethrower wouldn't have hesitated for a moment.

The silence stretched, all motionless in the long space, no sound save the soft clicking of the spinning lights as they continued their silent, orange-hued warning across the white walls. Eldredge took a cautious step closer. Schweitzer could smell his fear, different from the others around him, but fear nonetheless.

The guard and the man with her both began to speak at once, but Eldredge silenced them with a wave, squatted down on his haunches. Schweitzer could see the shimmering silver candle tips of his own eyes reflected back at him in the deep brown of Eldredge's. "What happened?"

Ninip stirred, looked at the flamethrower at the low ready, pilot light still burning, and thought better of it. Schweitzer tested his control over their shared body, found Ninip was letting him drive. He sat them back slowly, keeping their clawed hands well clear. He did his best effort at jerking a thumb over their shoulder, painfully aware of the bone spike making the motion menacing. "Fight."

Eldredge looked up now, taking in the woman's battered face, the scratches on the man's forearms. "I see."

Schweitzer stood their shared body up, careless now of how the others in the corridor shrank away from them. He'd done what he'd set out to do. Whatever ill end was evolving with those two, it wasn't going to happen on his watch.

Eldredge was saying something, the knot of soldiers breaking up and moving with the exaggerated purpose of those seeking to corral fear. The man and woman were talking over one another, pointing.

Schweitzer ignored them all. He took control of their shared arm and pushed the broken transparent cone back the other way, sending fragments tinkling to the floor and widening the hole enough for them to slip back through, landing lightly on their feet and returning to the pile of books. There was nothing else to do.

Schweitzer sat them back down on the floor, trying to wrap his head around what had just happened and why the aftermath felt so different.

Suddenly, a certainty tore through him. A gust of feeling. The smell of rosewater filling his nostrils, cloying. Sarah. Sarah floating in a lotus position, eyes closed. *I'll get past this. But I don't want to.*

He shook his head internally, noticed that his physical one had followed suit. Impossible. Sarah was dead. He'd seen the bullet take her.

He turned to Ninip but noticed Eldredge looking through the hole in the glass, eyes crinkling with, what? Sympathy?

"You did a good thing, Jim," Eldredge said.

Ninip paced, and Schweitzer tried to process the words.

He'd died, come back, shared his body like a close apartment with a thing out of hell.

And in the midst of it, done good.

CHAPTER XIV
HINT OF A LIE

It took Steve longer to call than she'd expected. The days stretched on, growing long and hollow, the space filled with a string of excuses not to return her mother's and sister's increasingly frantic calls. She endlessly turned the thought of pregnancy over in her mind before dismissing it. By her normal calendar, her period should have just finished, and it should have been fine. But the stress and injury had thrown her cycle into chaos, and there had only been spotting at odd times. *You should take a pregnancy test.* No. She couldn't deal with that, couldn't handle the answer either way. Not yet.

So she played with Patrick, searching for glimmers of progress, snatching at a word or an expression. The therapist assured her that, while it would take time, he would make way, that children were remarkably resilient. But all she could do was think of Peg's recounting of how she had slowly realized that her own son was autistic. It was the one time Peg had broken down in front of her, not so much crying as having too much liquid for her eyes to contain, running down a face whose expression showed no hint of grief.

No, Walter was fine. For the longest time he was fine.

Then . . . it was like something broke inside him. He started going backward. He wouldn't make eye contact, he stopped trying to talk to me. He . . . he regressed.

What if that happens to Patrick? Sarah's mind whispered, what Jim had called her inner reptile, the piece of her whose sole job was to jump at shadows, to plan for the worst, to overreact, to do anything it had to in order to keep her safe. They'd trained Jim's reptile mind until he lived in the space he needed to occupy in order to do his job. Sarah had worked not to follow him there. One family member in constant condition yellow was enough.

Not that it had done him, had done any of them, any good. When the threat condition yellow prepared them for had finally come knocking, readiness wasn't enough.

So she knelt in front of Patrick, lowered her head until her ear almost touched the floor. She trembled with worry until he finally met her gaze, and she saw recognition in his eyes. Then, relief would flood her with such force that she would lie on her side, panting, struggling and failing to hold back the tears, to be strong for her son.

Sometimes Patrick stared. Sometimes he ignored her. What he never did was come to her, crawl into her arms, ask why Mommy was sad.

It was in those small moments that she regretted turning Steve away. It would have been wrong to keep him, but in those troughs she thought that maybe any lie was better than the empty gulf that stretched across her days. Unwilling to leave Patrick, she'd stopped going to the gym, whiled away the hours in front of her laptop, scanning e-mails she couldn't bring herself to answer, watching her social media scroll by, a flowing current of a world that kept on turning as if nothing had happened, as if her life hadn't been suddenly snatched away from her, crumbled into a lumpen ball, and handed back with a note attached that read, FIGURE THIS OUT. GOOD LUCK!

Only one man had managed to pierce that fog, both for her and Patrick, and she'd kicked him out for his trouble. For at least the tenth time, her hand went to her cell phone, touched it, left it. No. She couldn't give him what he wanted. Not until she'd closed the door on Jim.

What the hell is wrong with you? she yelled at herself. *Jim is dead. It's time to accept that. Steve is alive. Patrick is alive.*

You are alive.

Her hand went back to her phone, drew it out.

She was so startled when the phone lit up that she tossed it in the air, then fumbled it a few times before finally settling it back in her hands, buzzing like an angry insect, the screen filled with an image of Jim and Steve, in uniform, arms draped across each other's shoulders. It was the profile pic she used for Steve.

She tried not to take it as a sign.

She brought the phone to her ear, the warmth of her cheek picking up the line. "Steve."

His voice was level, determined. "Don't hang up. I need you to listen to me."

"I'm not hanging up."

That, he wasn't prepared for. "Right . . . well."

"I've missed you," she said. She knew right away that it was the wrong thing to say even if it was true. "I don't want to . . ." She couldn't find the words. Be alone?

"Let me see you. I need you to see my face when I say what I have to say."

She closed her eyes. She dreaded that meeting as much as she hungered for it.

"Can you keep your hands to yourself?"

"I'll try not to be offended by that question," he said.

"Can you?"

"You know damn well I can."

"Okay, fine."

"I'll be there in thirty minutes," he said, and hung up before she had a chance to change her mind.

Patrick stared, expression unreadable.

"Uncle Stevie's coming over," she said. "Would you like to see Uncle Stevie?"

Patrick went back to his trucks without answering, his muttering a little louder now, a running interview in a language only he could understand.

She snatched up her laptop, leaned against the back of the couch, and tried to wait. Her mind seized in time with her stomach, and she realized it would do no good. She had to do something to fill the space while Steve drove I-64 at his usual breakneck pace.

She'd finally settled on another round of cleaning the already immaculate suite when she heard the soft chime indicating that she had e-mail.

Grateful for the activity, she propped the lip of the computer against her belly and flipped it open.

And froze.

The e-mail was the only unread one in her in-box, the bolded letters striping across the screen, boldly proclaiming the sender and subject.

The SENDER column read: PORTSMOUTH RAPID STD/ HIV/DNA TESTING. The subject was: ACCT. P00001224617 RESULTS.

She glanced at the can where it sat on the counter. They'd duct-taped it closed after taking their sample, put it in a plastic grocery bag. She'd forgotten all about it. *Be honest. You blocked it out. You know what that e-mail says, and what it means.*

It meant closure. It meant saying good-bye.

She was conscious of the pressure of her teeth digging painfully into her lip, forced herself to relax.

You couldn't have better timing, Steve. It wouldn't do her any good to face Steve just after reading confirmation of her husband's death. *Why? You know he's dead. What difference does an e-mail make? Having closure will help you move forward with a clear head.*

She thought of her dreams, the trail of rose petals, the unshakable certainty that he was alive.

Time to wake up. She swallowed and double-clicked the e-mail.

She read it three times, became slowly conscious that her mouth was hanging open, that a thin stream of drool was beginning to slide down her lip to drip onto her T-shirt.

She read it again. "The fuck?" Patrick looked up, his eyes widening.

"Ohmygod." She dropped the laptop onto the couch cushions.

The phone was already up, Steve forgotten, pressed against her ear.

"Comeoncomeoncomeon," she said as the thin stream of tones indicated it ringing.

At long last, "Portsmouth Testing."

"Hi, this is Sarah Schweitzer. You just e-mailed me test results on a couple of samples I brought in last week?"

The next few minutes seemed like hours as she waited to speak to the clinician assigned to her case.

Then another eternity of ringing, her stomach in knots that it might lead to an answering machine. If it came to that, she'd get in her car and drive there. She'd explain to Steve later. He'd have to understand.

When the other end of the phone picked up, she nearly sobbed with relief for the second time that day. "Yes, yes. Hi. This is Sarah Schweitzer."

The voice on the other end had a Virginia accent so thick she could barely understand it. "Yes, ma'am."

"I just got my results over e-mail, and . . ."

"Yes, ma'am." The voice was mildly amused. "I'm guessing you're going to want us to testify in court? Looks like your crematorium has some explaining to do."

"Are you sure there wasn't some mistake? I can't believe . . ."

"There's no mistake, ma'am. That's pig ashes you've got there. Not even close to a match for the semen sample you provided."

"I can't . . . the navy gave me these. How is it possible . . ."

"We get questions like this all the time, ma'am. We don't even try to answer them. For liability reasons, you understand. We can assert our findings, and that's as far as it goes. Now, if you want to use this as evidence in a civil proceeding, we have . . ."

"How can you be sure? Aren't pig and human DNA similar?"

The man responded with the vaguely irritated resignation of one who'd answered this question ad nauseum. "Yes, ma'am. Quite similar, but you have to remember we do this a lot."

"A lot? You test pigs a lot?"

"All the time. Livestock's about three-quarters of our business, I'd say. We get a lot more animal-heritage business than paternity cases. This isn't DC, ma'am. Lot of farming folk out this way. They live and die on their breeding lines, and I'm sorry to say that sometimes folks aren't as honest as they should be in setting their stud fees."

She didn't realize she'd gone silent until he spoke again. "Ma'am? Is everything okay?"

"Yes, yes. Fine. You are absolutely a thousand percent sure that was pig ashes."

"Yes, ma'am. We got lucky in that there were a few fairly good-sized bone fragments in that canister. It's rare to cremate someone all the way, but this was a rush job."

She hung up without saying good-bye, her mind and stomach doing loops in time. She looked back at the can on the counter, duct tape sealing in a lie. *Maybe there was some mistake.* What mistake? Do they typically keep pigs on navy bases? Cremate them? It didn't make sense.

She turned back to Patrick, who was standing now, coming to her.

And suddenly the sensation returned with such force that she staggered.

She'd seen no body, there'd been no funeral, no article in the papers. The navy had shrouded the whole thing in secrecy, and now there was a can full of pig ashes on the kitchen counter of her rented, extended-stay suite.

Jim was alive.

She swept Patrick into her arms, pressed his head against her thigh.

The doorbell rang.

Steve's timing had gone from fantastic to horrible in an instant. Or, had it? She had questions, and he was the logical place to start.

Patrick toddled to the door, hands raised and grasping. Normally, she'd at least go through the motions of lifting him, allowing him to pretend to open it. Now, she practically knocked him over in her rush to open the door. She swept Patrick up under one arm, beginning to squall as Steve came in.

He broke into a broad grin at the sight of the boy, and Patrick calmed as she passed him to Steve, who tossed him in the air as he made his way to the couch. "Hey, little man!"

She turned, closing the door behind her, leaned against it. Steve sat, settling Patrick on his knee before turning to her. His smile fled.

"Sarah, we're just talking. There's no need for drama."

She shook her head. "Never mind that."

"What? Let me put Patrick in his room for a minute. He can play with . . ."

"No, Steve . . ."

His face darkened. "Look, you can't just keep on . . ."

"Steve, will you shut the fuck up and listen for five seconds?"

He closed his mouth, set Patrick down. The boy wrapped his arms around his calf and pressed his head against his knee. "Nice language around the P-Train."

"That can of ashes. Where'd you get it?"

"What do you mean where did I get it?"

"Just answer the question. I'm in no mood right now."

"I told you. I got it on post. They gave it to me after I made a fuss."

"No. I mean, specifically. Who gave it to you?"

He looked at her as if she'd sprouted a second head. "Chief."

"And you trust her?"

"What kind of a fuc . . ." He looked down at Patrick, lowered his voice. "What kind of a question is that?"

"It's the question I'm asking you, damn it. It's the question I need you to give me a straight answer to."

"Yes. That woman has saved my ass on at least three different occasions. I've run ops with her since I pinned on. I would trust her with my life. I have trusted her with my life."

"She's never lied to you? She's never given you any reason to . . ."

"She's a SEAL, Sarah. She's cleared Top Secret. They polygraph her every five years. If a person can be proved honest, it's her."

"Did you see them pack the ashes?"

"What? No! No, I didn't see . . . Look, what the hell is this all about?"

She gestured to the laptop. "First e-mail."

He disentangled himself from Patrick, put the computer on his lap, and opened it. She watched his expression, the sullen anger and surprise, the slow fade first to concentration as he read and finally to disbelief as the meaning came clear.

"You . . . You had it DNA tested? What the fuck? Sarah, what the fuck is wrong with you?" All concern for Patrick's tender ears was gone.

"I might ask you the same question, Steve. I thought I was crazy myself when I had it run, but I gave myself permission to be crazy for once. Seemed like the right time for it. Now I'm glad I did."

"There has to be a mistake. The lab messed up."

"I just got off the phone with them. They seem pretty damn sure."

"Have them run it again."

She shook her head. "Do they keep pigs on Little Creek?"

He remembered Patrick, pulled the boy in, covering his ears with his hands. "What?"

"Just answer the question."

"No! Wait. Yes."

"Yes."

"Yes. For TCCC."

She was familiar with the acronym soup for Jim's day-to-day, but this one hovered at the edge of her mind, just out of reach. She cocked her head.

"Tactical Combat Casualty Care. We cut their femoral arteries to practice stopping arterial bleeding."

She wrinkled her nose.

"They're sedated," he said. "At least, when we're not trying to simulate a noncompliant case."

"What happens when you're done with them?"

"I have no idea. Maybe they serve them in the DFAC."

"So, it's possible they cremate them? That there was a mix-up?"

He was silent for a long time. "If it's a mix-up, it's one hell of one. I mean, I've seen some dumb shit go down, but this takes the cake."

"We have to go back there," she said. "We have to talk to Chief Ahmad and find out what the hell happened."

He was already patting the air with his palms, standing. "There is no *we* here, Sarah. I understand you're grieving, but you are not just walking onto our compound shaking your fist and demanding answers. Leave it to me, I'll get it figured out."

"I need to be sure, Steve. I'm going."

"Sarah, I understand this has you pissed. I'm mad as hell, too. But it's just ashes. It's not some conspiracy."

She bridled, embarrassed. Enough of her suspicions had leaked into her tone. "I didn't say anything about a conspiracy."

"No, you didn't. You just radiated it. Sarah, you said yourself you've been having dreams that make you feel like he's alive. But he's not alive. A screwup with his remains doesn't change the fact that he's not coming back. We both need to accept that."

"I do accept that," she said, fighting to keep the lie from her voice. "I just . . . I need this handled. You can get me into Little Creek."

"No way. You're going to have to trust me on this. It was

hard enough just to get that can in the first place. If I bring you back there in your current . . ." He stopped himself, blushing.

"In my current what? My fucking current condition? My hysterical, driven-mad-by-grief condition?"

Patrick started crying at that, and Steve lifted him to his chest, rocking him gently. He met Sarah's eyes over her son's shoulder. "I'm not taking you, Sarah. Not because I'm ashamed of you, or because I doubt you, but because it won't help. You want to find out what happened? Then you need to let me take care of this."

She went to him, gathered Patrick into her arms, felt Steve's hesitation in releasing her son. Patrick held on, cried worse when they were finally separated, drummed his tiny hands on her neck. Her heart broke at the sound, but she held him close. She felt the mother lion behind her eyes, staring Steve down. *You're not taking my boy.*

The silence between them stretched. "So," he finally said. "I'll go find out what's up. Then, after, we can talk."

"Fine," she said, her voice sounding foreign in her own ears, hard. "Thank you," she added. "I appreciate this."

He nodded, headed silently for the door.

"How long do you think it'll take?" she asked before he could leave.

He turned to her, exasperated, his hands already sweeping up into the broad motion that would say, *How the hell should I know? Calm down.*

"Please, Steve," she said, her voice husky now. "I need this to be over."

His eyes softened at that, and he nodded. "I'll head there now, and I'll text you as soon as I have something. Just . . . just hang on."

And then he was gone, leaving Sarah to rock her son into tearful sleep, and to hang on, as ordered.

CHAPTER XV
OCONUS

Schweitzer offered no resistance as they moved him from the damaged cold-storage unit to a reinforced cell farther down the hall. This one had no transparent panel, no slot in the door. A narrow cage occupied the center of the room, well away from the walls. The cage's bars were thick, stretching from the ceiling to the floor, where Schweitzer knew they were probably anchored several feet deep. He wasn't sure if he could bend them with his newfound strength, but he doubted it.

Burn and freeze nozzles covered the walls, newly painted, layers of deck gray that were unable to fool Schweitzer's enhanced vision. He could see the deep furrows in the reinforced concrete behind them, smell the faint, acrid odor that wafted from the scorch marks. The room's burn function had been used, and recently.

I think they're done fucking around, he said to Ninip.

No cage can hold us, Ninip answered, but the jinn's voice lacked its usual razor edge, seemed muted somehow. Quieter.

Schweitzer paused, tried to goad the jinn into speaking again. *I don't know, those bars look pretty thick.*

Ninip didn't answer.

You think you can bend them? Schweitzer tried again.

Perhaps, Ninip said.

Definitely quieter, and there was something . . . smaller about Ninip's voice, a hair less arrogant. There was the hint of a reverberation, as if the jinn were speaking from the bottom of a very wide well.

Schweitzer tentatively reached out into the darkness they shared. The presence still dominated it, but there was a bit more space for him to slide into. The sense of being pressed into the edge of their shared body had abated a fraction. Was the jinn some kind of vampire? Did he need slaughter to sustain himself? Had the revelation of the death of his civilization sapped his will? Schweitzer reached into the presence, fumbling for a grasp on the jinn's thoughts and memories.

Ninip came alive at that, snarling and slapping him away. Down but not out, then.

I was a millennium in the storm when your ancestors were a hope of generations distant. Do not presume to match your strength to mine. Your precious professionalism will not help you here.

Schweitzer raised phantom hands in a placating gesture. *Okay, okay.*

Ninip gave a final growl and settled back. It was a little while before Schweitzer realized with a start that the jinn hadn't tried to push him out again. For all Ninip's bluster, Schweitzer still had his extra share of the darkness.

He batted away a thousand questions. The only one who could likely answer them was the jinn. He could ask Jawid, or Eldredge, but he remembered his old adage from the counterintelligence portion of his indoctrination. *Need to know,* his instructor had said. *I don't care if it's the guy standing right next to you. The essence of compartmentalization is only revealing that which must be revealed. That*

*way, if your buddy's compromised, the mission isn't. Treat
everyone like mushrooms, keep 'em in the dark and feed
'em shit, until the mission absolutely requires otherwise.*

No need to tip his hand until he had a better grip on
what this meant.

The books were gone, and he didn't want to risk tangling
with Ninip again, so he spent his time reaching out into the
void, stretching for some hint of the tremor he'd felt before,
the intense feeling that Sarah was searching for him.

Ninip seemed content to let him, and the lack of resistance allowed him to push his consciousness easily outward into the freezing darkness that lay beyond the walls of
their shared body. The screaming assaulted him instantly,
and he felt the slightest tug toward the maelstrom of souls,
a hint of an undertow that he hadn't noticed before.

Most firefights were an enabling scenario for Attention
Deficit Disorder, a flashing series of peripheral engage-
ments that prevented focus on anything. SEALs trained for
that, expanding their peripheral vision, their ability to flit
from task to task, their focus everywhere at once. Master
Chief Green, in one of his rare metaphysical moments, had
quoted from the Samurai sourcebook *Hagakure. Taking
an enemy on the battlefield is like a hawk taking a bird,*
Green had said. *Even though it enters into the midst of a
thousand of them, it gives no attention to any bird other
than the one it has first marked.*

There was a time and a place for laserlike focus. A supported prone shot over long distance didn't require multi-
tasking. The ability to drill down to a single space in the
universe, to will a round to go into it, no matter how small
or far away, was just another tool in their toolbox.

Schweitzer summoned this focus now, drilling down
through the distractions, the cold and the screaming and
the gentle tug into chaos, searching for the echo of his wife.

It was harder than when he was alive. Schweitzer was
used to the smells and sounds of combat, able to slip into the
space where the primate faded back, and the artist stepped

up to do his work. The void was different. The shrieking pastiche nagged at his senses, tempting him to focus, to try to single out individual voices from the throng. It diverted his attention from the undertow, reeling him slowly closer as he focused, until he snapped back to himself, pushing suddenly backward, alarmed at how close he'd come. He knew that, once sucked in, he'd never escape.

Slowly, the voices slipped farther and farther to the edge of his hearing, going from scream to murmur and finally to the low buzz that masked everything when he focused, gunfire, explosions, radio chatter.

And there, at the bottom, was his sniper's lens. It arced out into the tangle of souls, swept through in search of its single target, the signature of the love of his life, the scent of her homemade perfume. The maelstrom was chaos of an order of magnitude he'd never experienced, but this focus was Schweitzer's own bit of magic, his artistry of the gun. It could put a bullet into a square inch at almost two thousand yards.

It could find anything.

He was dimly aware of Ninip rousing, reaching out to observe Schweitzer's focus, but that quickly receded into the low hum of everything around him, until it became so thematic that it was a kind of quiet.

And in that silence, he found her.

The smell of rosewater, faint, but unmistakable, and something more, a tremor, a pulsing, weak and rapid, but most certainly there. No, two pulses, one smaller than the other, regular rhythms in counterpoint.

Heartbeats.

Schweitzer jolted back into himself, whirled to face the jinn. *They're alive. My family is alive.*

The jinn's focus on Schweitzer had been nearly as intent as Schweitzer's focus on the void. Ninip startled back, paused for a moment before shaking his head.

No, they are not.

They are! I felt them. Their hearts are beating. I picked it out of the storm.

Nothing can be picked out of the storm. I was there for . . .

For thousands of years. I know. You bring it up every chance you get. I'm telling you, I spotted it. They're alive. I heard their heartbeats.

Ninip sighed. *Millennia mean nothing to you, but you must trust me that it is time enough to observe one's own surroundings. There are no heartbeats in that place. It is for the dead.*

Bullshit.

I know . . . I know your family is your purpose, but you must believe me. My helmet bearer served me since I became a man. When we fought the barbarians from the swamps, he took one of their poisoned arrows through his knee. The wound soured.

So you killed him.

He was a warrior and my friend. Ninip sounded hurt. *The priests took his leg from the knee down. They made him a harness to go around the stump, holding a bit of wood there, so he could walk in a broken fashion, like a camel gone lame. He was no longer able to fight, to be sure, but I made him my master of granaries, and he served me faithfully until his death.*

Is there a point here?

He swore to his dying day that, though he could look plainly and see that the leg was gone, he felt it as it were not. He felt himself stretching his calf, moving his toes. Phantoms. Illusions conjured by a desire so deep it can bend our seeing the world for what it is. I felt the same when I first came into the storm. That I could hear the voices, or feel the warmth of my people, my concubines, my sons. Phantoms, I tell you.

Schweitzer's joy curdled so rapidly that he could feel himself deflate. *That can't be it,* he said, even as he realized it was.

I am sorry, Ninip said. *Even if they were alive, even if we could go to them, what would you do?*

Schweitzer ran the scenario through his mind. His corpse-gray skin, the silver flames of his eyes, the Frankenstein scars. The broken remnants of his face, scraped over a steel frame until he could neither smile nor kiss.

Sarah would never recognize him. Patrick would be terrified. For the first time, since his death, he looked down at their cock, limp and gray, trailing along the inside of one thigh. He remembered desire, caught echoes of it in Ninip's lust, but the root of it was lost to him.

Ninip laughed at that. *Is that what you want? A woman?*

Schweitzer's sudden anger burned so hot that even the jinn was taken aback.

I am sorry, Ninip said. *That is likewise beyond us. We are an engine of war, nothing less than that. There are no more wives, nor children. The touch of a woman is yet another phantom from the life you have been cut from. You do not truly desire it. It is only an echo that will fade as you begin to see it for what it is.*

He was right. Schweitzer couldn't make love. He couldn't come home at night and chat about a day at work. He didn't truly inhabit the world of living, just a twilit corner of it, a shadow of life, forever cut off from the interactions that made the true living world worth enduring.

That's what his love was. A phantom limb.

He lifted the dog tags, looking at the image of Sarah and Patrick. The lines seemed clearer now, the rust scraped away in the jostling of his breaking through the transparent panel to his cell. But it meant nothing. They were shadows. Memories. They were gone.

The realization struck Schweitzer so deeply that he didn't realize he'd sunk into a reverie until Jawid's voice snapped him out of it.

Step into the cage, please.

Why? Schweitzer asked. Ninip coiled beside him, ready to spring. Without reaching for them, Schweitzer could see the images flashing through the jinn's mind as he recalled staring down the nozzle of the flamethrower, pilot light flickering beneath.

For your own safety, Jawid said. *Dr. Eldredge wishes to speak with you.*

Schweitzer could hear a dull hissing as the gate's bars sank into the floor. The long, slow slide told Schweitzer he had been right in his guess of how deeply they were anchored. He met Ninip's spiritual gaze in the darkness. The jinn's eyes seemed serpentine in his mind, golden orbs, split by a black chevron of a pupil. They dipped as the jinn nodded. If the world of the living was where Schweitzer's heart lay, then Eldredge was his connection to it, and Jawid the man who'd given him a chance to remain in it a bit longer. That counted for something.

As soon as he stepped into the center of the dotted square left by the retracting poles, they shot upward until they slid into the depressions in the ceiling and slammed home with a dull clank.

Thank you, Jawid said.

The door hissed open, and Eldredge stepped into the room, hand wrapped around a small plastic cylinder capped with a shiny, red button. Schweitzer guessed depressing it would trigger the burn nozzles, freeing him and Ninip both to chase their respective phantom limbs in the chaos beyond.

"Jim," Eldredge said, "I'm sorry about this." He gestured at the bars.

Schweitzer raised their shoulders a fraction of an inch, dropped them.

"How is . . . your companion doing?"

Schweitzer did the miniscule shrug again. Inside their shared body, Ninip crouched beside him impatiently, waiting for Eldredge to get on with it.

"It was a good thing you did, Jim," Eldredge said. "That would have gone ugly if you hadn't popped in. Thanks for that."

Schweitzer gave him nothing. He could hear the *but* in Eldredge's voice, see it in the set of his mouth.

Sure enough, "But there are . . . people higher up in the chain of command here who are . . . concerned about what they're seeing as an outburst. They're worried about the safety of their personnel. They don't see you the way I do, Jim. Unfortunately, they're in charge."

Will he destroy us? Ninip hissed.

Relax, Schweitzer said. *If they wanted to destroy us, we'd be destroyed already. He's here for a reason.*

"Fortunately, we've got our first lead on a Body Farm supplier, and they happen to be OCONUS. This kills two birds with one stone, Jim. It gets you out of the country, which will settle the nerves of my superiors, and it puts you on the track of whoever did this to you."

Schweitzer's heart leapt. The defeat and sadness of Ninip's revelation reversed course, suddenly fanned to a blaze. He couldn't be back with Sarah and Patrick again, but he could avenge them. For a brief moment, his own bloodlust matched Ninip's, and he could feel the jinn exulting, fanning the flames until Schweitzer shivered. He fought down the impulse, knowing it would do no good, but he found their shared body pressed up against the bars, Eldredge taking a fearful step back, thumb hovering over the button in his hand.

Schweitzer fought through the flood of eagerness that drowned him, took control of their lungs, throat, and mouth, managed to squeeze out a single word. "Intel."

"You'll get it with your targeting package once you're on the ground."

"Where?"

Eldredge paused. At last, he shrugged. "Waziristan. It's a . . ."

Schweitzer was already tuning him out. He'd run three ops in the lawless Federally Administrated Tribal Areas that composed a mountainous no-man's-land claimed by both Pakistan and Afghanistan. It was a broken sprawl of shattered mountains, stunted trees, and people mired in the dark ages in every respect save their access to modern weapons.

He began flashing the imagery to Ninip before the jinn could reach into his memories, *Talebs* with kohled eyes, rouged cheeks, and bad teeth, helicopter dustoffs from rocky outcroppings held together by the tough roots of stunted trees, hanging out over hundreds of feet of empty space. Crevasses, deadfalls, box canyons, a landscape that seemed full of its own malevolent life force, dedicated to making interlopers pay for their trespass.

The jinn's slow grin was so predictable, it made Schweitzer tired.

"We'll be staging you out of COP Garcia." Eldredge paused, searching Schweitzer's face.

The look confirmed that he knew Schweitzer had been there. The Combat Outpost was deep in the lawless semi-autonomous tribal regions and highly secret, technically a Pakistani "regulatory authority office" that was frequently used to stage US Special Forces teams on specific missions. Schweitzer shuddered to speculate on what it had cost the US to get it in place, but the government wanted a free hand to move ground troops around inside what was technically Pakistan. Garcia was the means to that end. Schweitzer had staged a single op out of there, his beard dyed black and his skin covered in makeup until he could be mistaken for a Pakistani provided nobody got too close. They'd run the op in Pakistani uniforms, using specially modified AK-47s.

"I take it you're familiar with it," Eldredge said.

Hill people. Ninip smiled. *I have fought them before. Did you win?*

Not in the way you think. They paid tribute and served in my army, and continued to kill my tax collectors whenever they went unescorted. That is as much of a victory as even a living god can have.

But we're not a living being anymore.

No. The jinn's smile grew. *We are not.*

CHAPTER XVI
ANSWERS

It felt wrong from the moment Chang's boot touched the asphalt outside the gate. He'd never truly felt like he belonged here even when he did, and the time convalescing had only intensified that sense. The sign hanging over the guard shack had once made him proud, the eagle and anchor surrounded by the words NAVAL AMPHIBIOUS BASE LITTLE CREEK. The red, white, and blue road beneath had always been the path he imagined himself on, the ideas of where it would lead never factoring in fragments of bone in his lung, letting his best friend die, failing to convince his best friend's widow to love him.

You're not a SEAL, Master Chief Green's voice echoed again. No, he wasn't. Not anymore. For a moment, he'd occupied a terrifying space where the man he'd known himself to be had vanished, leaving him suspended over a void of questions, with no clue where to go next. In times past, he'd run off that anxiety, pounding the pavement until he'd sweat himself dry, his stomach rebelled, and sheer exhaustion chased the demons away. But with his wound, that hadn't been an option.

But then there'd been the night with Sarah, the culmination of a fantasy he'd never allowed himself to admit to having, and with it, light in the darkness. He had something to live for. He had a woman, and he had a child.

He loved Schweitzer, missed him, but this had been his problem all along. Schweitzer's priorities had been screwed up, loving the job more than his own family. You couldn't keep a woman as amazing as Sarah that way. They were doomed from the start, and they'd both known it. His death had just brought the inevitable to a head more quickly and made him a martyr that confused matters more than they needed to be. Schweitzer had never been there; Chang knew he would be.

He wasn't a SEAL, but he could be a husband and a father. That was a thing to live for. Sarah herself had admitted that Patrick only broke out of his fog when Chang came around. That boy needed him. In the quiet hours before he drifted off to sleep, Chang admitted that he needed Patrick just as much, maybe more. And wasn't that what made a family?

Sarah would come around, she just needed closure. He couldn't believe they'd managed to fuck up the ashes, but it was good in the end. It had forced him to come back on post, to confront Biggs and Ahmad, to look them in the eye and hear what they had to say.

Sarah wasn't the only one who needed closure.

He flashed his ID to the guard and walked on without slowing. The man just nodded, used by now to the nonchalance and protocol skirting that the men and women who worked here regularly engaged in. Chang loved the teams, but he didn't envy those regular navy sailors who had to work with them.

The setting sun washed the road in dull orange as the base scrolled by. He acknowledged it tangentially. He hadn't had much use for it during his time here. People in the teams usually lived off post and on the economy, kept their own counsel. The last time he'd visited the PX was to get a good deal on a flat-screen TV that he'd broken a week later with a half-full beer can after the 49ers lost in the playoffs. He still hadn't bothered to replace it, the jagged crack reminding him of the cost of being drunk and stupid.

His attention zeroed as he approached the second gate, bearing a similar circular sign as the front gate. But this sign bore the arms that he'd always considered the crowning achievement of his life: the eagle, flintlock, and trident in the center of a ring of words: US NAVAL SPECIAL WAR-FARE GROUP FOUR.

There was no guard shack this time, no evidence of anyone, but Chang knew where the cameras were mounted, knew they were watching him as he waited, hands in his pockets, outside the gate. A moment later, there was a click, and the gate slid open, scattering a small cloud of midges who'd been resting on the wheel mechanism.

An intensely nondescript corrugated steel garage bay stood just beyond the gate. No posters adorned the walls, no flags flew, no music played. There was only a row of Humvees in a perennial state of repair, packed tightly together to obscure whatever work went on behind them.

Ahmad was in civvies, what they all wore when they weren't specifically on an op or in the final stages of prepping for one. She leaned against one of the Humvees, arms folded across her chest. Her ex-husband had gotten out a rumor that her rack used to be huge, but that she got a reduction once she found out she'd been selected for BUD/S. She'd wanted it that badly. For her ex, it was proof that she had no business being in a marriage, but to Chang it spoke of a level of dedication needed for true greatness. In retrospect, it was likely a lie told by a man hurting from the loss of the most important relationship in his life, but it was Ahmad in a nutshell. She got the job done, whatever it took. That was the person a SEAL needed to be, the reason why Chang couldn't be one anymore.

"There he is." Her tone was flat; her expression told him nothing.

He thrust his hands deeper into his pockets, looked at his feet. Silence was a bad thing out in the world, and most folks would say stupid things just to keep it away. But it wasn't that way with the teams. Sometimes that bugged him. He was grateful for it now.

"You've got another two weeks on your chit," she added. "Surprised to see you back now."

"Yeah," he said.

"YN1 told me you put in to lateral."

The hard part was coming sooner than he expected, that was fine. Better to rip the Band-Aid off. "Yup."

"I've been calling you."

"I know, Chief. I got the messages. I just needed time to be alone and think."

"Yeah, well, I could have helped with that. That's my job."

"Respectfully, Chief, I didn't want help. That would have just muddied the water."

"Maybe I just wanted to talk for myself. Maybe I needed someone to lean on. We all lost Jim. Not just you."

"I know that . . ." The truth was that he hadn't thought much about it, had been so consumed by his own grief that he hadn't made room for anyone else, even for these people who'd risked death with him, for him. *I'm sorry,* he thought, but he didn't say it. At this point, it wouldn't have made a difference.

"We can talk about it now," Ahmad said. "Chilly brought in a case of Coronas two days ago. Got 'em on ice in the BMF. Let me grab four, and we can go down to the water and chew it over."

He'd known that she'd do this. It was her job to do this. But that didn't mean it hit any less hard. He fought against a part of himself that yearned to take her up on that offer, to leave Sarah and Patrick to themselves, to throw himself back into the training and bonded comfort of the brotherhood, to forge a new path back to the bleeding edge that had made him a god of war so long ago. He met Ahmad's eyes, dark and hard as ever, caught the slightest tremor in the sclera.

"Steve," she said. "I'm not asking as a favor to you. I'm

not blowing sunshine, and this ain't pity. You're a good SEAL. Nobody wants to lose you."

Chang felt himself teetering on an edge. All he had to do was nod, grab a beer, and listen. Easy day.

"You're not the first operator to get fucked up," she said. "We can rehab you, requalify you. You can come back."

And then what? A few more years running and gunning through shitholes against shitheads until he was too banged up to go on? And after? Back to San Francisco to take care of his mom? To chase after his niece while his sister looked on disapprovingly?

The SEALs were his job. Sarah and Patrick were his family. He had to put them first.

"I can't." The words sounded lame, childish.

Ahmad's expression showed she agreed. "El-tee is going to want to talk to you then," she said, "and don't expect him to be all nicey-nice about it. He's not a softy like your old chief."

Chang smiled at that. "Yeah."

"He's in the head-shed," she said. "I'll be in the armory once he's done with you. Make sure you talk to me before you head out."

"I will, Chief," Chang said. "Thanks."

He made his way around the side of the repair bay to the long trailer that served as an office for Biggs and the senior enlisted. It was as painfully neutral as everything else in view of the gate. They'd even gone so far as to leave the sign of the rental company in place. Chang was told that there'd been a permanent office before he'd first reported to Little Creek, but they hadn't bothered to build it back after the third time a hurricane flattened it.

Biggs's huge frame was shoehorned into a fancy, swivel-backed chair. He looked comically large at the best of times, and the way the plastic armrests forced him to hunch his shoulders didn't help matters. He was in his kha-kis, which meant that there was a meeting either recently in his past or in his immediate future. He typed frantically with his index fingers, tongue jutting out of the corner of his mouth. Chang's heart swelled at the sight.

"Sit," Biggs said.

Chang didn't, crossing his arms and leaning against the doorframe. "Paperwork, huh."

"The root word of 'officer' is 'office.'" It wasn't true for Biggs. Chang had watched him take apart a room with seven dug-in narcoterrorists when they'd cut off his team's egress. He led by example. "How're you holding up?"

"I can't complain." Chang shrugged.

"Well you could, but then you'd be a pussy. You want a beer?"

"I'm good. Chief said you wanted to talk to me."

"I do. What's this shit about a rating change? You want to go back to A-School for . . ." A pause while he sifted through the mountain of paper on his desk. "Intel? The fuck you know about intel?"

"I've read some reports. They use little words mostly."

"You're gonna ride a desk for the rest of your career?"

"I've already got the clearance. Good prospects after I get out."

"You're not getting out."

"I am after this enlistment."

Biggs shook his head. "This pity pot only flushes up, bro. Lots of guys roll back in SQT. You earned the pin. You're in the club. You want me to kiss your asshole?"

"It's not that."

"Lots of guys get hurt."

"It's not that either, I . . ."

Biggs cut him off, something he almost never did. It meant he was trying to keep Chang from saying anything stupid. "And you can't work this job for long without losing someone. That's what this is. It gets better."

"Bullshit."

Biggs looked at his desk, sighed. "Yeah, that is bullshit. It doesn't ever get better. But that doesn't mean there isn't another way forward. You don't have to do this."

"That mean you're going to hold my paperwork up, sir?"

"Hell, no, Steve. You're a grown-up. I'm not going to stand in your way if this is what you really want, I just don't think it is. You need to take some more time and think this through. It's not a little thing. You can't unpush the button."

Chang was quiet at that. Biggs leaned forward, seizing the advantage. "I'll level with you. There are a lot of guys I wouldn't argue like this over. I'd just punch their ticket the moment they handed it in. You're not one of them, Steve. You can stick."

Steve shook his head. He could stick all right, and that meant cutting through this lovefest and getting done what he came here to do.

"I don't want to talk about that."

"Well what the fuck do you want to talk about? Your lousy football team? The stellar cut of my jib?"

"Jim's ashes."

Biggs's face fell. "What?"

"The can Chief gave me for Sarah. It's not Jim."

"Dude. Are you high?"

"She's hurting real bad, sir. She went a little crazy. Had the stuff DNA tested. Came back as pig."

"Like . . . the thing made out of bacon?"

Chang's anger rose into his face, and he pushed it down. Biggs was still his lieutenant, and he was, for now, still a petty officer. "This is off the charts for a fuckup, sir. Sarah's suffering, and this has really put her over the edge. How the hell is it possible to have mixed up his ashes with a pig's?"

"It's got to be some kind of mistake." Biggs had gone pale. "The people at the testing place must have messed up the samples."

"Do we even cremate the pigs we use in TCCC?"

"I don't fucking know!" Biggs's eyes moved quickly from his computer screen to his desk and back to Chang. A sinking feeling lodged in Chang's stomach, churned there. "You'd have to ask the Senior Chief Aning."

"Who oversaw the cremation, sir? I'd rather track this straight from the source."

"No idea on that either. Chief took care of it."

Chang's mouth felt dry. "I'll go check with her, then. I might need some officer muscle if people stonewall me."

Biggs looked up at him, eyes narrowing.

"I mean, nobody likes to admit it when they fuck up is all." Chang added, "Might help to hide behind your leg."

"Sure," Biggs said, already turning back to his computer screen. "Whatever you need."

"Okay, thanks, El-tee. I'll go chat with Chief."

Biggs grunted, pecking away at the keyboard again, eyes firmly in front.

Chang stepped back out of the trailer, his gut doing loops. *What the hell just happened? One second he's all baby-please-don't-walk-out-that-door, then he's too busy to talk.* He'd gotten basic field-interrogation training. It was bullshit, and everyone in the class knew it, but like all other bullshit, there was a grain of truth at the bottom of the steaming pile. It had taught him to look at a baseline in a subject's behavior. The deviations were the hint of the lie. He'd spent years running and gunning with Biggs, knew his baseline like he knew his way around his sidearm. Something was off.

He paused outside the trailer, looking into the shadows of the repair bay where Ahmad waited for him. The darkness was suddenly sinister, her inscrutability now full of secrets.

Sweat trickled down his spine, his consciousness dropping down into the zone where the warfighter lived. His peripheral vision expanded, his limbs relaxing even as the adrenaline began to pump. He calmed, ready to run, fight, whatever needed to be done.

Make sure you talk to me before you head out.

No, Chief. No, I don't think I'm going to do that.

Chang turned and made for the gate, walking quickly, but not so quickly as to tip anyone off to his haste. The gate loomed before him, and for a moment he had an image in his mind of its refusing to open, of him turning while Ahmad led other sailors to grapple him.

But it did open, the wheels squeaking as the barrier drew aside. Chang breathed a sigh of relief, walked slowly through.

"Chang!"

He froze, Ahmad was jogging up behind him. "Dude. I thought you were going to check in with me before you split." She could have been hurt, she could have been angry, she could have been about to ask to borrow five bucks. There was no way to tell.

"Sorry, Chief. I've gotta get back."

"Okay," she said. He turned to go.

"Oh, hey," she said. "The ashes. I don't know what's up with that. That DNA place must have shit the bed. No way that's pig ashes."

"How'd you know?" he asked.

"Biggs called me on the shop phone."

"Right. Thanks."

"He didn't talk you out of the rating change, huh."

"Nope."

"Well, don't do anything tomorrow. Give me another week to change your mind."

"Sure, Chief. Talk to you soon."

Interrogation techniques were 90 percent bullshit. But there was something deeper stirring as the gate shut between him and Ahmad, her eyes boring into his back.

He didn't think she really wanted another week to change his mind. He didn't think she wanted that at all.

CHAPTER XVII
INBOUND

Eldredge and Jawid accompanied Schweitzer and Ninip all the way to the Globemaster. The ramp was already down, exposing a cavernous interior, Ninip's twisted vision turning the shadows into crawling ghosts bent on murder. The plane grew as they approached, the cargo bay a giant dragon's maw, its horns the long, sloped wings, stretching out into the distance.

A soldier waited for them beside the aircraft, what looked like a fighter pilot's helmet tucked under his arm. He passed it to Eldredge, then walked off into the darkness without a word.

Eldredge raised it up, approached Schweitzer. "May I?"

What's this? Schweitzer asked Jawid through their link. It was easier than doing the heavy lifting of forcing their dead lungs and larynx to work. *It looks like it's made of cardboard.*

"He wants to know . . ." Jawid began.

"It's not for protection," Eldredge cut him off. "There will be personnel on-site who aren't privy to the specifics of this program, and we'd prefer to keep your identity hidden."

You don't care if they know who I am. You care if they know what I am, Schweitzer passed to Jawid.

Eldredge smiled. "You really are extraordinary. Yes, that's right. The lure of media exposure is too much for many. Do you remember when Bin Laden was killed, and the SEAL who shot him wrote an unauthorized tell-all?"

Schweitzer remembered, the cold anger it kindled in him alerted Ninip, and the jinn began his usual dig into Schweitzer's memories to bring himself up to speed on the subject.

"The Gemini Cell operates as well as it does because of strict secrecy. We can't risk that sort of thing here." Eldredge tapped the helmet. "You keep this on the entire time you're there. They can speculate as much as much as they like, but there's no need to give them evidence."

What if people talk to me?

Jawid's translation drew another smile from Eldredge. "You can manage monosyllables. Leave the rest to us."

Schweitzer nodded and slipped the helmet on. Eldredge reached in and snapped connecting tabs from the helmet's lower edge into the collar of his armor. The visor was tinted one-way: Schweitzer could see out easily, but the surface would show only darkness to anyone looking in.

Eldredge stood back, hands on his hips, surveying his work.

Does it make me look fat? Schweitzer sent to Jawid.

Eldredge laughed out loud at that. "It makes you look terrifying, which is the desired effect." He leaned in, slapping a patch against the Velcro surface on Schweitzer's shoulder. Schweitzer looked down, seeing a subdued American flag shrouded in the gloom.

"That should at least take the edge off," Eldredge said. "Let's get you to work."

Schweitzer was surprised when Jawid and Eldredge headed up the ramp along with them. *You're coming with me?*

This time Jawid answered. "Of course. You are our most independent subject. We need to be on hand to help you."

Eldredge nodded, gesturing to a huge steel cage in the

center of the enormous and empty interior. Ten men surrounded it, fire axes held casually over shoulders or head down on the deck plates. *No flamethrowers. They don't want to risk fire while we're in the air.* They were decked out in the armor that looked straight out of a documentary on the Middle Ages: thick leather riveted under steel plates.

Ninip looked at them eagerly, Schweitzer could feel his sense of recognition. Warriors with hand-to-hand weapons and metal armor? This was the world the jinn knew.

Only ten? the jinn asked. *That is no challenge.*

Schweitzer agreed. Even if they'd filled the hold with guards, Schweitzer would have given himself and Ninip even odds of taking them apart.

Jawid stiffened as he felt Ninip's mood, nodded to Eldredge, who smiled at Schweitzer. "I'd keep Ninip in check," he said. "The pilots of this aircraft have orders to scuttle it the moment they get word of a struggle back here. There are no parachutes on board. None of us want to die, Jim. But we are every bit as willing to give our lives for our country as you were when you lived. Remember that."

Jawid looked pale, but the axemen's and Eldredge's faces were utterly committed. Schweitzer projected an image to Ninip of the plane slamming into the earth and exploding into flame, or their shared body vaporizing, the storm of souls opening up to receive them.

The jinn growled in frustration but receded.

Eldredge gestured to the cage. "Now, for your own safety. Please."

As Schweitzer and Ninip approached the back of the cage, Schweitzer saw a small wooden stool piled high with books. At the top of the stack was a thick volume with a frayed dust jacket showing a group of women in hoop skirts gathered around a piano.

Oh, Ninip, Schweitzer said, *have I got a treat for you.*

Ninip was howling before Schweitzer had finished the first chapter. The jinn leapt at their shared hands for the third time, trying to force them to drop the book, but Schweitzer managed to hold on, limbs trembling, text remaining firmly in place.

Tedium, the jinn cried, *they are women without money. Their parents should have sold them to the priests. They could have served the fertility goddess. Instead they bemoan . . . Christ . . .*

Christmas presents, Schweitzer finished for him. *They want to buy Christmas presents for their mother.*

Why would anyone want to hear about peasant women? Your people are mad.

This is widely considered one of the great American novels. You should be more respectful. Schweitzer could barely keep the laughter out of his tone.

Ninip blinked at him incredulously. *You should take care. I am a lord.*

Yeah, you keep saying that. Schweitzer went on reading, Ninip's howling gradually receding as he found his rhythm in the prose. The truth was that he didn't like the book much more than Ninip did, but his mother had forced him to read it before she agreed to let him join the navy. He still remembered her face over her morning coffee, cigarette dangling from one lip, the cancer slowly consuming her lungs. *You have to read it because I will not have you grow into some pig-headed macho dickhead. That book created the concept we know as "the American girl," and every woman you meet has been influenced by it whether she knows it or not.*

It had been agony, but he loved his mother, and in retrospect, a part of him knew that she was dying, so he read it cover to cover. He remembered Sarah's expression changing when he told her he'd read it, the dawning interest behind her eyes. *Thanks, Mom.*

I know you were a king and a god or whatever, Schweitzer said, *but you had a family of your own. Why can't you even begin to wrap your head around this stuff? Didn't you have a wife?*

Several.

Oh, right. Well, what about a favorite?

Ninip quieted at that. When the jinn did speak, his voice was soft. *Yes, there was one.*

Schweitzer thought of the woman in the braided wig, bending over Ninip as his son fed him the poisoned fig. *What happened to her?*

She would have married my son, the jinn said. *Or he would have killed her.*

Schweitzer paused, searching for something to say.

It doesn't matter. Ninip beat him to the punch. *That is all beyond us now.*

Schweitzer thought of the jinn's animal bloodlust, tried to square that with the grief he sensed from Ninip now. *You were a man once. What happened to you?*

He could feel the presence fixing its eyes on him. *You have no idea how long I drifted in the soul storm. You cannot fathom the weight of all those years. It stripped everything. It is coldness, blackness, it is isolation. It is endless death, without even the shadow of life.*

There were men in my time who became enamored of the Plant of Joy, the jinn went on, *smoking the dried pods to the exclusion of all else, choosing delirium and dreams over their wives and children, over their lords and oaths. They became the husks of men, little more than animals.*

We call it heroin, Schweitzer said.

Whatever you call it, it steals men's hearts, drives them like cattle. Blood is the pulse of life, Ninip said. *You do not realize that it drives you with an even greater force than this heroin. In life, you never think on it, it is not until death, and the freezing darkness of the void that you realize how much you cherished it.*

And that's why you kill? Because you want blood?

I told you. Killing is still life. But it is more than that. Remember your . . . what is that story about the steppe count who drinks blood?

Dracula. You're saying you're a vampire?

No, not like in that story. But I can understand. When you cannot have a thing, sometimes you hunger for it any-

*way. The closeness of it, the taste of it, the feel of its heat.
It is a pale reflection of the truth, but a reflection is better
than darkness.*

That's not all, is it? Schweitzer asked.

There is vengeance, Ninip said.

Vengeance? For what?

I do not live. Why should they?

Schweitzer thought about that for a long time, understanding the answer, even as he was horrified by it. *You
can't kill everyone, Ninip.*

Not now, the jinn answered slowly. *Not yet.*

Schweitzer took a break from the book when he finally
felt the plane descending, and the axemen began to strip
off their armor, stowing it and their weapons in Pelican cases
to reveal army combat uniforms beneath.

A moment later, Schweitzer felt the dull thud and bounce
that indicated the plane had landed, heard the roar of the
backing engines as it taxied to a stop. Hydraulics hissed as
the ramp dropped, bright, artificial light flooding the bay,
chasing the shadows into the corners before extinguishing
them utterly.

Schweitzer felt the heat hit him, could see the soldiers
sweating. He smelled the familiar odor of diesel fuel and
burning trash. He was in the Middle East, probably at a tran-
sit point to refuel before making the final push into Afghanistan. Qatar, probably. Otherwise, Bahrain or Kuwait.

Eldredge walked over to the cage and punched a code
into a keypad. A soft click, and the door swung open.

"Out you come, now," he said.

He led Schweitzer and Ninip up through a passageway
that led to the cockpit, but turned off at an open hatch in
the fuselage. Schweitzer and Ninip stepped out to see a
Blackhawk spinning up on the tarmac. The cabin was
empty, save for a single crewman waving them in. Eldredge
and Jawid strapped on rigger's belts and clipped them into
the ring on the helo's floor. Schweitzer and Ninip sat on the

edge, feet dangling over as before, the inhuman strength in their abdomen keeping their shared body braced more tightly than if they'd been belted in.

They flew dark, the pilots relying on their night-vision goggles. The ground below was invisible to Eldredge and Jawid, but Schweitzer's enchanted eyes saw clearly. The ground rushed by them, veiled in shadow. They quickly cleared the airbase's edge, marked by tall, concrete barricade walls and plywood guard towers ringed with barbed wire, and soon found themselves moving over the kind of dense, quickly constructed village that sprang up around any US military installation in a foreign country. It was a hodgepodge of scavenged building materials thrown together around dusty, narrow tracks that could scarcely be called a road. Dogs and livestock prowled the quiet alleys while their owners slept.

And then even that hint of civilization was swallowed by the darkness, and the landscape gave over to broken, arid barrens dotted with tiny growths of scrub plant life.

They flew for an hour, with Schweitzer spotting only one person, a tiny figure wrapped in a single bit of dirty cloth, herding a small cluster of scrawny goats with a long stick. The air began to cool as they went on, the ground rising sharply, becoming richer with plant life. Soon the ground dropped off sharply into the ravines and peaks he knew from his time out here. His phantom stomach clenched instinctively, and his memories began to reel back images, fire coming from all directions, villagers who smiled at you and then shot at you once your back was turned. The nagging lack of finality, of being able to be sure that you were doing any good, of cutting off the hydra's head only to have four more rear up in its place.

Ninip observed the reaction with interest. *These are hill people. Here the professional is not enough. Here, you need a king.*

Schweitzer said nothing as the helo finally began to shed altitude. A tight ring of concrete barricades and piled sandbags hemmed in a postage stamp of a camp against the side of a rock face that looked like it had been ripped off a larger mountain and set there deliberately. Guard towers dotted the peak. Schweitzer's augmented vision made out a mortar position there, with spotters and shooters carefully camouflaged alongside.

They were waved in by a ground crew with dimly lit wands, which were extinguished immediately after the helo was in position, leaving the pilots to eyeball the rest of the descent and landing.

They were met on the ground by a group of Americans in Pakistani army uniforms, with thick beards and long hair. Schweitzer immediately recognized the steel-eyed confidence, the unflappable acceptance of the strange, the subtle notions, like civilian hiking boots and nonstandard drop-holsters. Minor augmentations to their Pakistani AK-47s. An ACOG scope, two magazines duct-taped together, a wooden butt stock replaced with a plastic folding one. Dogs came with them, Belgian Malinois with jet-black muzzles, eyes as hard and alert as their owners'.

Schweitzer couldn't be certain if they were SEALs, but they were cut from the same cloth, the community of hard operators he'd once called home. A pang of nostalgia dug at him, and Ninip snarled contempt while simultaneously hungrily taking in every detail about the men.

"Sir," one of the men said. He might have been an officer or a private, distinguished only by the fact that he was speaking. Rank was hidden and virtually meaningless in this world, as were all the tiny touchstones of uniform and protocol that the rest of the military swore by. These operators were professionals. They didn't need those parameters to do their jobs.

Artists, as Schweitzer had been.

As you still are, Ninip said, *as we are together.*

"So, this is him," the man said.

Eldredge was unclipping his carabiner, stepping out of the helo cabin. "This is him. Let's get him briefed up."

The men's eyes flowed over Schweitzer and Ninip's strange armor, their tinted visor, the modified weapon slung across their shoulders. "Looks like he's kitted up to go right now."

"That's because he's ready to go right now," Eldredge replied. "If conditions are favorable to taking the target immediately, we're ready to jump as soon as he's processed the targeting package."

The man nodded at Eldredge's words, but his eyes stayed locked on Schweitzer and Ninip's visor, as if his sight could bore through it.

One of the Belgians padded silently forward, sniffing at Schweitzer and Ninip's toe. A moment later, its hair stood on end and it backed away, a deep growl sounding in its throat. The other dogs joined it, then set up a chorus of sla-vering barks, lunging at their leads.

Ninip surged in answer, and their shared body trembled as Schweitzer fought him down.

When the dogs could not be calmed, their handlers walked them, still barking, into the distance. The man now stared hard at Schweitzer, eyes slits. "You don't talk much, do you?"

Eldredge opened his mouth to answer, but Schweitzer did the bellows dance with their dead lungs and throat. "No."

The man jerked his head back at the croak, made to say something else, but Eldredge cut him off. "Please. Com-mand wants this target actioned as soon as possible. We can't be delaying that because the chemical treatment in his armor frightens dogs. Let's get moving."

The man looked as if he would say more, then reluc-tantly led the way to a long, low shack that sheltered in a deeper pool of darkness cast by the shadow of the peak.

The shack and its interior were as familiar as a favorite chair. Cheap plywood under a corrugated steel roof, cov-ered in sandbags. It was standard architecture for the kind of longer-term temporary construction done by the navy's construction battalions, the Seabees who had built pretty much every structure Schweitzer had ever slept in besides his own home.

The smell of the cheap pine mixed with the standard

smells of spent fuel, cordite, and alcohol-heavy hand sanitizer to evoke the world he'd known all his professional life.

Cheap metal folding chairs ran in regimented rows before a rolled-down projection screen. A laptop was hooked up to the projector, suspended from the ceiling, displaying the first of a set of PowerPoint slides. OP NIGHTSHADE was written across the top of the screen, the bottom scrolled with all the standard warnings, stating the classification level of the briefing and the dire consequences that would surely befall any who let those secrets slip.

What . . . ? Ninip began.

Secrets, Schweitzer cut him off. *Always secrets.*

Ninip nodded. Apparently spycraft was as old a trade as warfighting.

Jawid paused at the doorway, his eyes ranging over the dark horizon, his brow creased, and a tenseness visible in his shoulders that made him look like a man expecting a blow. Ninip followed Schweitzer's gaze, slid into control of their shared nose, sniffed the air for Jawid's scent. It was acrid and metallic, much like the smell of fear, but this was different, heart deep and longing. Eldredge took his elbow, whispered in his ear. Jawid nodded, his shoulders slowly settling to level, then slumping in what looked like fatigue. He joined Schweitzer and Ninip as the three of them made their way to chairs in the back, took their seats.

The smell began to fade, but Schweitzer clung to it, tried to envision it as a trail, much as he had with Sarah's perfume. He receded back into the darkness, envisioned the path stretching out, connecting him to Jawid. Where Sarah's perfume evoked the pink and crimson of the crushed rose petals she used to make her perfume, Jawid's worry was yellow and jagged, the sediment of chemical runoff, an emotional buildup of yellowcake uranium. Schweitzer pushed himself along it, reaching out for Jawid. *What's bugging you?*

Jawid stiffened in the chair next to him, turned to look at him, eyes wide.

Ninip swarmed up behind him, scrambling up the link to the Sorcerer, reaching for him, ravenous. Jawid's eyes narrowed, and Schweitzer felt the man's concentration press inward, pushing back against them both before withdrawing totally as the connection was severed.

The fuck? Schweitzer whirled on the jinn. Ninip said nothing, only reaching with disappointment for the trail Schweitzer had created. *You fucking ruined it. I didn't know it was two-way. He's only contacted us before.*

Ninip shrugged, but Schweitzer caught a flash of something from the presence, a child's sheepish, smiling guilt.

And something else. A fleeting image from his connection with Jawid. A woman. A girl, really, no older than seventeen. Dark eyes glittering, her long hair peeking out from beneath a dark blue head scarf. She was smiling shyly. A sister? A lost love?

He reached deeper, but a man had stepped in front of the screen at the front of the display. He wore muddy blue jeans and a button-down flannel shirt. A ball cap sporting a subdued American flag packed down a tangle of unruly hair, dangling down along a patchy beard. A pistol occupied a hip holster, police-style. He'd likely tangle the handle under his body armor if he ever dried to draw it in a fight. His fleshy neck and chin stood out in stark contrast to the hard angles of the men in the Pakistani uniforms. This was no operator. Intel.

"Welcome to COP Garcia, sir. I'm Ty." His voice was deep, flat, the hard tones of a man trying hard to sound authoritative. While he lived, Schweitzer had been briefed by dozens of these types. They all talked with the same self-conscious macho affectation.

Ninip picked up on Schweitzer's disdain and sneered.

Lock it up, Schweitzer said. *This is our targeting package, and that's the expert on the target.*

Ty paused, unsure of how to proceed. This part of the briefing would usually consist of the team making small talk, letting them know how they were settling in, gently griping with their relief, or the base CO. It was the time to ask the new arrivals if they needed anything.

But Schweitzer and Ninip had been there for a few minutes. They hadn't asked for rack time, or a bathroom, or something to drink. They'd walked their shared body into the room, sat down, carbine still slung and helmet firmly in place.

Eldredge came to his rescue. "Thanks, Ty. I know this isn't SOP, but we've been told to light a fire under this. Command wants us in the field right away. Our operator has all the necessaries locked up. He just needs briefed and deployed."

"Right," Ty said. "So, I just got the cable on you guys a few hours ago."

"Secrecy is critical here," Eldredge said.

One of the Americans in a Pakistani uniform folded his arms across his chest. "Says no team, just him."

"Sorry, you are?" Eldredge asked.

"Sergeant Major McIntyre, sir," the man said. "I'm ops here."

"Got it," Eldredge said. "No team. Just him. We just need eyes from the air and little birds on standby in case any of the bad guys bolt."

McIntyre exchanged a look with his teammates, worked his tongue inside his cheek. Schweitzer realized he had a wad of chewing tobacco in there. He hadn't spit once since they'd landed. "Sir, we haven't hit that target for a reason. We don't have an exact count on the compound, but last count we were around . . ." He looked to Ty for help.

"Fifty," Ty answered. "Fifty people overall. More than half of that's MAMs."

MA . . .

Schweitzer cut the jinn off. *Military Aged Males. People who can fight back.*

Schweitzer could feel Ninip's grin in their shared darkness.

"It's not a capture mission, Sergeant Major," Eldredge

said. "Our man is going in to neutralize Nightshade and get out. Should simplify matters."

"You're sending one guy into that?" McIntyre asked, arching an eyebrow.

"There may be a lot of men in there, but he only has to kill one."

"Yeah, well," McIntyre said, "whatever you've got going on here is none of my concern."

Eldredge smiled, began to rise, nodding.

"But"—McIntyre wasn't finished—"what *is* my concern, is your guy getting himself neck deep in shit and me having to send a fire team in to extract him. We're exposed here. Our hosts, and I use the term loosely, are reluctant at best. Your guy gets pinned down in a burned-out car, and the QRF I send to get him out gets to join him, and all of a sudden we've got a situation that's not exactly good for bilateral relations."

This man is a . . . sergeant major? Ninip asked, double-checking Schweitzer's memories. *He does not make decisions for this . . .*

He's Special Ops, Schweitzer said. *The rules are different for us . . . for them.*

I will never understand the way you fight. You have no order, no honor, nothing one can call a way.

Schweitzer smiled. *Welcome to the modern world.*

Eldredge was standing now, dusting off the seat of his pants, putting his hand on Schweitzer and Ninip's shared elbow. "I wouldn't worry about that," Eldredge said. "He won't get pinned down, and you won't need to extract him."

"Can't extract him," McIntyre said. "I've made my concerns known all the way up to division. I am not risking the lives of my people by putting them on the ground in that compound, nor am I willing to risk our relationship with Pakistan by bombing it. Your boy goes in, he's on his own."

Schweitzer felt something stir deep in his soul. Those words might have come directly from Chief Ahmad.

Eldredge's smile widened. "That's just how he likes it."

CHAPTER XVIII
HONEY, I'M HOME

Chang had to fight against the instinct to run once he cleared the compound gate and made his way through the rest of the base to his car. The unease had settled in his stomach, curdled into something darker, until he swore he could imagine Ahmad slinking up behind him, eyes slits of rage, teeth bared, a wire garrote in her hands.

He fell into an old breathing exercise he'd been taught at SQT. In. Count to four. Out. In. Count to four. Out. Most times, it helped almost instantly, but now it only made him short of breath, his vision narrowing and his knees feeling weak. It was the wound. Goddamn that stupid fucking lung.

He comforted himself by watching the foot traffic by the PX as he passed it. Families shopping for groceries, fathers taking their children to pick out toys. All the trappings of a normal world, where nobody substituted pig ashes for those of your cherished friend. He knew it meant nothing, but it helped, and the darkness had receded to the edges of his mind by the time he reached his car.

He allowed himself one moment of franticness, whipping open the door and looking over his shoulder.

Nobody. A breeze made a crumpled plastic wrapper into a tumbleweed, bouncing along past his foot. A few seagulls cried hopefully above a green metal Dumpster.

He sighed and flung himself into the driver's seat, his hand dropping down to brush the side of the plastic Pelican case he kept beneath it. He fumbled for the catch and opened it, let his hand brush the smooth surface of the .45 1911-pattern pistol he kept in an operational state, one round in the chamber and ready to go.

As soon as his fingers touched the metal, his heart slowed, his breathing coming more easily, some of the sense of dread subsiding. He exhaled and let his hand drift deeper, feeling the screws in the wood grain handle pressing against his palm, the reassuring touch of a mother, a lethal reminder that, come what may, he could handle it.

He shook his head and pulled out his phone, dialed before he knew what he was doing, and lifted it to his ear. Soft, echoing chimes went on long enough for him to know that Sarah wasn't answering. Her voice mail was the old Sarah, before Jim's death, her voice confident and a little playful. "Hi! I know the automated greeting just wasted a few seconds of your life, so I figured I'd waste a few more. Thanks for having a sense of humor!"

Chang smiled. Sarah never ceased to amaze him. She gave the world the middle finger and embraced it simultaneously. She lived life entirely on her own terms. Who the hell else could go nose to nose with the mighty James Schweitzer and bring him to heel? God, how he loved her.

"Hey . . ." He stopped himself before saying "babe," but only just. "Hey, Sarah. It's Steve. I talked to Chief, and there's . . . there's some mix-up. She's looking into it now, and we'll get to the bottom of it. They're all really shocked, and sorry." He'd made that last bit up, but he figured it would help her to hear it.

"Anyway, this is getting long, but I'm coming over. I want to finish our conversation, and not about Jim's ashes this time. We need to talk about us. If you're out, I'll wait. See you in a few."

He hung up, put the phone in his pocket, and started the car. As he turned the key, his adrenaline-amped senses screamed at him, *You forgot to check the car for bombs! It's going to explode!* But the engine hummed into life even as he shook briefly from the dump of adrenaline.

"Jesus," he said out loud. That sort of thing wasn't uncommon for any warfighter who'd served in combat, but the uneasiness of his encounter with Ahmad and Biggs had exacerbated it. He tightened his grip on the steering wheel, shook his head, and got on the road.

The tires set up a heartbeat rhythm as he moved over the concrete seams of I-64. The highway passed him over the bridges that dotted the five-cities area, an improbable collection of minor population centers sprouted haphazardly in a maze of swamps, inlets, and sunken peninsulas. As darkness came on in earnest, he rolled down the window and smelled the salt air, the slight tang of garbage and creosote that spoke of the complicated berms, floodgates, and drainage ditches that made human habitation here possible. They were nasty smells, but they were familiar, and that was a comfort.

He didn't bother to turn on the radio, and instead let the night sounds of peeping frogs and the racing wind lull him. He felt almost normal again as he turned off the highway onto the tree-lined local road that would lead him to Sarah's, tapping on his brights to pierce through the thick darkness, made blacker by the tunnel of trees that seemed to shroud the lane, making it a narrow corridor of civilization through a primeval wood.

He slowed a bit to take the sharp turns, and also on the off chance that some overeager Portsmouth cop might pull him over. They might have let him go if he were in uniform, but it was unlikely now. The thrumming of the air through the window and the familiar shadows of the neighborhood put the whole situation in context. He needed to be reasonable. Ockham's razor. What was the simplest explanation: that Ahmad and Biggs were shocked and embarrassed by the screwup? That it was an awkward exchange to

begin with given his decision to get out? That he'd gotten a
little freaked-out for no reason? Or did it make more sense
to believe there was a conspiracy at work here?

He smiled, hoping the expression would force the dread
out of him, but it hung on in the corner of his mind, a sick
spike in his gut, so slight that he could almost believe he
imagined it.

Almost.

"Fuck it," he said, bending to turn the radio on. He made
sure the road was clear before allowing his eyes to flick to the
scan button, pressing it in the hopes of finding some Motown
in the midst of the ocean of preaching, gospel, and country
music that dominated the airwaves in this area. He tapped
the button, looked back up to the road, as clear as before, the
reflective paint of the stripes sliding along to his left.

He drove for a full minute before he realized that the
radio hadn't come on. No music, no static. Nothing.

He glanced down to see the digital numbers racing past,
running up to the top of the FM spectrum before starting
again at the bottom.

Which meant it couldn't find a signal.

"The fuck?" He glanced over his shoulder, but the
antenna was intact and extended, nodding in the breeze
like a pillar on the verge of toppling over.

He punched the radio lightly, nothing. The sense of
dread came roaring back into him, stronger than before, as
if it had only waited for the moment to pounce. He slowed
down, the feeling mounting to panic before sliding into the
calm alertness that always came over him in a crisis. Jim
had called it "bullet time" in deference to some video
game, but it seemed that time slowed, his heightened
awareness allowing him to note the waving of individual
branches, the tiny flicker in his headlights. His peripheral
vision expanded until he could feel the darkness at the side
of the road clambering up the berm to either side of the
road, as if it resented the light and noise his vehicle made,
sought to swallow them to purify the gloom.

Chang steered with his knees, his hand instinctively

dropping back to the unlocked Pelican case, feeling for the handle of the pistol. His mind clicked from hunch to certainty. Something was wrong. Something was dangerous. It was time to get off the X.

And that is when he saw the man.

He emerged from the woods, galloping on all fours like a silverback gorilla, head turned toward the headlights, coming level with the bumper before he leapt to his feet with the agility of a circus acrobat.

Chang only had time to take in the color of the man's naked body, the gray-white of a beached fish long after the sun had its way with whatever color had marked its living scales.

The man stepped fully in front of the car, mouth opening, issuing a groan that sounded at once pained and angry, and Chang hauled the wheel to his left, crossing the empty oncoming lane and brushing the guardrail, sending a shower of sparks that would have done a metalworker proud. Chang knew better than to pump the brakes, applying gentle pressure until he felt the pedal tap against his foot as the antilock mechanism engaged. He pulled the wheel back right, but the mud at the top of the berm had his tire now, hauling him by his momentum deeper and deeper into the woods.

A gap in the guardrail opened briefly on his left, and the front of his vehicle swung into the empty space, a horse making a break for the hole in the fence. He tried the wheel again, felt the car slide further, then cursed and turned into the slide, the vehicle just missing the next guardrail segment, catching the metal against his right headlight, which exploded in a spray of colored glass.

The remaining headlight did its level best to give him a good view of the ground sloping down the berm and the near solid wall of tree trunks just beyond. Chang abandoned attempts to steer, brought his forearms up to cover his face, locking his elbows against the wheel, jerking himself forward in his seat belt, forcing the locking mechanism to engage. He closed his eyes.

Bang.

The thunderclap sounded just below a sound like paper crumpling and an ocean wave breaking at the same time. He felt the air outside rush in, powdered glass spalling across his forearms as the windshield shattered. The seat belt suddenly dug into his chest and gut, a malevolent constrictor snake that made his wounded chest scream. His head whipped forward and down, a motion that would surely have damaged his neck if he hadn't braced his face against his forearms.

There was a smell of gasoline, melted plastic, and the wet night air. The engine died with a cough and a high screech as a rubber belt gave way and spun off its wheel.

Then, silence.

Chang opened his eyes. The remaining headlight had dimmed, showing the edge of a tree that now neatly bisected the front of his car, the fractured radiator bent around it, liquid spraying up in weaker and weaker pulses, a heart bleeding out its last.

Beyond the light was a solid wall of darkness, the slow rise of night sounds already filling the vacuum left by the stilling of the engine. Crickets chirping. Frogs calling for mates. Beetles foraging for food. The natural world raced in on his moment of weakness, answering the panicked crash with peace and softness. Chang felt the temptation to be lulled by it, to lean back into his seat and give the fog in his mind a moment to clear. But the alertness he'd conjured just before the crash came surging back.

A nude man stepped deliberately in front of your car. There was something wrong with the way he looked. He can't be more than a few hundred feet behind you.

Get off the X. Go.

Bullet time again. Chang's hand dropping down, yanking the handle of the Pelican case as his other hand thumbed the button on his seat belt. The button depressed halfway, then stopped dead, the tongue stubbornly holding fast.

He yanked once, the nylon still tight across his chest,

then moved his hand to his pocket, pulling out the knife and flicking it open in one smooth motion, the click sounding loud and alien in the midst of the rising night sounds. A duller knife would have taken some time, but even a lousy SEAL kept his honed to razor sharpness. He slid the blunt edge along his belly, working the blade behind the seat belt and cut it in a single swipe. His weight was already leaning hard to the left, and he rolled out of the car and came up in a crouch in the thick mud at the base of the berm, his back solidly covered by the uneven hardness of the tree trunk behind him.

He threw the knife down blade first into the dirt and flipped open the case, pistol and tactical light almost leaping into his grip.

And then he was ready. His mind was clear, his situational awareness as good as it would get. Whatever that fucker had hoped to do to him, he was going to have one hell of a fight making it happen. Chang raised the pistol, bracing the backs of his hands against one another, tactical light pointed outward in his left hand, thumb flicking it on. The tension of his hands stabilized his firing platform, his eyes falling naturally onto the gun sights, his finger indexed gently above the trigger guard. All in a single smooth motion, in the space of a few breaths. Silent, expert, professional.

Maybe not such a bad SEAL after all.

He didn't waste time with threats, idiot shouts of "Who goes there?" that would give away his position. His light flooded the side of the berm, washed up to the road's edge, confirmed that, so far, no one had followed him to the crash site. Then the light was off and he was moving, defying anyone homing in on the illumination to locate him. He crab walked sideways along the tree line, back up to the road, feeling the comforting brush of the tree branches across his shoulders. Not cover, but concealment at least.

He slid sideways, up the road toward where the man had appeared. He briefly considered running into the darkness behind him but knew it was a fool's temptation. The woods

went on for miles, a pitch-dark run of ankle-turning mud
puddles and tree roots, with no sign of human habitation.
Whatever was going on here, it wanted to work in the dark
of the woods. His best chance was to stick to the road,
where the chance existed that a passing state trooper or
someone out for a late-night milk run might stumble on the
wreck and call for help.

After he'd gone at least thirty feet from his last position,
he froze, listening. He didn't risk the light again. He strained
his ears, sorting out the animal sounds from the distant call
of waves breaking on the shoreline, borne on the gentle but
rising breeze.

The air was a gentle rushing sound, the soft, damp
swishing he'd come to know from years in the Tidewater.
Suddenly, the rushing accelerated, as if the wind strained
to accommodate a large object shooting through it.

Chang had heard that sound before as he sheltered in
place on a blasted hillside in Afghanistan. Indirect fire. A
rocket.

He got low, crouching almost prone. If it was a rocket,
he had no hope of outrunning it. The most he could hope
for was for the shrapnel to pass overhead.

But it wasn't a rocket. The dark silhouette of a man was
outlined against the lighter gray of the starlit sky, hurtling
through the air to land with a crunch on the hood of Chang's
car, his weight driving it down nearly a foot, crouching
deeply and gracefully as a gymnast, arms out to his sides.

The man from the road.

Naked, showing no sign of pain from landing bare-
footed on the broken roof of a car.

He'd jumped. He'd jumped across hundreds of feet of
road. He'd practically flown.

Panic and disbelief swarmed in the pit of Chang's stomach, but his training answered, surging through him and
pushing it back down, keeping him suspended in the state
of hyperalertness, of focused calm. *Later,* his mind told
him. *You can sort it out later. For now, stop the threat.*

The man crouched on the roof, then raised his chin, sniffed the air. His head sawed unerringly in Chang's direction, a low growl emanating from his throat, sounding more rottweiler than human.

Scary, sure. But the man made a perfect target, silhouetted against the night sky, spreading long-fingered hands to give Chang a perfect centerline for his shot.

He dropped his eyes back onto his gun sights and thumbed the button on the light. If that fucker was to die, let him die blind.

But the light washed over his target, and Chang's battle bubble popped.

The man's corpse-gray skin nearly reflected the light back at him, waxy and hairless as a store mannequin. It was crisscrossed with tiny scars, with yellow-white stitches clinging stubbornly to three puckered mounds over his left pectoral. Chang recognized them as gunshot wounds, carelessly sewn closed in the manner of an undertaker preparing a corpse for burial, knowing the rough work would be covered by clothing.

The shape of the man's body showed Chang he was male though his manhood had been cut away, the site stitched shut with the same sloppy carelessness. Horns sprouted from his head, uneven spikes of bone, piercing the skin of his scalp, matched by a broken mountain range of spines running down his back. What Chang had assumed were long fingers were claws, as if the bones of his hand had sprouted tapered branches, making him a thing of spikes, a human porcupine.

Across his chest, marred by the wound scars, was the faded remains of a tattoo: an eagle, wings spread, perched proudly above crossed cannons on a waving American flag. A banner scrolled beneath: DUTY, HONOR, COUNTRY.

The man growled again, his jaw unhinging like a snake's, his gray tongue lolling out a foot long, weaving in Chang's direction like a sentient thing.

His eye sockets were hollow, gray pits. Whatever meat

had resided in those depths was long gone. In its place, twin gold flames flickered, tiny balls of metallic, malevolent fire.

The panic surged in Chang again, an electric jolt up his spine, the tiny muscles along its length seizing in horror, his brain sparking as it tried to wrap around what it was seeing, a flood of words selected and discarded in an instant. Zombie. Ghoul. Wraith.

Devil.

Chang's conscious mind reeled, his subconscious mind did what it was trained to do. Devil or not, it had a man's shape, and he knew how to kill men. The target went blurry, the front sight post came into clear focus, and Chang snapped the trigger back three times. The gun kicked, but he held it steady, his solid frame pushing it back into place between each shot, eyes never leaving the jumping sights.

The fear and amazement must have been getting to him; the first shot came in low, punching through the top of the man's sternum, just under the hollow of his throat, but the next two shots impacted where Chang had intended, the first holing the man's gray Adam's apple, and the second pushing through his eye socket to explode out the back of his skull, carrying scraps of skin and fragments of bone with it.

Forty-five caliber rounds packed a hell of a punch. The man's head snapped back, and he practically somersaulted off the car's roof, landing with a thud behind it.

Chang wasn't dumb enough to race around the vehicle. Instead, he dropped prone in the mud, lining up for another shot before flashing his light through the undercarriage. The white beam flooded over mud and clumps of grass. No body. Nothing.

The whooshing sound again.

Chang looked up just in time to see the man hurtling down toward him. He launched himself back, stumbling to his feet as the man landed, swiping out with one clawed hand, sharp bone tips of his claws singing through his shirt, tracing shallow, bloody lines across Chang's chest.

This close, Chang could see the bloodless, black entry wounds his rounds had made. The bullet had passed through the empty eye socket without affecting the gold flame that flickered there, dancing hypnotically, as the man turned his head to follow Chang's movements.

Chang's brain had now switched monikers. Thing. Creature. Whatever this was, it wasn't a man.

He raised the pistol again, but the thing stepped forward quicker than a cat and brought its forearm down like an iron bar on his wrist. He felt the bones snap, his body barely registering the pain in the rush of adrenaline. The gun went tumbling from his limp hand.

And now his training betrayed him. His conscious mind understood that the thing before him didn't respond to the tools in his toolbox. A high-powered round through the eye wouldn't put it down. The only thing to do now was run. But his body wouldn't let him. Years of training had put it on autopilot, so that all he could do was stand and watch himself as he stepped into the attack, close as a lover, hooking two of his fingers over the thing's sternum, pushing in and pulling down, seeking the nerve cluster that he knew would have no effect because the thing was dead, and pain was nothing more than a distant notion.

His knuckles rocked into the entry wound as his fingers sank deeply enough that a living man would have dropped screaming in pain. But, of course, the thing showed no reaction, leaning casually aside and forward, the extended jaw clamping over his shoulder, the mouth bone dry. He felt the teeth sink into him, grinding against the bone beneath. No man's teeth were that long, that sharp. It gave a quick jerk of its head, like a hunting cat, and Chang felt hot blood spray up his neck. His arm went numb.

His blood. His arm.

Nonetheless, his body was in full control now, the training driving him even as his conscious mind acknowledged the fact that it was useless, that he had lost, that a dead thing could not be killed.

He twisted, feeling the flesh of his shoulder tear, ripping

clean of its mouth, the agony still a distant thing. He rolled across its shoulder, bringing his elbow down hard against its short ribs, felt the satisfying crack beneath that would have put any living man out of the fight. His face slid along the thing's triceps. It smelled of hospital antiseptic and something spicy that reminded him of the Arab suqs he'd been to in Qatar, Yemen, and Oman.

The thing lifted its arm, and Chang saw a dark scrawl down its side. He couldn't read it in the dark, but he knew it was tattooed lettering: blood type and serial number. He had it, too. Most operators did.

Not just a zombie. A zombie of one of his own.

And then his body did register the pain, and the claws slid up under his rib cage, rising through his lungs, his heart, beyond. He felt the hand follow, drilling into the wound, and all his strength suddenly left him. He couldn't breathe, couldn't move. His knees buckled, and he sagged in the creature's arms. It held him like a baby, its face hovering over his own, close enough that he should have been able to smell its breath. But it wasn't breathing.

The gold flames of its eyes bored into his own and it croaked something, a few words in a language that sounded like Hebrew, garbled and truncated, wind blown through an ancient chimney.

His vision went gray, collapsing into a tunnel that shut out all except those twin burning fires. His mind clung to a single thought, that he had been going somewhere, that this losing fight was all the more a tragedy because it had stopped him from something important that he needed to do.

Sarah, he thought as he slid further into the dark, even the light of the golden fires fading.

Oh, Sarah. I'm sorry.

CHAPTER XIX
ALIVE

Schweitzer and Ninip went in on foot.

The helo set them down around three klicks out, on a slope of broken scree that spoke of a rockslide in months past. The larger stones had all been carried off, which let Schweitzer know that there was a settlement nearby. If his memory served him, it was likely to be farther up the slope, back to a harder piece of the mountain, hidden and defensible.

Bring up the map again, Schweitzer sent to Jawid.

His vision went white as the Sorcerer reached out to him, channeling his own vision of the screen in the briefing room. Schweitzer could see Ty out of the corner of Jawid's eye, looking at the Sorcerer with something akin to fear.

Beyond him, the screen showed a drone's camera image of a large compound. It was built around a low house of at least three stories, judging from the tiered balconies. A higher wall ringed the open space beyond it, enclosing two smaller buildings and two towers. White dots clustered in a corner. Goats, most likely. A few darker points were likely people. Cars were parked in neat rows just outside one of the gates.

The bodies glowed bright white in the thermal-imaging lens. Two of the cars glowed white up front, the heat from their running engines lighting them up for the camera. The building corners glowed in stark relief, so brightly in some spots that Schweitzer could tell where the generators were stored.

All, save one.

A long, rectangular building, certainly a single story, was nestled alongside the main building's side, ringed with what Schweitzer guessed was tall fencing.

It was pitch-black.

That's where they're storing the bodies, he said to Ninip. *It's refrigerated.*

He could feel the jinn's impatience, but Ninip was slowly learning the benefit of taking his partner's counsel. *Why are they trafficking in corpses? Perhaps they have their own Gemini Cell.*

Eldredge did say there were other Sorcerers besides Jawid. Maybe there's another program, more Operators like us.

Ninip mused as they trudged along a ridge, keeping to the far side and just out of sight. *Us against another pairing, with an ancient soul of its own? That would be a worthy contest.*

Yeah, well. Hopefully that's not what we're running into here.

You hope for strange things. Schweitzer could feel the jinn's hunger rising as they closed on the target. Schweitzer kept their shared ears tuned, the incredible fidelity filtering through a sea of sounds. The wind sighed along the ridge, insects foraged in the scrub grass. He could hear the high whining of the drone's tiny engine, kilometers above them, the whispered conversation of the men back at the grounded helo. Somewhere to the northeast, a jackrabbit stomped its foot to warn of approaching danger. Schweitzer listened for a moment before deciding that it was at least a kilometer away.

Ninip ranged over the map as well, and Schweitzer was surprised to see him struggling with his own impulses, trying to consider the best breach point. *We should go in from the back of the main building,* the jinn suggested. *The wall looks high there. There are no windows that I can see, and it is taller than the towers.*

It's not taller than the towers, Schweitzer said. *You have to get used to looking at this kind of imagery. It's deceptive. You need to count balconies. Anyway, that's an awning.* He flashed Ninip a slice of the image, a light gray patch on top of the building's roof, closest to the far wall. *If they're at all security conscious, they've got men underneath it.*

Then we will kill them. Ninip couldn't resist falling back on his old habits.

Sure, we can. And wake up the whole damn place in the process. Here's where we go in. He indicated a long stretch of wall farthest away from the towers, just opposite the refrigerated building. Eyeballing it from the top down, he put it at around thirty feet.

Easy day.

Normally, we'd have to blow a hole in the wall, bring the whole place down on us. Now we can just jump over.

Ninip was already flashing images of slaughter, the presence quivering with anticipation of the hunt. Schweitzer felt the infectious thrill, the temptation to give the jinn rein, to lose himself in the gory dance. Why bother acting the part of the hard operator when his body wasn't his own anymore? There were only two marriages for him now, either to the feral monster who shared his body, or to the legions of screaming dead in the void beyond.

It was a familiar set of choices that any SEAL was long used to, bad or worse, frying pan or fire.

Despair and panic rose in him, stubbornly sticking in spite of his attempt to put them off with the old drill: tip the hat, do the job. Ninip, lost in his frenzy, didn't bother to try to stop Schweitzer as he reached behind the armor and pulled out the engraved dog tags, looking at the outlines of his family's faces, smiling as if the world were a wonderful place where all you loved wasn't snatched away from you in an instant. The lines seemed clearer still, some of the rust shaken off against their chest.

He forced their dead lungs to draw a breath, deep and long, like he had used to. Ninip growled at the sight of the dog tags, began to resist, forcing the arm down. Schweitzer let him, focusing on the breath, the old reflexes, muscles moving, tissue expanding and contracting. He almost felt alive.

Which was why this way was better. Not for the chance at revenge. Not for justice. But because it was what Sarah would do. Because it was the best chance to visit his family's graves someday, to see people inhaling and exhaling as he had just done. To hear voices speaking, music playing, to turn pages and stretch limbs. It wasn't life.

But it was as close to a second chance as he'd ever get.

And if the price of that was that he kept doing the job he'd loved all his life, with just the one added task of keeping a muzzle on this rabid dog inside him, well, that wasn't so bad.

There was still a ways to go before the compound, and Schweitzer found himself wondering about Jawid's village. Was it close by here? Did it have the same broken landscape? He tried to remember the images of the burning wreckage of Jawid's home that the Sorcerer had shown him when he'd first awakened into his new life.

He felt a stirring as the channel opened up between him and Jawid, as it had when he sat in the COP waiting for Ty to begin the briefing.

You are learning, Jawid said. *You can reach out to me now.*

Ninip stirred, began to sniff at the channel linking them, but Schweitzer didn't want to lose this chance to speak to the Sorcerer and shoved the jinn sharply back.

I've always been a fast learner. I saw a girl last time, Jawid. You were thinking about her. Who was she?

Grief filtered through the channel between them, but Jawid only sighed. *That's lost to me now.*

Ninip said the same damned thing.

I gave you your answer, the jinn snarled. *Leave the goatherd in peace.*

He is right, Jawid said. *Focus on the op.*

Jawid, we've got another klick to cover at least before we reach the compound, and I can hear a rabbit taking a dump in the next valley over. Nobody is going to catch me with my pants down.

There is no sense in looking over our shoulders, Jawid said, sounding angry now. *The past is the past.*

You still sound just like Ninip. What is with you guys? You were both human beings. Hell, you still are.

I am not, the jinn groused. *Do not compare me to that pathetic lot.*

But you were, Schweitzer said. *What the hell happened to him, Jawid? Is this what magic does to you? Turns you into a dried-up, bitter douche bag? Because I don't see that happening to me.*

The void, the soul storm, is magic, Jawid said. *It is the wellspring, the source. I brought Ninip back just after you died, while your soul was still tied to your body. When Ninip came back, so did you.*

So?

So, the void is a cauldron of magic. You . . . soak in it. It goes into you, changes you. It makes the soul of a man . . . something else. The longer you soak, the more you change. And when I bring the soul back, the magic comes with it.

Schweitzer thought of the horns, the claws, the burning silver of their eyes.

How long exactly was Ninip soaking in the soul storm? Before you brought him back? Schweitzer asked.

A long time, the jinn said.

A very long time, Jawid agreed. *The longest of any jinn I have ever known.*

And that is the root of our strength, Ninip said.

Would it happen to me? Schweitzer asked. *If I . . . soaked in the void long enough?*

It is happening to you, Jawid replied. *You are steeping in the magic as we speak. It comes to you through the jinn.*

I am your cauldron now, Ninip said.

Schweitzer thought of Ninip's talk of an addiction to slaughter that was stronger than pure heroin. *You've got the wrong guy,* Schweitzer said. *You two can chuck your humanity in the trash all you want. I am James Schweitzer, and that is never going to change.*

You will learn, Ninip said, and Jawid sighed and closed the channel between them.

As the ridge finally gave way to arid plain, Schweitzer dropped them into a low crawl, pushing back against Ninip's desire to run toward the compound. He shifted their vision into the infrared, seeing the faint heat outlines of a trio of jackals prowling about a klick out, the tiniest wavering lightness indicating the compound in the distance.

Eyes on, he sent to Jawid. *Approaching from the northeast, entry on target at point bravo.*

Roger, Jawid sent back. The military radio jargon sounded silly coming from him with his beard and robes. A moment later, he came back with, *Overhead reports no pickets in your zone of approach.*

I already knew that, Schweitzer thought, but didn't send, as they rose to a crouch and began to make their way more quickly toward the wall. The jackals lifted their heads, sniffed the air in his direction, bolted the opposite way.

Ninip swung the carbine onto their back and forced them down on all fours, loping along like an ape. It was faster than the duck walk, so Schweitzer didn't bother trying to wrest control back.

A moment later, Jawid came back, his voice wooden, repeating words someone was saying to him. *Adjust your approach to the east, enter at point delta.*

Schweitzer pictured the map. Delta marked the back of the building, what Ninip had wanted. *There's an awning up there,* Schweitzer said. *That approach is covered.*

Negative. You're misreading the imagery. That's your approach.

Fuck that. Not doing it.

Command has called point delta as the app—

I heard you the first time. I'm not doing it. Fire me.

Being dead had its upside.

Ninip moved them across the intervening distance, allowed Schweitzer to slow them back into the crouch, then finally rose from it, steady-stepping to the base of the wall, carbine at the low ready.

He could see the heat signatures in the nearest tower, but the man wasn't looking his way, or if he was, Schweitzer and Ninip were lost in the thick shadows that swarmed the plain. They crouched and sprang, watched the wall lengthen, then shrink as they crested it, landing in a light crouch that barely hinted at their impact. Their peripheral vision caught the man in the nearer tower. The enemy had tied a shemagh around his face to keep the blowing dust out, and a light-colored baggy tunic and trousers reflected the starlight, obviating Schweitzer's need for infrared vision. An enormous antimateriel rifle was slung across his chest, a high-end nightscope perched on its Picatinny rail. Expensive stuff, and one hundred percent American manufacture.

Schweitzer filed the information away, sighted, and fired. The carbine emitted only a dry click, and the man gave a single short gasp as the back of his head came off, arcing out over the tower before clearing the wall and falling to the ground. The rest of him dropped, disappearing behind the tower's low railing.

Schweitzer and Ninip crouched, listening to see if the shot had been heard, the casualty seen. The only sounds seemed peaceful enough; a muttered conversation between a man and a woman, a low-horsepower motor running steadily, goats in the courtyard crowding together for warmth.

He was beginning to believe that all was clear when

Ninip asserted himself, forcing control of their limbs and leaping out over the tower railing, claws extending.

No, you fucking idiot! he shouted at the jinn. The ground was already rushing up at them, he glanced about wildly, trying to assess the layout. Heat signatures flashed by far too quickly for him to fix any one of them.

And then solidity under their feet, crunching, then soft, liquid spraying around him, a high, inhuman wail sounding up between his legs.

They'd landed on a goat. Ninip was even now driving a fist down into its skull, cutting the wail short. The rest of the goats were scattering in all directions, bleating madly. Ninip snapped their teeth at one of them, breaking through the chinstrap and knocking the helmet askew. Schweitzer raised one shared hand to rip it off and cast it aside while Ninip took control of the other, lashing out and slashing through one goat's hindquarters, spraying blood and sending the animal screaming, dragging its limp hindquarters along the ground.

Congratulations. You've maimed a goat, Schweitzer said, but the jinn was senseless in his search for slaughter, and Schweitzer found himself yanking back on him to keep them from racing after the nearest animal, whose voice was joining the terrific noise that now echoed through the court-yard.

The first shot caught them in the back of their right shoulder, coming in from a high angle that told him the shooter was in the other tower. There was the weird sensation of the liquid against their skin suddenly going brick hard, and then they were rolling facedown through the dust as the force of the high-powered round bowled them over.

Ninip howled and spun them back to their feet, the heat signature of the shooter flaring in Schweitzer's vision. He swung the carbine back around and raised it to fire.

But before he could draw a bead, Ninip crouched them deeply and leapt so high and long that Schweitzer briefly thought the jinn's magic had enabled them to fly. For a moment, Schweitzer thought they would fall short by inches, slam face-first into the tower's side, but then he felt their shared fingertips catch on the railing's lip, gain purchase, haul them up until their boots came down on solid footing.

Their enemy was backpedaling to the far railing, his rifle hanging between his legs, barrel tangling in his baggy pantaloons. Ninip grinned, reached out with one shared finger, the bone spike entering the man's eye, pushing through. Schweitzer could feel the brief resistance of the back of his skull before it gave way, and the man went suddenly limp, a rag hung on the clothesline of their claw. The jinn whipped their shared hand to the side, and the man flew from the tower, landing with a dull thud among the panicked goats below.

Shouts from the main building now. Ninip answered them with a shout of his own, deep and primal, their jaw unhinging, horns and spines sprouting, the thick tongue lolling out. The monster in full form.

Enemy in contact, shots fired, Schweitzer passed along to Jawid. *We're dynamic.*

Roger, Jawid replied, *do not engage any targets but Nightshade.*

Ninip was already making them leap, clearing the tower's edge, angling for the nearest balcony of the main building. Schweitzer knew they were going to miss it before they'd gone a quarter of the distance, watched the wall rise up as they fell, figures rushing to the balcony's edge, pointing, aiming weapons.

He looked down just in time to see the long building beneath them, dark and cold, the low thrumming of a refrigeration unit sounding from the roof. The flimsy surface gave way as soon as they slammed into it, thin metal parting to drop them onto the concrete pad below.

The concrete held, the slight spring indicating the rubber pad beneath it that would protect the building against the cracking and shifting of the dry ground below. Expensive work, requiring skilled labor.

Ninip sniffed the air, smelled no life, snarled. Schweitzer looked around the room, a nasty familiarity dawning in him at the sight of the stainless-steel racks, the puddled shadows, the chemical smell of embalming fluid. The space was roughly the same size as the shipping container he'd seen the night before his death. Only three bodies lay still and silent, gray skin a field of rough scars where mortal wounds had been stitched closed. Two were male, one female, all with the Kushite features that told Schweitzer they were likely Pakistanis, or Waziristani locals.

And then Ninip's lust for blood rolled through him like a tide, launching them backward and around, until they crashed through the door and back out into the courtyard.

Two men rushed toward them, firing rifles from the hip, undisciplined bursts of panicked fire that were in no danger of hitting their target. Ninip's bloodlust became so intense that it blotted out Schweitzer's vision, an orgasm in every dead nerve in his body, sweeping him under as the jinn took control of their shared body and rushed the enemy, decapitating one with a sweep of their claws and pinning the other to the ground through his knee, eliciting a shriek of agony that reverberated through the inner space the jinn and Schweitzer shared. Schweitzer and Ninip floated on the sound, delicious music.

Schweitzer struggled to free himself, come back to his senses, but the bloodlust was so intense that he lost the boundary between his own consciousness and the desire to kill, to drink in the screams of the dying, to taste the coppery tang of their blood.

It steals men's hearts, drives them like cattle, Ninip had said. *Blood is the pulse of life. You do not realize that it drives you with an even greater force than this heroin.*

Ninip lunged, pushing Schweitzer to the edge of their shared space, and this time he didn't fight, couldn't, staggering and drunk, heedless of the void beyond.

Ninip pressed their opponent to the ground, twisting the claws in his knee, slowly tearing his leg in half. The man cried out now, words that Schweitzer couldn't begin

to try to understand, as his entire being vibrated to the
intoxicating screams. Ninip moved their hand to grab the
man's face, turning it toward them, staring into their enemy's eyes and reveling in the terror written there. And then
the jinn leaned their shared head forward, jaw stretching
wide, and the screaming stopped with a snap.

Light flickered from a small, square window in the side
of the building, light-dark-light, figures moving in front of
an incandescent bulb. More screaming, high and distant.
Women, maybe children.

Ninip lifted their head to look up at it. Schweitzer could
feel the rent meat of the man's throat sliding down their
chest, red threads drooling from the corners of their mouth.
He fought to keep from shivering with pleasure, tried to
drag himself a millimeter back toward their humanity. Ninip
barked something and set off running. Schweitzer felt a hiss
of air as a round streaked past their ear, the fluid shear solid
as another grazed their thigh, and then Ninip was making
them jump again, stretching their hands out over their head,
their legs behind, a diver moving in reverse, up into the sky.
Ninip turned them gracefully, the momentum carrying
their body through the window. He tucked their chin, rolling across the floor, popping up into a crouch, spinning the
forgotten carbine in its sling out of the way of their hands.

The screaming of the goats had been nothing. The tight
quarters of the spartan room reflected high-pitched terror
at them, their amplified hearing sorting through the
sounds, pinning down individual voices. For a moment,
Schweitzer was reminded of the chaos waiting for him in
the storm of souls. The thought was sobering, granting
him a fraction more sense of self. He pushed deeper into
the shared space, grounding himself to resist the jinn.

And realized he would have to stop him right now.

The room held three women, none of them over twenty,
and at least twice as many young children, now dashing
behind the skirts of their mothers, or sisters, or cousins.
The girls' faces were tear-stained, eyes wide with terror.

Schweitzer had seen scenes like this on every op he'd run in this area. The scum whose actions merited a visit from the SEALs always bedded down with women and children, knowing that it was a better defense against American forces than any hardened bunker.

Ninip coiled to spring, Schweitzer tried to shrug off some of his torpidity, forcing himself into control of their shared limbs.

He didn't stand a chance. The jinn's blood was up, the thrill of the hunt singing through him, while Schweitzer was still drunk on the heady sensation of violence and endless power.

The jinn launched them forward, breaking through what little resistance Schweitzer offered as easily as a fist through paper. The girl before them stumbled backward, reaching out to yank on a cheap table, moving it into their path. They tripped over it, claws slicing through air, bare inches from the girl's nose. The rest of the children scattered. The girl backed away, alone, until she hit the wall hard enough for her head to rebound, her eyes huge and red-rimmed, cheeks wet. Schweitzer could smell the salt tang of her tears, it was intoxicating. He could feel phantom saliva in their dry mouth.

Ninip paused to revel in her helpless terror. Schweitzer feebly yanked against the jinn, akin to hauling on a mountain in his drunken state. He watched in open horror as Ninip slowly lifted their shared clawed hand, reached for the girl's neck.

And suddenly she was dancing, red flowers blooming across her chest, spraying across the wall. Schweitzer felt their armor go hard as rounds tore into it, staggering them a few steps forward until they pinned the girl against the wall, looking into her eyes, the terror gone from them now, staring sightlessly into the distance as her death rattle sounded.

Ninip made them toss her corpse aside, whirl to face the new threat.

Once of the boys, Schweitzer guessed he was about nine,

stood holding a smoking assault rifle. It was a cheap Chinese knockoff of the old Russian favorite, long, curving magazine straining the boy's scrawny arm. The sling trailed at his feet. He was awkward, gangly, all scabs and sharp angles, the kind of boy that Patrick would have become if he'd lived.

The thought should have made Schweitzer angry, vengeful, but it didn't. It wouldn't bring his son back. Nothing would. The sadness was sobering, he shook himself and leapt after Ninip, trying anew to drag the jinn aside.

The boy ignored them. His eyes were locked over their shoulder, on the result of his attempt to shoot Schweitzer and Ninip in the back. The body of his sister, or his mother, slid down the wall, leaving a sheet of trailing gore as she went.

"Khoor!" the boy sobbed, dropping the gun as if it had turned into a poisonous snake. *"Khoor!"*

Ninip made them lunge.

Schweitzer's rage galvanized, he leapt at the jinn with everything he had, hauling the presence back from control of their body, stopping them cold. The jinn raged and pushed, but their shared form only shook. He battered against Schweitzer, trying to break free, then suddenly stilled, silent. The silence troubled Schweitzer more than the insensate rage. It meant the jinn was thinking.

Schweitzer reached out to try to read those thoughts as the jinn turned on him, not battering him out of their shared body this time but assaulting his senses with imagery of slaughter. It was a pastiche of horror, a flood of still images ranging across time. Here was a man Ninip had tied to a wagon frame, his executioner working with a curved skinning knife, slowly and deliberately. Here was a woman buried up to her chest, her head slowly deforming into a red slurry beneath a growing mound of stones. The visuals were accompanied by a flood of smells, the sweet scent of corruption, the fetid stink of an opened stomach. And under it all, the now-familiar metal tang of blood.

His earlier inebriation had been nothing. Schweitzer's

senses exploded in response, every wisp and tendril of soul vibrating in rapture. He drowned, swooned; gone were all thoughts of right and wrong, of Patrick and lost youth, of anything other than the paradise he wanted to last forever.

In that moment, Ninip could have killed the world. The jinn could have gored Sarah and Patrick, and Schweitzer would only have looked on in stupor. He thought no more of restraining Ninip than he did of planting turnips.

Ninip grinned, Ninip turned.

And Ninip cut the boy in half.

The horror blossomed in Schweitzer, the sudden realization of what had happened, of what he'd allowed to happen. The child was no threat. Each life he took in the past had been part of operational contingency, the eggs broken to make the omelet that kept his family alive.

But his family was gone. And each life he took carried him further from himself, pushing him by inches to the edge of the slim territory that tethered him to the living world.

In the darkness they shared, Ninip faced him, and smiled, and gave a final push.

Schweitzer tumbled.

The edge of himself slipped and passed, the cold and screaming gripped him.

And then he was drifting, watching his own body fall away, seeing himself from above, standing over the child's corpse, turning to pursue the others. Ninip rose, alone in Schweitzer's skin, reaching a clawed hand behind his armor, pulling out the engraved dog tags that were the last of Schweitzer's wife and child. Even through the growing distance, Schweitzer could see the surface was completely marred with rust, the etched lines that sketched the image of his family now filled in and covered up. With a quick jerk of his hand, Ninip snapped the chain and tossed them aside.

And then Schweitzer was tumbling, drowning in screams, tangled in the hordes of shrieking dead, spinning end over end into the pooling dark.

CHAPTER XX
RUN

Sarah exited the movie theater in a daze. For an hour and a half, she'd bundled Patrick against her chest. All her life, she'd hated mothers who brought their young children to the theater. How the hell had she become one of those people? But it hadn't mattered. Patrick had sat silently, gazing at the seatback in front of him for a solid hour.

Steve's departure had left her alone with a churning stomach and a dreadful certainty. It was as if the attack on her family had split her in two. There were twin Sarah Schweitzers living side by side now, sharing a body. One of them was the Sarah she knew, the one everybody knew. This Sarah was as focused as a scalpel, wary of the institutions to which she belonged, ordering the world around her. This was the Sarah who had been brave enough to pursue a career as an artist, good enough to be successful at it, strong enough to keep with it in the face of patronization masked as concern for her welfare, the tone-deaf questions: *But what will you do for money, dear? You know, during the day?* That Sarah eschewed the metaphysical, rejected religion, superstition. She didn't have time for it, didn't need it.

But the other Sarah, the new Sarah, had one foot firmly rooted in the weird land of shifting shadows that haunted her dreams since she'd first woken in the hospital. This new Sarah's gut spoke to her, not in the language of hunches but in clairvoyant certainty. This new Sarah knew things, was sure she knew things, without ever seeing them. This new Sarah kept the old Sarah awake long into the night, pinned her wrist behind her back and whispered in her ear. *Your husband is alive,* this new Sarah said. *Here is the path that leads to him.*

Your son is dying. If you do not figure out a way to reach him, you will lose him forever.

And now, ever since Steve had walked out the door, *The only real friend you have left is gone. You will never see him again.*

This new Sarah was a stranger to her, and as with all strangers, she wasn't sure if she could trust her. She still allowed herself a moment to sift through the strange sense of dread, of certainty. There was no way she could know that Steve was gone, truly gone, in the way that Jim was, but she was. It was as real to her as the night sky, the solidity of the parking lot under her shoes.

Bullshit. She'd call him, set it right. Put this new Sarah in her place. She reached into her pocket and brought out her cell phone. The screen displayed a missed call and voice mail.

Steve.

The feeling of certainty swamped her again. She shook it away. *Of course it's him. Who else calls you these days?*

She punched through the selection screens to replay her voice mail, conscious of her fingers fumbling across the virtual keyboard, forcing her to type her passcode three times before she got it right. Steve's voice was tinny, hesitant. He told her there'd been a mix-up, that Jim's unit was going to look into whatever caused the mistake. A routine visit, an old shipmate asking for a favor from his colleagues.

So why did he sound so frightened?

"Anyway," he said, "this is getting long, but I'm coming

over. I want to finish our conversation, and not about Jim's ashes this time. We need to talk about us. If you're out, I'll wait. See you in a few."

The message had come about an hour ago, while she was sitting in the theater, trying to pretend her son was interested in what was unfolding on the screen. Steve would be outside her apartment now, waiting in the dark. She swallowed, equal parts relief and apprehension. She was glad to know he was okay, that this strange new Sarah didn't have complete control of her life, but neither was she ready for yet another tense heart-to-heart about where he stood in her life. She didn't have the energy.

She opened the car door, began arraying the Gordian knot of child-seat straps over Patrick's chest and hips. He was already nodding off to sleep, sucking contentedly on the side of his hand. He used to make getting him tied into the car seat a challenge that made her wish she had double the arms. She'd have been grateful for that problem now. But just as there was a new Sarah, there was a new Patrick as well, sullen, silent, withdrawn.

She held the phone to her ear as she started the car, vaguely conscious that this was against the law in Virginia, thumbing the REDIAL. Steve's phone went directly to voice mail without ringing, his old gravelly voice, Steve Chang before the wound and the death of his best friend had cracked his spine. "Chang, speak."

"Steve, it's Sarah. Look, I . . . I don't have the energy for another fight right now. If you want to talk sanely and quietly, then fine. But if you're looking to get laid or have some kind of crying marathon, then it's going to have to wait. You also have to take 'no' for an answer, okay? See you in a few."

He was probably playing games on his phone, or dealing with the intermittent signal that came along with living outside a major city.

She navigated the winding road through the woods back to her apartment, shadows coiling around the tree trunks, pressing as close as they could before the blades of her headlights cut them away. The darkness shifted as it folded over and under the light beams, shifting until the woods around her seemed alive with movement, all of it malevolent, all of it aimed at her. She risked a quick glance over her shoulder. Patrick was pale and still in his car seat, his lips blue in the gloom.

She faced forward, her stomach clenching. *Don't be stupid. He's fine. This is just the other Sarah fucking with you. Don't let her win.*

But she knew she'd lost even as the thought crossed her mind. She put gentle pressure on the brake, slowing the car to a stop on the shoulder, then turned. "You okay, baby?"

Patrick didn't answer, his head had slumped forward. The shadows outside the car ate up the space left by her headlights, until black smoke seemed to waft over the windows.

"Baby?" She didn't like the shrill panic in her voice, couldn't stop it. She undid her seat belt, reached back, lifted her son's chin, gently rocked his shoulders. "Baby? Come on! Wake up!"

He screamed then, kicked feebly at her hands, bawled. Awake all right. He'd been sleeping peacefully and was now scared into consciousness by his panicked mother. Nice going.

She cursed herself and crawled into the backseat, gently rocking him until his crying subsided. "Mommy scared me," he said over and over.

"I know, baby. I'm sorry. Mommy just got scared. That's all. Everything's okay."

But everything was not okay, and Patrick knew that as well as anyone. She swallowed the ball of dread as she slid back into the driver's seat and started the car.

She had to get out of here. She had to find another place to start over. She didn't know what she was doing waiting here, in the same old place around the same old people. There was nothing in Little Creek but memories and what few contacts she'd made in the tiny sliver of an art world that clung on tenaciously in Norfolk. She'd talked to Jim before about the possibility of Austin, or Asheville, or even

New York City. She'd panicked and stewed and grieved long enough. Look at what it was doing to her. She'd tell Steve tonight. Saying the words to someone else would help make them real.

This thought was definitely first Sarah, the one she wanted in charge. It comforted her as she turned the last corner and pulled into the dark parking lot outside her apartment door. She watched the headlights wash over the vinyl siding, clouds of bugs racing for the false moonlight. She waited for them to illuminate Steve, shoulders leaning against her doorjamb, face set in a welcome smile.

Nothing.

She parked, busied herself with unstrapping Patrick, her mind only half on the task, the other half busy with a sweep of the parking lot, looking for Steve's beetle green sedan, gray blue under what little moonlight penetrated the clouds.

Again, nothing. His car wasn't here.

First Sarah was simply disappointed, but second Sarah seized her opportunity, choking her with a combination of a surreal sense of drifting outside herself along with a dreadful certainty that something awful had happened, was about to happen.

Why? Were you looking forward to seeing him after all? Was it just because you didn't want to be alone?

Patrick buried his face against her shoulder as she hoisted him on her hip and carried him inside. He'd said he'd be there, that he'd wait for her. That meant he'd be there. She'd never known Steve to not do a thing he'd said he would.

Maybe he'd just gotten fed up with waiting. Maybe he got a call and had to take care of something else. She dug in her pocket for her cell phone, looked at the screen. No voice mail.

Steve would never have left without leaving a voice mail.

First and second Sarah agreed with a suddenness that churned her stomach. Something was wrong.

She kept it together as she unlocked the door, fighting the urge to rush inside and lock it behind her. She kept the smile on her face as she gave Patrick his bath, read him his story, his favorite picture book about a pig who wanted to be kosher. Patrick asked no questions, only staring at the ceiling, his hand firmly planted in his mouth.

When she finally tucked him in and gently kissed his forehead, he stirred, kissing her back and throwing his arms briefly around her neck. She stifled a sob of relief.

"Mommy?"

"Yes, sweetie?"

"Can Daddy come give me a kiss?" It was the first time he'd spoken of Jim since his silent reaction to the news of his death.

"No, sweetheart. Not tonight." She cursed herself for being unable to make the words definitive, for leaving the door open to the possibility of Daddy's coming later. *But he might come later,* second Sarah said, *because he's still alive, and you know it. Just as you know Steve is dead.*

Patrick only rolled onto his side, wadding the blanket into a ball in front of him.

Sarah returned to the living room and slid open the counter drawer below the spot where the can of Jim's ashes had once stood. A thick folder lay inside, untouched since she'd first put it there. He'd given it to her a week after their honeymoon. *I don't want to scare you or make a big deal about this,* he'd said, his eyes taking on a darkly serious cast, *but you know what I do is dangerous. Everything you need is here. If I go missing. If I get zapped. Put it somewhere where you won't ever see it, but always know where it is.*

So she had. She'd labeled it with red magic marker: YOU WILL NEVER NEED TO OPEN THIS, and of course, during one of Jim's deployments, when she was stuck on a project, she had, just to see what was inside.

Nothing surprising. Power of attorney, a will, account numbers, phone numbers, everything she'd need to make the unthinkable run smoothly. She sorted through the papers, ignoring the irony that she was opening them now, after weeks of failing to deal with Jim's passing, after doing everything but applying for death benefits, transferring funds, making sure that the navy gave her her due.

The paper was right where she remembered, third from the top, a phone number circled, with Jim's crabbed handwriting below. CALL IF YOU CAN'T FIND ME. Above the number where the words SPECIAL WARFARE DEVELOPMENT GROUP—OOD.

She looked at the green ghostlight of the digital clock over the microwave: 9:00 P.M. Nobody would be able to help her now, but hadn't Jim said that his people never slept?

Second Sarah would not be denied. She lifted the phone and dialed the number, listened to the faint ringing. One, three, five. Weren't these people supposed to be alert at all hours? What the hell was . . .

"Watch, Ahmad." Ahmad's voice was stony, hard.

"Hey, Chief." Sarah paused, unsure of what to say next.

"Ms. Schweitzer, it's great to hear from you. We've been worried about you." Ahmad sounded distracted. An engine was throbbing in the background, boots tramping.

"Yeah, well. I just haven't been fit to talk to anyone."

"I understand, ma'am. I don't think I'd want to talk to anyone either."

"Right . . ." She lost her words again, stammered.

"Ma'am, is everything all right? Did you want me to send the chaplain, or did you need . . ."

"Where's Steve?"

"Ma'am?"

"Steve Chang. Where is he? He's not answering his phone."

There was a long pause. The engine coughed and died. Someone cursed.

"He didn't tell you, ma'am?"

"He told me he'd meet me at my apartment. He didn't. That's not like him."

"Well, he can't, ma'am. He's deployed."

"He's . . . what?"

"Petty Officer Chang is responding to a contingency, I

figured he'd have let you know, but maybe there was something in the spin up that precluded that."

"That's . . . that doesn't make any sense. He didn't say anything before that would . . ."

"Ma'am, you've been in this community long enough to know that sometimes things pop off awfully quickly. I'm sure he'll get in touch as soon as he's able. Now, why don't you let me get a chaplai . . ."

"I don't need a fucking chaplain!"

Another pause. "Sarah, I understand you're . . . stressed right now. Tell you what, there's a Starbucks on post. Can I meet you there? We can talk. No Chief Ahmad, just us girls."

The thought of a "just girls" conversation with the hard-as-nails chief actually brought a smile to Sarah's face despite her fear and frustration.

"No, thanks. Just . . . if you hear from him, just tell him I'd like to know that he's okay. Get a message to me."

"Of course, ma'am. He's fine, I'm sure. You just sit tight. Call me at this number if you need anything. I'm on watch all night."

"Okay, thanks."

She hung up the phone and doubled over, the fear becoming a spike twisting in her gut.

Because she knew it was all wrong.

She wasn't one of the old-hat navy wives, women who'd spent decades trailing their husbands from station to station until they practically wore the uniform themselves. But she'd been with Jim long enough to know a thing or two.

First, she'd never heard of a chief getting stuck on watch. It was a duty reserved for junior personnel.

Second, Jim had left suddenly before, but never so suddenly that there'd been no word. There'd always been a short phone call, a cryptic text message or e-mail. Never this.

And lastly, something in Ahmad's tone that she'd never heard before. And those words: *You just sit tight.*

Second Sarah swam to the surface, blooming into a

shimmering warning in the back of her mind, finishing the sentence.

You just sit tight. We're coming to get you.

She raced to the bedroom and snatched up a blanket, threw it over her shoulder before going to retrieve Patrick. He nestled against her shoulder, made a questioning sound in sleepy tones. "We're going to see Auntie Peg. Won't that be fun?"

But Patrick was silent, chasing the quiet corner of sleep that shut out the world. She left him to it as she raced out of the house, not bothering to lock the door, getting into her car, buckling him in, and heading out for the highway as fast as she dared.

The sodium lights of the parking lot receded, taking the shadows with them, leaving all washed in gray. The clouds had pulled back from the sky, and the stars lit everything desert bright, laying down miles between her and what she only now realized she'd considered home.

CHAPTER XXI
REDEMPTION

Schweitzer watched his body shrink in the distance, the cold of the void giving way to numbness, the chorus of screaming sliding through the range from buzz to silence in the space of a few moments. There was peace in it, of no longer having to fight to hold on to himself.

The room, the women and children were all gone. He floated in the darkness, looking down on his animated corpse. He'd never seen himself from this angle before, broad back and strong shoulders straining the STF armor, arms swinging deliberately. *Enjoy it, buddy.* He knew the jinn could not hear him. *Use it in good health.*

Ninip didn't answer, and he noticed that he felt a pang of loneliness at the realization. The jinn might have been a monster, but it was impossible to share such tight quarters and not grow connected.

He spun into the storm of souls, his view of himself tumbling away, replaced with something white and narrow, shutter-flashing by. It was followed by another flash of white, then another. A torso? A leg? They spun past so quickly, he couldn't focus on any single one. It was a film shown in stop-motion, the frames moving just quickly enough to keep him from locking on to any single image. A face, oddly familiar, eyes deep and haunted. A hip. Another arm. The images taunted him, flashes of possibility, a promise of an end to isolation, of other people with whom to connect, if he could only slow down enough to see them.

He could feel the magic all around him, a current like Jackrabbit's but a thousand times more intense. He could feel the force of it bathing him, pushing through him. Was this what had turned Ninip's human soul into a jinn? And if Schweitzer tarried here long enough, would he become the same?

It is the wellspring, Jawid had said. *The source.*

He felt a tugging, a faint but definite current drawing him backward, slowly and unceasingly deeper into the storm. He kicked against it, rolling himself over, catching a glimpse of his body again, this time shrouded by the whirling bodies of the other souls in the chaos around him. He kicked again, felt himself move forward slightly, the current putting on strength like a living thing, petulantly refusing to let him go.

The storm seemed to turn on its side, his body spinning like a fighter jet doing a barrel roll. His body receded to an oblong black dot, covered and uncovered and covered again. His bearings flew away as he tumbled, the current becoming more and more insistent.

Why was he still fighting? What was there to swim for? A place in another fight? That bare room full of blood and the screams of children? The other bodies folded over him, and the first tendrils of shuddering exhaustion began to make themselves known. This was simply a different horror than what he'd just known. There was no reason to resist it. The thing was done.

No. The thing was not done. He kicked harder against the current, straining back toward his body. He cast his mind out toward the world fading in the distance. There was something there, something he had to do. The bodies whirled around him, the current spun him, the screams buzzed in his ears, addling his brain. He couldn't focus. He drifted deeper, battered more incessantly by the other souls whirling past him, through him.

At last, even the black speck that was his body vanished, and he turned away, spinning deeper into the morass. A knee coursed past, followed by an earlobe, torn where some jewelry had been savaged out. A disembodied hand, long fingernails cracked and blackened. A throat, the hint of an Adam's apple bobbing. A face, something stuck over one eyelid. The back of a knee . . .

Schweitzer spun, trying to turn back to the face, to find it in the spinning throng. Something had been stuck to its eye, something that wasn't part of its body. He didn't know much about the rules that governed this haunted expanse, but he hadn't seen anything that wasn't a body part in all the time he'd looked on it. The souls lost here carried nothing but their bodies, no jewelry, no clothing.

He grasped, swam, clawed his way through the throng. The screaming intensified, as if the storm sought to drown out his thoughts. The sounds began to push deeper, until they crystallized as the shreds of thoughts filling his own mind, threatening to pull him away from himself.

I'm sorry I'm sorry I'm sorry
Why did I do that so stupid
Oh father think kindly of me
That yellow bastard I can't believe he got the drop on me

Schweitzer gritted his teeth, trying to hold to his own consciousness, to pick it out from all the others. The spinning mass of limbs stretched out in all directions now, endless. He'd probably imagined that spot over that eye. Even if he hadn't, he'd never find it.

He rolled over onto his back, was it his back? All sense of direction was lost to him now.

And there it was again.

It was clear to him now, a tiny spot of crimson in the midst of the whirling chaos. Set against the semiopaque pallor of the whirling dead, it glowed like a star. It moved counter to the invisible currents that crossed and recrossed, whipping the souls along. Where the dead cascaded and eddied, this thing slowly swayed, gently falling, a late-spring leaf finally succumbing to the rigors of autumn.

A rose petal.

And there, cutting through the sound and the tumult, a gentle scent, slight but unmistakable, the soft rosewater that meant wife and love and home.

The voices pressed into his mind, the invisible wind and current dragged his spirit, but nothing assailed his smell. The trail was stark, definite.

It could be followed.

He knew it led somewhere important, back to a thing he'd left undone. He tried to focus. He'd been good at focusing once, before the legion of voices had crowded into his mind, passing themselves through him, drowning out his own thoughts. But the smell was enough. He didn't remember what it was for anymore, but it was different, something other than the chaos around him. He latched onto it, kicked off.

The current bit hungrily into him, the tugging now shifting into something akin to pain, as if it were a thinking force, angry at the thought of losing him. He clung to the smell, a rope now, a lifeline, drove himself along it inch by agonizing inch. The storm continued unchanged, the bodies and faces flashing before him, his mind full of the regrets and shock of last moments spanning centuries. And then the chaos thinned, the screaming receded, and he could think again.

There, far distant, was that speck he knew was his body, growing steadily. The smell had gone, but he no longer needed it. He had the bit in his teeth now, each moment bringing him closer to himself, the memories of who he was. Sarah and Patrick and Peter and Chief and his first kiss and his first day of school and on and on and on. All the hard-won skill from Coronado. How to focus, how to fight.

With a final shout, he broke free, threw himself down the intervening distance, rocketed across the void, scrabbling along the edges of himself, feeling the jinn's presence filling the space beyond.

Ninip was drunk on carnage, bent on slaughter and unready for Schweitzer's bulling himself back inside, stretching himself into a small pocket of the darkness, spreading out, pushing against the jinn, racing up to their shared eyes, looking through them once again.

What felt like eons had been a fraction of a second. Their shared body still stood over the split remains of the boy, the assault rifle at his side, tendrils of gray smoke still curling up from the barrel. The screams of the void were once again replaced by the screams of the women and children, racing out through the open door, Ninip even now turning to go after them.

Schweitzer instantly felt the drunkenness, the addictive high of the jinn's feral hunger. But the chill of the void was still in him, the echo of the shrieking souls still ringing in his ears, the smell of Sarah's perfume still a hint in his memory. He still felt the magic tingling in the fibers of his soul.

One of the girls bolted the wrong way, racing away from the door, toward the open window. Ninip twitched out a clawed hand to intercept her, and Schweitzer hauled it back, pinning their arm flat against their side. The jinn noticed him now, screamed, pushed against him, but Schweitzer was dug in. Ninip abandoned his efforts and turned back to the girl as she ran to the window and threw herself out.

Schweitzer let Ninip have rein then, knowing the jinn would follow.

But not before he forced them to reach out a hand and retrieve the dog tags from where they lay on one of the few remaining dry spots on the floor. He thrust them back behind the armor's breastplate, felt them slide down his chest to lodge behind the tight fit of his web belt. It would have to do.

They dove through the window, the girl already falling, arms waving madly, eyes closed. She hit the ground a moment before them, her shattering bones audible through the slim envelope of flesh around them.

They landed beside her in a deep crouch. Ninip saw her dead, looked up for other prey. A bullet sang through the air, kicked up a pocket of dirt beside them, and the jinn was off. Bullets meant living people and the predator's high the jinn sought.

The gate to the compound was open, a small knot of men running through it. Four in the middle were clustered tightly around another figure, herding him along. Schweitzer had seen those tactics from dedicated Protective Security Details throughout his career. Hardened men, willing to give their lives to protect their charge.

Nightshade.

Eyes on target, Schweitzer sent to Jawid, *engaging,* then Ninip had them up and running.

One of the figures detached himself from the column, steady and calm. He stopped, raised his weapon, and took careful aim.

The round caught Schweitzer and Ninip in the throat, striking just an inch above the collar of the armor. Schweitzer felt the round punch through the hollow of their throat, through the dead remains of their esophagus and larynx, piercing the vertebrae beyond.

It was an incredible shot, one Schweitzer would have been proud of. In a world that made sense, Schweitzer would go down and the shooter's skill, training, and dedication would have been rewarded.

But Eldredge had said it best: The world was changing. Schweitzer and Ninip reached the shooter in three strides and bit his head off.

Two rounds thudded into their armor, both center mass, knocking them back a couple of paces, the fluid cells going hard and heavy from the impact. They needed to lower their profile. Schweitzer shot Ninip an image of a loping gait to the target, and Ninip obliged, all too happy to revert to his preferred means of getting to the fight.

Ninip galloped them forward on their haunches and knuckles, snarling now, imitating Schweitzer's bellows dance when he tried to speak. The battle cry went out internally first, as Ninip channeled it up their shared windpipe. *Alalai! Ashtar!* But the punctured larynx let the air out before the sounds could be shaped, so Ninip's words twisted into wheezing barks, a coughing shout.

Then they were through the compound's gate, out among the neat rows of parked cars, starlight dappling dented hoods, piles of spare tires and junked parts piled on clumps of tough grass that defied the dry soil.

The group splintered.

Schweitzer knew immediately that this was rehearsed. This was not a mad scramble, it was a scripted retreat, the wings of the escort flanking out to put them in enfilade, the High Value Target pushing on while his PSD dropped back one by one to delay the pursuit.

Schweitzer flashed the images to Ninip, showing him the tactics classes he'd learned in SQT, the shoothouse scenarios where mistakes like this got a team wiped out in less than a minute.

But the jinn had the bit in his teeth. He charged them on, lunging for the first of the escorts, while Schweitzer stretched their peripheral vision, trying to track all the contacts at once. Two of them were digging in the open bay of a golf cart to his right, pulling a tarp aside. Schweitzer didn't like the look of that, but Ninip was already on, the line of sight broken, and Schweitzer was forced to look forward again as they snatched up a man who fired uselessly over his shoulder and brought him down on their knee with enough force to snap his spine.

Ninip had them toss the body aside, as Nightshade threw open the door of a jeep and dove inside.

And then the world exploded.

He'd been blown up before, and not far from here, knocked off the top of an MRAP on one of the few godforsaken lanes of broken stone in this part of the world laid smoothly enough to be called a road. He'd tumbled through the air, end over end, his ears ringing, his vision gone white, the stars exploding in his eyes and his head too thick and too bright to allow him to get his situational awareness back. If not for his teammates, he would have died.

Schweitzer flew now, but there was no ringing, no stars. His vision was clear. Their right side was burning, the armor coated with gasoline from the car struck by the explosive round. Spalling glass and metal fragments had punched through the liquid cells too fast for them to react, peppering their legs, hand, the side of their head. Were he living, the agony alone would have sent him spiraling into shock, followed closely by death.

But as it was, Schweitzer rolled them into the momentum of the blast, letting their body glide through the air, landing roughly on their stomach, the shock spreading out across their body. Some ribs snapped, he could feel cracks in their cervical vertebrae where they'd been weakened by the bullet, but that wouldn't impair their functionality. The rest of the bones, the ones they needed to keep moving, held. Ninip had them up again in an instant.

The escort was good. Schweitzer could see the shooter kneeling alongside the golf cart, keeping his eyes on the sights of the RPG, his companion already fitting another rocket in place. Schweitzer knew they couldn't cover the distance in time, that their body, even charged by magic, would be shattered by the explosive charge, the copper lining inverting, melting into a metal carrot that would be propelled through them at over a klick a second, the hypersonic speed alone grinding him to powder.

He pressed them down, trying to force their shared body flat on the ground, knowing it would be futile, that they'd be incinerated regardless. The irony wasn't lost on him, he'd fought his way back into his body from the void, only to enjoy his body for a few brief moments before losing it again.

Ninip saved them. The jinn resisted Schweitzer's efforts with a sudden ferocity, his contempt at the thought of crawling on his belly breaking through Schweitzer's

defenses, smacking him aside. The jinn seized control of
their arms and grabbed the back bumper of the jeep as the
engine roared into life and the tires began to spin, scattering dust as they sought traction on the dry ground.

Ninip slammed their chest up against the vehicle,
adjusted their grip and torqued their waist. Schweitzer
caught the RPG man out of his peripheral vision, lowering
the weapon, unwilling to risk hitting his master, crab stepping sideways to get a clear shot. From his other eye, Schweitzer saw Nightshade lean out of the driver's side
window, waving a pistol. Ninip locked their back muscles
and heaved as the tires finally found purchase and dug in.

Schweitzer felt their shared shoulders and back, the
dead muscle snapping tight across the bone. His old corpse
began to tremble, and he felt certain that they would snap
their spine in two and be left sprawled in the dust while the
jeep sped away.

But the tires spun, clicked to a stop, spun again. Schweitzer felt the jeep's weight shift. Nightshade screamed.

Even with the magic, they didn't have the strength to
throw the car through the air. It tumbled along its axis,
rolling and bouncing, tires still spinning ineffectually,
reaching for a surface continuously snatched away. The
man had enough time to drop the RPG and scream before
the car landed on him, knocking his companion sprawling,
crushing him flat. Ninip leapt the remaining distance,
vaulting over the smoking wreck of the jeep, ignoring the
dead RPG man, landing on his stunned companion, driving
their shared knee into the man's stomach with such force
that the wall of the abdominals gave way, his spine crunching against their patella. The man was unconscious, cheat-
ing Ninip of his sport, and the jinn snarled, rising, looking
for the next victim.

No one. The compound was suddenly and eerily silent,
the wind still, even the normal night sounds of animals
and insects faint and distant. Ninip sniffed the air, straining their augmented ears for a tremor that would indicate

more human prey. Schweitzer used the distraction to seize control, turning them back to the jeep.

Target down, Schweitzer sent to Jawid. *Jackpot Nightshade.*

Well done. Make sure he is dead, then get out of there.

The jeep lay on its side, the windows shattered, one wheel still spinning slowly. Schweitzer could smell the pungent odor of gasoline, was painfully conscious of the nearness of the still-smoldering patches left by the last RPG blast. But he let Ninip clamber them up the jeep's side, sticking their shared head into the driver's side opening, reaching in to . . .

Nightshade was alive.

The man sagged in his seat belt, head lolling, blood trickling from the corner of his mouth. His eyes were opening, unseeing, his breathing coming in hitching gasps. Schweitzer saw a long, jagged shard of glass emerging from his forearm. The fluttering eyes turned, took in Schweitzer and Ninip, widened. Nightshade began to moan, trying to shrink away, held fast by the nylon of the seat belt.

Ninip grinned, flexed their clawed hand, and cocked it back.

Schweitzer raced forward, grabbed the limb, forced it down. Ninip pushed back, first halfheartedly, then with sudden violence when he didn't break through. He began to pulse images to Schweitzer again, the same carnage-joy that had drowned him when Ninip had slaughtered the boy.

But Schweitzer's head was clearer now. The chill of the void was still with him, the trail he'd followed home still lingering. He felt the hunger, responded to it, but with distance now, an itch he could bear not to scratch, knowing it would speed the healing.

Schweitzer hung on, and the arm didn't move. *We take him in.*

Those are not our orders! We were sent here to destroy him!

He's alive. That's intel. Orders change.

Intel? Ninip raged. *We are not spies! We are a god of war.*

And Schweitzer paused because he knew Ninip was right. He didn't care about intel, neither did Eldredge. Whatever intel the Gemini Cell had on Nightshade had already convinced them to take him out, just as it had convinced them to send Schweitzer and Ninip after Jackrabbit. Schweitzer and Ninip hadn't been sent in to gather information, they'd been sent in to wreak havoc. They could do the damage of an army, leaving no blood of their own to analyze, no helicopter wreckage or tire tracks to study, no risk of blowing the op and getting captured, appearing later to babble on the evening news. An army come and gone in a puff of smoke, leaving carnage in its wake, a void of questions answered by the ferment of the human mind: rumors and wild speculation, talk of ghosts, or aliens, or secret weapons. The fog of war, panicked, dread-addled thinking that made sure the truth was never known.

Schweitzer didn't want intel. What Schweitzer wanted, dearly and desperately, was to cling to what was left of himself, what tiny fragments were free of the jinn and the magic and the Gemini Cell. His life was shattered into shards so tiny, they could be confused for grains of sand. But the grains were all he had left. Here was one called "decency" and another called "standing up for people weaker than you" and another called "integrity." Here was the grain of dogged persistence that had seen him through BUD/S and SQT. There was the grain of shutting up, listening, and not offering solutions when Sarah just needed to talk. Here was the grain of patience when Patrick stepped on his balls and put his fingers up his nose.

And there, jumbled up with them, was the grain of not killing the defenseless. Not when it wouldn't compromise the mission. Not when it wasn't necessary.

It wasn't about intel. It was about identity. It was about survival.

And whatever it was about, it funneled through Schweitzer, filling him with urgency and determination, pouring what he had into that right arm, keeping it still, then slowly forcing it down. The jinn screamed and pushed, and Schweitzer ignored him, the shouts fading to a buzz, much as they had in the storm of souls. He shouldered the jinn aside, expanded his room in their shared darkness, and Ninip went quiet, struggling weakly against him as he reached out with their shared hand, sliced their claws along the nylon strap of the seat belt, cutting through it, catching Nightshade as he fell into the recesses of the jeep, lifting him out and slinging him over a shoulder. The man kicked weakly, then his eyes fluttered shut, and his head lolled along Schweitzer and Ninip's back. If not for the faint and uneven rhythm of his breathing, Schweitzer would have thought Nightshade was dead.

I have the target, he sent to Jawid. *Proceeding to exfil point.*

Target is actioned? Jawid sent back. *Confirm.*

Negative, Schweitzer responded, Ninip's rage suddenly cool and silent. *I'm bringing him in.*

CHAPTER XXII
EXFIL

Schweitzer and Ninip walked the rest of the way to the extraction point. Jawid projected himself into Schweitzer's mind, trying to share the view through his eyes. Ninip snatched weakly at the Sorcerer, and Schweitzer pushed him the rest of the way out. *What the hell are you doing?*

We can't see your tracker.

Schweitzer touched the back of his neck and felt something crunching just beneath the surface. He sliced a small flap with the tip of his claw, felt the small cylinder there mostly melted, crisped wiring peeking out from the cracked, ruggedized plastic. *Got a little cooked back there. It's dead.*

Where are you? Jawid asked.

On my way. Inbound.

Stop, Jawid said, his voice taking on the wooden tone that told him he was translating someone else's words. *You may be followed.*

Schweitzer thought of the trail of human wreckage Ninip had left on their way to Nightshade. *Nobody is following anyone. Tell the bird to sit tight.*

He did a quick check of their body as he walked, feeling for breaks in the bones, tears in the muscle, but the structure seemed whole. There was no danger of their failing to make the long walk home or to take care of any opposition they might meet along the way. Nightshade flopped on their shoulder like a bundle of rope. Schweitzer again dialed down through the spectrum of sounds until he caught the small, ragged sound of Nightshade's breathing.

Ninip coiled in a corner of their shared internal space, sullen, silent, much as he had been after Schweitzer had intervened to save the guard outside his cell.

The fuck's your problem? Schweitzer asked him. *Didn't get your fill of killing back there?*

You bring that bag of rags back home like a bride stolen from the enemy camp, the jinn said. *Will you have us bugger him next?*

After Schweitzer had saved the guard back in the States, the jinn's voice had sounded weaker, smaller, a faint vibrato echoing to him through a tunnel's length. The same effect was back but twice as pronounced.

Schweitzer reached out, pushed against the jinn experimentally.

Ninip gave way, fluttering madly as Schweitzer moved him toward the edge of their body, the void nipping at him. The jinn was a moth in a jar, gossamer wings flapping in panic, powerless to affect the shell around him.

What's the matter there, big guy? You spent? Schweitzer gave another experimental push, and the jinn yielded before him, an incoherent growl rising from him, faint and tinny.

Schweitzer reached inward again, feeling their muscles. Their shared limbs felt heavier, much of the magical strength he'd taken for granted leached from them. The battered bones ground together along the fissures, the tears in their flesh ripping wider as motion and chafing pulled at them. With Ninip's diminishment, their power ebbed.

Perhaps the jinn was spent, perhaps the killing had sated him and Ninip had no energy left to hang on to his position inside Schweitzer's corpse. But that didn't make sense. Ninip had been stronger after they'd taken Jackrabbit, and had killed no one when they saved the guard. He'd slumped, sulking, while Schweitzer had pulled the dog tags from inside their armor and . . .

Schweitzer almost dropped Nightshade as he thrust their hand behind the breastplate of their armor, still slick from where the fluid had leaked out of the punctured cells. He could feel Ninip stir, but it was a cringing motion, the jinn making no move to stop him as he reached their hand down, fumbling for the dog tags, panicking at first when he could not find them, then finally extracting them from just above their useless prick, pulling them out and holding them in front of their face.

The lines were as clear as the day they had first been etched. Sarah smiled at him, the love and joy shining in her eyes, visible in the lift of her cheeks. Patrick was open-mouthed, babbling some nonsense stream that meant, "I am happy, and I love you."

There was no oxidation at work here, only magic.

Eldredge's words returned to him, the solemn respect in his voice after he'd seen what had taken Schweitzer through the glass of his cell and spilling out into the corridor beyond. *You did a good thing, Jim.*

Schweitzer glanced over at Nightshade, marked for death but still breathing.

A good thing, indeed.

Do not, Ninip said.

The push wasn't experimental this time, Schweitzer gave the jinn a sharp shove, pressing him steadily toward the edge of the space they shared.

Do not! Ninip shrieked.

Why the hell not? You did it to me. It's what you were after all along. You want the whole thing, don't you? I float in the void while you walk around in what's left of my skin. Game's changed, asshole. Time to vacate.

He redoubled his efforts, pushing Ninip to the brink, where the jinn dug in fast. Schweitzer could feel him hold-

ing on, as if his limbs splayed out over a doorframe, his
body dangling over the space beyond. The jinn didn't have
much strength, but he was ancient and steeped in magic, he
could hold.

Get out! Schweitzer shouted. *Go twist in the storm, you
fucking devil.*

You will go with me, Ninip said. *It is my being that ani-
mates your body. My magic that makes us run and fight and
leap as ten men. Without me, you drop, and this shell rots.
Without me, there is only the storm. You may hate me, but
you need me. You need me if you want to go on.*

Schweitzer felt the jinn's magical current washing
through them, had felt it engage to keep the muscles in
their back from tearing as they rolled the jeep. He'd felt it
when they ran and jumped the wall. He'd felt it when his
vision and hearing shifted spectrums.

He felt it now, ebbing faster, weakness flooding them as
Ninip's hold on their shared body slipped with each shove
Schweitzer gave him. Schweitzer paused.

Ninip crept forward, moving into the shred of space
that Schweitzer gave up when he'd ceased to push. He
sounded relieved. *You are the body. I am the magic that
keeps it moving. You need me.*

Schweitzer had full control of the body now. He moved
an arm, opening and closing the hand, wiggling the fingers
before closing them again into a tight fist. The jinn made
no move to stop him, couldn't have if he'd tried. Schweitzer
tuned their hearing, moving past Nightshade's breathing
and out over the hardscrabble plain to where the sounds of
animals were beginning to return again.

Everything still worked, for now.

But that didn't mean that it would continue to once
Ninip was gone.

Jawid. Schweitzer reached out for the Sorcerer. His voice
was stronger now, his sense of the pathway that linked them
more acute. He had fumbled for it before, but it came clearer
now, a road as vivid and sharp as the one that had led him
out of the soul storm before.

Jawid.

I am here. The Sorcerer sounded shocked. Schweitzer could feel his surprise funneling down the channel that connected them.

Do I need Ninip?

What?

Do I need him? Without him, what happens to me?

The jinn began babbling, reaching out to the channel to Jawid, but Schweitzer slapped him down, sending him sprawling back into his corner. *Do I need him? What happens if it's just me in here?*

Silence. Schweitzer could feel Jawid still in contact, but the Sorcerer didn't answer. He was thinking, maybe conferring with Eldredge, the others in the command center.

At last he came back, his voice wooden. *You die,* he said. *The great death. The last one.*

Schweitzer turned back to Ninip. *You will never avenge your family,* the jinn said. *You will be quit of this world forever.*

It's almost worth it, Schweitzer said, pushing against the jinn again, eliciting a squeal of terrified rage. *Almost.*

He kept the jinn there, a part of him pressed against him, keeping him hemmed into a tiny sliver of the darkness they shared. He trotted the rest of the way back to the helo, reveling in the feeling of control, Nightshade gently bumping against his back. His body was weaker, but it responded solely to him, much as it had in life. The spray of stars glowed overhead, the crunch of his boots on the hardpack sounded in his ears, the wind played over his gray skin.

It's a beautiful night, he sent to Jawid.

He could feel the Sorcerer's surprise and confusion. *What?*

I said, it's a beautiful night. Are you outside right now? Can you see it?

Yes, Jawid answered after a long pause. *There are many stars.*

You're alive, Jawid, Schweitzer sent. *Don't underesti-*

mate what that's worth. You look up at those stars, and you remember that.

He looked up at the stars himself as he went. It was a taste of the world as he had known it, without Ninip's poison filter hovering halfway over the experience. He had all of the sensation he wanted, without the pain or fatigue, his body reporting the injuries he'd sustained from the round through his throat, the RPG blast that had tossed him like a toy, but all of it vented, filtered, powerless to affect him. It was the world without pain, and it was glorious.

The jinn was still a splinter in his mind, hanging on the edge of his experience, a reminder of death and hell. It kept Schweitzer from truly thrilling in the world about him, a loose tether, but one he could still feel.

Small price to pay for second chances. Schweitzer shifted his grip, trying to ease the bouncing of his shoulder against Nightshade's broken bones. He wasn't certain what it was that gave him command over Ninip, but he knew it was tied to who he was. The more he asserted his own self in thought and action, the more he became himself in the physical world. Or was it selflessness? He'd saved two lives. Each one had brought the jinn low, had made him the master of their shared form.

Is that how it works? he asked the jinn. *You take lives to rule, and I save them? Is it just two sides of a coin? It can't be that easy.*

The jinn only slouched in the slice of their shared space that remained to him. Schweitzer could see the presence, sullen, an outline in his mind: drooping chin, arms hugged around a narrow torso, eyes shut tight. *I do not know how it works,* Ninip said, and the agony in his voice spoke of honesty. *We fight for the body, it is true, but we can find balance. We will. You will teach me your footman's ways, your "professional" war. I will teach you valor and nobility, our place at the head of all things. Together, we will make a mighty work and . . .*

There is no mighty work together, Schweitzer cut him off. *There is you making with the magic and me letting you*

*stay for as long as you do. There's you fucking with me
and me punting you into the soul storm for your trouble.*

We are joined, the jinn said. *There is no life without me.
If you push me out, you follow. The Sorcerer himself has
told you.*

Schweitzer leaned close, letting his presence hover over
the jinn's, filling up all but a fraction of the darkness they
shared. *Try me,* he said. *See if I'm bluffing. I'm fucking
begging you.*

Ninip looked at him now, eyes yellow slits in the darkness that flashed as he dipped his spiritual head.

Schweitzer turned his focus back to the outside world.
He changed his grip to cradle Nightshade, head lolling
against his wrist, the rest of the way back to the helo. He
watched the bearded face, skin lined from hard use, cracking at the corners of the mouth. He wondered what he'd
done to merit a visit from the monster that was Schweitzer
and Ninip. Why was he smuggling those bodies? Had it been
like Jackrabbit? Was it a deal gone sour? A recalcitrant
who'd refused to play ball? What was his real name? In
life, Schweitzer's job had never been to ask questions. He
was a moving weapon. The navy pointed him at a problem
and pulled the trigger.

But he felt his single-minded command of his limbs for
the first time since he'd died, looked at Nightshade's face,
looking almost as if the man slept, and realized that he had
to ask the questions now. The alternative crouched in the
darkness beside him, reduced but present, alert and ready
for his moment.

More, he had to have answers that mattered, had to weigh
them himself. He sniffed the rosewater in the air, stronger
than ever, and thought of Sarah. *The whole world told you
who to be,* Schweitzer thought. *Wife, mother, homemaker.
You gave them the finger, took what you wanted, and made
something better than they'd ever imagined.*

He had to be like Sarah, whose artistry had shaped his
own. Death had only raised the bar. He had to be better.

He saw the pickets long before they saw him. They lay

on their bellies, covered by dried bushes, heaps of rubble and tumbleweeds masking the barrels of their .50 caliber long guns. Their spotters crouched beside them, eyes fixed to their field glasses, motionless as stones. Schweitzer could hear the buzzing of the drone miles above him. Perhaps it had his position now, was relaying it to the spotters. Perhaps it was still searching for him, pinging his tracker uselessly.

The helo was a lump behind them, rotors folded and covered with camouflage netting. He could sense Jawid now, the spicy musk of his magic rising as Schweitzer approached. Schweitzer wondered if the pickets would fire on him, decided that his utter lack of stealth would put them as much at ease as men that vigilant ever were.

We see you, Jawid sent when Schweitzer was practically on top of them. Had his own faculties been so weak in life? Could an enemy have gotten so close to him without being spotted? He remembered the lopsided fight on the tanker, Chang going down, his breathing as rough and shallow as Nightshade's. Maybe he had gotten so used to fighting as a dead man, he'd forgotten what it had been to fight as a live one.

You see me? I thought I told you to look at the stars? Schweitzer sent back to him.

He felt the pickets' fear as the men rose, guns at the low ready, and advanced to him, postures so alert he thought they might fire their weapons if he so much as sneezed. He didn't envy them their uncertainty, their hyperconscious mortality. It was a thing about life he would never miss.

He stepped out of the shadows, the starlight washed over his bare face, and the men froze, horror and the resulting tangled decision plain in the trembling muzzles of their weapons.

His helmet, he remembered with a start. It was gone.

Jawid, Schweitzer sent, *you might want to call off your dogs before they punch more holes in me.*

Ninip made a weak flail toward attacking them, easily slapped aside. For a moment, Schweitzer saw himself as they must see him, stepping out from the shadows and laid plain in the starlight, ragged wound of a throat, horror of a face, contorted and stretched into a mockery of their own.

Black pits, balls of silver flame in their depths.

Even hard operators were human. This wasn't a sight they'd been trained to process.

They were taught as he had been: that it was better to be judged by twelve than carried by eight. When in doubt, shoot.

Schweitzer lifted Nightshade's body toward them, a peace offering. The gun muzzles rose.

McIntyre jogged out of the darkness behind them. "Stand down, stand down."

He stopped short at the sight of Schweitzer's face. "Jesus fucking Christ."

Schweitzer tried to answer him, even a monosyllabic word of assurance, but his larynx was flayed now, and the wind whistled hollow from his throat, the sound of a tea-kettle on low boil.

He knelt instead, laying Nightshade down as gently as he could, standing as Jawid and Eldredge joined them along with three more Americans in Pakistani uniforms. He watched Eldredge's expression harden as he took in the horror on the operators' faces, pointed an emphatic finger at the man lying in the dirt.

"Why the hell is this man alive?" McIntyre asked, indicating Nightshade.

"That is a very good question," Eldredge added, looking meaningfully at Jawid.

Tell Eldredge my throat is shot out. I can't talk.

Jawid only pointed.

"Can't talk, eh?" Eldredge asked. "Okay." He turned to McIntyre. "Sergeant Major, I'm afraid you've just become privy to a special access program that is going to require some additional discretion on the part of your people."

McIntyre shook his head with the resigned disgust that Schweitzer had seen on Ahmad every time she shut out a contingency, focusing on the core tasks needed to get a job done. "I figured. That doesn't change the fact that your man was supposed to push a button on this bitch. Instead, he is lying in front of me engaging in a repugnant behavior that looks suspiciously like breathing."

Eldredge smiled, turned to Schweitzer. "The sergeant major would like to know why you elected to capture the target you were sent to kill."

Tell him I got him intel, Schweitzer sent to Jawid.

"Intelligence," the Sorcerer said, his eyes never leaving Schweitzer, his face taut with shock.

"This fucker isn't going to talk"—McIntyre gestured at Nightshade—"and we already know anything he'd tell us. We needed him put down."

So, put him down, then, Schweitzer sent to Jawid.

"He says then you should shoot him," the Sorcerer translated.

McIntyre looked at Schweitzer, his eyes appraising now. "You are one ugly motherfucker."

Schweitzer reached down and grabbed the soft webbing between the liquid cells that covered his crotch, squeezed.

Eldredge laughed, and McIntyre threw up his hands. "This is your problem, Eldredge," he said, heading back to the helo. "You handle it."

Eldredge stepped close, traced his fingers along the ragged edge of the hole in Schweitzer's neck. "This is going to take some work to patch up. Don't think we'll be able to get your speech back either, not all the way."

That's fine, Schweitzer sent to Jawid. *It's not like any of you are particularly stimulating conversationalists.*

Jawid translated, and Eldredge laughed again. "You're amazing, Jim. In all my time on this program, I have never seen one of our Operators so . . . so human."

What were the rest of them like?

Eldredge responded to Schweitzer, answering Jawid's question. "The rest of them were . . . the more recently deceased side of the pairing was weaker. The jinn had more control."

All SEALs?

"Not all, but all of them pipe hitters like you. A few of them only lasted minutes before the jinn won out."

Schweitzer turned to Ninip. *You hear that, buddy? This time, the good guys win.*

Jawid translated, and Schweitzer waved his hands.

"You're talking to Ninip." Eldredge nodded. "I know. How's he . . . handling all this?"

He's unhappy, but we seem to have reached an understanding.

Eldredge stepped back, apparently satisfied with his inspection of Schweitzer's wound. "So, it's you who wins out. That's never happened before."

What do I win?

Eldredge paused, shrugged. "You get to go on. That's something isn't it?"

It's not a whole lot. Who is this guy? Why did you send me to kill him?

"We didn't send you. We sent a new entity that is a combination of you and Ninip. And the jinn was the only part who did his job."

Not good enough.

"And what if I don't tell you?"

Maybe I'll fucking kill you. Maybe I'll head back to the FOB and kill everyone in it. Ninip would like that. Indeed, the jinn stirred at the words. Jawid's eyes widened at that. He took a step backward, the fear scent thickening.

Eldredge only snorted. "You're not going to do that, Jim."

How the hell do you know? The question was genuine, Schweitzer's curiosity piqued by the fact that Eldredge was absolutely right.

"Because you broke into a hallway and faced down a flamethrower to save a complete stranger. Because you spared this scumbag even when you'd been expressly ordered to kill him. Because you're a killing machine who wants to read books and visit his family's grave.

"Because you're a good guy, Jim. And somehow, that makes you different. Somehow, that makes you stronger. It may make you the most powerful asset this program has ever produced.

"I have to get you back to the US yesterday. We're out of here just as soon as I make sure this particular band of brothers understands the importance of keeping their fucking mouths shut."

Why?

"You're something new," Eldredge said. "I have to understand why."

CHAPTER XXIII
ON THE LAM

The miles disappeared beneath spinning tires. The landscape grew steadily more rural as Sarah angled northwest, her GPS instructed to avoid highways at all cost. She flicked her eyes to it as much as she dared, alternating glances between the tiny screen, the road, and the rearview mirror, with its view of Patrick, sleeping fitfully in the backseat.

She used to love driving, letting her subconscious navigate the roads, the gentle vibration of the motor massaging her, her conscious mind free to think and plan, to draw sketches in her brain that she would later commit to paper. Now she focused entirely on the task at hand, ensuring she wasn't followed, that where she was headed wasn't obvious.

Jim had taught her the basics of countersurveillance, how to make and shake tails, more as a fun exercise than because of any real need, and now she was grateful. She kept to five miles over the speed limit, generally meandering toward her goal, doubling back from time to time. The trick was to obscure her route without seeming like she was obscuring her route. Jim had told her that it was a balancing act that you could never know if you had gotten

right. She stopped once to refill her tank, being sure to pay
with cash. She always kept a hundred-dollar bill Scotch-
taped to the back of her library card for emergencies. Jim
had teased her about it, saying it was a waste of money, but
again, she was glad of it now. That money should see her to
Peg's. Just barely, but enough.

She picked up her cell phone to call her sister, then
dropped it onto the seat beside her. A moment later she
picked it up and turned it off, set it down. A moment after
that she picked it up again, pulled the battery out, stuffed it
all in the glove compartment. She didn't know if she could
be tracked by her phone, but it stood to reason that she could.
Better not to risk it. Peg would be surprised but pleased to
see her.

You're being paranoid, she thought. *You have no reason
to believe you're being targeted.* But she thought of
Ahmad's cool tone, of her insistence that they meet. Her gut
churned with terror, her blood racing as if the cells themselves were crying out in warning. They had killed Steve.
They were going to kill her, too. She knew it in her bones.

Just like she knew Jim was alive.

The certainty shook her, as concrete as the metal frame
of the car around her, as the pressure of the dark sky. Jim
was alive. He was alive, and he was searching for her.

My God. I am going crazy.

Fine. If she was crazy, then she was crazy. It was her they
wanted. Patrick was too little to say anything to anyone and
be believed. She would leave him with Peg, then . . . and
then she had no idea. Get a tent, a pack, flee into the forests
of West Virginia. Live on trail mix until she figured everything out. It was a terrible idea, but she didn't have any others just now.

She glanced in the rearview at Patrick again, saw the
glowing bands from the lights along the highway striping
his pale cheeks. Rage surged in her. *They won't hurt him. I
won't let them.* She recalled the canvas-cutting knife twisting in her hands as she plunged it into the man's throat, the
stubby wooden handle suddenly slick with his blood. She

would get a gun. Jim had taken her shooting, ensured she
knew her way around the full range of options, short and
long, shotguns and carbines and high-caliber pistols. They
might be SEALs, killers of long experience with the force
of authority and technology that could make a man into
something more.

But she was a mother protecting her son. She would
take at least one of them with her.

The night stretched on, and she calmed, the rhythm of
the road giving her some small measure of peace. And
with it came the first gentle touches of fatigue. The divid-
ing lines striped her vision, forming a blinking, hypnotic
pattern that lulled and distracted. After another hour she
found her eyelids growing heavy. She needed to stop. She
needed to sleep, if only for a few hours.

She couldn't use a hotel. They would need ID, a credit
card; they would be suspicious of a cash payment. Hadn't
Homeland Security instituted some kind of requirement?
She was too tired to remember. They'd have to sleep in the
car. Patrick was passed out, snug in his car seat; it was for
her to make do. Pull over in the middle of the woods? Risky.
She needed a semipopulated space. A small town where the
one cop was asleep but where she'd have recourse if some
lunatic happened upon her.

She turned off the road and headed to where the lines
thickened a bit on her GPS map. After another fifteen minutes, she found what she was looking for, a wider road,
mostly gravel and broken asphalt winding through a section of sparse trees, narrow trunks showing the land had
been logged just a few years back. She could make out two
farmhouses in the distance, dark and silent, abandoned for
all she knew. Still, the evidence of human habitation comforted her.

She stopped the motor, killed the lights, and cracked
the window ever so slightly. She pushed the seat all the
way back, looking up through the sunroof at the stars, so
intensely clear this far from any light pollution.

Jim, I'm here. She pushed her thoughts out up to them.

I'm here, and I need you. She pictured the thought as a tossed piece of paper, caught in a wind, tumbling as it blew, pushed along by the breath of those stars, across the long miles until it reached him.

The certainty gripped her again, so strong that her chest tightened and her breath came in hitching sobs. He had heard her. He was alive and he was coming. *I'm crazy. I've lost my mind, and I'll never get it back.* But it was a comforting madness, and she took refuge in it as she let the chorus of chirping insects and peeping frogs lull her into a shallow and restless sleep.

Sarah sank into a kind of wary half-life. She was aware of her closed eyelids, of the deeper and slower rhythm of her breathing. Her muscles were relaxed, but her senses wouldn't rest. Her hearing reported the night sounds, pattering of tiny feet on the unpaved road around her car as opossums and raccoons investigated, drawn by the unfamiliar smells. Her other senses worked as well. She could smell the pungent odor of gasoline, the rich, wet decay of the woods around her. She could feel the firm pressure of the car seat against her back and shoulders.

Jim had described it before, explained that on some of the more grueling ops, he'd literally learned to sleep while standing up, even while walking. She'd never understood until now, aware of the weird dichotomy of her body simultaneously at rest and prepared for danger.

Which was why she noticed as the pattering of animal feet silenced, was replaced by a steady, heavier crunch.

Footsteps.

Sarah resisted the impulse to bolt upright. She glanced down. She'd put the keys in the well beside the driver's seat, closed the cover. She'd have to move, make noise to open it. She cursed herself for not having the foresight to leave them in the ignition. *Stupid stupid stupid. Stop it. That won't help.*

She satisfied herself with reaching one hand beside the

seat, getting a firm grip on her steering wheel lock. It was a heavy and unwieldy club, but it was all she had. *Easy. You don't go there unless you have to. If you can get out of this with a simple excuse, so much the better. Maybe whoever it is will go away.*

But they didn't go away. The crunching drew closer, finally stopped just outside her window. She heard a click, light flooded in.

No sense in staying still now, she flung her arm over her eyes, giving a moan that she hoped sounded groggy, tensing her grip on the club.

The light moved away. "Sorry, ma'am." A man's voice. Older. Kindly. She relaxed a fraction.

"Whatcha doing on the road here?" Her eyes were already readjusting to the darkness, and she made out a man's face, jowly and long, with a neatly trimmed beard. Something dark and peaked covered his head, a baseball cap, she guessed.

Patrick began to stir, moan. "Sorry," she said, opening the door and pushing it outward, hoping to force him to move away from the vehicle.

It worked. He took three steps backward as she got out, relieved to find he was stooped and weak-looking, of a height with her. If it came to it, she was confident she could take him without too much trouble. His right hand held the flashlight. His left was empty.

She relaxed a bit more. "Sorry," she said again. "I was planning to drive straight through to my friend's place. Tired kinda snuck up on me. Was just planning to take a catnap and drive on."

He nodded, said nothing. Patrick began to blink, started crying. She unbuckled his straps and gathered him into her arms, swaying gently. "What are you doing up so late?" she asked.

He jerked a thumb over his shoulder at the farmhouse up the hill behind him. "My place," he said. "You should know better than to sleep in a car on a road out here with your boy in the back. Ain't right."

A needle of guilt pricked her, followed by anger. *Who is this old fucker to tell me how to raise my child.* She fought it down. He wasn't wrong.

She said nothing, bouncing Patrick, telling him it was okay. He cried harder, shoving his face into her shoulder. "Thirsty," he said.

"You got much farther to go?" the man asked.

She sighed. "Yeah, I'm afraid I do."

"Well," he said, "come on up to the house. We can give your boy a glass of milk and maybe a cup of coffee for you. Slaughter the fatted calf?" She could see his cheeks crinkle into a smile.

She could have been a serial killer, a thief on the run for all he knew. She was continually amazed at how the sight of a woman with a child disarmed men. It was at once honoring and insulting. And right now, damned convenient.

"That's kind of you, but you don't have to do that. I'm sure we can make it to a hotel."

"Nearest hotel's more'n thirty miles out, and it's a flophouse you wouldn't want to have your boy in. Come on." He gestured up the hill toward the house, lighted now around the doorway.

"Who else is up there?" Sarah asked, cursed herself inwardly for the question. It showed suspicion, but the words had escaped before she'd had a chance to check them.

"For now? Just the wife and me. But we're expecting company tomorrow. Church group, if you feel like stickin' around."

She smiled in the dark. "Not really all that religious."

"We don't judge." He shrugged and turned for the house without waiting to see if she had followed.

She didn't. Patrick had begun to quiet, strained to turn fully to see the old man, eyes wide with fascination.

The man turned, noticing she hadn't followed, saw Patrick's interest. The smile returning, warming his creased face. "Well, hello there, young fellah," he said. "You want a cup of juice?" He pointed out a finger, slowly and careful not to touch.

Patrick smiled back, said nothing.

"Cat got your tongue?" the man asked.

Patrick only smiled and looked, before turning and plunging his face into Sarah's shoulder. "Sorry," she said. "He's a bit of a flirt." The truth was that he hadn't done something like that in a long time, and the sight of him interacting normally made her weak with relief.

"Come on," the man said. "Name's Drew. I'm not a freak or a killer or a thief. Just a nice guy with a habit of taking in strays. No harm'll come to you."

Patrick turned to look at him again, and Sarah nodded. "Okay, thanks so much. That's very kind of you."

"Christian thing to do," Drew said. "Martha's the missus. She'll spoil your boy, I warn you."

"I'm sure he'll love it," Sarah said, walking behind him, up the wide track that led to the house, front door wide, soft light warm and inviting.

She shifted Patrick into the crook of one arm, allowed her right hand to drop to her pocket, fingering the knife nestled there, clip arm keeping it up toward the opening, ready to pull at a moment's notice. It was a gravity knife, technically illegal, though Sarah doubted any cop had made an arrest for it in the history of the ordinance. Jim had taught her how to use it, and she'd gotten into the habit of practicing during idle hours watching TV. Pull, flick, feel the snap and lock of the blade into place.

After a while, it had become second nature. She'd never beaten Jim's time, his hand a blur, knife quivering in a tree trunk before she'd even seen him release for the throw, but she could clear the blade in a respectable three seconds.

She patted the knife, the cold metal reassuring her as she followed Drew's bobbing shoulders.

She knew she wouldn't need it.

But it was nice to know it was there.

CHAPTER XXIV
ROCK STAR

Schweitzer began to flex his newfound muscles before they'd even boarded the plane home. Jawid attached himself to Eldredge's side and kept an open channel at all times now, facilitating a steady stream of questions and answers that Schweitzer knew Eldredge was mining in a desperate effort to understand what made Schweitzer tick.

"When we get back"—Eldredge was seated across from Schweitzer in a metal folding chair in COP Garcia's ready room, waiting for the weather to clear so that a helo could return them to the air base for the flight home—"I'm going to need you to work with a psych doc. Get a baseline profile. It'll be nice. Therapeutic."

Who was Nightshade? Why did you send me after him?

"Are we going to go through this every time we run you now, Jim? Are you going to be my first operational prima donna?"

You want to know what makes me work? This is part of it. You promised me the next op would point toward my family. What was with the corpses?

Eldredge frowned, arms folded across his chest. "This is highly . . . irregular."

Bowels are irregular. This is singular. I'm one of a kind. I'm pretty sure my contract with the navy expired when that bullet tore up my brain. New contract now. This is a negotiation, and a full stake is my price.

"I know you're not going to hurt anyone. Why should I tell you anything?"

Maybe I'll go for a walk down Pennsylvania Avenue naked at high noon.

"We'd torch you."

Maybe I'll save you the trouble. Push Ninip all the way out and join him. Leave you to run your program with whatever second-rate goods you were working with before I came along.

Eldredge chuckled. "Jesus. You're like a picky rock star. You want me to make sure you have a bowl of only green M&M's in your trailer?"

I want you to bring me into the decision-making process. I get a say in where, when, and how I deploy. We start with Nightshade, and we start right now.

"What if you don't like the answer?"

That's a risk you have to take. Ninip's not my only partner now. You hold the trump card in the end. You can push the button on the burn room. Start fresh.

"If you let me."

You said it, not me.

"We never learned Nightshade's name. We always knew him as Abu Naeema. You know these guys always take *noms de guerre.*"

Schweitzer nodded. He did indeed. It was a pattern they'd learned back in the War on Terror, and had kept it up even when that dark period slid smoothly into an epoch of insurgent crime.

"He was a supplier. He kept us in corpses. The program requires more bodies than we can get . . . in house."

You mean grave robbing your own?

Eldredge raised his hands. "You guys are pretty hard to

kill, you know. A lot of times, conventional units get ahold of the corpse before we can retrieve it. We don't dig up graves, Jim. We got lucky with you."

Can't you just . . . requisition bodies?

"There are exactly two people who know of the Gemini Cell's existence, Jim. It's funded out of a classified line item. I'm not entirely sure how it works, but I think Congress thinks the money is going to the CIA. There aren't a whole lot of people we can ask for help, and anyway, you know we need specific bodies for this, or souls rather. We can't use window washers. Hell, we can't even use Olympic athletes. You think hard operators in the prime of their life drop dead every day? With their bodies in pristine condition? With no families demanding an open casket? It's a rare commodity."

So, what did Abu Naeema give you?

"Hell if I know. Dead operators. Russian Spetsnaz mostly. A couple of Polish GROM. Plenty of Pakistani SSG. He even scared up a Japanese SST corpse once. I have no idea how, and I didn't ask."

Was he affiliated with the Body Farm?

"Tangentially. I think he played both sides of the fence, ancillary supplier to them. We knew about it. Tolerated it because it doubled as intel we could use to intercept their shipments."

Shipments where? To whom?

"Well, that's the thing we were trying to find out. And the reason you were brought in."

Because he stopped supplying you?

Eldredge nodded. "But kept supplying the Body Farm. We offered him a chance to give up his sources, to tell us where the bodies were going. When he refused, we found them on our own."

And he was no use to you anymore.

Eldredge sighed, shook his head. "Yes, but that's not why he had to go. The negotiations fell apart recently, Jim. We decided to solve that problem before he figured it was safer and more profitable to sell out his dealings with us to the Body Farm."

Schweitzer's anger was so hot and sudden that it nearly broke Ninip loose from his enclave and brought him surging back into control of their body. He sat silent while he struggled to contain the jinn. After a moment, he succeeded. *Is that how my identity got leaked? Is that how I got killed? How my family got fucking killed?*

Eldredge raised his hands again, as if his palms could ward off Schweitzer if he decided to cross the distance between them. "We don't know how that happened, Jim. You have my word. That's what we're trying to find out. You asked me to put you on ops that would lead to your murderers. I have done that. Abu Naeema was the first step."

So, question him.

"What will he tell us? These guys are pros. They don't give details to a third-rate supplier like Nightshade. He's a grave robber with mud under his fingernails. These guys know how to compartment information. We have to go slowly. We have to be patient. You know that."

Ninip growled, and Schweitzer realized that some of the jinn's haste had rubbed off on him. He'd lost focus.

So the Body Farm is . . . well . . . farming bodies.

"Yes." Eldredge looked uncomfortable.

I always thought it was a term for sex trafficking, child slaves, that sort of thing.

"It was. It is. Partly."

Why? Why the hell are they doing this?

"Why do narcoterrorists ply their trade, Jim? Why does al-Qa'ida farm poppies for heroin? Why does the United States sell fighter jets to Israel? Money, power, and the ability to project ideology beyond one's own immediate circle. It doesn't matter. What matters is that they play ball and don't threaten the security of this nation we're both sworn to defend."

So, where are the corpses going if they're not coming to the Gemini Cell?

Eldredge tugged awkwardly at the corner of his moustache. "That's the million-dollar question, isn't it?"

There's another Sorcerer, isn't there? Not an American Or, at least one not under American control.

Eldredge spread his hands. "Are you surprised? Jackrabbit was the first of many. This cell has been operating against rogue magic use for years now, and the cases only get thicker, more numerous, tougher. This is a tide, Jim. It's building, and I don't know where it stops. It makes sense that it wouldn't be confined to this country.

"Yes, there's another Sorcerer, and he or she is doing something with these dead. We need to find out who and what and most importantly . . ."

Who pulls their strings.

"I'd almost be relieved to find out it was a state actor, even an enemy, but there's no guarantee of that. We found Jawid by sheer luck. What if there's a Chinese Triad or a Greek terrorist group building Operators like you? That's some serious shit right there."

Depends on what they use them for. Maybe they'll liberate oppressed villages from corrupt party bosses.

Eldredge gave him a look. "You've read Homer, I assume?"

I was a SEAL. You don't get far in our line of work without knowing about Achilles.

"The blade itself incites to deeds of violence."

Meaning?

"If you have it, eventually you're going to use it, just because you can. Otherwise, you eat yourself alive. And weapons are built to do one thing."

Schweitzer remembered Ninip's sympathetic tones, catching him off guard, maudlin over the thought of his brother. *Let the branches do as the root commands,* the jinn had said. *You are a warrior. Fight.*

The anger returned as Schweitzer realized what the sympathy had masked. He turned inward, to where the jinn cowered. *You little fucker. You thought you could trick me into being a fucking animal like you? Was that it?*

I was giving you strength. It is what battle brothers do, Ninip whined.

We're not battle bro . . . We're not anything. Right now, you're a fucking battery. You clever little shit.

"Jim?" Eldredge's brow furrowed with concern.

Sorry. Just having a chat with my partner here. He gave me the same line of shit.

"What line . . ."

About being a weapon. I was never a tool. I was an artist. I was also a husband and a father. I was a friend. That fancy carbine you gave me? Doesn't do a whole lot without someone behind the trigger. That's a weapon, Eldredge. I'm a man.

"I'd say that's debatable now, but you don't need me to show you a mirror. You're something new, Jim. What exactly, we're still trying to determine. Anyway, do you have your answers? Will you play ball?"

This leads to the people who killed me, who killed my family.

"It does. Eventually. It's what we have for now. That's got to be enough."

Fine. I'm in. But first, I want to see their graves.

"Their . . . Your family."

That's right.

"Jesus, Jim. I can't just put a hat and an overcoat on you and send you . . ."

You're forgetting this is a partnership. You can sit here and bluster, or you can meet my baseline demands. You either show me my family's graves, or we have nothing to talk about.

"It'll take time, Jim. I'll have to clear it with some people. I'll also have to figure out where they're buried."

She has a sister, Peg. Lives out in the Shenandoah Valley. She'll know.

"Okay. Give me some time."

Light a fire under it, Eldredge.

"I thought we were partners, Jim. This isn't how you treat a partner."

It is when you're sick of their shit.

Eldredge put his head in his hands. "I'm not so certain

that this newest development in our program is altogether positive."

In all the other cases, what happened? The jinn won out?

Eldredge sighed, nodded. "That's right. Either the orig inal soul bound to the corpse was destroyed or completely overwhelmed by the bound jinn. Either way, we lost con tact with them."

You mean they wouldn't talk to Jawid anymore.

"That's right."

They were forced out.

Eldredge's face lighted, he looked up, the exasperation vanishing. "You're sure?"

It's a constant sumo match in here. Or, it was. I was forced out earlier. I found my way back.

"How?" Eldredge had produced a small notepad and was scribbling on it frantically.

Sarah.

Eldredge froze. "What do you mean?"

I followed her in. It's like there's a . . . a link, a path. I keep having this crazy notion that she's alive, like a phan tom limb. You know it's cut off, but you can still feel it.

Jawid's translation faltered here, as he attempted to cob ble the words together using his more limited command of English.

"And this is why you want to see their graves? Because you think your family is alive?"

I know they're not. I want to see their graves . . . because I want to see their graves. They're my family. I should be able to kneel there and cry.

Ninip's contempt was tiny, insignificant, but Schweitzer felt it nonetheless.

"You can't cry, Jim. You have no moisture in your body. You have no eyes. No tear ducts."

I can mourn. I haven't had a chance to do that yet.

He felt the urge to touch the engraved dog tags, but stopped himself with an effort. There was no need to play his whole hand just yet. Eldredge already suspected that good deeds made the difference between him and the other

Operators in the Cell, though Schweitzer thought it had more to do with simply asserting his own personality. Maybe he was a good man. Maybe the deep sable of Ninip's shadow merely made him seem good by comparison.

Schweitzer remembered a night with Sarah, before Patrick was born, finishing an op down south and flying back to MacDill Air Force Base in Florida. He took leave there, Sarah flew down to meet him and they lay in the darkness on the post beach, feet tangled together in the sand, her head on his chest as he gazed up at the wheeling stars.

"Why do you call them bad guys?" she'd asked.

"Because they're bad." He hadn't been paying attention; otherwise, he'd have recognized the tone of her voice that meant it was a serious question.

"Do you really believe that?"

"Sure. Sometimes. No. It doesn't matter. We have to think that."

"Why?" He felt her head shift, knew she was looking at him now.

"Because you can't do the job if you're thinking about their mothers, or their kids. You'll choke up. You'll get yourself killed. You'll get your teammates killed."

"I don't believe in bad guys."

"Huh?"

"I don't think there's such a thing as evil. Some people are crazy. Others are terrified. Others are stupid or too proud to reverse what they know is a bad course. Nobody's evil. Not in the moustache-twirling way."

"It doesn't matter."

"It does matter."

"No, sweetheart. It doesn't. The scalpel isn't the hand that moves it. You can't be both the hand and the blade, Sarah. That's how you get juntas. I don't worry about the nature of evil. There are no good guys or bad guys. There's only alive or dead. Mission objectives accomplished or failed."

But he couldn't be the scalpel anymore. That shining instrument had been sucked from his side, spinning away into the maelstrom of the screaming lost, the price of his return. Now he had to know, now he had to think.

He pictured Ninip, stripped from all he'd known, tumbling in a freezing, shrieking hell, until the screaming became his own, until loneliness and boredom and terror congealed into something he could never get out. Until the man he'd been was scattered dust, tiny fragments that only archaeologists could identify as something more than mud.

That wasn't evil. That was tragedy.

And it changed nothing.

He turned back to Jawid, sent another thought to relay to Eldredge. *What happened to the other Operators?*

"I told you, we destroyed them."

Destroyed them? We're a precious asset. Why would you destroy them?

"They were little more than rabid dogs, Jim. They couldn't be communicated with. Couldn't be controlled. The first few times it happened, there were incidents. Lives were lost. We had one break out just a week before you came into the Cell. We had no option."

You burned them.

"Most of the time. Once we had to cut one up until there weren't any parts left large enough to hurt anyone. Crude, but effective."

That won't happen with me.

"I know. And if we can figure out why you've won out over the jinn, we can duplicate it. Then, it won't happen to any of them."

But Eldredge had missed Schweitzer's meaning. Schweitzer thought of correcting him, then decided to let it stand.

Ninip made a few halfhearted attempts to expand his presence, but Schweitzer found it all too easy to kick him back into place. He still felt the weakness, the thrumming of his strength muted, his senses still stronger than they had been in life but nowhere near the powerful gradation he'd known when the jinn's strength was at its height. Smells ran together now, sounds tumbled over one another. At night, when the corridor lights went down and his cold-storage cell drifted into darkness, he could still see as if it were day, but heat signatures no longer registered. It was a small price to pay, but he wondered at the cost when he was run on his next op.

Schweitzer pushed, made demands. *We're partners,* he sent through Jawid. *That means I don't live in a cell.*

"Jesus, Jim," Eldredge said. "I'm not the only person involved with this program. I have superiors. I have to answer to them."

In the end, they'd compromised. Eldredge's boss had permitted Schweitzer a larger cell, still refrigerated, walls still dotted landscapes of burn and freeze nozzles, but several floors up. The walls were painted blue, and there was the crisped remains of a chair railing.

"This was our first attempt at a containment unit," Eldredge said. "It's as low security as it gets."

The door looked plenty formidable to Schweitzer, but he imagined the sky a few floors closer, felt it as an almost physical lifting of pressure, a slice of his humanity that much closer. Stupid. Another phantom limb. But it would do until he could push Eldredge for more. Slow was smooth, smooth was fast.

As low security as it gets is me not in a cell.

"I can't just let you wander around here, Jim. You'll scare people."

This is my problem, why?

"Because if you scare enough people, it could become a problem for me. Help me to help you, Jim. We'll get there."

We need to get there soon. I'll stay in here, but you want to meet me to run your tests or answer your questions, you're going to do it in another room.

"Jesus, Jim. You're really starting to chap my ass."

Life's rough all over. I want to go for a walk.

Eldredge hung his head. "It's a good thing my hair is already gray."

It's white. You look like Mark Twain.

"Yeah, I get that a lot. Where do you want to go?"

We can start with the command center.

Eldredge finally shrugged, sighed, and led him back down. It wasn't anything that Schweitzer hadn't seen a hundred times before. A busy watch floor, one twenty-foot wall covered with monitors, horseshoe-shaped long desks extending outward like ripples on a pond, busy analysts seated at terminals, ceasing all work to gawk at the monster in their midst.

The command center was suddenly still. Schweitzer could feel the shock, could smell the sudden sour tang of fear in the air. Ninip roused, pushing experimentally, the fluttering remains of his hunger stirred by the presence of so much weak and vulnerable flesh.

Eldredge folded his arms across his chest. Jawid stood beside him, looking around worriedly. "This what you wanted, Jim?" Eldredge asked.

Schweitzer nodded, tried to think of a way to reassure the analysts that he was no threat. He decided to clasp his hands beside his back as he strolled down the main, central aisle. He realized after a few feet that he looked like a dictator general inspecting troops and sighed inwardly. He was a monster. Any posture would be lipstick on a pig.

Tell them it's all right. I'm not going to hurt anyone, he sent to Jawid.

The Sorcerer did as he was bid, but the tension in their shoulders didn't ease, the high smell of fear didn't abate. Schweitzer turned to his right, walked to the analyst there. She leapt out of her swivel-backed chair, making a small noise and nearly upsetting the monitor in front of her. "Sorry," she squeaked.

Schweitzer could feel Ninip, pushing harder now, his hunger starting to fog the edges of Schweitzer's senses. He turned inward and smacked the jinn down. *No fucking way,* he said to Ninip. *Don't even think about it.*

Why? What good are these people to you? the jinn asked.

Schweitzer ignored him, channeled his thoughts to Jawid instead. *Ask her what she's working on.*

Schweitzer bent to examine the screen. It looked like a personnel roster, overlaid against a wide map, zoomed in too far for him to recognize the locale. Three gold-colored triangles flashed on it. They were labeled, G-41, G-18, and G-22. In the upper right corner of the screen, six more gold triangles sat unblinking in two orderly rows of three.

Beside them was a single silver one. S-1.

The analyst looked at Eldredge, and the older man nodded once.

She turned back to Schweitzer, biting down on her words to keep the tremor out of her voice. "That's you," she said.

S-1?

She nodded.

What are the G-series?

"Those are . . . all the others," she said. She looked young, hair cut unfashionably short, Coke-bottle glasses. Pale and soft. Not someone who worked out often, or ever. She reminded him of the code breakers and math dorks who'd helped crunch the numbers that built their targeting decks back in his living days.

Ninip pushed again, backed down at a twitch from Schweitzer. *Who are the others?* Schweitzer asked.

"Operators like you . . ." she said. "Only, not like you."

These are the ones who are still under control?

"Some control," Eldredge answered this time. "Enough for us to use them in less delicate situations than the ones we've run you on."

So the "S" is for silver? He thought of his eyes.

The analyst looked askance at Eldredge again.

"'S' is for singular, Jim," Eldredge answered. "You're the first we've ever had where the original soul, the one belonging to the corpse, won out."

I want to meet one of the others.

The analyst's fear stink grew stronger. "You wouldn't like them, Jim," Eldredge said. "They're not . . . as personable as you are. I said we can control them, but that doesn't mean a whole lot."

Still want to meet one.

Eldredge shrugged. "Won't kill anyone. I think. Sure."

Schweitzer turned back to the analyst. *What's your name?*

The analyst's fear stink became cloying once Jawid had translated the question. "Um . . . what? He wants to know . . ."

"He wants to know your name," Jawid said again.

Why do you care what this thing is called? Ninip sneered. Schweitzer ignored him, tried to look into the analyst's eyes. They kept roving, darting from Eldredge to him and back, finally alighting on the far corner of the room. Schweitzer turned and followed her gaze.

Six men lounged against one of the desks closer to the wall of screens, machetes casually dangling from lanyards around their wrists. Behind them two men stood by with what Schweitzer could only describe as halberds.

It was to be expected. He couldn't be offended by precautions. People who knew nothing about war thought it hinged on risks, brave and singular acts of heroism. That was how Ninip thought. Schweitzer knew better. You won by doing it by the numbers. You won by hedging.

He turned away from Eldredge's hedge and back to the analyst. There was probably a manual that specified the number of men and the number and type of armaments required depending on what room he was in. That was simply how the military did business.

Your name, he asked again.

"Gerald," she said.

Your name is Gerald?

"We don't use real names here, Jim," Eldredge answered. "All the females have male names, and all the males have female names."

So Eldredge isn't your real name?

"I stay with the program, Jim. These lucky fellows

might rotate out someday. Best to keep things as compartmentalized as possible."

He turned back to Gerald. *Well . . . Gerald, I'm Jim.* He extended a hand, keeping a watchful inner eye on Ninip, sensing the jinn's desire to extend his claws. *It's nice to meet you.*

Gerald stared at his hand. The fear stink spiked, slowly abated. She didn't move.

I won't hurt you, Schweitzer sent, but she had already reached out and taken his hand in hers, her thumb sliding gently over his palm. She forgot to pump it in her fear, and they stood in awkward silence for a moment, holding hands, all eyes in the command center on them.

"It's nice to meet you, Jim," she said. "You really are an amazing . . . man. It's such a pleasure to work with you."

But the words barely registered. Schweitzer was lost in the sight of her skin touching his, healthy pink clasped to dead gray. He could feel the gentle pulse of her blood through her palm, not with Ninip's predatory hunger, but simply as a warm thing, vital and close. Her hand was sweaty, the moisture formed a gentle seal between their skins.

He glanced up to find she was smiling.

Schweitzer realized with a start that this was the first time he had touched a person other than Eldredge, other than to kill them, since he had died.

I . . . thank you, Gerald, he sent to Jawid. *I look forward to . . . working together.*

He felt her grip slacken, the gentle tug as she tried to draw her hand back.

He kept ahold of it, even though the fear stink rose and she began to tug harder. Even though he had to push back harder against Ninip, surging in response to the nearness of blood.

Not because he wanted to hurt her. Not because the bloodlust surged in him as well, though it did.

But because he was touching a living person. Another living person. Not running. Not screaming. Not shooting or fighting.

Holding her hand.

What good are these people to you? Ninip had just asked him.

He looked down at the hand, tugging more frantically now.

And he knew.

CHAPTER XXV
JOB OFFER

The corridor was only wide enough to admit a single man at a time. Schweitzer could see alternating burn and freeze nozzles at regular intervals projecting from the walls, ceiling, and floor. Every twenty feet, a thick slot retreated into darkness, from which he assumed thick steel doors could drop to seal off the corridor by segments.

It felt like a cattle chute. He could feel the heaviness of the packed earth above him, the thickness of the metal on all sides.

"To the end, Jim," Eldredge said. "Stop outside the door."

I thought you said you had control over them.

"The ones we have the best control of are out working. You can't meet them. This is the one you can meet."

You can't use this one?

"I keep holding out hope, but I don't think so."

Then why keep . . . him? Her? It?

"It was a him," Eldredge said. "Air Force PJ. Was up for a posthumous Medal of Honor. Missed it by an inch."

So . . . why not destroy him?

"I said I was holding out hope," Eldredge said. "He's

still one of our own. He has good days and bad. Sometimes I think he's getting the upper hand."

Over his jinn? What's his called? Is it another anc—

Jawid cut him off this time, saying something briefly to Eldredge before turning inward to Schweitzer. *He does not speak.*

Schweitzer's senses were still amplified enough to sense Eldredge nodding behind him. "I said he has good days, Jim. You have great days. On his best day, he can't manage speech. Whatever is in there with him, it's not interested in the finer points of conversation. On the good days, it wants to kill what we point it at. On the bad days, it wants to kill everything."

So, what are you hoping will happen?

"I don't know. But I'm convinced that whatever it is, you're the key to it. I want him to be like you, Jim. I want them all to be like you."

How are they different?

"You'll see." Eldredge pointed down the corridor. "He's an animal. More monster than man. We need Operators who can think, who can reason."

Who can be relied upon to obey.

"A thinking creature is far less reliable than an animal," Eldredge said. He put his hand on Schweitzer's shoulder. "This is a partnership now, remember? I'm not some cartoon villain, Jim. There's more administrator in me than secret agent. I am genuinely sorry about what happened to you, about what happened to your family. But the truth is that there are forces at work here that we don't entirely understand, and you are the only way I know to keep them at bay. I am terrified of the thought of creatures like the one you're about to meet being the only thing that stands between this country I love so much and creatures like Jackrabbit and Nightshade. Please believe that."

And Schweitzer found that there was no guile in Eldredge's eyes, and that he *did* believe him, in spite of everything.

He remembered Sarah's face, her cheeks hot with anger,

during their last argument on the night the Body Farm had
shattered his home and life and family.

*Why do you do it, Jim? What do you get out of it? I
mean, apart from the adrenaline rush,* she'd asked.

I'm good at it, he'd replied. *Really, really good at it. It's
like you with the painting. You touch it, it's amazing. You
don't even have to try. I know you do, and damn hard, but
that just makes a good thing better.*

If he wasn't a SEAL, and he wasn't a husband and
father, then he didn't know what he was.

"So, yes," Eldredge said. "I want them all to be like you.
Every Operator in the program."

It was something that was not a SEAL or a husband or a
father.

It was something that was not Ninip.

They were silent for the rest of the walk until the hallway ended at a thick, steel door, painted in diagonal stripes
alternating red and yellow. Schweitzer could smell the
Composition B explosive lining the edges, the ammonia
stink of the nitroamine so strong that Ninip was roused.
There was a lot of explosive all around him. Probably
enough to bring the entire room and corridor down around
them.

The burn nozzles, the control points, the pounds of explosive. Layer upon layer, what the SEALs called defense-
in-depth.

Whatever was behind that door, the Gemini Cell sure as
hell wanted to be able to snuff it out in a hurry.

Schweitzer could feel the current again, the weird sense
of standing in a tunnel of flowing liquid. The magic. There
was magic behind that door.

Ninip was awake now, pacing his tiny corner of their
shared space, looking for his chance to break out. Schweitzer ignored him, lost in the sense of the current washing over him.

"Ready?" Eldredge asked.

What was his name?

"What?"

His name. I want to know what he was called when he was alive.

"He's not going to answer to it, Jim."

Doesn't matter.

Eldredge sighed and Schweitzer could feel him shrugging. "Cameron. His friends called him Cam."

Schweitzer nodded, kept an eye on Ninip, and faced the door. *Ready.*

A slot in the door slid aside with a bang. It was only wide enough for a tray to pass through, and Schweitzer could smell the explosive packed around it with such strength that he tried to filter it out. After a moment, he gave up. Ninip's diminishment had robbed him of many capabilities, this among them.

He leaned forward and pressed his eye to the slot. His view was distorted by a cinder-block thickness of transparent palladium. Beyond was a tiny room, scarcely more than a large closet. It was completely white and so clean that the angles where the walls met the floor melted into one another, joining the thick, transparent pane in giving a weird, distorted impression of a window into the interior of some round ball. The only break in the otherwise uniform expanse of white were the ubiquitous burn and freeze nozzles, interspersed with metal boxes that Schweitzer guessed contained more Comp B, or Semtex, or something else that could turn whatever was in the room to dust with the touch of a button.

There was nothing else. Schweitzer pressed closer to the slot, turning his head sideways to better see the room's hidden corners. He could feel Ninip looking through with him, trembling with excitement.

He instinctively tried to switch to heat vision, and Ninip tried to press forward to assist, but Schweitzer pushed him back again. There was no way it would be worth it to let the jinn reassert himself just to see around a corner.

I can't see anyone . . . Schweitzer sent to Jawid, heard the Sorcerer translate to Eldredge behind him.

"He's there, trust me," Eldredge said. "He likes to . . ."

The heavy door reverberated as something huge and dark slammed into it. Schweitzer's augmented reflexes sent him leaping back, knocking Eldredge into Jawid. He heard them cry out, but it was as faint as Ninip's voice, receding in the spectrum of sounds as his hearing shifted to focus on the space in front of him, scanning for threats.

The jinn was pushing again, and Schweitzer noticed his claws were out, his jaw hanging lower, tongue lolling, fangs lengthening. It wasn't much of a struggle to rein Ninip back in, but that didn't mean it was effortless, and Schweitzer froze as he turned his attention toward forcing Ninip back into the sliver of space he'd marked out for him.

By the end of that moment, the thing that hit the door had begun battering at it. Schweitzer could hear the shriek of something sharp being dragged along the metal between each blow.

Ninip was trembling. The jinn flashed thought after thought to Schweitzer, a tangled, semicoherent string of images. Excitement over meeting another like him. The thrill of an even contest. Schweitzer opening the door. Schweitzer tearing it off its hinges.

Schweitzer pushed the jinn away and turned his focus back to the door.

It thumped, rattled.

I don't think it's going to hold, he sent to Jawid.

It will hold, he will calm in a moment, the Sorcerer came back.

And if he doesn't? You're going to incinerate us all?

If he doesn't, we will freeze him solid. We have done it before. He will thaw.

But true to Jawid's words, the battering was already slowing, possibly as the man inside the body wrestled with the jinn, got the upper hand, or as the jinn gave up the effort as futile. The bangs against the door came less frequently, and finally stopped altogether, and the thing in the room moved away from the slot and into view.

There was little left of the man he once was. Rough, raised purple ridges covered in baseball stitching showed where both arms and a leg had been severed and reattached. Metal reinforcing cables protruded from the flesh, snaked along a few inches, and disappeared below the skin again. Another Frankenstein line of stitching formed a neat X over his stomach.

He loped, squatting deep on his haunches, strong thighs supporting him. His hands were raised above his head, long claws extending almost to his shoulders, fanning out like an umbrella stripped of its fabric. His teeth were comically long, slicing through his lips, which hung in ribbons between them. His jaw nearly touched his navel, gray tongue spread out on the floor like a carpet runner.

Tattoos covered him. Death had grayed his dark skin, but it was still difficult to make out the black lines of the ink. Schweitzer could see an Air Force logo on his thigh, a scrolling banner on the opposite leg wrapped around, but Schweitzer could make out the words, REVERES HONOR. A tattoo on his arm was the brightest and easiest to make out, the background marred by the stitching and cabling that held the arm in place. A beautiful woman was done in the likeness of a Benin noble, heavy iron circlets covering her long neck and graceful wrists. A pectoral covered her breasts. Her dreadlocked hair was piled in a tall, iron crown. Her arms cradled two children, their faces done in such realistic detail that Schweitzer knew the tattoo artist had taken them from life. Three names were written below: MALIKA, COLIN, WINNIE.

His family. The man this monster had once been.

Cam's tattered body crouched at the back of his cell, face turned intently toward the door, every muscle tensed to spring.

His eyes were gone. In the black pools of the sockets burned two marble-sized flames. Bright gold.

No. There were threads of silver in the fire, like the gouts of blue that entered the flames from a propane tank teetering on the edge of empty.

What's that?

Jawid didn't need him to explain. *That is the man he*

once was, losing to the jinn he soon will be. He heard Jawid repeating the conversation to Eldredge, a low buzz in the background, insects at play.

That's what's happening to me?

"No, Jim," Eldredge answered. "That's what *should* be happening to you. Jinn are thousands of years old. That much time beyond life makes them incredibly strong. This is another reason why we pair them with hard operators. They are the few people with the mettle to hang on to some shred of themselves in the face of such power."

I'm more than a shred.

"Much more. I want to understand why."

Schweitzer lifted an arm, pointed at Cam's face, which weaved to track his finger like a cat tracking a mouse. *What happens when his eyes turn all gold?*

"Then he is gone, Jim. Then what little Cam is left will be lost."

And you can still use him?

"In extreme circumstances, maybe. In most cases, they have to be destroyed."

Why?

"They're animals, Jim. If you have a dog you know is capable of writing poetry, but all it does is bite you, you don't wait around for it to spit out a sonnet.

"You put it down."

Schweitzer returned to his cell, sat in the corner of his cell.

Eldredge observed him through the transparent metal pane after the door had shut. Jawid leaned against the corridor wall behind him.

"So, you've met Cam. What do you think?" Eldredge asked.

I told you, no questions while I'm in here.

"Oblige me, Jim. I think I've been meeting my part of the bargain."

That's true. Okay, one question. And not about Cam. I'm still processing.

"Okay . . ." Eldredge paused, thinking. "Why do you sit?" he finally asked.

Huh?

"You don't need to sit. Your body doesn't feel fatigue. I notice you doing this a lot. Things you don't need to do. Nodding or shaking your head. Looking at people even though you're talking to us through Jawid . . . living things."

Schweitzer thought a moment before answering. *Sarah forced me to read a comic book once, about a masked freedom fighter who unseated a totalitarian government. They made a movie out of it.*

"Comic books don't seem your style."

I loved comic books. I was just more into superheroes. Anyway, Sarah always got what she wanted, so I read it.

"And? You liked it?"

Yeah, I did. There was a scene where a prisoner passed a letter to another. "It is the very last inch of us," she said of integrity, "but within that inch we are free."

There's so little left of me that's human, Eldredge. Sitting is my last inch.

"There's more humanity in you than many living men, Jim," Eldredge said. "Good night." He left, Jawid at his heel.

Schweitzer sat for a long time, thinking about Cam and Eldredge and humanity. His last inch. It would be good to read that comic again, to see if the lines were as he remembered them. He stood, reached out to Jawid to ask the Sorcerer to request the comic . . .

. . . and found the Sorcerer was already opening the link to him.

That link was a tunnel connecting Ninip-Schweitzer and Jawid, allowing communication to travel both ways. Jawid was doing his level best to sound casual. Schweitzer had heard it at least a dozen times before in brush passes and back-alley midnight meets with intel contacts. They were inevitably men who had gone rogue for money or some misplaced belief in redemption. Always, they quickly discovered they were in the company of genuine killers with no way out but forward. Always they affected the same casual tone. Always they failed to hide the terror beneath it. When it came to killing, a man could only harden himself so much. There was something deeper that helped you pull the trigger when you had to, and to forget about what the round did after. Some people had it, most didn't.

We are almost ready for your next run, the Sorcerer said. The link connecting them was more powerful than speech, conveyed emotion with a clarity that no expression or tone could match. Jawid's fear was as thick as summer fog, riding on a current of desperation so keen that Ninip stirred, reaching back up the link toward the Sorcerer.

Schweitzer felt the jinn extending himself, his presence reaching out for the emotions that filtered down the link from Jawid. Ninip dipped into Jawid's fear, coiling around it, using it as Schweitzer had used Sarah's rosewater scent, a path that could be followed back to its source. Schweitzer felt Jawid recoil from Ninip's exploration, and he reached out to push Ninip back. The jinn resisted briefly, but Schweitzer was much too strong for him now.

What's the op? Schweitzer asked.

It is back to the Baluch, Jawid said. *Near to where you were . . .*

I know where it is, Jawid. I've been there enough. I thought I made myself clear. This is a partnership now. You don't call the op and send me. We call it together. That's how this goes.

The Sorcerer was silent.

Where's Eldredge? Schweitzer asked. *Get him back in here.*

He is coming soon, Jawid said. *I wanted to talk with you first.*

The Sorcerer's fear traveled down the link with such strength that Schweitzer felt buffeted by it. There were two ways to deal with a frightened man, go nuclear and cow him, or go easy and make him feel safe. Both were dependent on the subject's personality, both carried risks, and both were disastrous if you guessed wrong as to what the other person needed.

Schweitzer made his choice. *You can tell me, Jawid. I'm not about to go tattling on you to Eldredge.*

The Sorcerer hesitated. Schweitzer felt the moment balance on a knife's edge. Either Jawid would shut the link and cut the connection, or he would talk.

I know I can trust you, Jawid said. *I am less sure about him.*

Ninip? Schweitzer asked. *He's done.* He felt a pulse of anger from the jinn at that but no movement.

I . . . wanted to talk to you, Jawid went on. *We are both prisoners here.*

Schweitzer muffled his surprise. He could feel the vibration of the link that connected them, understood that as Jawid's emotions were flowing to him, his were flowing in reverse. Was the Sorcerer as powerful as Ninip when the jinn was in control of their shared body? Ninip had been able to read Schweitzer's thoughts and emotions with ease. He didn't know if Jawid had the same ability. Schweitzer had only ever known the steady rhythm of their communication, Jawid faithfully translating until he faded into the background, Schweitzer barely noticing he was there.

I can't imagine that they'd want someone with your abilities having weekends off, Schweitzer said, hoping Jawid couldn't see into Schweitzer's mind, discover that Schweitzer was attempting to manipulate the Sorcerer into opening up.

I am given my rest, Jawid said, *but I am always watched.*

Schweitzer felt Jawid push his consciousness down the link between them, pressing into Schweitzer's thoughts, trying to white out his vision so he could tell another of his picture stories. This time, Schweitzer pushed back, closing himself off and forcing Jawid to recoil back into himself.

He felt the Sorcerer's shock. Schweitzer was getting better at this whole being-dead thing.

No, Schweitzer said. *You don't walk into my mind anymore. You want to tell me something, then tell me.*

I was going to show you my home, where they keep me. I'm sure it's very nice.

I have seen your home. Before the attack. From pictures, not from invading your mind. I swear it.

I believe you. Schweitzer realized that he did believe him, that he could feel the honesty vibrating through the link that connected them. There was so much to learn about how this new unlife worked, about what he could do.

I think we are the same this way, Jawid said. *Denied family. You asked me about the girl you saw . . . in my mind, back in COP Garcia.*

You said that she was lost to you, that it was pointless to look over your shoulder.

Schweitzer could feel Jawid's embarrassment. *Before the Talebs took me, I was promised, betrothed. I would be married now were I still in my homeland. I will never have her now, or the children that would have come of it. We have both lost loved ones.*

Schweitzer felt his anger spike at the comparison. He felt Jawid shrink from the rage resonating up the link to him. Schweitzer hauled on the emotion like a line, brought it in.

Schweitzer calmed himself with an effort, then spoke. *It's not the same thing. I lost people I'd built a life with. You're mourning a vision that might never have come to pass.*

Of course, I'm sorry. Schweitzer could feel Jawid's anger giving the lie to his conciliatory words, mingled with disappointment. The Sorcerer wasn't sorry. Jawid wanted something else out of this conversation.

What was her name? Schweitzer asked. *The girl you were betrothed to.*

Jawid's shock resonated down the link. The Sorcerer clearly hadn't been expecting the question. It took him a long time to answer. *Anoosheh. She was called Anoosheh.*

You ever see her?

I think I did, once. My father beat me for that.

Schweitzer knew enough of Jawid's culture to understand that seeing unmarried women was forbidden. Children could get away with it, but by the end of adolescence, a woman's skin exposed to sunlight was treated like pure gold and toxic waste in equal measure.

Beat you badly, huh? Schweitzer asked.

I lived. Jawid's voice was light, but Schweitzer could feel the pain in the memory.

Why are you talking to me about this? Schweitzer asked. *Can't you . . . you know . . . talk to someone alive?*

They force me to talk to their psychologist, Jawid said. *I meet her each week. She is kind.*

That help?

She is . . . her questions . . . She is not seeking to help me. She is seeking to keep me calm. To know my intentions. To ensure that I keep working, that I do not flee.

Schweitzer had been off to see the wizard enough to know that the psych docs' open smiles and soft voices could never conceal their mission: to determine if you were still fit to keep the government's secrets and to do its dirty work.

You didn't need magic to see that.

My guards do not speak with me, Jawid went on. *The analysts here do not even use their real names.*

Eldredge?

Eldredge is . . . all that man does is work. I have never seen him sleep. I have never seen him gone from here for more than a few hours. He is a machine.

So, you've got nobody to talk to. You want a buddy, is that it? Schweitzer asked, but he knew it wasn't. The emotions traveling down the link told him that Jawid wanted something specific. He was feeling Schweitzer out.

I thought . . . you are a father, Jawid said. *I thought you would understand.*

I was a father, Schweitzer replied, *and that's why I do understand. Family is everything.*

And as Schweitzer said it, his own words rocked him.

All those years, his pride in his profession, his commitment to his art. Lying beside Sarah as she drifted off to sleep, fearing that loving her would strip away all in the world that made him great.

All of it possible because of her and Patrick. Her standing at the top of the stairs to her loft studio, grinning down at him. Patrick, before he could walk, seated in his pack and play, cooing and reaching. Each after action, Schweitzer marinating in the realization of what he'd done. What he'd accomplished. What he'd endured. Telling himself he was hard, that it didn't matter, that he could shrug it off.

It had been Sarah and Patrick, hadn't it? Before Sarah, he had been strong by leaning on his brothers and sisters in the teams. And after, he'd leaned on her. Even as he'd told himself he was being strong for her. His family was the foundation on which everything he'd achieved rested.

Sarah and Patrick, always.

Peter's face flashed before him. Schweitzer remembered being chased by a dog as a little boy, running into his brother's arms. Peter had swung him into the air and into safety. In a way, he'd never let him go. *Proud of you, bro.*

That no person made it on their own was hammered into SEALs from the first day of training. They were a band, they were a team. They won together or they fell together. They left no man behind.

Always leaning. Always.

He'd never truly appreciated it until this moment. Now that family was utterly beyond him, he finally understood their significance.

Family is everything, Schweitzer said again, and this time he let the emotion kindled by those words, his amazement at how much his family meant to him, reverberate up the link to the Sorcerer. He felt the emotion touch Jawid, envelop him. He felt Jawid respond to the feeling that he had never known, had always desired, savoring it much as Ninip savored fear and pain. This was a thing Jawid and Schweitzer shared, uniting them through the silent language that all men knew, the love of home and hearth and of the ones who came up with us.

Jawid had wanted to know what it was to have a family of his own, and now he felt it through Schweitzer. The Sorcerer drowned in the sensation and dropped his guard entirely. The link between Schweitzer and Jawid opened wide, the fear momentarily dissipating and leaving the link as wide as a corridor, a tunnel between their two souls.

Without knowing what he was doing, Schweitzer stepped into the link, pushed his presence up the channel of communication with Jawid, following the instincts of his new existence, flowing like water through the path of least resistance.

Schweitzer found himself in two places at once. Half of him remained in his own corpse, locking Ninip firmly in place as the jinn leapt to follow him. The other half of Schweitzer's consciousness passed up through the link and into Jawid's consciousness.

Jawid felt Schweitzer's invasion of his inner space. The Sorcerer ripped himself from his reverie, his rapture shifting to anger, surprise, and panic. He pushed madly against Schweitzer, trying to force him back down the link that connected them.

But Schweitzer would not be moved. Jawid lay open to him, his thoughts and memories bare, just as Schweitzer had been vulnerable to Ninip when they first woke up together, sharing Schweitzer's corpse. This was what Ninip must have seen. This was what it must mean to be the jinn in another's form. Schweitzer could feel the sense of violation, the gut-wrenching revulsion gripping Jawid. This violation, the raping of memory and experience had been the worst of what Schweitzer had suffered since he'd been paired with the jinn. He knew that to delve into Jawid's mind was cruel.

But Jawid was part of the reason that pairing had happened in the first place.

The Gemini Cell had been a labyrinth since Schweitzer had awoken under its thrall. He had backed Eldredge into a reluctant partnership, held him there only through the promise of his future utility. And now Jawid came to him with another op decided on, Schweitzer's cooperation assumed. What else would he do? What else was there he could do? He was a monster, a dead thing created to make more dead things.

The truth wasn't much, but it was something. Maybe that it was different from what he had was enough.

Schweitzer reached out, felt the membrane of Jawid's memories resist him, felt the Sorcerer's defenses shift from the futile attempt to push him out of his body to a scrambled defense of his mind.

Too little, too late.

Schweitzer plunged into the stream of Jawid's thoughts. The images of Jawid's memories flashed through Schweitzer's mind now, all but blotting out his vision, faster and more vivid than they had ever been in any communication Jawid had willingly sent.

Schweitzer replayed Jawid's memories. He saw through Jawid's eyes as the Sorcerer stood in the command center beside Eldredge, watching the silver triangle that represented Schweitzer's movements track across a map sketched out in black and glowing green. Schweitzer flashed to another memory of Jawid standing beside Eldredge and a young woman in jeans and a T-shirt, talking animatedly over an open file with Schweitzer's picture paper clipped to one corner. His psych reports. The young woman was a "human terrain" analyst, trying to predict Schweitzer's motivations, to explain to Eldredge why Schweitzer thought the way he did, to decode who he was.

As with all of the analysts, she was young, plucked from one of the best schools in the nation. Jawid's memory told Schweitzer that the Sorcerer had been terrified of her, obscenely aroused by her. Schweitzer realized that Jawid had been thrust from a world in which he never saw women at all into a daily routine where he was surrounded by them, and in dress that in his homeland would have been considered scandalous.

And as with all of the analysts, her name was not her own. Jawid called her Jack.

Schweitzer didn't stick around to learn more, he pushed further back through Jawid's memories, going deeper into the Sorcerer's past, not sure what he was looking for, pulled on by the satisfaction of finally learning about the events surrounding his resurrection.

Schweitzer left that memory and moved to another one. Jawid red-faced and arguing with Eldredge. *I did everything you asked me!* Jawid had said. *It is not such a great request. Let me go back, just for a night. You can send soldiers with me.*

Eldredge's sad eyes, looking old and tired. *I'm sorry. We can't risk that. You know I'll push for it. I've been pushing for it. We'll get there Jawid. You just have to be patient.*

Schweitzer pushed on, examining an older memory. Jawid sitting cross-legged on the end of his narrow bunk, feeling the currents of magic flowing around and through him. Jawid cast himself out into the void, feeling his way through the darkness, drifting along the wave tops of the currents of magic all around him. The Sorcerer slowly became aware of other consciences, whirling in the distance, tumbling over one another, so that Jawid only caught a snatch of each presence before it spun away to be replaced by another.

Schweitzer knew what Jawid was seeing: the soul storm, the whipping, screaming chaos that had almost claimed him.

But where Schweitzer was dead, his disembodied presence moving through the void, Jawid was alive, and using his magic to project his will outward. Jawid hovered along the edges of the void, unable to push farther, feeling the long miles, a distance between planets, still separating him from whatever lay beyond.

Then, a pulse. One voice growling deep and low and stronger than all the others, clawing its way to the surface of the storm of souls, reaching out. Powerful, wicked.

Schweitzer could feel the fear curdling in Jawid's gut. Sweat tickling his neck, his spine, before soaking into the band of his trousers. Jawid remembered warnings from his grandfather. Superstitious cautionary stories about the evils of magic. Old tales to make children obedient, until they'd become real.

The memory was as real as if Schweitzer were living the experience himself. He could feel Jawid swallowing, forcing the fear into a tight ball that sat in his stomach. Schweitzer could feel Jawid reminding himself that without magic, he was a goatherd. Without magic, he was a victim, shivering under Abdul-Razaq's sweaty bulk, biting down against the pain. *You're so beautiful,* the Taleb had crooned over and over again, *like a deer. My little deer.* Abdul-Razaq had conjugated the nouns in the feminine. Jawid shook, knowing that to relax would make it hurt less, but fearing that if he let this bastard make him into a girl, he would be one forever.

So Jawid had let his muscles fight. And he had suffered.

Magic put an end to it. Schweitzer could feel the reminder giving the Sorcerer steel, Jawid reaching out to the stronger voice in the storm, extending the magic, pushing a tiny thread of his presence across the fathomless dark. The magic obeyed, the arcane currents ceased their aimless eddying, moving purposefully now, carrying Jawid's signal on and out, a hand extended in invitation.

Schweitzer saw it all. The hand at the other end, grasping, locking on. Jawid reeling in.

Schweitzer saw through Jawid's eyes, open now, looking down at a corpse on a cold, metal gurney, hand on its chest. Jawid's magic current flowed out, the jinn, the presence out of the storm, moving past and through Jawid, reaching out strong arms and digging in, trying to find purchase in Jawid's body, preferring the pulsing of his living heart to the cold emptiness of the dead one on the gurney before him.

The memory played on, and Schweitzer could feel Jawid grinding his teeth together so hard that his jaw hurt, the coppery taste of blood flowing into his mouth, pushing the jinn on, until it was past and through, flailing and clawing as Jawid's magical current bound it into the corpse. Jawid felt the faint signature of the soul of the original owner of the corpse still clinging to it, haunting its former home, as it would for a few days, or a few hours, before

moving off into the storm. Jawid performed the final binding, linking the ancient soul from the void to the newly
dead one in the corpse.

Schweitzer watched through Jawid's eyes as the memory went on. Jawid examined the corpse: a Caucasian with
epicanthic folds on his eyes, an indicator of steppe heri-
tage. The dead body jerked, fingers flexing, chest rising
and falling once.

Schweitzer stayed with the memory while Jawid waited
for his latest experiment to wake. Hours passed in the
memory.

At last, the eyes opening, flames dancing in the depths.

Silver at first, but flickering faintly, slowly overcome.

Then, at last, gold.

An axe rising. Falling.

Schweitzer abandoned this memory and pushed deeper,
delving further back, trying to find something of himself,
of his family of . . .

He saw through Jawid's eyes as the Sorcerer stood beside
Eldredge, watching video-camera footage of a hospital room.
The image was grainy, distorted, but Schweitzer could see
a woman sitting on a bed, cradling a child in her arms. She
was weeping. A doctor crouched at her side, trying to find
comforting words, clearly failing.

Schweitzer felt Jawid fight harder, flailing desperately
as Schweitzer replayed the memory fully, focusing on the
figures on that hospital bed, reconciling the chronology of
the memories, playing them back in order.

Back further, to Jawid observing the wreckage of Schweitzer's home just after Schweitzer's corpse had been
carted off.

Fast-forward to the memory of Schweitzer's psych profile. Back again to the wrecked apartment, forward slightly
to the hospital room, to the grainy image of the woman
and child, hauntingly familiar.

The haunting dissolving into sudden certainty.

Schweitzer pulled back from the stream of Jawid's
thoughts, snarling. He hovered just outside Jawid's body, at

the very edge of the link that connected them. Jawid pushed against him, but sick rage had made Schweitzer unmovable. *They're alive!* Schweitzer screamed at the Sorcerer. *You fucking little motherfucking bastard! They're alive!*

Schweitzer poured his anger out through the channel connecting him to the Sorcerer, white and hot and senseless. Ninip leapt at it, riding the emotion up through the link and scrambling gibbering to the very edges of Jawid's soul. Schweitzer let him, holding the snapping, ravenous presence of the jinn mere inches away from Jawid's inner space, letting the Sorcerer feel his nearness.

They're alive, Schweitzer said. *Where are they? Why did you . . . ?*

Jawid's body was moving, Schweitzer could see through the Sorcerer's eyes now. The Sorcerer jumping up from his desk, eyes scanning the wall, coursing over a field of buttons set in a stainless-steel panel, finding the palm-sized red circle, square plastic shield clapped over it.

White letters etched in the surface: BLOCK-6E—BURN.

Schweitzer lunged, tried to force himself back into Jawid's body, to stop the Sorcerer's thighs from engaging, to stop his arm from reaching out. But the Sorcerer was a living thing, and Jawid's magic was still pushing back against Schweitzer, gaining momentum now that Schweitzer had left the Sorcerer's memories.

Schweitzer felt the steady drumming of Jawid's heart, felt the pulsing flow of his blood rousing Ninip to madness. Jawid's soul fed on that vitality, that pulse of life, enormous, transcendent, filling every last particle of the Sorcerer's body. Schweitzer's beachhead in Jawid's conscience was powerful enough, but the Sorcerer's living body was another matter. It thrummed with power, bursting with the energy of electrochemical signals. Muscle fibers expanded and contracted. Cells divided.

Life.

Schweitzer changed angles, scrambling for Jawid's mind, struggling to find something to freeze the Sorcerer in his tracks, to make him sleep, to give him doubts.

Nothing. Jawid's memories came thick and fast, images from his past, flashes of emotion, but observation was not control. Schweitzer could read, but he couldn't write.

At last Schweitzer gave Ninip full rein, allowed the jinn to slip out of his sliver of their shared space and come surging up the link to Jawid.

At Coronado, they'd taught Schweitzer never to take desperate gambles. *Each decision point should be like a marriage proposal,* Master Chief had said. *Before you pop the question, you should already know the answer.*

Schweitzer didn't know the answer here, wasn't sure he could rein Ninip back, regain control of his body again. He didn't know if it would help at all.

But he was determined to try anything, no matter what the cost.

Because Sarah and Patrick were alive.

Ninip surged, ballooning into his sudden freedom, mad with the nearness of Jawid's vitality. Schweitzer felt the jinn arc through the link to Jawid, the jinn's presence so great that Schweitzer had to fight to maintain his connection to the Sorcerer, to not be pushed out by Ninip and back entirely into his own self.

Schweitzer watched through Jawid's eyes as the Sorcerer ran the few paces to the wall, scrambled for the plastic cover, fumbled the catch, buying Schweitzer a precious second.

Ninip blazed against the perimeter of Jawid's self, burning with bloodlust, a blooming red flower. He shrieked, pouring himself into the link, driving himself into Jawid's body with all he had.

The jinn surged, lunged.

And rebounded.

Ninip's power was tremendous, his pent-up aggression burned so hot that Schweitzer's spirit reverberated with it.

But it couldn't change whatever strange laws magic obeyed. The jinn could share a dead body with its owner but not a live one.

Ninip could read enough to know what the word on the

red button meant, what it would do if Jawid pushed it. He redoubled his efforts, hurling himself into Jawid with greater and greater frenzy.

Schweitzer watched in horror as Jawid flipped the plastic case open. *Not like this,* he pleaded, *not now. Not when I know they're alive.*

I'm sorry, Jawid sent back, hovered his fist over the domed red surface, punched it home.

As much as it was possible for a soul to wince, Schweitzer did. Ninip howled, anticipating the wash of the flames that would scour away their link to the land of the living and send them both back to the void and the shrieking storm that awaited them there.

Instead of the whooshing roar of fire, Schweitzer heard a whining hiss.

He pulled back from Jawid, Ninip coming with him. Schweitzer fell back into control of his own body again, turning his head.

The freeze nozzles were firing, liquid nitrogen smoking into the atmosphere. A patina of frost was already spreading along the wall behind the stainless-steel heads, blue-white spikes crackling outward. A few of the nozzles were jamming, the tips silent as whatever mechanism drove them failed under the pressure of the gas.

Schweitzer felt Jawid's shock as the incineration protocol didn't fire, observing from a video feed in his cell, most likely.

Ninip cooperated as Schweitzer threw their shared body as far from the nozzles as possible, slamming into the narrow door.

We are not . . . He did not . . . Schweitzer had grown used to the tinny faintness of the weakened jinn's voice. This new Ninip, stronger and nearer, was a shock.

Schweitzer didn't show it. *Eldredge didn't trust Jawid,* he said. *He wasn't going to let us be burned. Not when we could be saved.*

Schweitzer was dimly aware of an alarm sounding, the flashing of a Klaxon through the thick panel of transparent palladium alloy that gave him his view of the corridor outside. He felt the cold already taking effect, stiffness in the tips of their shared fingers and toes, the glycerol in the cells struggling to keep them pliant, but failing rapidly as the temperature in the room plummeted.

Shouts reached him, boots pounding in the hallway outside.

He flattened their body against the door, compressing as much as he could, as if the mere inch he gained could somehow save them. The cold gripped them mercilessly, the outer layers of his body refusing to report to him, their joints going rigid. As Schweitzer watched, the frost blooms spread to encompass the entire room, leaving it a sparkling cavern of diamonds. The burn nozzles crackled and popped as their internal pilot lights went out.

Ninip tried to seize their shared fist, pound it against the door behind them. Schweitzer could feel the increasing fragility of the cells, going hard, brittle. He swatted the jinn back, pushed him further into a smaller pocket of their shared space. *Stop! You idiot! You'll snap it off!*

Perhaps Ninip's resurgence had regained some of their lost sensory ability, perhaps he imagined it, but Schweitzer heard a tiny cracking sound from beneath their fist. The jinn ignored his warning and pounded again before Schweitzer could push the jinn back again.

Crack. Definitely not his imagination. The sound came from higher up over their shoulder. Not their body. The wall.

Schweitzer poured all his will into their legs, forcing them to taking a lurching step forward. Their frozen limbs obeyed as best they could, but didn't lift as high as he needed. Their toes curled under, and Schweitzer felt the two smallest snap off, the arch of the foot breaking. It didn't matter, he didn't need it.

He planted their still-solid heels and launched their body high and backward.

They collided with the door, and Schweitzer felt the skin all along their spine, their neck to the base of their skull, split open with the light sound of breaking glass.

The tracker sizzled and broke away from its anchorage against their spine. The door shuddered. Schweitzer felt their bones shiver, the momentum straining a structure suddenly gone brittle. He channeled his rage and frustration into the hit, railing with an abandon that would have made Ninip proud. Their frozen body would break. The fragments would scatter. His family would be lost to him again, just as he'd learned there was hope. The thought made him insensate with rage, eroded the quiet professionalism that made him who he was.

Schweitzer gave in to it. For the moment, the animal ruled, and he lost himself in a cry of rage that shattered the stretched remains of their lips and sent a shivering crack through their face.

Then there was a wrenching, a splintering sound, and he felt their body sailing through a wall of cold, rolling out into the corridor behind and a sudden heat that felt like an inferno.

The shattered door top pelted down around them as their cells suddenly expanded, took on moisture, fought their way back to their original shapes, missed, became something lumpen, a grotesque imitation of their prior form. A living man would have howled and died in agony.

Their shared peripheral vision picked up the shapes of men, guards racing into the corridor around them. They were men and women just doing their jobs, contractors and uniformed service members dedicated to defending their country, just as he had been, as he still was. Schweitzer knew they saw him as a monster, as a threat. They were good people.

But they were people who wanted to stop him from getting back to Sarah and Patrick.

And for that, they had to die.

Schweitzer rifled through his options. Disabling wounds or an effort to render them unconscious would require exposing himself, leaving to chance the possibility that their shared body would be damaged too badly to escape this facility and get back to his wife and child. There was no way he was going to take that risk.

They had lied to him, they had imprisoned him. They would keep doing it if he let them.

Ninip pulsed, and Schweitzer let the jinn have full rein. *I'm sorry,* he started to say to the soldiers around him, then realized he was not.

He wasn't sorry. He was angry. He was desperate. He was not going to miss this chance.

Schweitzer rolled them to their feet as an axe blade whirled past their head to rebound off the wall beside them. He caught the flicker of a blue pilot light out of the corner of their eye, and once again allowed Ninip to surge to the fore, the jinn's bloodthirsty edge suddenly utile. The jinn flooded their limbs, and their warming arm snapped out so quickly it was a blur even to Schweitzer's augmented eyes. It closed around the barrel of the flamethrower, bending it upward, the metal crumpling in their dead hand, some slick liquid sheeting across their knuckles, catching fire as it was exposed to the air, racing back up the line.

Schweitzer pushed off again, leaping them forward as the man detonated, the corridor suddenly engulfed in white-hot flame, dancing with screaming figures, little more than black blurs dissolving in the fire, so that the fire seemed a living thing itself, screaming at him to run.

And so they ran, Ninip casually decapitating Mr. Axe as they passed, his burning body slumping to the ground, the jetting blood sizzling and popping in the heat.

The jinn let their shared body flee now, knowing there was nothing behind them but flames, any slaughter to be had lay ahead. Schweitzer could feel their back smoking, the skin doubtlessly badly burned, but they had only been seconds out from nearly freezing solid, and the dropped temperature had spared them the worst of it. The flame had even done double duty in partially cauterizing the split in the skin along their spine, melting the gap closed in sections. What mattered was that the bones had held, that the muscles were connected enough to keep them moving and fighting.

Because the echoing screams reminded him of the finality of the move. His captors burned behind him, soldiers, G-men. The good guys. Those deaths would have to be answered for. There was no capturing him, no putting him back in a cage. There was no more partnership. They would destroy him if they could.

But they couldn't. Because Sarah and Patrick were alive, and hellfire and wild dogs and all the firepower on earth wouldn't stop him from getting back to them.

He gave his body over to Ninip and let the jinn take up his loping knuckle-walk, moving faster than Schweitzer could drive them upright. The corridor ended at a pair of steel doors just beginning to swing open. Ninip and Schweitzer barreled through them, knocking them apart and feeling the weight of the people on the other side. Shouting, panic, then Ninip and Schweitzer were among them.

Schweitzer turned away and let the jinn do his work. He turned his attention inward, trying to square the layout of the place. He remembered the detention blocks at the Forward Operating Bases he'd deployed from in the past, cheap structures of barbed wire and plywood meant to provide a quick and convenient means to detain and debrief those enemies the SEALs managed to take alive.

He felt their body whirling, pushed away Ninip's intoxicating exultation, the hot blood washing over them, the bone spurs lengthening into teeth and claws. The screams were a buzz in his ears, waves crashing on a distant shore. Schweitzer was dimly aware of the callousness of turning away from the carnage, knew he should be trying to restrain the jinn, to protect the lives of innocent people just trying to do their jobs.

But they had lied to him and kept him prisoner while Sarah and Patrick had been alive. When he could have been with them. Could have protected them. Instead, he had been . . .

They had created the thing that now gibbered and shrieked and drained their blood. Let them enjoy the fruits of their labor.

When he finally returned to their shared eyes, there wasn't a moving body in sight. The steel doors had swung shut behind him, shutting out the screams, the flames already beginning to die down. They stood in a wide, plain room. Rows of benches marched out until the far wall stopped them, another identical door splitting its otherwise blank face. A giant whiteboard was covered with dry-erase scribbling in bright color. An American flag stood in one corner. An orange light hung from the ceiling, spinning out its warning beams, reminding the severed heads and limbs that the Schweitzer-Ninip Operator was coming to kill them.

They galloped through the opposite pair of doors, turning sideways to skid through a second set of sliding gates just before they slammed home behind him, before louvering down and turning abruptly solid, seamlessly blending into the wall, so that any normal human would have to squint to see that the surface was unbroken.

They were standing in the lobby of an office. It looked for all the world like they'd come into the receiving room at a software company. A pleasant-looking secretary in a smart suit was slowly rising from her swivel-backed chair, hand going to her mouth. A fake plant spilled the banks of a cobalt blue ceramic pot. Raised stainless-steel lettering behind it arced across the wall: ENTERTECH/PHASE III, INC. Below it, smaller letters read: SERVING THOSE WHO SERVE.

The fear stink hit their nostrils and Ninip lunged for the woman, but Schweitzer caught him and hauled him back. It was a struggle, but far easier than it had been. The jinn howled and shook, but Schweitzer was able to back their shared body away, heading for the second set of sliding steel doors, a spray of glowing pinpricks showing through the double thickness of glass.

Stars.

They'd put him on the first floor after all.

Schweitzer stepped in front of the doors, waited for the

electric eye to recognize his presence and slide them open.
Nothing.

He turned them back to the woman behind the desk.
Raised a finger, pointed at her, took a step. She screamed,
hand hammering something behind the desk.

The doors slid open behind him, and they were out into
the coolness of night.

Schweitzer left the body to Ninip, allowed the jinn to take
them at a blurring pace while he examined their surroundings.

The building behind them was low and long, with an arcing roof like an airplane hangar. Orderly rows of box elder
had been trimmed to form a green fence around the front
entrance, gap-toothed now from the hole that Ninip had
punched through rather than simply change their course to
make for the deliberate opening.

Beyond was a parking lot with only a few cars squatting
between the freshly painted white lines. Solar-powered
sodium lights rose on twenty-foot poles, dark for now. The
corporate logo Schweitzer had seen inside was written
across the building's front as well.

The parking lot stretched off into the distance, where
Schweitzer could see the beginnings of what looked like an
office park, carefully manicured lawns surrounding low,
glass-fronted buildings so deliberately inconspicuous that it
screamed the government's hand to any who saw them.
Thick woods lined the parking lot on the remaining three
sides.

Schweitzer put energy into their legs, guiding Ninip as
the jinn vaulted them over a car and made for the office
park.

No, Schweitzer said. *That's going to get us taken out.*

The jinn responded with a feral grunt. He didn't need to
speak. That was where life was likely, where the most
blood could be spilled. Schweitzer pressed again, and the
jinn turned, not wanting to risk being shoved back into the

far corner he'd occupied since Schweitzer had gained the upper hand. They sprinted into the trees, disappearing under the thick canopy just as rotors began to beat the air overhead, and Eldredge's voice began to call over a loudspeaker. "Jim! Come back! You're making a mistake!"

Ninip tried to turn them instinctively at the sound, angling back for the building they'd just escaped, responding to the sound of prey reflexively. Schweitzer pushed him back on course, and they forged deeper into the woods as the rotors began to beat the air directly over their head.

In movies, the fugitive was always hounded by barking dogs, dodging between bright circles of focused light. Schweitzer knew that in real manhunts, the dogs were trained to move as silently as their handlers, that the men in the helos above him were staring through night-optical devices, the world below them tinted green and in perfect focus, their night vision preserved for the ugly work ahead.

He knew, because he'd done it. The green haze of the night-ops world had been one of the foremost colors on his palette, right next to the ochre red of blood.

The rotors came louder, lower. Two birds, keeping pace. They weren't flying a search pattern, and that meant they'd seen them. The softer patter of the rotors told him they were light helos, Little Birds most likely, which meant there was probably a sniper broadside, lining up his shot. .50 cal rounds or 20mm airburst ammunition if they wanted to make sure there weren't any pieces of him left big enough to cause any trouble. Schweitzer had trained for months to fire broadside out of a moving helo at an obscured target. It never took him more than a few seconds to get the shot off.

The clock was ticking.

Schweitzer funneled the images to Ninip, the helos above them, crammed with beating hearts, pulsing blood, lungs expanding and collapsing. He mainlined the coppery smell of gore, the canvas-ripping sound of flesh coming apart.

Ninip shivered, shrieked, scrambled in a circle looking for the carnage he so desperately sought.

Up, Schweitzer pushed to him. *Up.*

Ninip went up.

The jinn leapt them in a straight line, clearing twelve feet before grasping a thick limb above them. The limb drooped and cracked under their weight, but the jinn was already swinging them up and off, the pressure tearing the tree limb free but sending their shared body sailing another ten feet in the air to impact with a thicker section of tree trunk before launching off it.

Ninip leapt them from tree to tree, sometimes springing, sometimes swinging from branch to branch. They soared faster than if they'd been fired straight in the air. Schweitzer could see the trees shaking around them, knew the pilots would be seeing it, too, but by then it would be too late.

They exploded from the canopy, launching skyward with a shout.

Schweitzer had been right, two little birds hovered alongside one another. The sniper was seated at the edge of the cabin, boots on the skid. He cradled a carbine in the crook of his elbow, sighting down it toward the canopy that rapidly receded below Schweitzer-Ninip's feet. The sniper's finger was indexed along the trigger of the grenade launcher below its shortened barrel. He was already coming off the sights, eyes widening as Schweitzer-Ninip arrowed toward him. Ninip extended their arm, claws lancing out from extended fingers.

Schweitzer felt the man's eyes pop under the pressure of the bone spikes, punching the skull plate behind to slide into his brain. He flopped like a fish, jerking back into the cabin and into another man, who leapt for the tree canopy rather than face the monster suddenly in his helo. Ninip turned long enough to skewer one of the pilots through his helmet. The second pilot fired a pistol blindly over his shoulder, and Schweitzer felt the helo lurch, spinning.

He shouldered Ninip aside, grabbing control of their body and gripping the cabin's edge. He swung them out of the open door and caught the tail boom, their weight dragging the helo earthward. He could feel the wind from the spinning tail rotor, cutting the air inches from their mock-

ery of a face. The helo canted over and began to spin
wildly. Schweitzer opened their hands, letting go and falling backward down into the canopy.

The leaves covered them, but not before Schweitzer saw
the helo whirl sideways, the blades of its main rotor shattering against the cabin of its partner before both blossomed
into bright balls of flame.

Schweitzer felt the heat of the blast, the patter of smoking debris bouncing off their head and shoulders. He let
them turn then, just as the first tree branch snapped beneath
their weight, reached out a hand, and gripped the trunk,
fingertips wedging into the grooves of the bark and locking expertly on, the inhuman strength already slowing
their descent as they scraped along it.

By the time they reached the ground, all was silent save
for the crackling of flames from the burning canopy above
them.

The jumper had gambled and lost. He lay on the ground,
one leg bending the wrong way, the trouser leg dark with
blood. A splinter of tree branch projected from his arm.

Schweitzer knelt them over him. Ninip raced to the
fore, leaning their head in, long tongue extending.

Schweitzer hauled him back. The jinn shrieked and
fought, but it was much easier to control him now.

*What are you doing? If you do not kill him, he will tell
where we are!* Ninip said.

They already know where we are, Schweitzer said, unbut-
toning the man's shirt and stripping it off him. It was filthy,
soaked with blood and sweat, but the ripstop fabric was only
moderately torn. It would be clear that something was wrong,
but Schweitzer knew it was better than standing nude before
an onlooker, their corpse flesh burned to a slurry, digits
snapped off, the flesh split from their skull to their buttocks
as if someone had been attempting to cut out their spine.

And if he was going to find Patrick and Sarah, they
would need to walk among people again.

*He deserves death, worse than death! He kept your fam-
ily from you, he was trying to destroy you!* Ninip shrieked.

As if he could hear their conversation, the man groaned, and said, "You better fucking kill me, because as soon as I knit up, I'm going to light your freak ass up, you little bitch."

Schweitzer didn't doubt he meant it. He was a hard operator, unused to losing. He believed in his cause. He would attempt to follow through on his threat.

He was the kind of man that, in life, might have been Schweitzer's friend.

He lives, Schweitzer said. He knew how it worked now, that to slaughter this man would be to restore Ninip to control. That the jinn wanted it was the surest sign that it was the wrong move.

Instead, Schweitzer stripped the man of his trousers and boots, rushed them into the clothing. They were tight, but they fit. They stood to go, looked down, knelt. Ninip raged while Schweitzer forced them to grasp the man's thigh just above the knee, and the calf of the broken leg with the other hand.

He did the bellows dance again, working the air into a wheezing cough through their shattered voice box, hoping he made a convincing enough sound. "Hurt."

The man looked at him, nodded. "I know, get it done."

The leg snapped back into place with the sound of splintering wood. The man didn't scream, only went unconscious, head lolling back and eyes staring sightlessly.

It was all Schweitzer could do. The man's colleagues would be here soon enough. Schweitzer sprinted them off into the foliage.

The ground rose sharply, the trees beginning to thin as the stony soil gave under their stolen boots. Their augmented ears began to hear the sounds of car engines, the whine of air conditioners.

They crested a ridge, bursting through the foliage and stopping short as the ground fell away. A river moved below, current ripping hard under the nearly full moon, white-topped wavelets dancing under the light.

In the distance, a city thrummed with life, twinkling lights blotting out the stars. A highway snaked past it, a

double loop of traffic, moving smoothly at this late hour.
They heard distant snatches of music. Ninip took it in, awe
momentarily replacing his desire to kill. Schweitzer
remembered that the jinn had never seen a modern city
before, even one as small as the patchwork of buildings
that sprawled below them.

Then Ninip stared through their shared eyes at a single
spire rising from the low field of lights, more than twice
the height of anything around it. Recognition flared. *Where
are we?* the jinn asked, his boyish tone so out of step with
the situation that it almost made Schweitzer laugh.

Of course he recognized it, Schweitzer thought. Of
course. *It's not what you're thinking. That's a replica. It's
built to imitate . . .*

The lighthouse, Ninip said.

They named the city after it, Schweitzer said. *Or, maybe
they built it because of the city's name. It's Alexandria.*

Ninip tried out the word. *It was called Ra-Kedet. And
the lighthouse was ten times the size.*

*They renamed it after Alex . . . after a guy who con-
quered it. And yeah, it's only a replica.*

This was no time for history lessons. Schweitzer forced
their eyes away from the tower and back down to the river
again. He knew it now. It was the Potomac, the current ripping south, winding past Maryland and out to the Atlantic
beyond.

He was looking north, the Pentagon squatting just out
of view, the dome of the nation's capital beyond.

He knew where he was. What he didn't know was where
to go.

But he knew what his best bet was if he wanted to throw
off the hunt.

Schweitzer grabbed control of their legs, leapt. The cliff
face disappeared behind them, the wind rushing in their
ears, the sparkling line of the river stretching below, still
for a moment, then rushing up to meet them.

Schweitzer extended their hands, tucked their head,
locked what remained of their abdominal muscles. They

arced gracefully down toward the water, and Schweitzer felt something rising inside him, strange and familiar, a distant memory, faintly recalled. It felt fantastic. It felt like joy.

The silver surface of the water expanded in his view. He felt their hands cut the surface.

And then his vision blacked out, their nerves dead, their body suddenly refusing to report to him. Even Ninip faded into the background, as all Schweitzer's senses tuned to a single signal.

Sarah's voice. Forlorn. Lost. But alive.

Jim, I'm here.

The sound shivered through him, more felt than heard. It seated in every cell of his dead body and rooted there. *I'm here, and I need you.*

And then it was gone. The water embraced them, and they coiled under, turning and righting before swimming for the surface.

Schweitzer shivered as the echoes of Sarah's voice reverberated through him. He had heard her. The scent of her perfume hadn't been his imagination. His sense of her was no phantom limb. There was a trail through the void. Perhaps it was nothing more than the magical equivalent of a homing pigeon's instinct.

But Schweitzer knew it was more than that. He felt their love like a physical thing, a rope, infinitely long, infinitely strong, linking them wherever they were, soul to soul. He realized now that he had always felt it, that it had taken losing her to see this thing that had been a part of him since the day he'd first watched her sleeping beside him, head on his shoulder, and realized it would be her and no other. He had always felt this thing that the magic had made into a compass needle, unerringly pointing the way to the love of his life.

He knew he was defining something that he didn't understand, trying to bound it in a way he could grasp. The truth was that he didn't know what to call this thing, this certainty, this sense of direction.

But whatever it was, it was something he could follow. It was a way back to her.

Schweitzer stopped rising before their head broke the water's surface. He was following instinct, doing what a living man would. They had no need to breathe. Slowly, he let the dead, airless weight of their body sink to the bottom, until their feet touched down on trash-strewn silt. Precious little light penetrated here. The thickness of the water jealously guarded its secrets, shutting out all senses, sound and smell and sight all exiled to the air-breathing world.

But there were two things it couldn't obstruct.

The first was the smell of Sarah's rosewater perfume, so strong it was nearly cloying, so clear Schweitzer felt he could reach out and touch it.

The second was the feeling of Sarah's presence, a light that was her glimmering soul, distant and focused and shining like a polar star.

CHAPTER XXVI
REUNION

Drew was as good as his word.

Sarah guessed the house needed tens of thousands of dollars in repairs. The paint was so patchy and peeled that there was more siding exposed to the elements than not, and the slate roof had gone to mold in such spectacular fashion that it practically glowed green under the moonlight. The foundation sagged so badly that the windows on the upper story were canted, giving the house the look of a stroke victim, one side of the face slack and sagging. A tractor shed leaned drunkenly against the house. Sara didn't doubt it would have fallen over but for the support of its sagging neighbor.

But a candle burned in each window, and the walk up to the entrance was lined with ceramic pots bright with flowers. The grass was neatly mowed for a solid twenty feet around the house, then immediately gave over into overgrown fields dotted with big, gray shapes that she guessed were round bales.

Martha stood in the doorway in a pair of sweatpants and stained T-shirt. She looked a few years younger than

Drew, and smelled of old perfume hastily applied. But her smile was genuine and she hugged Sara as if she'd known her for years before turning to Patrick with a warmth that could only belong to someone who'd raised children herself. The boy buried his face in his mother's shoulder with a forced shyness that Sarah knew meant he was delighted.

Drew made introductions, then led the way into a scene from an *Architectural Digest* shoot of folksy Americana. The wide-planked wooden floor gleamed under soft light from iron floor lamps. A wooden American eagle stretched over the fireplace above a sword, its gold paint covering it considerably better than the exterior of the house. The fireplace was dark, but the iron grate held a planter stuffed with herbs.

An ancient yellow Lab thumped his tail against the floor, too lazy to lift his head from his paws.

"It's beautiful," Sarah said. "It's like something out of a movie."

"Oh, that's very sweet," Martha said. "We've been here since we got married. My grandfather built it back before the Civil War." They stood in silence for a moment before she said, "I'll put some tea on, and let me pour Patrick a glass of milk. Do you let him have sweets?"

"Thanks for asking. Not normally, but I figure a night stuck out in"—she stopped herself before she said *in the middle of nowhere*—"unfamiliar territory warrants a treat."

"Cookies it is," Martha said. "Are you hungry?"

"'Course she's hungry," Drew said, guiding her to a dark, wooden kitchen table that looked as old as the house but considerably better maintained. "We got any of that brisket left?"

Martha smiled an affirmative and set herself to bustling in the kitchen while Sarah and Drew made small talk, Patrick staring at the old man in fascination. From what Sarah could glean from the conversation, Drew and Martha had both been federal bureaucrats in DC before retiring to open a bed-and-breakfast that turned out to be more work than either of them were interested in. Instead, they rented

the acreage out as a hay mowing, and that income com-
bined with their retirement allowed them a nice place from
which to watch the sunset.

Patrick ate and drank his body weight in milk, chocolate
chip cookies, and tiny bits of the best brisket Sarah had ever
tasted. She talked with Drew and watched in amazement as
Patrick nestled in Martha's arms while she sang softly to
him, staring up at her until he nodded off once again.

"That's amazing," Sarah said. "I've never seen him that
comfortable with a stranger . . . well, ever."

Martha's smile showed genuine pleasure. "Well, I've
raised three of my own, you know. Got some practice."

"Got five grandchildren so far," Drew said. "Our cup
runneth over, truly."

"Any of them coming tomorrow?" Sarah asked.

"The middle one," Drew said. "The boy. He's in the
army. You'll like him."

"My husband was navy," Sarah said without thinking.

Drew and Martha exchanged a glance before Drew
turned to her. "Was. He got out?"

"No," Sarah said, "he was killed." *You're lying,* she
thought. *He's alive and he's coming. You know it in your
bones.*

"I'm sorry," Sarah added quickly, "I didn't want to
make this personal. I know you don't know me."

"Afghanistan?" Martha asked.

"No . . . he was here. I'm sorry, this is so personal."

"We don't mean to pry," Drew said. "We were just wondering what really brought you out here in the middle of
the night with your boy in the car. You've got a hatchback,
Sarah. I didn't see a suitcase in there."

"I keep a change of clothes at my friend's." Sarah could
feel the lie in her words, could see that Drew and Martha
felt it, too. They exchanged another glance, and Drew
looked at his lap.

"As I said, I don't want to push you here," he said, "and I
promise we won't turn you out or call the law, but we're

bedding down under the same roof, and I think Martha and I have a right to know what kind of trouble it is you're in."

"I'm not in any trouble."

"Sweetheart," Martha said, her voice taking on the firm tone of a schoolteacher, "Drew told you we take in strays. This isn't our first rodeo. We know trouble when we see it, and there's trouble here."

Sarah stood, reached out to gather Patrick. "I'm sorry to have disturbed you, thanks very much for the hospitality. I'm feeling awake now, and I'm sure I can make it the rest of the way . . ."

Drew stood, patted the air with his palms. "Hold on, now. There's no need to . . ."

But Sarah wasn't listening. Her eyes were locked on Martha, who had turned her torso, holding Patrick away from Sarah as she bent at the waist to pick him up.

The kindly old woman vanished. All Sarah saw now was a blurred enemy curled around her child. She vaguely wondered if this was how James saw the world when he ran ops. Her hands twitched, her heartbeat seemed to slow.

"Give. Me. My. Son."

"All right," Martha said, fear blossoming behind her eyes. "Wasn't going to keep him from you. Just caught me by surprise is all."

Sarah collected Patrick, held him in one arm, kept the other hand free and hovering over the pocketknife hidden in her pants. "I should go," she said again.

"Please don't," Drew said. "I'm sorry, we were prying. If you want to go, that's fine, but we'd really prefer it if you stayed. You're tired and in the middle of nowhere. We'll lay off the questions. Think of your son."

"I am thinking of my son," Sarah said. "I am always thinking of my son. That's why I am out here, that's why I'm driving in the middle of the night. For my son. Because no matter how many cookies you give me and no matter what nice things you say, I'm still the one who has to take care of him." The words tumbled out, petulant and nonsensical. Her stomach fluttered, her veins felt like fire flowed in them, a jittery rush rising in her, as if she'd been funneling espresso instead of sipping hot tea.

Something was coming.

Her body was amping up in preparation. Her gut sank with the same dead certainty she'd felt so often over the last few days. The sense of pending arrival was mixed, dreadful and joyous, equal parts exultation and foreboding. Martha and Drew were already fading into the background, Sarah's senses alert to the windows and the door, the darkness pressing against them like a physical thing made of purple black mist.

"Sarah," Drew was saying. "Before you go, will you do one thing for me? Call it payback for the food."

"Sure," Sarah said, distracted. The front door seemed far away, her vision of it fish-eyed, a bulbous, distorted tunnel. The door's edges seemed to vibrate almost imperceptibly.

"Will you pray with me?" Drew asked. "That's all, just a few minutes with your head bowed. You don't even have to believe it, just indulge an old man who's worried about you."

"Pray?" Sarah moved to the window. There was a low growl sounding in the distance, so faint that it might have been mistaken for wind, but Sarah's hearing had changed, had tapped into the currents in the air around her, the tiny hairs in her ears vibrating madly, pushing the air down, bouncing it off the onionskin of her eardrums below.

A low, throaty growl. At first she thought it a roaring lion. Her mind accepted this without a moment's cognitive dissonance. The bullet that had felled Jim had taken reality with him, leaving Sarah to float in this weird miasma of tangible dreams, precognition, and the shimmering tinctures of her past. In this world, roaring lions could charge up a deserted country road in the middle of the night.

"Sarah?" Drew asked, standing.

He stiffened, Martha's eyes narrowed, and Sarah knew they heard it, too.

The roaring lion resolved into a rumbling bass. An engine, a loud big twin.

"Someone's coming for you, aren't they?" Martha asked. She turned to Drew, her eyes pleading.

He shook his head. "If whoever is coming is dangerous, now would be a good time to tell us."

Sarah could feel him inching backward, elbow brushing a sagging bookcase and fumbling for the closet door beside it.

But it didn't matter because whatever it was had arrived. Sarah's vision contracted to a pinhole, the rest of the world vanishing, time slowing to a crawl inside the tiny circle before her.

Through it, she saw a thin, insectile chopper rolling slowly to the foot of the driveway, easing to a stop, narrow front tire crunching on the shattered gravel. The gas tank was badly dented, the chrome refracting the starlight where it should have glittered, signs that the motorcycle had fallen at speed, skidded on its side for a few feet before coming to a stop. The metal funnel of the exhaust had turned a deep indigo from the heat of the sliding friction.

The rider lent credence to the idea. He was a big man, the large bike looking comically small between his thick legs. He swung one over, didn't bother with the kickstand, let the motorcycle topple over and flop on its side with a crunch. His clothing was tattered, the evidence of a long scrape on the pavement written across him in melted leather and frayed denim.

His head was hidden behind a red motorcycle helmet, a long white stripe showing where it had scraped along the pavement until the curved surface had been sanded flat. The man took a shuffling step toward her, a zombie shamble, and two things happened.

First, a low buzzing click outside the pinhole focus of her senses told her that Drew had thrown open the closet door, pulled something out.

Second, the dread vanished, the joy consumed her, making her giddy, rising behind her breastbone until she felt her shoulders pin back and her breasts lift, as if she would float off the ground. She took a step forward, banged her knees against the wall below the window, turned to the door. Drew and Martha were both talking at once, a low rumble in the far distance. She heard a mechanical click-clack, a gun's action working, but it didn't matter, she was to the door, opening it, stepping out into the thick night air.

The man did his zombie shuffle up to the base of the front steps. The porchlight fell on him and she saw why. The boots were at least a size too small, unzipped only a few inches before the protrusion of his anklebone punched out over the metal teeth. The leather jacket was likewise a size too small, the cured surface bulging and stretching to accommodate his muscular arms. It hung open, revealing skin so pale it reflected the light, the blue-gray of fish scales. His belly and chest were crisscrossed with rough white scars, the evidence of ham-fisted surgical stitching. His head had been forced into the helmet, the thick pillar of his neck bulging comically out below the lower edge.

She set Patrick gently down, felt the boy scramble away. The sensations came as if from a long distance, actions taken by another person who looked like her. Her attention was locked in the pinhole, watching the man at the foot of the steps.

Sarah could smell him as he shambled closer, the pungent odor of chemical preservative, engine oil, dirty leather. But the smells were like the rising panic in Drew and Martha's voices, background noise, outside the tunnel of exultation that linked her to this strange man. The tunnel's edges widened to accommodate him as he came up the steps, taking on a pinkish cast, until Sarah imagined that they stood together on a path of rose petals, echoes of her dream made real.

He was a slab of tortured muscle stretching beneath skin the color of a fish's underbelly. He shambled like a zombie. But it was Jim. The thing that bound them was undeniable. She could feel it coursing through her, eddying across the space between them. Not bound at the hip, but at the soul. It was the same way she'd known he was coming. He could have been walking on all fours and had a tail, she would still have known it was him.

At last, she let go of the idea that she was crazy and gave what linked them a new name.

Magic.

Their love, their history, their bond was magic. Somehow, it linked them, over any distance. It didn't make sense, but it didn't have to. He was here.

She gathered him into her arms, letting the tears come now, nestling her head against the cold, waxy surface of his chest, wrapping one arm around him, feeling the jacket sink unnaturally over his spine, as if he was split there.

"Oh, Jim. Oh, baby. I knew you were alive. I knew it I knew it I knew it."

He stiffened, froze. For an instant, she felt doubt gnaw at her, fear beginning to bloom in its shadow. But no, the certainty was there, her stomach still doing cartwheels of joy. It was Jim. She'd known he was alive and here he was and she was holding him and so what if it didn't make sense and was crazy. So what. He was here. That was enough for now.

She heard the leather creak, felt his arm rise behind her.

Felt his thick, gray hand find the back of her neck, gently grasp it, pushing her into him.

Like Jim had done, and only Jim. He'd said it was the one thing he liked about her preference for shorter hair. It gave him a better grip. The tears came fresh, with such force that she shook, steadying herself against the solidity of him, a pillar, as he'd always been.

Her forehead knocked against the lower lip of his helmet and she leaned back, reaching up to lift the visor.

His hand moved again, quickly now, grabbing her wrist, painfully at first, but letting up immediately.

"Babe . . ." she began. *I don't care what you look like under there. It doesn't matter. I want to see you.*

But his hand was a vise supported by an iron bar. The helmet inclined, and she could tell he was looking at her, thought she saw just the faintest shimmer of dancing lights behind the visor, as if candle flames flickered there. More strangeness that wasn't strange. Not in the rose-tinted tunnel they shared.

His neck began to flex, air whistling up and drawing her attention to a badly patched wound in his throat. Air whistled out of it as a breathy word sounded from inside the helmet, echoing out to her, a rasping grunt that gave no hint of the voice she'd known. It didn't sound like Jim at all, but the word was unmistakable.

"No."

She opened her mouth to reply, and suddenly she was being pulled away from him, a hand on her shoulder hauling her backward. Something long and dark was sliding past her vision, invading the sacred space she shared with Jim. She shook the hand off and the tunnel went with it, her vision suddenly expanding into the harsh corners of the world, flooding her with the sickly light of the porch lamp, clouded with insects questing for its false moon.

Martha was pulling her back into the house, yelling at Jim to get back. Drew was moving forward, his body inexpertly hunched behind a fowling piece, the wide barrels chipped and rusting, pointed out at Jim.

"No!" she shouted. "Drew, don't!"

The old man ignored her. His face was purple, his terror congealing into a shaking anger that made wide veins stand out on his forehead and nose. He was shouting incomprehensibly at Jim, thrusting the old gun at him as if it were a spear.

Jim's hand slapped down, faster than she'd ever seen anyone move, grasped the double barrel. Claws had sprung from his fingertips, long, sharp, the yellow-white of old bone. The tip of a long gray slug slithered from below the helmet's lower lip, dusty and dark. After a moment, she realized it was his tongue.

She lunged for Drew, shaking off Martha easily enough, the old woman's grip falling away. Her arm snaked out, her rabbit punch connecting poorly, bouncing ineffectually off the old man's shoulder, careening up into his neck. He cursed, shuddered.

Boom.

The old gun exploded. She felt the heat flash and smelled the rotten-egg stink of cordite, flailed backward, tumbled, fell.

She blinked, saw only darkness. She felt something soft beneath her, was dimly aware of Martha sobbing.

She eased herself up, straining her triceps to take her weight, keep the pressure off the old woman beneath her. She blinked again. The darkness resolved to white, then burst into splinters of shattered glass, dissolved into stars and finally she could see again. Martha weeping, curled in a ball, streaks of black powder running up her cheek, blood on her shoulder, her hands, her hip.

Drew stood over her, hands crushed to his abdomen, horror and pain mingling in his strained expression. His eyes were fixed over Sarah's shoulder, bulging, comically wide. Sarah crouched, followed the direction of his gaze.

Jim alone stood stock-still, looking down at his hand, still clutching fragments of the broken gun. Slivers of metal had shredded his jacket arm, the flesh beneath. Sarah could see them embedded there, smoking, smell the cooked meat stench of his burning flesh. The jacket had been shredded to the shoulder. As she watched, he shrugged loose of it, leaving it to pool behind him.

It landed beside the motorcycle helmet, knocked off by the blast, the visor cracked and burned where some hot metal shard had unseamed it hinge to hinge.

The crown of Jim's head was split, nubs of bone horn piercing the scalp, rising through rubbery skin the color of a beached fish. Slowly, Jim raised his head, looked at her.

It was him. That much was clear. His beautiful face was still intact enough to recognize, but only just. When zombie movies had become popular, she'd toyed with an online game that allowed you to "zombify" yourself. You fed the program a picture, and it turned you into a zombie. Jim was zombified. His face was a flat expanse, his features stretched and warped. His nose was gone. What remained skewed at a hard angle over a jaw that now jutted out in an underbite that would have been comical if not for the wicked, tusklike teeth rising from it, the gray snake's tongue lolling out the side. His face looked part dead, part mechanical, a cyborg built from stainless steel and corpse flesh.

And his eyes. Oh God. Jim's beautiful eyes. Gone. They were gone. They were empty holes, lit by flickering silver flames. She could feel them boring into her nonetheless, and fear suddenly gripped her. This was a monster facing her. It felt like Jim, bore traces of the face she loved, but . . . she shuddered as the totality of it hit her. She reached out again, felt with the same clairvoyant certainty that it was him, felt the same spike of love. She could feel the rose trail, the magic that linked them, shimmering in the back of her mind, flowing out to him. No matter what Jim looked like, that connection hadn't changed, couldn't change.

She remembered the old C. S. Lewis quote. *You don't have a soul. You are a soul. You have a body.* Her soul loved James Schweitzer's soul with everything she had. His body was a wrapper, a suit of ill-fitting clothing draped across the thing she loved. He was Jim. Nothing could ever change that.

His new form was terrifying, but the connection between them vibrated with the love he felt for her. A monster, maybe, but a monster who would never do her any harm.

She swallowed her revulsion, stood to go to him, but the body around her soul demanded its due, and she couldn't keep the reaction off her face.

He reached a hand toward her, his expression creasing in sympathy as her horror registered on him. The shift was repulsive. His brows tried to furrow, the stretched skin only spreading and gathering around the black pits of the sockets, the corners of that vicious wood-chipper mouth dipping in what should have been an arc of concern, and instead became a hungry, predator grin.

"S-rah," he croaked. *Sarah. He's trying to say my name.*

She looked at the smoking shards of metal, embedded deep in his arm, his neck, his chest. She saw the ragged wound in his throat, the gray slashes across arterial pathways.

Maybe her husband wasn't alive after all.

Patrick was screaming. The little boy huddled against the closet where Drew had retrieved the gun, hands over his head. If he recognized his father, he gave no sign at all. Jim's eyes finally moved from her to his son. He froze, trembling.

Drew shouldered her aside, standing fully over his wife. Jim showed no reaction, his burning eyes fixed on Sarah, tracking her as she staggered, shifted, regained her balance. Sarah felt a tugging tension in him. He was at war with something, but for now at least, he had the upper hand. Her body screamed at her to run, to put miles between her and this shambling corpse that had once been her husband, but Martha's moaning wouldn't permit it.

She swallowed and knelt, tried to find the source of the blood. Drew was shouting. Martha rolled pleading eyes in her direction. Sarah's hands traced the rips in her clothing, trying to locate the wounds.

". . . the hell away from here! You hear? Git!" Drew's voice had taken on an hysterical edge.

"Stop!" Sarah yelled up at him. "Your wife is hurt!"

Drew looked down at Sarah, pausing in his ranting long enough to kick her aside, turn his wrath on her. "Get off her!"

Jim turned, snarled. The expression suited him, far more natural to his new face than the attempted sympathy was. He cocked one hand, the blades of his fingertips lengthening as he reached out with the other, grabbing Drew's neck, turning the old man's shouts into a sudden choked gurgle.

And released him.

Jim stepped back, his head sawing, trying to look in all directions at once. He crouched deep, clawed hands out at his sides, eyes scanning the room for a defensible position.

She heard a faint slapping in the distance, pairs of bare feet smacking on tarmac, crunching over leaves. Getting louder as they drew near.

Something was coming.

Somethings.

They didn't have much time.

CHAPTER XXVII
EVEN ODDS

The signals reached out of the darkness, pulsing in Schweitzer's mind. It felt much as it had when he had seen Jawid reaching out into the maelstrom of churning souls. Pulsing signals, the magic firing like lasers through the ether, long, glowing lines converging on a single point.

Him.

Ninip went mad at the signals' touch, straining and pushing against his bonds, his strength seeming to grow at the nearness of them. He was drunk on the anticipation of battle, on the nearness of worthy opponents. Schweitzer had been with the jinn the last time he was so roused, when they stood outside the cell containing the animated remains of the former PJ known as Cameron.

Schweitzer looked up at his son. Patrick had gone white-faced with terror, his fear passing the red line from screaming adrenaline and into catatonic paralysis. Trauma heaped on trauma. He shuddered to think of what this would do to Patrick as he advanced through the years into manhood.

But that manhood would only come if the boy lived. Schweitzer would worry about the trauma later. For now, he was going to keep his wife and son alive, stick with them, and protect them as he couldn't when he had lived himself.

Sarah was coming back to her feet, ignoring the old man, screaming out his lungs in a vain effort to summon courage. Bravery didn't work that way.

The signals began to tighten, to converge. Schweitzer turned his attention inward, shoving Ninip back into his corner. The jinn seemed to be drawing strength from the coming tide. It was getting harder to contain him. Ninip was ranting, but Schweitzer didn't take the time to listen.

The old man turned his vitriol on Sarah, standing protectively over his own injured wife. There was no time to deal with his histrionics now. The threat was too imminent. Too great.

Schweitzer grabbed a handful of the man's shirt and threw him across the room. He landed on his ass and skidded across the floor to slam into the cabinets under the kitchen sink with a grunt. He wasn't hurt badly, and, more importantly, he was out of the way.

Schweitzer turned to Sarah and pointed at their boy, who'd slid down the wall to a sitting position, his tears dry now, skin chalk white. He squeezed his lungs, pushed the whistling air up and through his ravaged throat, managed to make a gurgling whisper: "Pah-ik." He prayed she would understand, pushed his will down the corridor that linked them. *Hide him. You can't face what's coming.*

Sarah nodded, ran, scooping Patrick up under one arm and flinging the closet open with the other. She cast a worried eye over at Martha. It was clear that she was torn over leaving the old woman still injured, but Sarah moved with purpose, getting a better grip on their son, rummaging frantically for a weapon.

She's a SEAL born and bred, Schweitzer thought. Mission over man. Triaging in a crisis. Making the hard call to protect her own.

Schweitzer turned to face the door, scanning the room for a defensible position as Sarah found the closet empty, fled to the kitchen, stepped gingerly over a groaning Drew before giving a short bark of victory and brandishing a good-sized meat cleaver in her free hand.

They are coming. They are coming, Ninip exulted. *They are coming, and now you will see what we are.*

Something landed on the roof with a thud loud enough to shake plaster dust out of the eaves.

Schweitzer looked up, tried to keep Sarah in his peripheral vision, pushed back on Ninip. There was nowhere to go. Maybe the door beside the kitchen led to a cellar? Maybe he could hide them . . .

The wall exploded.

Something heavy collided with Schweitzer's stomach and he spun across the floor, digging his claws into the hardwood to stop himself. Straining to see through the cloud of dust where the bay window and front door had once been. He shifted through the vision ranges, some of the power returning to him as Ninip reasserted himself.

A shape skidded through the dust, resolving as it slid into the light of the kitchen, clawed toes shredding the linoleum, bringing it to a shuddering stop.

It wasn't Cam.

But it might as well have been. Schweitzer had time to make out the naked form, well muscled, scarred, twisted out of humanity by the jinn's supremacy. This one was female. Her skull had blossomed into a ring of horns, circling her entire head like the petals of a hideous sunflower. Her breasts had been cut off, rough purple X's marking where the surgeon had stitched the incision sites shut.

Her eyes burned gold. Was she G-3? G-5? Schweitzer wondered who she had been in life. She sniffed in his direction, burning eyes lighting on him. He could feel her magical current reach out to him, washing over him before she pulled it away. The current scanned further, settled on Martha.

She hissed and vaulted over him, making for the old woman, a single bone spike protruding from the back of her balled fist.

Ninip raged, but Schweitzer wasn't surprised. Of course she had gone for the old woman. Schweitzer couldn't slake her lust. He had no blood to give, no screams to utter.

He flung himself up onto the balls of his feet, took note of Sarah, beside the old man with Patrick tucked under her arm, her head sawing frantically as she searched for an exit. Then he launched them after the Gold Operator, flinging one hand forward to catch her trailing ankle.

He knew instantly that he wouldn't reach her. He was weak from holding Ninip in place, the jinn's reduced presence draining his power as much as his struggle to keep him locked down. The Gold Operator sailed through the air, bone spikes growing along her spine and finally sprouting into a nub of flexible tail just above her buttocks. She shrank as the distance between them grew, her shadow falling over the old woman, who screamed, throwing her arms over her head.

Schweitzer seized Ninip, gave over control, hauled the jinn into the fore.

The jinn came forward with a shout. Schweitzer made way for him, feeling Ninip fill the shared space, the hunger flooding him, dulling his senses, tingeing their shared vision with red. The air seemed to reverberate, and Schweitzer could feel their left foot touch down, dig claws in, push off.

They flew forward, missing the ankle, and instead crashing into the Gold Operator's back. They tumbled through the air and crashed into the broken remnants of the wall. "Go!" Schweitzer shouted to Martha, heard his own voice sound as nothing more than a grunt.

The Gold Operator hissed beneath them as they locked their legs around hers, grabbed ahold of the ring of bone spikes around her face. Ninip howled with joy, setting their shoulders wrenching, flashing visions of twisting her head off her shoulders.

Schweitzer strained and pulled, Ninip's strength doubling his own.

Her neck didn't budge. They might as well have tried to rip a building off its foundation.

She hissed again, her tongue lashing out like a whip, wrapping around Schweitzer-Ninip's head as she kicked her legs out, breaking their grip as if they were a weakling child. The tongue heaved, and Schweitzer felt them lifted into the air, flying end over end until they crashed into the sink, ripping the faucet from its moorings and sending water arcing into the air.

He spun them over, leapt to their feet just in time to see the Gold Operator throw herself across the old woman, sinking her head down low, the bone spikes cutting deep, her whip tongue changing direction. The old woman shrieked, gurgled, was silent.

Schweitzer could see Sarah throwing open the back door, slowly edging around the corner as he had taught her, refusing to rush blindly into danger no matter how frightened she was. He swallowed the spike of pride and love. The Gold Operator would be done with that old woman soon, looking for fresh prey. He marshaled Ninip, flashed an image of springing forward, claws first.

But the jinn had other ideas. Before he could stop him, the jinn had turned their body, crouched to spring at Sarah's back, Patrick cradled in one arm.

Schweitzer pushed madly against the jinn, battering him with everything he had. At first Ninip resisted, their wills locking until Schweitzer felt as if their ghostly foreheads touched, sweating and wrestling in the darkness. The jinn gained ground, and Schweitzer screamed as their body began to turn again, moving in the direction of his wife.

No! Not now. He couldn't bear to see his wife and child slaughtered at his own hand. He would far rather spend eternity in the soul storm than that. He gave a shout and threw himself at the jinn once more, the thought of killing his own family charging him to heights approaching madness. Ninip wailed and gave way, Schweitzer battered him back and back, until the jinn clung to only the tiniest sliver of their shared body, a thread's span from being pushed out entirely.

You will end us both!

Better that than you touch her.

He heard the Gold Operator turn to face him, utter a screaming hiss, then the ceiling collapsed and something fell on him.

He heard Sarah shout, saw her turn, and then he was borne to the ground. Spikes pierced his shoulder and chest, punching through his flesh and bone and piercing deep into the floor beneath him, the fist that drove the spikes sinking deep into the cavity occupied by his dead lungs.

His enemy was enveloped in a cloud of dust from the broken ceiling, swirling around him. Schweitzer could make out two golden pinpoints through the swirling grit, a gray grimace slowly beginning to come clear.

He heard another hiss, a whooshing of air. *Sarah!* But the scream that sounded from beside him was the old man's, punctuated by a wet ripping sound that drew his shouts into a crescendoing howl.

Schweitzer attempted to grab the Gold Operator's hips, using a combatives maneuver to throw it off, but Ninip bulled forward again, seizing more of the shared space, interfering. The jinn's animal instincts added to his strength, his speed, but as always, they interfered with his ability to bring his training to bear.

Instead, Schweitzer opted for a simple maneuver, punching their arm up, driving their claws into the flesh of the Gold Operator atop them, the weakness engendered by Ninip's diminishment robbing the blow of its power. The motion cleared the rest of the dust, revealing an umbrella armature of needle teeth, cutting the lips to ribbons.

Cam.

Cam's eyes focused, lost interest. Schweitzer was a dead thing, of interest only insofar as he presented an obstacle. Cam's head lifted, sniffing the air, freezing as he found a target.

No! Schweitzer flailed against his grip, feeling the claws rip deeper into him. Cam withdrew them, rising to kill Schweitzer's wife and child.

Thok.

Cam's head rocked to the side, the meat cleaver embedding so deeply that Sarah almost cut his head in two. He rolled off Schweitzer-Ninip and came to his feet, the cleaver still quivering where it had stuck, the flames of his eyes covered by its width like a metal hat brim. He made no sound, only tensed.

Beside him, the female Gold Operator was rising, soaked in gore. She was slower, torpid with two kills to her tale, but Schweitzer knew it wouldn't save Sarah and Patrick. He heard the thump of shoes on wood and knew that his wife had pelted out the back door, was running. *Good, baby. Go. Go.*

Ninip was shouting, the soft buzz of his voice a gnat buzzing around Schweitzer's ears. Schweitzer ignored him, sending them diving for Cam's legs as the Operator sprang after Sarah.

The Gold Operator's knees buckled and he collapsed backward across Schweitzer-Ninip's back, growling. Schweitzer could hear the female Gold Operator leaping over them, scrambling out the back door, racing after Sarah.

Cam arched his back, shoulders pinning them to the floor. The Gold Operator reached out to grab their ankles. Schweitzer pushed up for all he was worth, their dead muscles stronger than any living man's, but still pathetically weak with Ninip's help impaired. Cam didn't budge until he was ready, then he whipped his arms forward, hurling Schweitzer-Ninip through the air for the third time that night.

Schweitzer felt the wall give as they burst through it, the coolness of the night air, the wet touch of the grass as they skidded into the dirt, all directions becoming a mad jumble. The tractor shed beside the house spun like a washing machine's load and finally settled as they rolled to a stop on their back.

Ninip was shouting something, but Schweitzer ignored

him, his eyes locked on that female Gold Operator, loping like a hunting dog toward the tractor shed just as the doors slammed and the wooden bar was dropped into place. Sarah was inside. The wooden slats of the walls looked thick and sturdy, but Schweitzer knew they wouldn't hold for very long.

Schweitzer rolled them to their feet, weakness and weariness suffusing him, their pace maddeningly slow as he forced them to pursue the female Operator. Something was grinding in their thigh, where a bone had snapped.

She had reached the shed's edge, was clawing at the boards, a high, whining cry of hungry anticipation issuing from her dead mouth. The whip tongue draped over her shoulder, twitching in excitement.

There was a roar from inside the shed, an engine coming to life. Maybe the old man had a car in there? The flare of hope was brief. At the height of Ninip's power, Schweitzer knew they could outrun a car. He didn't doubt that the Gold Operator could, too.

With a shout of triumph, the Gold Operator ripped the first board away, railroad-tie thick and gray from creosote. She threw it over her shoulder, tumbling through the air. Schweitzer-Ninip caught it on the fly, stumbled, skidded to their knees as another board came away, and another.

Then all the boards burst apart as a gigantic tractor shouldered its way through the weakened shed wall.

Schweitzer could see Sarah in the driver's seat, her face a mask of determination, Patrick shaking in her lap. What the hell was she thinking? Was she going to run it over? That wouldn't help.

Then he saw the spinning blades of the wide hay mower attached to its front forks, and realized that it would.

But the Gold Operator wasn't going to stand still and be cut to ribbons. She spit contempt at his wife and crouched, her tail quivering as she prepared to vault over the blades to join Patrick in Sarah's lap.

Schweitzer shouted, poured all his will into their twisting torso and threw.

Please. Oh, dear God, please, he thought as the chunk of

wood spun through the air, level with the ground, its shadow blotting out the reflection of the starlight on the damp grass as it went, making the ground shimmer beneath it.

It caught her feet squarely as she leapt, turning the jump into a stumble and then a fall, the bone-framed head pitching forward into the grass just as the hay mower passed over it.

The body jerked and spun, sucked into the whirling blades with amazing speed, the Gold Operator's shrill scream suddenly cut off as her throat, her lungs, her torso were ground to chuck and vomited back out.

Schweitzer got them on their feet as tiny chunks of meat and bone spattered them, a rain of flesh that had once been a thing of magic and death.

Sarah was screaming, though whether from victory or terror he couldn't tell. Something hard collided with them and they went facedown in the grass. Cam, on their back, claws piercing their head this time, holding them in place, eyes canted, giving them a full view of the house's intact side, the edge of the driveway beyond, a third Gold Operator galloping up it, gaze fixed on Sarah, chanting a litany in a strange language Schweitzer couldn't understand.

Ninip's voice finally reached him. *Let me help you! You cannot face them alone. You are too weak. Let me . . .*

Schweitzer felt his own exhaustion. His spirit was leaden, his phantom limbs too heavy to lift. He knew he couldn't resist the jinn should he let him fully out again, knew that Ninip would turn him against his family. He had always thought of the jinn as predators, but he had forgotten the primary rule of how predators operated. The wolf never took on the strongest buck in the herd. It chased down the young, the sick, the isolated.

It didn't like fair fights. Given the choice between the hot blood of Sarah and Patrick or the cold force of the Gold Operators, Schweitzer knew which Ninip would choose. He couldn't bear the thought of Sarah and Patrick dying, not when he had just found them. It was the worst thing he could possibly imagine.

Save his being the instrument of that death.

Schweitzer pushed with everything he had. Cam's claws held them firmly in place. He couldn't move their shared body an inch. He felt Cam's knees lift off their back, replaced by the new Gold Operator's feet as he prepared to leap for Sarah and Patrick. Two ribs snapped under the weight.

And, at long last, the artist, the professional, the victor of scores of life-or-death contests, gave in. Ninip's voice receded back into a whining insect buzz.

Oh, Sarah, you fucking hero. You brave warrior. You give them hell. Schweitzer forced the thought out to her, sending it down the link that connected them. He hunted for the smell of her perfume one last time.

I'm sorry I failed you. If there's a way to find you in that mess, I will. I swear I will.

Ninip had gone silent, Schweitzer felt horror dawning through the jinn as he realized what Schweitzer intended to do. *No!* Ninip wailed. *Do not . . .*

Schweitzer thought of his son, his youth a question mark, a life about to unfold. He mourned that potentiality, the man that he would someday become. *Close your eyes, little man.* Then, he fixed his wife's face in his mind, tracing the hard line of her jaw, her narrowed eyes blazing defiance at her enemy. Sarah the warrior queen. His love, his light, braver and stronger than he ever could hope to be.

Good-bye, baby. I love you.

With the last shreds of will left to him, he turned on Ninip, pushed with all he had left, and forced the jinn all the way out, sending him tumbling free into the void, drawn inexorably to the storm beyond.

Schweitzer shut his eyes, pulled his senses inward, readied himself for his own tumble, the edges of the nothingness rushing in hungrily to take him. He steadied himself against the cold, tried to find the calm that had come to him before. Failed.

He pushed his will out to his ears, dialing his hearing down through the spectrum so that he could hear the min-

ute scramblings of the ants beneath him. He listened to the
deafening click of their mandibles and the pounding of
their marching legs, grateful for the noise. Anything that
would keep him from hearing Sarah and Patrick's screams.

He realized two things.

The first: His power over his hearing was as acute as it
had ever been with Ninip, his control as fine.

The second: He was still in his body and in complete
control. The fatigue and despair had left him. His left hand
sprawled over a stone. He flexed his fingers experimentally.

The rock split and fell away in halves, the fine powder
of its remnants gusting off his palm.

Schweitzer felt Cam leap off his back, and exploded
onto his own heels, propelling himself after Cam.

The strength in Schweitzer's legs was incredible, as
strong as it had been when Ninip had been in control. He
felt the same strength flowing through him, his presence . . . larger, more vital than before. Almost . . . alive.

He came down on Cam, bearing the former Air Force
PJ to the ground just short of Sarah, his head crunching
against the steering console, the embedded cleaver snapping free.

Schweitzer could hear the other Gold Operator lumbering toward them, painfully slow, it seemed now.

But now Schweitzer's training came surging to the fore.
Without the jinn's jabbering battle lust, he was free to concentrate. There was no rage now, only the cold artistry of
the professional warrior he had once been.

Schweitzer placed his knee against Cam's neck and
grabbed his arm, pivoting and locking it back as his combatives instructor had taught him, as he had practiced hundreds of times. There was no need for strength. The torque
of his position overpowered Cam's flailings, a perfect pivot
point between his pinning knee and his pulling arm. Schweitzer took his time, leisurely bending the limb back,
twisting, tearing. He moved slowly.

Because now, he understood.

It had been lies. Lies from Ninip, from Jawid, from Eldredge, from everyone.

It was a lie that Ninip made him stronger. The jinn kept Schweitzer in check, and then, when Schweitzer had asserted himself, sapped his power. With the jinn gone, Schweitzer's self was ascendant.

He had never needed Ninip.

The millennia the jinn had spent "soaking" in the void made no difference. The only thing all those years had grown was Ninip's evil nature, his addiction to death and blood, his desire for violence. To die was to touch the source of the magic, to become imbued with it, to bring it with you when you were returned to a body. Whether you were dead two hours or two thousand years, Schweitzer was "jinn" every bit as much as Ninip was. He had the same power as any jinn, as all of them. From the moment Jawid's magic had returned his soul to his corpse, he always had.

"Jinn" was the word Jawid used to describe the souls he summoned back. In the absence of anything better, it was the word that all in the Gemini Cell used. But the truth was that they didn't know what Ninip was, what the things that drove the Gold Operators were.

Schweitzer didn't know either, but he knew one thing— Schweitzer was different from the rest of them. He had one critical advantage.

He'd learned it from Sarah.

And that tipped the sum, so that there was no difference between Ninip and Schweitzer. Dead was dead. Souls were souls.

He gave a final heave, and Cam's arm came away, trailing fronds of broken sinew, the joint dangling wetly. He brought it down just as the other Gold Operator reached the tractor, climbed up.

The limb hit him hard enough to knock the Gold Operator backward. Schweitzer followed with a peroneal kick, what he commonly used when he wanted an opponent down. It connected with a crack, and the Gold Operator tumbled, his shoulders skidding through the turf, sending clods of soil arcing.

Schweitzer reveled, not with the base rage of Ninip but in the joy of his years of training once again responding to his command, now paired with the power of the void's magic. The two divided made him a blunt instrument, the two joined made him a scalpel again, precise, focused.

Deadly.

Schweitzer made his way down to his remaining opponent slowly, leisurely. *Now I'm going to rip off your own arm and beat you senseless with it.*

But as the Gold Operator rose, he had another idea.

The Gold Operators fought like wild animals, as he'd been forced to fight when he'd shared his body with Ninip. Now, he fought like a finely tuned machine.

He caught his enemy's clumsy punch at the wrist, leaning aside and jerking the arm taut. Then, he brought his right elbow down on his enemy's forearm, using his full weight. He'd broken many an arm on ops with this technique. The Gold Operator's bones were magically enhanced, but so was Schweitzer's strength. The radius and ulna snapped like twigs, his opponent's fist dangling loosely. Schweitzer's claws, horns, and spines were gone, his jaw was clamped tightly to his skull, tongue firmly in his mouth. Those extravagances were Ninip's calling cards, the flailings of a soul driven mad by too many years in the storm. He didn't need them.

Schweitzer was a footman. Years with the teams had taught him discipline, the quiet valor of a professional.

But it was Sarah who had truly taught him right from wrong, in the soul-deep way that allowed ethical action in an instant, when the pressure was on. Ninip would have said it was womanish, weak.

But Schweitzer felt the strength of it flowing through him, powerful enough to make the might of the Gold Operators not insignificant but finite. A thing with limits. A thing that could be beaten.

The monster in his hands drove its head forward, fangs

clamping over him, piercing through his shoulder and chest, lodging there.

Ninip would have raged at the insult, pride wounded by an enemy's gaining purchase on his body. But Schweitzer the professional recognized the tactical advantage. The move held the enemy fast. Schweitzer punched his own hand forward, not bothering with claws, allowing the rigidity of his pointed fingers to puncture his enemy's abdomen, walking his fingers past the wall of muscle, over the dead organs, until he found the spine at the lumbar vertebrae and gripped it tightly.

They'd lied to him. They'd told him Sarah and Patrick were dead. They'd told him that without Ninip he would go back into the void. They'd told him that his short time in the void made him weaker than Ninip with his thousands of years of death.

All lies. He'd believed every one.

The betrayal, the silver-tongued talk of service to the nation, the wasted time. Rage grew in him, and Schweitzer pushed it down. *Focus. Mission first. Emotion never helps.* He tightened his grip, felt the bones grinding in his palm.

The Gold Operator divined his intent, worked its jaw harder, trying to bite through him.

Schweitzer didn't give it the chance.

He yanked with all his might. At first the bones held, and he struggled with the momentary panic that he might have overplayed his hand, left himself vulnerable to his enemy's counterstrike. He felt the sharp teeth grinding against his scapula, his ribs.

But then he felt the spine bend, snap, and finally come dragging out through the thing's stomach, leaving it to fold in half like an old coat suddenly off the hanger.

He turned as Cam rose, reaching for Sarah with his remaining arm, and stabbed the handful of bone and gristle into his buttock, lodging it there, a handle he used to drag the monster back down to the ground, where he planted one foot on its back, shoved it roughly toward the blades.

Sarah sat in the driver's seat, staring. Finally calm, Schweitzer could concentrate on his own augmented senses. He could smell the slight tang of sweat in his wife's perspiration, the sweet scent of her breathing, tiny traces that would have normally been overpowered by the oil and vinyl stink of the tractor under her. He dialed down, digging through the odors until he found what he was looking for.

The perfume was so faint it could barely be called a trace, a tiny patch of skin behind her ear, where she hadn't scrubbed enough during the last shower.

But to Schweitzer it was overpowering, it was all.

He felt the slight ache, the hollow left by Ninip's absence, bulge and fill out, a fender dent pushed back into form, buoyed from within by the expansion of his own fullness. Now, in death, Schweitzer felt more alive than ever before.

And now, without Ninip's competition, he truly knew his power. The strength suffused him, the lightness in his limbs made him feel as if he could float. Every fiber of his body answered him, reported its condition, every atom in the world around him pulsed with information, pulsing at his touch. He tasted the air, he vibrated with the tiny tremors of the ground beneath him.

Jim Schweitzer the SEAL was an artist.

Jim Schweitzer the jinn was a god.

He itched to test his control, to find the limits of his power. But Sarah still sat in the tractor seat, Patrick was still bundled under one arm, awake and staring.

Cam still struggled feebly under his boot.

Schweitzer leaned back, gave Sarah a mock bow, gestured at the blades. He channeled the air, his lungs obeying him easily now, the muscles around his rib cage answering with precision, stretching to drop the pressure, then squeezing tight with precise control to send the air spiraling up his ragged trachea, the muscles of his throat crushing down around the wound to shape the words he needed. No more power, just greater control. But it made all the difference in the world.

"Well," Jim Schweitzer said, in a gravelly approximation of his old voice. "You going to do the honors? I can't hold him forever."

Sarah gaped for another moment, then stepped on the gas.

Schweitzer stepped aside as Cam jerked and thrashed into the whirling knives, one leg shooting off into the darkness as the rest of him dissolved, and the tractor jumped with the effort of rendering him down.

Sarah killed the engine, sat staring.

"It's okay, baby," Schweitzer said. "I'm okay."

She stared. Patrick mewled, kicking backward. The cries became words, the first Schweitzer had heard the boy utter since he died. "No no no no no Mommy no."

Schweitzer knelt, tried to use his fine control to coax something of a smile from his ruined face. There were limits to his power. With so little muscle to work with, he gave up trying almost immediately and reached out a hand instead.

The world lighted as his arm came into view. The gray surface of his skin had deepened into even sable, smooth, frictionless, liquid. The light tracery of his veins were barely visible beneath, tiny runnels of glowing silver, a network of glycerol pathways that mapped the course of his old life.

He wasted little time marveling at it. He was growing tired of marvels.

"Come on, man," he said to his son. "You know me."

But as much as he willed it, it didn't make it so. Whatever connection linked him to Sarah hadn't formed in Patrick. Schweitzer's son shrieked all the more, crawling so deep into Sarah's armpit that she had to fumble to keep from dropping him. *Oh, Patrick. All of this has hurt you.* Grief for his son's lost childhood swamped him.

He dialed his senses up the spectrum until he found what he dreaded, the high stink of the hormone dump that was prepping Sarah's system to fight or run for her life, the rapid pulsing of her heartbeat. Whatever magic had brought them together had done its work. The rose trail had ended, and they would have to find their own way from now on. Her pupils were dilated, her veins constricting beneath the skin, the air around her sweetening as the sugar content of her blood spiked.

But Schweitzer still felt the link, the magic connecting them, specter of a trail that had haunted him from the moment he'd awoken to his new unlife. It had led him to her, and now, so close, he felt it attaching them. He knew Sarah felt it, too, could see it in the mixture of fear and longing on her face, could sense it in the chemical cocktail that poured off her. She knew who he was.

"They told me you were dead," he said. "I would have come sooner, but they lied to me."

She nodded, her eyes wet now. But the fear stink didn't subside. Schweitzer could see the battle etched out on her face, her love of him warring with her physical instinct to run.

She was terrified.

But she didn't move. Her muscles tensed to spring and didn't.

She was trying.

And that was something.

All his newfound power did little to help him muster the effort to stop himself from reaching toward his family, to stand, to step away.

"Okay," he said. "It's okay. I won't hurt you."

"I know," she said. She stood, gathered Patrick, stepped to the ground. Stared up at him. "What is this, Jim?"

"I don't know, baby," he said, "but I'll tell you what I've figured out so far, and we'll hammer the rest out together, like we always have."

She was quiet, looked away. Schweitzer could see the tears sliding out of the corners of her eyes. His new powers had their drawbacks, too, it seemed. He knew the lie in his own words. He was a walking corpse, a dead thing made animate by magic he didn't understand. He had found them, his wife and child, but how could he be a husband and father to them now?

"I . . . I thought you were alive," Sarah said. "I was so sure. Are you?"

Sarah had changed, but not so much that he could lie to her. "No," he said. "This isn't life."

"Then how can we figure it out like we always have?"

He thought of the Gemini Cell, receiving satellite reports of the defeat of the Gold Operators, spinning up the secondary team, sending in drones, activating whatever plan B they surely had in place.

There wasn't much time.

"Because we have no choice. Whatever I am now, I can protect you."

"I can protect myself, Jim."

"Not against what's coming, Sarah. This is different."

She shook her head, looked up at him. "I know."

"You don't, and I don't have time to explain it to you now. So, know this. There are more of those monsters, many more, and they're coming. They won't stop until they have you and Patrick."

"Why? Why do they care about some widowed artist and her son?"

"Because you know what I am, Sarah. And now you know there are others like me. You honestly think they're going to let you live?"

"We'll go to the authorities," she said, her tone indicating she knew the foolishness of the statement.

"They are the authorities, Sarah. There is no help coming. You saw what they can do. You need a monster to defeat a monster. I'm the only one who can keep you safe now."

"A monster . . ." She was weeping openly now. The sight tore at him. He would have joined her if he could.

"A monster who can keep Patrick safe. Sarah, if you won't let me protect you, at least let me protect him. You can't do it alone. Not now."

She sobbed, nodding. "I love you, Jim. I love you so much. But . . . this makes things different."

"No, baby," Schweitzer husked. "Please don't say that. I

love you. Dying kills the branches, Sarah, but the roots hang on."

"You promise to keep Patrick safe?"

"Promise. With everything I have, Sarah. I will not let them hurt either of you."

"There's something between us . . . there's a link, Jim. I always knew you were . . . still here. I always knew you weren't gone. How is that possible?"

"I don't know, baby. It's magic. I don't think it's supposed to make sense. But I know that I love you, and that love ties us together."

She paused, mastered herself. She put her hand on her chest, indicating the invisible connection there, the one she knew they both felt. "If I die, will I become like you?"

And he did extend his hand now, his dead heart swelling with longing, with grief for what was lost, with gratitude for what had been saved, with hope for what was coming.

Sarah swallowed, took his hand.

Hell rose behind them, the stars circled overhead, and the woods swallowed them. The tree trunks closed in as they ran, sealing off the outside world, an oddly fitting door slamming on all they had finally lost.

All touchstones vanished, all notions of the familiar were erased by the thick darkness and the raging chorus of chirping insects and peeping frogs. This new world was as alien as the void had once seemed to him.

Pete's face rose again in his mind, his deep-set eyes smiling. *Proud of you, bro.*

Schweitzer spoke to that ghost, words he'd never said aloud to anyone. *Pete? I don't know what to do. I'm scared.*

And he was.

But he had himself now, wholly, truly.

And he had his family.

It was enough.

GLOSSARY OF MILITARY
ACRONYMS AND SLANG

ABC'S—Airway, breathing, circulation. First responders check these vital signs to ensure a patient's vitality. Direct-action teams check them to ensure a target has been neutralized.

BIRD—Aviation asset such as a helicopter or fixed-wing aircraft.

BMF—Boat Maintenance Facility.

BUD/S—Basic Underwater Demolition/SEAL training. The six-month training course that all sailors must graduate to become US Navy SEALs. BUD/S alone does not make one a SEAL, and additional training is required. BUD/S is intensely grueling, with an 80 percent attrition rate.

CARBINE—A long gun with a shorter barrel than a rifle. Carbines are better suited to combat in close quarters than their longer cousins.

CAS—Close air support. Action taken by fixed or rotary-wing platforms to assist ground troops.

CHEMLIGHT—Also known as "glow sticks." A short plastic tube filled with chemical compounds in separate compartments. When the stick is bent, the barrier between the compartments breaks, allowing the compounds to mix. The resultant chemical reaction causes the tube to emit a strong colored glow.

CLEARED HOT—Authorized to open fire.

CONDITION YELLOW—A state of hypervigilance where a person is constantly anticipating sudden violence.

CONEX—A type of intermodal shipping container.

COP—Combat Outpost.

CQB—Close quarters battle. Refers to the tactics of breaching and clearing confined spaces, such as a building or ship.

DANGER CLOSE—Indicates a friendly force in close proximity to a target of fire, usually from artillery or close air support.

DFAC—Dining facility.

DYNAMIC—An operational state wherein the enemy is aware of the assault team's presence, rendering stealth unnecessary.

EMBED—Embedded or one who is embedded.

"EYES ON"—Indicates the speaker is observing the subject of the sentence. "I have eyes on the door."

FNG—Fucking New Guy/Girl. A person who is newly assigned to a military unit. This friendly pejorative is meant to indicate the likelihood that the described will make mistakes.

GROM—Grupa Reagowania Operacyjno-Manewrowego. Poland's elite counterterrorism unit.

HAWK—Armed aviation asset such as a helicopter or fixed-wing aircraft.

HVAC—Heating, Ventilation, and Air-Conditioning.

K-9—Canine. A unit that employs working dogs for law enforcement or military operations. The term is also used to refer to the dogs themselves.

KC—Kill-Capture. A direct-action mission wherein the team's first goal is to capture a human target. If the team is unable to capture the target without risking harm to their own number, they will kill him/her. A successful KC must conclude with the target either captured or dead.

MAM—Military aged male.

MANPAD—Man-portable air-defense system. A shoulder-mounted missile launcher.

MEDEVAC—Medical evacuation. An emergency retrieval and removal of a casualty from a crisis zone. The patient is stabilized and transferred as quickly as possible to a medical facility where adequate care can be provided.

"MIKES"—Minutes.

MWR Morale, Welfare, and Recreation center.

NODS—Night Optical Devices. Mechanical devices that permit the user to see in the dark.

"OFF TO SEE THE WIZARD"—Slang used to indicate a visit to a mental-health professional.

OP—Operation. Refers to any military undertaking with a discrete beginning and end.

OPERATOR—Members of special forces elements who engage in special operations. Term connotes members of direct-action elements whose primary tasking is breaching hardened targets and neutralizing a dug-in enemy.

PAX—Passenger or passengers.

PIPE HITTER—A fighter. A person whose principal occupation is the use of force.

PJS—Pararescue jumpers, also known as "pararescuemen." A special operations element within the United States Air Force.

PLATOON—A military organizational unit consisting of twenty-eight to sixty-four members.

QRF—Quick Reaction Force. A standby troop of warfighters positioned to respond rapidly to an emergency.

SEABEES—CBs, the construction battalions of the United States Navy.

SEAL—"Sea, Air, and Land." A special operations force of the United States Navy.

SQT—SEAL Qualification Course. Secondary instruction for SEALs that follows graduation from BUD/S.

SQUIRTERS—A colloquial term for those enemy who flee a targeted location.

SSG—Special Services Group. Pakistan's Special Operations forces.

SST—Special Security Team. An elite counterterrorism unit in the Japanese Coast Guard.

TCCC—Tactical combat casualty care. First-responder medical training given to operators. It is designed to allow non-medical personnel to engage in triage under fire, and to stabilize casualties for medevac.

TIC—Troops in contact. Indicates that the speaker is engaged and fighting with the enemy.

WIA—Wounded in action.

YN1—Yeoman First Class. A senior enlisted member of the US Navy or Coast Guard specializing in administration.

THE ULTIMATE IN FANTASY FICTION!

From magical tales of distant worlds to stories of those with abilities beyond the ordinary, Ace and Roc have everything you need to stretch your imagination to its limits.

Marion Zimmer Bradley/Diana L. Paxson

Guy Gavriel Kay

Dennis L. McKiernan

Patricia A. McKillip

Robin McKinley

Sharon Shinn

Steven R. Boyett

Barb and J. C. Hendee

THE ULTIMATE WRITERS OF
SCIENCE FICTION

John Barnes	Jack McDevitt
William C. Dietz	Alastair Reynolds
Simon R. Green	Allen Steele
Joe Haldeman	S. M. Stirling
Robert Heinlein	Charles Stross
Frank Herbert	Harry Turtledove
E. E. Knight	John Varley

penguin.com/scififantasy

ACE RoC

M3G0511

For Murph, the Protector.
You made the right call, and then you made the right call.

Drew Reyes, Master Chief Thomas LePage, Senior Chiefs Patrick O'Sullivan and Michael Callanan, and all the rest in the Chiefs' Mess. Peter V. Brett is always last and never forgotten. I choked up thanking him in person when I accepted the Compton Crook, which I hope conveys how much I mean it. I hope each book shows you all those hours on e-mail and over the phone were time well spent.

ACKNOWLEDGMENTS

If there's one thing military service teaches you, it's that no one does anything alone. Even the most independent operator is the tip of a very long spear, made up of thousands of support personnel, from administrators to food-service workers to logisticians and intelligence officers. Writing is much the same. Readers of my work may be getting tired of hearing the same folks thanked over and over, and that's just fine by me. Nobody ever got a hernia from gratitude. The book you're holding has been made possible by an army of publishing staff: the folks at Ace/Roc and Headline. It would never have even made it to publication without the concerted efforts from my US agents at JABberwocky and my UK agents at Zeno. It would have been a terrible book if not for the incredibly helpful feedback from Justin Landon and Carrie Vaughn. I would have gone insane without the support of a small army of friends: publishing professionals like the Drinklings, and writers like the disciples of the Holy Taco Church, named here because I haven't named them before: Kevin Hearne, Wesley Chu, Sam Sykes, Brian McClellan, Stephen Blackmoore, Delilah Dawson, Django Wexler, Jason Hough, and Chuck Wendig (actually, I have named him before, but throw me a bone here). I also want to thank Maria Dahvana Headley, for reasons she knows. Thanks also to Yosef Lehrman, Tony Bulathwelage, and Gilbert Flecha, whose humor and discipline have helped me to lock it up and get back to work to keep Gotham safe. Thanks also to my command staff at US Coast Guard Station New York, who daily keep me from walking off cliffs, flying off the handle, or engaging in other stupid junior-officer tricks: Chief Warrant Officer

Ace Books by Myke Cole

*Blessed be the Lord my strength, who teacheth my hands
to war, and my fingers to fight . . .*

—PSALM 144:1

AUTHOR'S NOTE

The events in this novel take place in the early days of the Great Reawakening, many years before the first book in the Shadow Ops series, *Control Point*. While I'm thrilled to welcome back fans of the original trilogy, and think it'll be fun for them to see the SOC in its infancy, I also want to extend a warm welcome to new readers. If you're looking for an entry point into my universe, here's another one. Thanks for reading.

A glossary of military acronyms and slang can be found in the back of this book.

PROLOGUE
DAMN, SHE'S GOOD

"Sarah has been working for four years to get this show." Though Biggs was his lieutenant, James Schweitzer didn't call him "sir." They didn't stand on formality in his corner of the navy. "I thought we were stood down. This will kill her."

He glanced over his shoulder at his wife. Sarah had noticed the call but was doing her best to keep the irritation from her face.

"That was before I got word that our ship might be coming in." Lieutenant Biggs sounded grim. "Now, suit up. We're mustering."

"Might be coming in, or *is* coming in? Damn it, she's already on her last nerve with the pace of operations. Do you know how hard it is to get an art showing in Norfolk? There are critics here from every paper in the Tidewater. She needs me. I can't leave unless it's going to count."

Biggs was silent a moment. "Still waiting on the intel watchstander. If this is the right one, we're going."

"Then call me when you're sure it's the right one."

"God fucking damn it, Jim, I am not —"

"I'm a fifteen-minute drive from Station. I can be there before you finish boat checks. Call me when you know." Schweitzer killed the call and stuffed the phone in his pocket before Biggs could say anything else.

Schweitzer took a deep breath, willing the knot in his stomach to settle. This was Sarah's first show in Norfolk, and she was nervous as hell. Hopefully, the watchstander would be slow in confirming the target, or Biggs was wrong altogether. Schweitzer turned, putting on a smile, shaking his head as he walked to where his wife leaned against the art-gallery door.

"Everything okay?" she asked.

"Biggs dug himself another hole. This is the thing about junior officers, they need us to keep them from walking off a cliff. It's fine."

She frowned at him, her dark eyes narrowing beneath her bright pink bangs, the two purple streaks framing her face, so beautiful she still made his breath catch after all these years. "If he needed help, why didn't he go to Chief?" she asked.

Schweitzer winced internally, struggled to find words.

"Jim." She spoke as if to a little boy. "Do you know where liars go?"

"To the movies?"

"To the couch for the night. Without getting any."

"You are a coldhearted woman."

"I am a beautiful angel who can see through your bullshit like it's clean glass."

Schweitzer sighed. Lying to her was a necessity of his job, but he knew better than to think it would ever work. "You need to focus on your opening. We can talk about it when we get home."

She drew her lips into a hard line and breathed out through her nose. "So, that means we're going home together. As in, you're staying for the whole event."

"We've only got the babysitter until eleven. You know Patrick isn't really going to sleep until you come in and kiss him good night."

She grimaced. "Oh, right. Let me call before we go in."

He touched her elbow. "Babe, you called her ten minutes ago."

She looked up at him. "I did? I did."

He pressed his forehead to hers, inhaled her rosewater perfume. "You know what you're doing?"

"What?"

"You're trying to get your mind off this opening by worrying about something else. That's fear talking. Mission first. Focus."

"Mission first." She was smiling now.

"Mission first," he said, "and people always. You are a fantastic mother and a better wife than I could ever hope for. I love you so much it hurts. Now, get in there and show them what I see every day."

"Love you, too," she answered. Her face composed, the smile smoothed.

They turned together and stepped into the gallery.

The crowd inside applauded as Sarah entered. Her paintings lined the walls, hanging from clear line, looking as if they were floating amid tastefully arranged sprays of white orchids. Schweitzer caught himself scanning the crowd for threats, noting the exits and blind corners. *Stop it. You're not at work. This is for Sarah. Be present.*

"Sarah!" squealed a tall woman wearing diamond earrings likely worth more than their car. She stretched her arms to embrace his wife, and Sarah returned the hug with precisely the correct blend of affection and forbearance, turning to Schweitzer as they parted. "Jim, this is Bethany Charles. This is her gallery."

Schweitzer smiled, extending a hand. "Thanks so much for hosting us."

Bethany dragged the proffered hand until Schweitzer was wrapped in a tight hug. Her pale neck smelled like oranges and alcohol. He met Sarah's eyes over Bethany's shoulder and made a face. Sarah rolled her eyes and grinned.

"Sarah's told me all about you," Bethany said when she finally released him. "She says you're in the navy, but

absolutely will not talk about what you do! I've been in Norfolk long enough to know how it is with you intel folks."

Schweitzer let her error pass as she put the back of her hand to her mouth and spoke in a stage whisper. "Your secret's safe with me!"

A man approached out of the crowd. He wore too-thick glasses and a beard that rivaled Schweitzer's own. "Ms. Schweitzer," he began.

Sarah took a step toward him and shook his hand. His smile froze at the close contact. Schweitzer winced internally. Guy was the shy type, liked more personal space. Sarah immediately released his hand and took a step back, smiling as if that was her intended approach all along. "Sarah Schweitzer, nice to meet you."

The man's face relaxed, and his smile turned genuine. "Leo Volk, I write for the *Virginian Pilot.*"

"Ooooh," Bethany whispered to Schweitzer as Sarah and Leo spoke. "That was a good save. He's not one you want to disappoint."

Schweitzer shrugged. "She's a natural. She should have joined the navy. We could have used her in intel." He smirked internally. No harm in perpetuating Bethany's assumption.

"Well, one sailor per family is plenty." Bethany gestured to Schweitzer's chin. "Don't they give you grief about letting your beard grow?"

Schweitzer smiled. "I'm on leave," he lied. "I'll shave it when I get back to base."

Bethany followed Schweitzer's gaze to his wife. "She really is quite socially adroit."

"She's had a lot of practice." It was a gross understatement. The practice was born of years of dedication to her craft and the networking that surrounded it, until it had become as natural as breathing.

Sarah wrapped up her conversation with Leo and headed into the crowd. She looked over her shoulder at Schweitzer, cocked an eyebrow.

You're good, he mouthed.

I know, she mouthed back, gave an exaggerated wink.

He missed Bethany's next question, intent on Sarah, circling and smiling and engaging with such ease that you'd never know this was her first big show, her "coming-out" in the Mid-Atlantic arts scene. The stakes were high.

But that was when Sarah Schweitzer locked on. When it mattered. She was a professional.

Like him.

"I'm sorry?" he asked Bethany.

"I was asking if you like art?"

"Depends on what you mean by 'art.' I like her paintings," he answered. *And I love the painter.*

Sarah was speaking to another man now, Schweitzer recognized him as an art critic from one of Sarah's magazines. She was matching his style effortlessly, leaning in at the same angle, nodding recognition at a point he was making. He laughed like an old friend, put unconsciously at ease by her smooth reading of his signals. Sarah looked lit from within, like she was having the time of her life.

But Schweitzer caught a glance out of the corner of her eye, then another. She was looking to see if he was still there.

He could stare down a gun barrel. He could run until his lungs burst. He could always find a way. But to give Sarah what she needed, he'd have to stay, *really* stay. And that would mean giving up the one thing that made him as powerful as she was.

Sarah was approaching him now, her hand on the elbow of a man in his midthirties, a mop of Dylanesque curly hair hanging in his face. He wore a corduroy jacket and an expression of cool boredom. "Honey, do you remember the sculptor I was telling you about?"

Schweitzer did, the man made scale replicas of major monuments entirely out of gun parts. His work was amazing. What was his name . . .

Sarah was smiling as the man's hand came up to shake Schweitzer's. "This is my husband, Jim."

The pride in Sarah's eyes sounded in her voice. She

wasn't just showing off for her husband, she was showing her husband off. Schweitzer blinked.

"I've heard great things about you. My name is . . ." the sculptor began.

Schweitzer's pocket buzzed. The bosun's pipe ringtone sounded.

Sarah's expression changed as Schweitzer lifted his phone to his ear, sliding from shock to recognition to hurt to anger and back to composure in an instant.

"I'm sorry, baby," Schweitzer said as he hit the ANSWER button, his stomach doing somersaults.

"It's fine," she was saying, the professional mask already back in place. "Do your job."

Her big night. The one she had worked four long years to get.

Schweitzer prayed it was a wrong number, or the babysitter calling to say Patrick wouldn't go to bed.

"It's our ship," Biggs said. "We're going."

"It's fine," Sarah said again, reading Biggs's words in Schweitzer's expression.

But it wasn't fine.

It wasn't fine at all.

CHAPTER I
STORM AT SEA

An impossible shot, and a risky one. Schweitzer took it anyway.

The small boat rocked beneath him. His target paced the cargo deck of the freighter, rolling with the swells, obscured by darkness and fog. The man was just a speck at this distance, at the limit of Schweitzer's effective range, with five hundred meters of heaving water to cover.

But Schweitzer's boat would cover that five hundred meters in short order, and deliver the SEAL team to the target. And that man couldn't be left alive to sound the alarm before they arrived.

Petty Officer First Class James Schweitzer closed his left eye. The Night Optical Device mounted to his helmet turned the world into a shifting haze of green witchlight. NODs bent shadows, distorted depth perception.

They made it harder to hit what you were aiming at.

He squeezed the broom-handle grip under his carbine's barrel, and a pencil-thin beam shot across the intervening distance, visible only to those wearing NODs. The boat's modified engines turned soundlessly underwater.

The silence and darkness rendered the craft nearly unde-
tectable.

The distance was too great. The beam diffused far short
of the target. Schweitzer breathed deeply and relied on his
training. *Lead the target. Fire between breaths. Slow,
steady squeeze to the rear. Don't anticipate the recoil. Let
the shot break.*

The carbine was silenced, but if he missed, there was
nothing he could do to stop the noise of the bullet slamming into the freighter's metal hull, or the side of one of
the stacked shipping crates behind the man making his
way along the cargo deck toward the superstructure. That
noise would inevitably raise the alarm. Up close, the man
might look like an ordinary seaman, part of the freighter's
deck crew, but Schweitzer knew that he was a hardened
enemy operator. A killer, not so different from Schweitzer
himself.

Schweitzer was a professional, a product of years of rig-
orous training. Shooting people was what he did. But even
professionals had to step out on a ledge and take a chance
sometimes.

The man stepped clear of the last container. Nothing
but open air behind him.

He exhaled, waited half a moment, then pulled the
trigger.

His rock-steady frame absorbed what recoil wasn't
already mitigated by the carbine's padded stock and weighted
bolt. The gun barely moved.

The bullet rocketed across the intervening distance,
racing toward his target at thirty-one hundred feet each
second.

It would be the greatest shot of his career if he didn't
miss. Behind Schweitzer, the four other SEAL operators
held their collective breath, straining into their scopes to
keep an eye on the bobbing speck that was Schweitzer's
target.

The speck hovered for a moment, stiffened.

Then fell.

SEAL teams were meant for foreign warfare. They could only conduct operations in American waters when there was a qualified terrorist threat. While the "nexus to terrorism" made the operation legal, Schweitzer's skill made it possible. He'd been a mediocre student, of middling looks. He'd never been a good hand at painting or music.

But out here, he was an artist.

Chief Petty Officer Ahmad let out a breath, the slight shudder in her exhalation the only indicator that she'd been nervous. "Okay, so you can shoot."

Schweitzer lowered the carbine and allowed himself a moment to face her and the rest of the team. Ahmad never smiled, but Chang's balaclava looked lumpy at the corners, the black fabric barely concealing his grin. "That was fucking amazing, dude."

"Secure that," Ahmad said, glancing down at her watch. "We've got another . . . fifteen minutes without air cover. Stay locked on. Watch that deck."

"I don't like this vague-ass target," Chang groused. "Shipping container full of what? Bad guys? Explosives? Aliens? What's in there?"

"We don't get to pick the target," Schweitzer answered. "You're not the lieutenant, Steve. You want to call the shots, rank up."

Ahmad jerked a thumb in Schweitzer's direction. "What he said."

Chang shook his head and was silent.

Ahmad looked at her watch again. "Fourteen minutes to air cover."

Even so, they had time before they reached the target. The kill had earned them precious breathing room, taking down the only eyes on the freighter's starboard beam. The enemy didn't know the team was coming. Schweitzer's shot ensured it would stay that way. Chang ceased smiling and returned to overwatch, sighting down his carbine's thermal scope at the deck. Schweitzer released his carbine and let the sling take the weapon's weight as he folded down the ruggedized minicomputer mounted to the front

of his body armor. Compact and useful, the minicomputer
would do double duty slowing an enemy round before the
armor's interceptor plate had to do its job.

Schweitzer propped up his NODs as the screen flashed
into low light, showing the specifics of his target. The
computer reeled off details of the Body Farm's operations,
from drug smuggling in Southwest Asia to trafficking sex
slaves in Eastern Europe. But the vast majority of the hits
were the kind that called for Schweitzer and his team,
attempts to bring terrorists into the country:

> NOV 13—0843z—MINI-CONEX DROPPED BY
> PARACHUTE (INTEL DRVN.)—CNT. 2 MANPAD
> ANTIAIR SYSTEMS.
>
> NOV 29—1117z—SCALLOPER WITH HIDDEN
> COMPARTMENT (K-9 ALERTED)—3 PAX—ALL 3
> MILITARY-AGED-MALES (MAMS)—ALL
> WATCHLIST HITS (CLICK FOR DETAILS)

Intel could never prove that those missiles were meant for
those men or what their target might be. Frankly, Schweitzer
didn't care. His last op had been smoking-gun conclusive—
terrorists being smuggled into the country. It resulted in a
chain of follow-on raids, and the skipper had waived crew
rest regs, working him nonstop for a month. Sarah had put up
with it stoically, but he could tell it weighed on her.

But follow-ons were normally rare, and provided there
wasn't one here, Schweitzer could finally put the burden
down, at least for a little while.

Ahmad was looking at her own computer, NODS up, no
doubt frantically checking in the hope that the air cover
would be available sooner than expected. She caught Schweitzer's glance and misread its intent. "I've got you, shipmate," she said. "I'll pull Landry if there's a follow-on.
You get leave after this. All you'll be responsible for is the
after action and passdown."

Schweitzer was embarrassed that Ahmad had caught him.

He *was* thinking about getting off duty. *Unsat. Focus. Missions fail because operators lose the bubble for a split second.*

But the thought wouldn't be denied. The past month of constant work was just one of many months like that, over a long string of years. Sarah had endured it all, filling her lonely days with Patrick and painting in the makeshift studio she put together, avoiding the gossip of the navy wives who wondered why she wouldn't come to their socials, to church, to anything. But even Sarah had her limits. She hadn't gotten married to be alone. Ducking out in the middle of her big show hadn't helped.

With her pink hair and sleeve tattoos, Sarah wasn't navy-wife material. She was a rare bird, maybe even a unique one.

Which was why Schweitzer loved her.

"She won't put up with it, Chief," Schweitzer said. "She'll split."

His hand went to his chest, pushing against his body armor. Beneath it, he could feel the set of dog tags pressing into his chest. They were engraved with an image of his wife and son, and pressing his armor until he could feel their comforting pressure against his chest had become a ritual every time he suited up.

"I know," Chief Ahmad said. "I'll keep my word. After this, you stand down."

Last op. No follow-ons. He would be home.

"Don't sweat it, Jim," Chang said. "If you get zapped this run, I promise to marry Sarah."

"Fuck off." Schweitzer smiled. In his heart of hearts, he knew that if the worst ever came to pass, Chang wouldn't hesitate to look in on her. But Chang didn't know Sarah like he did. She didn't need looking in on.

"Hey man, the Somalis do it all the time. Brother goes down, the other brother marries the widow. All SEALs are brothers, right?"

"You want to go back to Mogadishu, I'll make it happen," Ahmad said. "For now, shut the fuck up."

Chang winked at Schweitzer. Schweitzer shook his head, but he still felt comforted. Because in a sense deeper than biology, Chang really was his brother. His six was covered. Sarah's, too, whether she needed it or not.

Schweitzer swallowed a knot of emotion and toggled the screen of the minicomputer, switching to the air-assets heads-up. It was blank. Radar showed the freighter growing larger on the horizon as they sped toward it. Their own radar-dampened support craft were out of range, but ready to respond if the enemy fled or the mission went south. He craned his neck skyward, taking in the thick, roiling cloud cover that had swept in just after their boat launched, leaving the skipper with a choice, scrub the mission or accept that air cover would be stymied. Skipper had risked the mission like Schweitzer had just risked taking the shot.

Professionals knew when to make the hard calls.

"Last look," Ahmad said. "Confirm your target. There are a lot of conex boxes on that deck. Be sure we're moving to the right one."

Schweitzer glanced back down as the computer brought up a layout of the deck, illuminating one of the conex-box shipping containers, a forty-foot steel rectangle at the bottom of a stack of five that soared fifty feet off the rolling freighter's deck. Intel had managed to secure images of the thing, which displayed it from all angles, showing every scratch, dent, and patch of rust. The Body Farm labeled all its freight containers with the same front-company logo: a stylized face of a grinning Asian child, the word SHAN written underneath. Intel was vague as to what was in it, but if this was anything like past ops, it would likely be anywhere up to five bedraggled and stinking men, exhausted and half-starved, ready to build bombs or sling rifles after they'd been released into the country.

Or it could be bricks of explosives, vials of nerve agent, maybe even canisters of materials that would set off the radiation detector clipped into a pouch on his body armor.

Schweitzer wasn't a fan of Chang's giving voice to his doubts, but he couldn't deny the truth behind them. In his

entire career, he'd never had a targeting package this vague. Just a shipping container with no indication of what was inside. They were going in blind.

Schweitzer looked for obvious cracks in the container's sides, screened "drainage" pipes. Years of running these ops had trained him to recognize such anomalies as disguised air vents, indicating living cargo. He didn't see anything, but the images weren't exactly clear.

"Everybody got it?" Ahmad asked.

Schweitzer didn't have to look behind him to know that everybody did.

"Body Farm has this ship," the chief said. "The able seamen on there aren't able seamen. You treat them as hostile."

Schweitzer's training had long since taught him to dispense with stupid notions of fearlessness. Professionals acknowledged fear, tipped their hat to it, and got the job done anyway. As with every op, Schweitzer felt fear's slow crawl from his balls to his belly. He swallowed, noting its presence, letting his training compensate. His body was rock steady as the boat surged forward.

The bulk of the freighter rose before them, a black wall lifting out of the pitching sea. Dan Perreto, the Coast Guard rep with the team, chucked Schweitzer's elbow, but Schweitzer ignored him, closing up the computer and picking up the Jacob's ladder from the bottom of the boat. Ahmad finally lowered her NODs and joined the rest of the team in covering him as the boat closed the rest of the distance and drew up alongside the freighter's starboard beam, where the deck dropped low enough for the ladder's hooked top to reach.

Ahmad whispered their position into the radio mic suspended over her mouth while Schweitzer extended the ladder, hooking it to the ship's side and deploying the narrow netting that would serve as rungs. The loose black fabric was a challenge to climb, doubly so with all their gear, but the SEALs were professionals.

Schweitzer came last, swarming up the ladder as if he were floating. The coxswain, Petty Officer Martin, was a

religious fanatic whose preaching made Schweitzer's hackles rise, but he kept the boat perfectly alongside the freighter, keeping pace with the vessel's slow swing around its anchor line.

Schweitzer took a knee on the deck, covering their six while the rest of the team got their bearings. The deck stretched off into the darkness, the stacks of conex boxes shrouded in the gloom, moon and stars blocked by the thick cloud cover. Schweitzer squinted up at it. The blanket of clouds looked unnaturally regular, as if painted on by some divine hand. He looked back down. A foot farther on, his target lay in a spreading pool of blood, folded over his dropped assault rifle. He wore a faded T-shirt and jeans, the colors washed into pale green by Schweitzer's NODs. He'd been blown out of his flip-flops, which lay on the deck about a foot distant. Schweitzer's round had tumbled, utterly pulping his head. The bullet looked like it had entered through the ear, leaving a ragged pit of an entry wound. The long distance and the impact with the body had attenuated most of the bullet's force. If the tumbling trajectory had struck the superstructure after leaving the man's head, it had done so quietly enough.

Schweitzer allowed himself a brief moment to appreciate his work. Hell of a shot.

Ahmad made certain the team was in place before flashing a hand signal and moving toward the bow. They'd be moving directly under the windows of the bridge tower, which rose at least five stories off the deck, but the towering stacks of conex boxes worked with the darkness to screen them from view. The goal was to ensure the target conex was in the specified location and verify the contents before unleashing hell.

Command wasn't interested in dealing with the inevitable public scrutiny and legal wrangling that would surely accompany a counterterrorism operation in US territorial waters. Not to mention the lost opportunity to gather critical intel. That meant quiet, and quiet meant Schweitzer's

team. It was riskier this way, but if they were spotted, they could always call in the helos early.

If the cloud cover ever broke. The combat weather team had assured them it was passing, but a quick glance at the sky showed Schweitzer a thick sheet of black cotton. He spared a quick glance over his shoulder to ensure the team was moving, then rose to go with them.

There was the clunk of a wheel spinning. The watertight hatch on the superstructure's side opened and light flooded out behind a figure. He stepped out, blinking as his eyes adjusted to the dark. His first step put him on the deck, the second slid in the slowly spreading gore from Schweitzer's kill.

The man lost his balance, grunted, went to one knee, eyes widening as he took in his fallen comrade. A military-grade shotgun hung from a sling around his torso, banging against the deck. Ahmad was right, able seamen didn't carry weapons at all, let alone the sleek black killing tool this man bore. They were accurate, deadly. Expensive.

And loud.

So close to his target, the superstructure behind the man would ring like a bell if Schweitzer took the shot. Instead, he raced across the intervening deck, grateful for the nonskid surface that gave his boots traction and increased speed. The man was just drawing breath to yell as Schweitzer closed, leaping over the corpse and dropping onto the palms of his padded gloves, kicking out at the man's knees. The bottoms of his boots connected perfectly, popping the man's joints sideways and sending his head banging into the superstructure with a resounding crack. It was louder than Schweitzer would have liked, but it stunned him, keeping him from crying out as he fell to the deck, rolling in the blood and fumbling for his weapon. Schweitzer pinned it with one hand, then pivoted off it, bringing his elbow down to impact the man's throat. The firm flesh yielded, folding inward under the pressure of the elbow guard, closing his windpipe. The man flailed, claw-

ing at his neck, eyes bugging out, making choked, gurgling sounds.

Schweitzer rolled over on top of him, smothering him with his own body, smelling the blood of the corpse beside him, still warm, feeling it soak into his uniform. The man shuddered beneath him. Schweitzer covered him with his bulk, letting the weight of his body armor, weapons, and gear hold him in place, crushing his forearm down on his opponent's throat, making sure the airway stayed closed.

Schweitzer saw movement in his peripheral vision, glanced up.

Another crewman, this one unarmed, had emerged from the stacks of conex boxes and was staring at him in wide-eyed horror.

Schweitzer didn't even bother going for him. He'd never make it before the man had a chance to raise the alarm. Better to stay on top of this target until the job was done, then face this new threat without an enemy in his backfield.

The crewman crouched to run, turned toward the superstructure.

Time slowed. Schweitzer could see the crewman's chest rising, jaw dropping open as he gathered the air to shout a warning.

"Nope," Perreto grunted, passing a garrote around the crewman's throat and pulling the wire tight. The scream didn't even have time to shift into a choked gurgle, and the only sound the crewman made was the dragging of his feet across the deck as Perreto pulled him into the shadows of the conex stacks and finished the job.

Schweitzer gave silent thanks and returned to his own target, pressing down until, at long last, the trembling stopped with a sigh, and his enemy lay still.

Ahmad's voice came through his earpiece. "Schweitzer, quit fucking around over there. We're moving."

Schweitzer got to a knee and looked up to see Perreto emerging from the darkness, covering over Schweitzer's shoulder with his carbine. Once Schweitzer had got to his

feet and raised his own weapon, Perreto nudged one of the corpses with his boot. "That's two arrests you've cost me."

"What'd you do with your guy?"

Perreto jerked his chin in the direction of the darkness where he'd dragged his victim. "Well, we talked it over, and he's repented his evil ways. He's waiting for the end of the op to come home with us and surrender to a federal magistrate."

"Cut the chatter," came in Ahmad's voice, as they rejoined the team and began weaving through the piled metal containers. The ship groaned beneath them as it drifted around its anchor and the swell began to hit it directly on the beam. The cloud cover was thick above them. *When the hell's it going to clear?* With nearly no ambient light, the shadows coiled in every niche and recess among the stacks of conex boxes, putting Schweitzer's reflexes on edge.

The bridge's windows were dark, but Schweitzer knew that meant nothing. A crewman of the watch was most certainly on duty, hopefully sleeping, his binoculars resting on his belly. He glimpsed the windows one last time, the signal mast rising above it, before it was lost from sight as the towering stacks covered them.

They moved as if along a rain-forest floor, through a tunnel of rust-flecked steel, stacking on a corner as Ahmad extended a wand and peeked it around the edge, raising her NODs, dropping the minicomputer from her chest, looking down at it.

She turned back to the team while Chang covered over her shoulder and flashed a series of hand signals. *Two contacts. Hard targets. Port and starboard of the hatch.*

Schweitzer acknowledged with a tap on Perreto's shoulder, which the Coast Guard operator sent on down the line until it reached Ahmad, who nodded and turned back to the corner. She flashed two more hand signals. *Anchor position, come up. Buttonhook with me.*

Schweitzer was the anchor, and he acknowledged with another tap, picking his line around the corner. Chang pulled a chemlight off his belt, broke and shook it, sending

muted neon red shadows dancing around the team, before throwing it around the corner, sending it careening off the target container and hopefully distracting the enemy.

As soon as Ahmad heard the clicking bounce, she left cover. Schweitzer moved behind her, buttonhooking around the corner and raising his carbine to take the shot as she came into view and took a knee.

The chemlight lay on the deck off to one side of the target container, sending its distracting glow cascading over the short space between the corner and the hatch of the target container.

But the enemy wasn't distracted. Both men were ignoring the short plastic stick, dropping to their knees and raising military-grade carbines, fitted with modified sights and extended magazines as advanced as the gear the SEALs carried. They looked nothing like the armed seamen Schweitzer had taken out. They wore black bodysuits, NODs mounted to high-quality Kevlar helmets, torsos enveloped in military-grade body armor that would stop most rounds fired into their center mass.

But Ahmad and Schweitzer were SEALs. They didn't shoot center mass.

Their bullets took the enemy in their faces, exploiting the three inches of open target between the top of the armor collar and the brim of the helmet. SEALs lived and died by their Close Quarters Battle training. While most troops on the range were firing at whatever parts of the target they could hit, to pass CQB you had to put rounds in that same three-inch triangle each time, every time.

The enemy jerked backward as the backs of their heads came off, sending their helmets spinning and painting the target container with blood, gray matter, and bits of bone. The SEALs' rounds clanged into the container, making a dull ring that probably wouldn't alert the ship's crew this far from the superstructure.

The rest of the team rolled around the corner, carbines tracking for targets, but finding none, the enemy already down and twitching on the deck.

After a moment, Ahmad let out her breath. "Well, that was . . ."

Shouts. A voice was crying out behind them, ragged and coughing, but loud enough to do the job.

Chang rolled back around the corner, returned a moment later. "Your guy, Coastie."

Perreto's jaw dropped. "He's dead. I choked him out."

"Well, you might want to make sure he's a little more dead next time," Chang said.

"Are you absolutely sure you finished the job?" Ahmad asked. "Sometimes they're just passed out. Did you check his pulse? His airway?"

Perreto's muttered curse was answer enough.

Light flooded the deck. A siren began to wail on the bridge.

"Fuck!" Ahmad's voice through Schweitzer's earpiece. "Get on that hatch!" Anger and frustration surged at the thought of Perreto's blunder sending the op south. Schweitzer crushed the sentiment, letting cold professionalism dominate. There was no mistake, merely a change in mission parameters. *Focus.*

The team took up position around the hatch as Chang moved up with bolt cutters and bit into the lock. It was a fancy cipher job with a reinforced shackle, but the chromium and molybdenum-infused jaws worked through it. Schweitzer glanced along the container's length as Chang worked the jaws, matching up the scratches, color, and label to the image he'd seen on the minicomputer. This was definitely the right container. He supposed it was possible that there were air vents topside, but he doubted it. That meant explosives, poisons, or fissile material. Maybe some kind of infectious bioagent. The thought of exposure made his stomach clench.

He forced the discomfort down. Intel hadn't said anything about bioagents, and while that didn't mean it was so, Schweitzer had no choice but to trust them. He was a professional. Professionals didn't get a vote. They did their job.

Hatches began to bang open on the ship's superstructure,

and Schweitzer heard shouting. He looked up at the still-solid blanket of clouds. They were still out of the air-cover window. There was no way that Martin could have missed the commotion. Even now, the coxswain would be muttering prayers, bringing his small craft alongside the ship's bow where the gunnels were higher off the surface of the water, but closer to the action if the team had to make a sudden break for it.

Which was looking pretty damn likely. Perreto echoed Schweitzer's thoughts. "This is going to get interesting."

"Shut up," Ahmad said, as Chang finally got the lock free, and the two of them set to wrenching at the hatch handles. "Focus."

The locking bars groaned, shed rust, and finally slid aside and the doors swung open just as the first enemy appeared. They had climbed up the backs of the container stacks opposite the team and now aimed down from the high ground, dialing in their sights and firing off a few experimental rounds, probing range and cover. Some of them were crew in T-shirts and jeans, but more were kitted out like the professional-grade operators Schweitzer and Ahmad had just taken out. For all their gear, they lacked SEAL training, and their shots flew wide despite the fact that the team was hemmed in around the target container. Many of the crew fired their assault rifles in three-round bursts, muzzles dancing wildly. The setting was effective for making enemies keep their heads down, so long as you weren't hoping to actually hit anyone. Schweitzer never used it.

The SEALs returned fire single shot by single shot, each one unerringly finding its target. The first few men were plucked from their perches on top of the stack, the rounds drilling neatly through the three-inch box that SEALs were trained to target. But, as more enemy came pouring around the corners, Perreto and Chang's fire was drawn off to keep their flanks clear, leaving only Ahmad and Schweitzer to engage to the front and cover the con-

tainer in case Schweitzer was wrong and it did contain living threats.

Within moments, they both abandoned the tight target box and let their shots roam in the interest of being able to put more bullets in more people more quickly. Schweitzer shot one of the enemy operators in his gut—miserable aim by his standards and likely stopped by the body armor, but the force drove the man off his feet and he tumbled from the top of the stack, shrieking, to slam into silence against the deck below. Schweitzer's eyes tracked and moved, sighting targets and shooting them, his hand mechanically releasing his empty magazine and shuffling it over two inches so the full one, duct-taped alongside, could move into the gun's smoking ammunition well with barely a second lost before the carbine's bolt slid home, and he was shooting again.

Bang. Target down. On to the next. Move. Bang. Target down. On to the next. Move again.

Part of Schweitzer ran through his killing drill. Another part marveled at the number of the enemy. The ship's hold must have been crammed with a small company, at least a large platoon. In this business, you lived and died by the details. The tiniest slipup could bring down hell. Schweitzer had run op after op alongside Perreto. The man was a master at his trade. And even masters lost the bubble from time to time.

Schweitzer just wished it weren't this one.

Bullets whined off the deck around him. He could make out Ahmad as he lowered his weapon to slide around her. Her eyes were completely focused, her face slack with concentration, the only indicator that she was in the middle of a gunfight was a thin runnel of sweat working down the outside of one ear.

Corpses lay atop the stacks, at the corners where the team had entered. Bang. Target down. Move. Beside the dead man, two others were unsnapping a tripod and mounting some kind of larger weapon atop it. Schweitzer's roving

eyes didn't settle long enough to figure out what it was, but it couldn't be good.

"Schweitzer." Ahmad glanced up at the impenetrable cover overhead. "Check that container. Nothing living in there, blow it. Give us five minutes for egress."

Schweitzer spun and moved to the container. Cold air slapped him in the face. The interior was refrigerated, the chill blotting out the thermal detection of his NODs, turning the green contours black and leaving him blind. But it didn't matter, in this cold there was no way there was anything alive in here. Refrigeration meant bioagents, and he felt his skin crawl with revulsion as he pulled the charge from his pack and took a knee, swapping magazines again before turning to fire without the aid of night vision. He didn't need it. The lights from the bridge silhouetted his enemies perfectly, making them stark black shapes against the gray sky. Bang. Target down. Move.

He turned back to the container, the shadowy interior coming into focus. The scratched, rust-bucket exterior was a lie. The interior walls were clean white plastic, the floor built from shining cross-hatchings of skidproof stainless steel. Stainless-steel racks lined the walls floor to ceiling. Two more dominated the center, with rows in between just wide enough to admit two people walking abreast. Vents in the floor and ceiling fogged cool air into the space, wafting over Schweitzer's shoulders and out past the open doors, mercifully cooling his neck and reminding him of how hot he'd gotten from fighting under all that gear. Somewhere, a motor churned, probably the refrigeration unit.

The racks were lined with corpses.

They were laid out toe to head, perfectly preserved, save where stitching marked a bullet or knife wound that had been sewn carefully shut. They were shaved of all hair, blue lips and closed eyes looking bruised even in the darkness. Their waxy skin stretched taut over solid frames. Nearly all the cadavers were male, and all had been elite athletes in life. Tight muscles bunched beneath the dead skin, as if the bodies would notice the intruder at any

moment, springing off their racks, reaching, dead hands eager to punish the intruder.

For a brief instant, the cold darkness in the container swamped him. The shadows coiled in the recesses of the racks, thick and malevolent, reaching out to him. He could hear the creaking of the metal as the bodies shifted nearer, hear the hissing of their rancid breath as they reached . . . He couldn't move. Couldn't breathe.

Schweitzer felt himself in the midst of a current, a tide of energy eddying around and through him. His nostrils filled with unfamiliar smells: the chemical reek of embalming fluid and something else: a musky odor of ancient spices, a burned-sugar stink of bridled power.

And then he was back to himself, shaking his head to clear it.

He had run at least three different ops that intercepted bioagents. He had seen compressed cylinders, metal racks filled with vials, even powders compressed into the shape of children's toys.

But dead bodies? He'd never heard of moving anything that way.

The feeling of supernatural unease lingered. If there'd been candle stubs and pentagrams, he'd have thought he'd stumbled onto the set of some cult ritual, hooded priests raising the dead. Killing men in a hopelessly outnumbered gunfight hadn't bothered Schweitzer at all, but now he felt the slow crawl of terror up his gut again for the second time that night. And for the second time that night he tipped his hat to it and got back to work.

He bent to set the charge as the flank Perreto was defending collapsed and the Coast Guardsman backed into the container mouth. Perreto's carbine had either jammed or run dry, and he'd transitioned to his pistol, letting the long gun dangle from its sling, slapping his thigh as he backed up. He was grinning, as he always did in a gunfight. "My scintillating personality just doesn't seem to be cutting it here."

Schweitzer felt the current in the nervous humor. Per-

reto knew he'd fucked up, was already beating himself up
over it. Not good. It couldn't be fixed now, and the man
needed his head in the fight.

An enemy crewman charged around the container corner with a machete, screaming.

"Police officer!" Perreto shouted as he shot him in the
face, then kicked him in the chest, sending him reeling
into the man behind him, one of the enemy operators. Perreto shot that man in the chest twice, sending him sprawling
while the Coast Guardsman changed magazines. "You're
all under arrest," he finished. "If you surrender, your cooperation will be noted."

Schweitzer fumbled with the charge as another enemy
took one of Perreto's rounds in the shoulder when he tackled the Coast Guard operator into the container. The two
men sprawled, knocking the charge out of reach, forcing
Schweitzer to go back to his carbine to prevent the enemy
from pouring into the team's backfield.

He dropped back onto his carbine's sights and stared
into a mass of enemy surging around the container's side.
He'd been right. The entire ship's hold must have been
crammed with them. What the hell was going on? He
cursed and thumbed the fire selector switch to three-round-burst mode. It wasn't like he could miss anyway. He swept
the barrel as he fired, trying to make the rounds find as
many different targets as possible, knowing that was futile.
The heat from the barrel was beginning to register through
the top of his glove. The patter of spent brass around him
was a reminder of how quickly he was tearing through his
limited supply of ammo.

Chang grunted and staggered into view, his body armor
smoking where he'd been hit. He collapsed into a sitting
position against the side of the container, still firing at the
enemy. Whether the round had penetrated or not Schweitzer couldn't tell and didn't have time to consider.

With Chang and Perreto sewn up, they were cut off.

Now, the only way out was through.

Perreto tapped Schweitzer's shoulder and knelt at his

side. He'd taken care of the man who'd tackled him and taken his shotgun. The Coast Guardsman racked the slide, firing a blast of shot at close range into the attackers on the flank. They fell back, howling, and Schweitzer returned to Ahmad's side, just as the tripod-mounted weapon on top of the stacks opened up, drilling heavy-caliber rounds into the deck and forcing them back into the container.

Ahmad's expression was even. She wasn't even breathing hard as she turned to Schweitzer. "You find a back door?" The rounds thudding into the deck outside provided a stuttering reminder that the front was no longer a viable exit. Chang collapsed in alongside him. Schweitzer still had no way to tell how bad Chang's wound was.

Schweitzer shook his head at Ahmad. A small part of him was amazed at how quickly the op had gone south. There had been so many unexpected turns. The number of enemy belowdecks for one.

Ahmad glanced up, noted the bodies, stiff and silent on the steel racks. If the sight affected her, she didn't show it. She only blinked and turned back to the mounting odds against them.

It didn't matter. She'd go down fighting. They all would. That was part of the job. They'd known it when they'd signed on. Schweitzer's only regret was that he wouldn't have the chance to make things right by Sarah, wouldn't see his son's sudden smile when Daddy walked through the door. He kept firing, imagining he saw the tracery of his wife's dyed hair in the filtering starlight that had begun to dapple the bullet-scarred deck outside.

Starlight.

The cloud cover.

Schweitzer didn't wait for Ahmad's say-so. He toggled channels on his radio. "White, white. Blue is pinned down with one WIA and TIC. Request CAS run. Your brief, stack, mark, and control."

Again, Ahmad gave no sign she noticed, other than to reach into a pouch on her tac vest and produce a targeting beacon, which she hurled out the container doors. Schweitzer

followed suit, throwing his as far from hers as he could, to give the sortie a range. Chang, still shooting one-handed, added his out the container's far side.

"Blue, blue. This is white," fire control responded. "Two hawks in the air."

"Paint is on target," Schweitzer replied. "We're danger close forward of the mark. You are cleared hot."

"Roger that. Hawks are cleared hot. Birds away. Hold on." They held on.

The tight confines of the container limited their maneuver, but the racks provided some cover. The SEALs moved seamlessly. Bang. Target down. Move. Somewhere along the way, Schweitzer noticed that Chang had stopped firing and was lying against the container wall, his carbine resting across his lap like he was taking a nap. *Unconscious, he's unconscious. He's not dead.* Ahmad tossed a grenade outside, and the team took cover. Schweitzer dragged Chang behind a rack as they weathered the backblast.

"How the hell are you supposed to take care of Sarah if you die, asshole?" Schweitzer asked him, trying to see if his brother SEAL was still breathing. The heavy body armor and tactical vest made it impossible to see the rise and fall of his chest.

Or lack thereof.

Screams reached him from outside, and he stepped back into the smoke. He fired, the carbine's bolt locking to the rear to remind him that he had no ammunition left. He dropped the long gun and wrenched his pistol from its drop holster, firing again.

Silence. The blast had bought them some time.

Hopefully, enough.

He bent to check on Chang, but Ahmad called to him, firing out of the container entrance as the enemy began to regroup. Boots tromped, voices shouted. Even with his adrenaline pegged, Schweitzer had been fighting nonstop for too long. His hands began to tremble, his limbs feeling heavy. He swallowed. The fear and fatigue, the worry about Sarah, the painful tide of missing his son, all slid down his

throat and into his gullet. He tightened his abdominal muscles and crushed the emotion, held it there, freeing his mind
and hands to do what they had been trained to do. What
they had been born to do. Bang. Target down. Move.

The knot of enemy formed a solid black mass outside
the container, surging inward. Too many. Way too many.

"Shipmate . . ." Ahmad began, her voice hinting at the
first strains of emotion he'd ever heard from her.

"Shots on target," Schweitzer's radio buzzed. "Take
cover."

The team hit the deck as thunder erupted around them.
The steel of the deck outside the container churned like
liquid and the black mass of attackers suddenly vanished.
There were no screams, only the thunderous roar of the
guns followed by the dull thumping of the helicopter rotors
as the birds finished their strafing run and turned to sweep
back over.

The SEALs weren't the only professionals. The aviators
put their fire precisely on target. Spent bullet casings
rained down across the shattered freighter deck, pelting
off the stacks of conex boxes and smoking in the shredded
remains of the enemy lying among them.

But not a single bullet fell forward of the target. The
team sheltered in place unnecessarily. They could have
walked to the edge of the storm of rounds had they chosen,
reached out, and felt the bullet contrails skim past their fingertips.

The helos made another run, then turned their attention
to the bridge. They had eyes on the target now and no longer needed direction from Ahmad's team. The thundering
of the miniguns ceased, and Schweitzer began to hear the
crack, pause, crack of single shots as the snipers on the
helos began to pick out individual targets on the deck,
among the stacks, through the bridge windows.

Ahmad moved to the container mouth and scanned outside. After a moment, she nodded, radioed that the target
was clear, and returned to check on Chang. The operator
breathed shallowly, his pulse normal. Schweitzer stripped

off Chang's body armor and probed the wound behind it. An ugly patch of purple had spread across the unbroken skin over his chest. "What do you think?" Ahmad asked.

"Broken ribs. Probably in his lung. Fucked up his air. That's why he passed out. He'll make it if we hurry."

Thank God.

Ahmad nodded and called for a medevac as the first members of the regular boarding team fast-roped to the deck, boots resounding loudly, the need for stealth long past.

Schweitzer looked back up at Ahmad, whose game face was back on again. The sound of gunfire had stopped. The battle was over.

The charge lay undetonated, but the interior of the container had been shredded by bullets, the corpses lying in heaps, torn to pieces by the sheer volume of fire. Whatever the Body Farm had wanted to do with these cadavers, it wasn't happening now.

He turned back to Ahmad. "So, Chief, how about that leave?"

Ahmad shook her head, but Schweitzer found himself smiling.

Because Chang would live. Because he knew Ahmad would be as good as her word.

Because he knew they'd all be going home after all.

CHAPTER II
HOMEWARD-BOUND

Chang was conscious and joking with the pararescuemen before his medevac helo even lifted off. The senior airmen lifting his stretcher into the helo confirmed Schweitzer's suspicion. The round had cracked Chang's ribs, driving them into his lungs and depriving him of oxygen. But the oxygen mask over his face made up for it, and his eyes were in focus as Schweitzer squeezed his shoulder.

Perreto's face was a mask so rigid that Schweitzer could tell he was holding back tears. "God, Steve. I'm so sorry. I fucked up, brother."

"Jesus, Dan," Chang said. "Shit happens. You didn't choke him all the way out. I blocked bullets with my chest. Even perfect people make mistakes."

His chuckle quickly turned into a cough, his smile melting with pain.

Schweitzer winced, tried to distract him. "Hell of a fight, Steve. You went down shooting. Badass."

Chang found his smile, wheezed through the mask. "Just needed a nap. Would have finished things up if you hadn't pussied out and called in the cavalry."

Ahmad snorted and called down to Martin, telling him to shove off. The team would take one of the helos out.

Schweitzer smiled and nodded to the pararescueman. "Take good care of him, Doc. We need him back on the line so I can take leave."

Then Chang was off into the helo, and Schweitzer followed Ahmad and Perreto to the freighter's helipad, where a large gray Seahawk was landing, keeping its rotors spinning, ready to take off again.

"Dan," Schweitzer began.

"Stow it," Ahmad said. "No plan survives contact with the enemy. We made it. That's what counts."

Perreto kept his eyes straight forward. "I fumbled the ball. I'll take what's coming." As the Coast Guard liaison, Perreto already caught a rash of shit from the all-navy unit, and every action he took reflected on the Coast Guard. Until tonight, he'd covered his service in glory. In a way, Schweitzer thought, he'd gotten it worse than Chang.

Chang would heal. Mistakes like Perreto's never went away.

The intel and medical teams were already scouring the freighter, along with security forces, securing any enemy left alive.

There were precious few of those.

Perreto gratefully left the SEALs to join the regular boarding team, lending the Coast Guard's police authority in case any of the Body Farm operatives turned out to be United States citizens.

Lieutenant Biggs sat in the Seahawk's interior, typing fiercely on a ruggedized laptop. He was bigger than all of them, a giant of a man who Schweitzer knew had been a ground operator himself before successive promotions had taken him out of the action. He looked up as the team came aboard, barely acknowledging them, focusing on completing his work. The team clipped into the floor ring and patched their helmet mics into the helo's system as it slowly lifted off. Biggs looked up, still typing, and cocked an eyebrow at Ahmad. "You look tired, Chief."

Ahmad shrugged. "Intel got the enemy numbers wrong."

"I heard," Biggs said. "Sounded like a lot."

"A few." Ahmad shrugged again.

It was almost a whole fucking company, Schweitzer thought. *Why would they commit that much firepower to guard a box of dead bodies?*

Biggs looked over her shoulder and down at the freighter's deck, still littered with corpses and living men being forced to their knees and into zip-cuffs. "A few," he said.

"Cloud cover was a problem," Schweitzer added.

Biggs waved a hand. "Skipper's call. How's Chang?"

"He'll be okay," Ahmad said. "SAPI plate caught the round. Broke some ribs."

Biggs nodded. "You take care of my lamb."

Schweitzer nodded along with Ahmad. Biggs referred to every SEAL under his command as one of his lambs. "Always."

"Anyone want to tell me why that turned into a stand-up fight?"

Schweitzer shut his mouth. He wasn't going to talk smack about a teammate. That the blunder was inexcusable didn't change the fact that that kind of thing could have happened to any of them. "Perreto didn't finish his target. He garroted him out, but left him breathing. Bad guy raised the alarm after we moved on."

Biggs frowned. Schweitzer wouldn't want to be Chief right now, but shitty tasks like owning up to your team's failures were part of the job she'd signed up for when she'd pinned the anchors on.

"How the hell did that happen?" Biggs asked.

"Perreto didn't check the target's ABC's. He thought he'd killed him. Target was just passed out."

"Fucking Coastie," Biggs growled.

Ahmad smoothly interrupted. "What do you want? Bad guy had an iron neck. It was a good hit from where I stood."

Biggs shook his head. "Well, he'll have to answer for it."

Ahmad said nothing. She knew that. Perreto knew it, too.

"So, corpses," Biggs said.

"Yeah. There was a refrigeration unit to keep them cold," Schweitzer said, grateful for the change of subject. "I'm guessing twenty to thirty at least. Got chewed up pretty bad in the gunfight. Any idea what that's all about? Who the hell pays for shipments of corpses?"

Biggs shrugged. "Not our problem."

"I've never seen anything like that," Schweitzer said. "If its bio stuff, there are more easily concealed ways to move it. Someone had put some effort into prettying them up, too. They were cleaned, stitched. If you're just moving bioagents, why the hell would you do that? And why use people?"

"I'll say it again," Biggs said. "It's not our problem."

Schweitzer frowned. "Okay, boss."

"You misunderstand me," Biggs added. "I mean it's officially not our problem. As in, we're not to talk about it." He pointed down at the laptop. "That's what this e-mail is about. Comes from the skipper himself. The intel team is being stood down. No follow-ons. No tactical questioning. No document exploitation. Langley's sending in their own people to go over the ship. Civilians."

"Civilians?" Ahmad asked. Schweitzer's own curiosity was piqued as well, but it was overridden by another thought: *Please don't let this turn into another long paperwork drill. I need to get home. I need to see Sarah and Patrick.*

But that thought was followed by another, more urgent. *Something is wrong here.*

"Boss, this doesn't . . ."

"Operations is your job, Petty Officer," Biggs said, steel coming into his voice. "What comes after is above your pay grade."

"Yeah, but shouldn't we at least debrief with the intel team? I mean . . ."

"Holy shit, Jim. We are not having this conversation. Is that clear?"

Biggs had never talked to him like this before. He

shrugged with a nonchalance he didn't feel. "You're the boss."

"I've got Non-Disclosure Agreements on here." Biggs tapped the laptop again. "I'll need digital signatures from both of you, and we're still going to need you both to write your statements for the After-Action Report. Chief, you'll have to get Chang's once he's recovered."

Schweitzer and Ahmad shrugged simultaneously. SEALs weren't exactly known to be people of many words. That part would be short. A human-trafficking organization selling corpses, with more firepower than some armies, and the government stepping in to keep it quiet. Schweitzer began turning it over in his mind, then dismissed it with a will. *Not your problem. Get home and take care of your family. You've done your job here.*

"One last thing," Biggs added. "I'm sorry to do this to you, but it's protocol for big firefights. I've got to send you off to see the wizard once we land and you clear medical."

Schweitzer groaned inwardly. He knew the corpsman and would clear the physical checkup in no time flat. But a meeting with the psych doc would take hours, and he'd have to wait on post to get an appointment.

Ahmad came to his rescue. "Boss," she said, "Schweitzer's due for a break. You're really going to have to send him off to see the wizard if you don't let him get home as soon as he clears medical."

Schweitzer shot her a grateful look. Good chiefs took care of their sailors, and Ahmad was the best he'd ever known. Biggs paused. Ahmad never countermanded her officers unless it was critical. Biggs turned to Schweitzer.

"It's Sarah." Schweitzer shrugged. "I really need to get home."

"Okay." Biggs nodded. "I'll handle it on our end. File your report and go home. You're lucky they ordered no follow-ons. I'll stand up section 3 for the next two weeks."

Ahmad nodded gratefully. With their section stood down, everyone would get some much-needed rest. "Outstanding," she said, leaning in to sign the electronic NDA.

"Remember," Biggs said as Schweitzer added his signature, "this is compartmentalized now. They're not screwing around. No gossiping about it, no speculating. No e-mailing anyone, even on the classified network. You don't talk about the Body Farm. You don't talk about what we found. You don't talk about what happened on this raid."

Schweitzer nodded as he signed. "When Chang . . ."

"Chang will be fine. I'll call you the second I hear anything."

"Thanks."

"Jim," Biggs said, "I'm not fucking around here. I am counting on you keeping mum about this. You got that?" Schweitzer nodded again, but Biggs's words came to him as if from the bottom of a well. They didn't matter. Sarah's face was filling his mind. He was an artist in his way, and she was in hers. Painting, papermaking. She smelled of rosewater that she made herself from the dried petals. He could almost smell it now over the high chemical reek of the Seahawk's burning fuel.

Once I see her, I can fix this. If I can just touch her, she'll know.

The Seahawk banked again, eating miles, each twist of the rotors carrying him closer to home.

Schweitzer bounded up the steps three at a time, heedless of how the thumping of his boots might wake the neighbors. When the corpsman had come to him in the squad bay, Schweitzer simply shook his head, hoping his eyes would convey his need. The corpsman understood. He made some marks on a piece of paper, tore off the yellow carbon copy, and handed it to Schweitzer. "Welcome back," was all he said, before moving on to check Ahmad. Schweitzer had looked numbly down at the yellow paper. FULLY MEDICALLY READY, it read.

He'd tucked it in his pocket and headed to the armorer to stow his gear.

Schweitzer fought impatience as he went through the